P9-EEK-783

BEST
SCIENCE FICTION STORIES
OF THE YEAR
Tenth Annual Collection

ABOUT THE EDITOR

Gardner Dozois was born and raised in Salem, Massachusetts, and has been writing and editing science fiction for over ten years. His short fiction has appeared in most of the leading science fiction magazines and anthologies. He has been a finalist numerous times for the Nebula, Hugo, and Jupiter awards and among the books he has written are *Strangers*, a novel, and *The Visible Man*, a collection of short fiction. In addition to *Best Science Fiction Stories of The Year*, he is editor of *A Day in the Life*, *Future Power* (with Jack Dann), *Another World*, *Beyond the Golden Age*, and *Aliens!* (with Jack Dann). Mr. Dozois, a member of the Science Fiction Writers of America, lives in Philadelphia.

BEST
SCIENCE FICTION
STORIES
OF THE YEAR
Tenth Annual Edition

Edited By
GARDNER DOZOIS

E. P. Dutton | **New York**

Acknowledgment is made for permission to print the following material:

"The Ugly Chickens," by Howard Waldrop. Copyright © 1980 by Terry Carr. First published in *Universe 10* (Doubleday). Reprinted by permission of the author.

"The Green Marauder," by Larry Niven. Copyright © 1980 by Larry Niven. First published in *Destinies,* February-March (Ace). Reprinted by permission of the author.

"The Feast of St. Janis," by Michael Swanwick. Copyright © 1980 by Michael Swanwick. First published in *New Dimensions 11* (Pocket Books). Reprinted by permission of the author and the author's agent, Virginia Kidd.

"The Last Answer," by Isaac Asimov. Copyright © 1980 by Conde Nast Publications, Inc. First published in *Analog Science Fiction/Science Fact,* January 1980. Reprinted by permission of the author.

"Nightflyers," by George R.R. Martin. Copyright © 1980 by Conde Nast Publications, Inc. First published in *Analog Science Fiction/Science Fact,* April 1980. Reprinted by permission of the author.

"Strata," by Edward Bryant. Copyright © 1980 by Mercury Press, Inc. First published in *The Magazine of Fantasy and Science Fiction,* August 1980. Reprinted by permission of the author.

"Slow Music," by James Tiptree, Jr. Copyright © 1980 by James Tiptree, Jr. First published in *Interfaces* (Ace). Reprinted by permission of the author and the author's agent, Robert P. Mills, Ltd.

"The Finger," by Naomi Mitchison. Copyright © 1980 by Naomi Mitchison. First published in *Edges* (Pocket Books). Reprinted by permission of the author and the author's agent, Robert P. Mills, Ltd.

"War Beneath the Tree," by Gene Wolfe. Copyright © 1980 by Omni Publications International Ltd. First published in *Omni,* December 1980. Reprinted by permission of the author and the author's agent, Virginia Kidd.

"Unicorn Tapestry," by Suzy McKee Charnas. Copyright © 1980 by Suzy McKee Charnas. First published in *New Dimensions 11* (Pocket Books). Reprinted by permission of the author.

Published in the United States by Elsevier-Dutton Publishing Co., Inc.,
2 Park Avenue, New York, N.Y. 10016

Library of Congress Catalog Card Number: 77-190700

ISBN: 0-525-06499-0
Published simultaneously in Canada by
Clarke, Irwin & Company Limited, Toronto and Vancouver

10 9 8 7 6 5 4 3 2 1

First Edition

For Trina and Peter, John and Ginjer,
Jeanne, Wanda and Rick and Raya, David K., Robert T.,
and in memory of Joan —
staunch New Yorkers all.

CONTENTS

ACKNOWLEDGMENTS

The editor would like to thank the following people for their help and support: Jack Dann, Michael Swanwick, Susan Casper, Virginia Kidd, David G. Hartwell, Jim Frenkel, John Douglas, Pat LoBrutto, Susan Allison, Victoria Schochet, Steve Roos, Edward Ferman, Roy Torgeson, Kirby McCauley, Robert P. Mills, Bruce McAllister, Charles L. Grant, Peter Pautz, Terry Carr, George R.R. Martin, Edward Bryant, Howard Waldrop, Isaac Asimov, Larry Niven, George H. Scithers, Sharon Jarvis, Stuart Shiff, Tom Purdom, Tom Whitehead of the Special Collections Department at Temple University, J.B. Post, Fred Fisher of the Hourglass SF Bookstore in Philadelphia, Trina King, Melissa Mia Hall, and special thanks to my own editor, Roxanne Henderson.

Thanks are also due to Charles N. Brown, whose newszine *Locus* (P.O. Box 3938, San Francisco, CA 94119 — $12 for twelve issues) was used as a reference source throughout the Summation, and to Andrew Porter, whose newszine *Science Fiction Chronicle* (P.O. Box 4175, New York, NY 10163 — $15 for twelve issues) was also used as a reference source throughout. Also used as reference sources were *Science Fiction Review*, edited by Richard E. Geis (P.O. Box 11408, Portland, OR 97211 — $7.50 for one year, six issues), and *The Bulletin of the Science Fiction Writers of America*, edited by Richard Kearns (841½ N. Vendome, Los Angeles, CA 90026 — $10 for four issues). Thanks again to all.

INTRODUCTION

Summation: 1980

Nineteen-eighty was full of contradictory signals and ambiguous omens as to the economic health of the field, a year when SF often seemed to be walking a shaky tightrope over the abyss of economic collapse and retrenchment.

On the negative side, a mentality of fear, a siege mentality, now exists among many SF editors and publishers. A lot fewer risks were taken in the marketplace this year than in other years, and books that were considered to be less than sure-fire commercially, books that didn't fit into an easily discernible subcategory, books considered to be "too good" or "too literary," books by unknown new writers, were all much more difficult to sell. "Wait until next year, or the year after, when things loosen up," was a refrain heard frequently along Publisher's Row. Big-money advances were less common, although a few were made. It was hard to tell whether sales were down across the board or not, although certainly some sales were down. SF and fantasy calendars and art-books, particularly those that were spinoffs from movies, were reported to have done very poorly at Christmastime this year, usually the biggest sales period for such items. Advertising and promotional budgets for SF have been slashed at several publishing houses. The availability of backlist titles declined throughout the industry, thanks in part to the famous Thor Power Tool decision by the IRS. The tax law as interpreted in view of that decision makes it unprofitable — indeed quite expensive — for publishers to store backlist titles past the end of the year. As a result, the effective life in print of an SF title is much shorter now than it would have been a few years back, and mail-order sales of backlist titles (once nearly the only way most SF books ever reached backwoods and small-town America) is becoming a much less important part of the SF publishing scene. Several publishing houses made further cutbacks in their SF lines, including Harper & Row, Berkley, and, at the beginning of 1981, Doubleday. Gregg Press postponed its 1981 line of hardcover library reprints until sales improve. A few publishers, like Baronet and Dale Books, went out of business entirely. Several SF magazines, including the thirty-year veteran *Galaxy,* died in 1980. At least one major anthology series is dying. And rumors persist that at least one major publisher is thinking of dropping its SF line altogether.

On the positive side, SF sales in general don't really seem to be down all that much, certainly not enough to justify the gloom and hysteria along Publisher's Row, and in fact many SF and fantasy titles continued to sell very well indeed. Most of the cutbacks can be seen as trimming unnecessary fat from SF rather than striking at the heart of the genre; SF had certainly become overextended and somewhat bloated during the last few years, so there is fat there to trim. For that matter, in spite of the cutbacks here and there, there doesn't seem to be a really noticeable lessening of the number of SF titles on the stands. New publishers are becoming interested in SF and fantasy even as the interest of some of the older houses declines. Some publishers are even *increasing* their SF lines, swimming against the tide of the times. For instance, 1981 will see the appearance of at least one major new SF line: *Jim Baen Presents,* under Baen's editorship, a subcategory of the newly formed Tor Books, to be distributed by Pinnacle. Jim Baen and Thomas Doherty, former Senior Editor and Executive Vice President, respectively, of Ace Books, left Ace this year to start the new line. Susan Allison, who replaced Baen as the editor of Ace, announced recently that Ace, which had cut its list from ten to six titles a month in 1979, would expand its list to ten titles a month again in 1981. In addition, Ace is reviving its old Ace Specials line, once again under the editorship of Terry Carr, and this alone could have a powerful positive effect on the SF scene of the next few years. The Pocket Books and Simon & Schuster SF lines, both under the editorship of David G. Hartwell, are being combined into Timescape Books, with promises of increased efficiency and greater promotion.

New magazines and anthology series were being born even as old ones died. Good books, even literarily daring and ''noncommercial'' ones, continued to be published. And although SF has demonstrated an increasing tendency to become a field almost solely composed of a handful of best-selling big name authors, good new writers continued to force their way into the field during 1980. The year saw the publication of a number of excellent first novels by writers such as Robert Stallman, David Brin, Paul F. Preuss, and Paul Hazel, and, in the short fiction market, stunning debuts by new writers such as Michael Swanwick and Pat Murphy.

As I said, ambiguous omens. Although the big SF boom of the late seventies does not seem to be continuing, neither have we, yet, gone completely bust, and I begin to have hopes that SF may muddle through after all. At the very least, we are, to paraphrase the old Chinese curse, living in interesting times.

Things were changing again, and not necessarily for the better, in the magazine field it was somewhat weak in 1980, publishing a smaller percentage of the year's top-flight stories than at any time since 1976, when the so-called "SF magazine renaissance" began.

Looking back, it is easy to see that talk of a magazine renaissance was premature. Of the new magazines founded during the tag-end of the seventies, only *Isaac Asimov's Science Fiction Magazine* and *Omni* survive — *Cosmos* died in 1978, *UnEarth* in 1979, and 1980 saw the demise of *Galileo* and *Asimov's SF Adventure Magazine,* as well as that of longer-running magazines such as *Galaxy* and *Fantastic.* If one omits *Omni,* which is not primarily an SF magazine (although it does regularly publish SF), *Amazing,* which is still in a semi-somnolent state (although lately it has shown signs that it is trying to come back to life), and the "semi-prozines" like *Whispers, Eternity,* and *Shayol* (which have negligible circulations), then we are left with only three surviving genre magazines: *Analog, IASFM,* and *The Magazine of Fantasy and Science Fiction.* This was roughly the case in the early sixties, when the magazine field was considered to be moribund, although then the Big Three were *Analog, F&SF,* and *Galaxy.*

Of the present three survivors, *F&SF*'s economic position is somewhat precarious, and *IASFM* and *Analog* are now both owned by the same company, Davis Publications, two eggs in one economic basket. A further stiffening of the recession or another upsurge in inflation, particularly one that hits Davis hard, could easily wipe out the surviving genre magazines.

Nor have we yet seen the proliferation of slick, high-paying, large-format SF magazines that many commentators thought would follow *Omni*'s amazingly successful debut in 1978. The *Omni* imitators have hit the newsstands, all right, a half-dozen or more of them — *Next, Discovery, Science 80,* and so on — but they are all strictly science-popularization magazines; none of them publishes SF, all having chosen to ignore that particular part of the *Omni* formula.

On the positive side, it does seem to me that SF is being used more frequently of late by the major "men's magazines," perhaps because of *Omni*'s example. *Playboy* has always published a certain amount of SF, but (although this is entirely a subjective opinion) it seems as if there is an increased emphasis on it there as well in the last couple of years; this probably has a great deal to do with the fact that the new Fiction Editor of *Playboy,* Alice K. Turner, is a long-time SF reader. *Penthouse, Oui,* and *Gallery* also seem to be using more SF now than they did a few years past. "War-gaming" magazines like *Ares, Questar, Space Gamer,* and a number of others, are also using SF on a regular basis, although as yet few of these magazines have published anything of real value. SF is also turning up more frequently in "literary" magazines, especially experimental pieces that are having a difficult time selling to the increasingly conservative genre magazine market — the collection *Their Immortal Hearts* (reviewed below), made up of such pieces, is a good example. There are a number of new "semi-prozines," most of them with *very* low circulations, and now even some small-budget Canadian SF magazines.

We may be seeing here a slow, underground shift in demographics, in the *kinds* of places where SF gets published, in evolutionary compensation for the dwindling genre markets. None of these markets, though, not even the slick national magazines, not even the original anthology markets, will be able to adequately make up for the loss of the genre magazines, if such a loss is in the cards. The death of those magazines would be a disaster for SF, a blow that might, in time, even prove to have been fatal.

For the present, though, those genre markets are not only still alive, some of them are relatively bright-eyed and bushy-tailed.

Omni had another successful year commercially, but the quality of *Omni*'s fiction was down somewhat in 1980 from 1979's high-water mark. With the exception of stories by Sturgeon and Brunner, little of real quality was published in *Omni* during the first half of the year. Things picked up somewhat during the last half of the year, with the final few issues of *Omni* for 1980 containing good work by Edward Bryant, Orson Scott Card, Robert Silverberg, Philip K. Dick, Norman Spinrad, Walter Tevis, and others. Opinions differ as to the reason for this slump — some fans of "hard" SF blame new Fiction Editor Robert Sheckley for it, claiming that Sheckley, whose leanings toward experimentalist SF are well-known, has de-factoly "banned" hard, technologically oriented SF from *Omni*, to the detriment of the magazine. Others see Sheckley as "opening up" the magazine, broadening *Omni*'s literary spectrum. I personally feel that all such judgments are premature, and that there is still no firm evidence in just what direction Sheckley *is* taking the magazine, or with what measure of success. As an old magazine hand, I'm well aware that it takes any new editor at least a year, sometimes considerably longer, to develop a distinct editorial personality, and that it is also quite possible, in fact likely, that a good deal of what was published in *Omni* in 1980 (and that Sheckley was either blamed or praised for) was actually former Fiction Editor (now Executive Editor) Ben Bova's inventory from the year before. The grapevine tells me that Sheckley has bought some first-rate fiction for upcoming publication in 1981, and by then the shape of the changes in *Omni* may be clearer.

I am much more concerned by the impression I get that the space reserved in each issue for fiction has been sharply reduced since last year. The two best stories to appear in *Omni* in 1979 — George R.R. Martin's "Sandkings" and Suzy McKee Charnas's "The Ancient Mind at Work" — were both in the 14,000-word range, and the persistent shoptalk rumor in professional circles is that both stories, if submitted now, would be too long for *Omni* to accept. If this is true then the quality of *Omni*'s fiction is inevitably going to suffer, as most of the best work in SF today is being done at novelette length. Only time will tell.

Isaac Asimov's Science Fiction Magazine was up somewhat in overall quality in 1980, although a lot of what they publish still is not to my taste. *IASFM* has developed a distinct stable of writers over the past few years, and that stable was more strongly in evidence in 1980 than ever before, with the same four or five young (and sometimes uneven) writers dominating issue after issue, occasionally contributing nearly all of the fiction published in a single issue. Even some long-term *IASFM* fans have been discomforted by the ubiquity of this stable during the year, and at least one letter in the *IASFM* letter column sardonically urged that the title of the magazine be changed to *Somtow Sucharitkul and Barry Longyear's Science Fiction Magazine.* Most SF magazines develop a stable of regular authors at some point (or, more precisely, a succession of different stables over the course of the magazine's life), nor is there anything reprehensible in letting new authors work out their apprenticeship in print — almost all SF writers learned their trade that way. No, *IASFM* differs from the norm only in that its stable is not composed of big names or practiced old hands, but is made up instead almost entirely of uneven new writers, and that instead of quietly doing their apprentice work in the back of the magazine in the time-honored way, these writers are dominating the magazine, their work comprising not only the lead fiction in most issues but sometimes nearly the only fiction. I can't help but feel that this is a mistake in judgment, that eventually the readers are going to get tired of seeing the same old faces, that *IASFM* badly needs to attract a more diverse selection of writers, particularly a higher percentage of seasoned professionals. On the other hand, *IASFM* claims that its circulation is up from last year, to nearly 130,000 copies an issue now, and it's hard to argue with success. Again, only time will tell.

On the positive side, Editor George H. Scithers does seem to be loosening up somewhat in his definition of an acceptable *IASFM* story, and he is to be sincerely applauded for getting some different types of material into the magazine. For instance, *IASFM* published a sophisticated, erudite, and very funny straight fantasy novella by Avram Davidson in 1980 — way off the beaten path of what is usually considered an "*IASFM* story" — as well as several other good stories that smacked of the unconventional by such writers as Pat Murphy, Gene Wolfe, Carter Scholz, and Lisa Tuttle. Personally, I find it a very hopeful sign that *IASFM* is still fluid enough to be broadening its horizons; it augurs well for the future. Good stories of a more traditional sort by Jeff Dunteman, David Andreissen, Juleen Brantingham, and others also appeared in *IASFM* this year.

Analog, long a publication of Conde Nast, was sold in 1980 to Davis Publications, the publishers of *IASFM,* a move that could have a profound effect on the magazine's future. The long-term effect could be good — Conde Nast had clearly lost interest in *Analog* in the past few years, and an interested new publisher could help to spark a revitalization of the magazine. For the moment, the immediate changes have been minor: Both *Analog* and *IASFM* will receive new logotypes, both magazines will publish thirteen issues a year instead of twelve. *Analog* has also slightly changed the emphasis and design of its covers, and somehow, without the changes being drastic or obvious, come to look something like *IASFM*.

I was glad to see George R.R. Martin back in *Analog* in 1980; he was represented there by two of the year's best stories, his own novella "Nightflyers" and a long novella or short novel called "One-Wing" in collaboration with Lisa Tuttle. Good fiction by Isaac Asimov, Ben Bova, Rick Gauger, Donald Franson, Leigh Kennedy, Charles Sheffield, Clifford D. Simak, and others, also appeared in *Analog* this year. On the whole, though — and I've said this before, other years — I found most of the short fiction in *Analog* to be gray, bland, and overly familiar. *Analog* does not seem to be taking many risks anymore, does not seem to be pushing at the boundaries of its own formula anymore as it did from time to time under former Editor Ben Bova, and the market that doesn't take an occasional risk is a market on its way to stagnation. I'm not suggesting that *Analog* suddenly turn itself into *New Worlds*, but there are new directions in which even the hard-science story can legitimately go, and several stories published this year by other markets explored some of those directions, notably Michael Swanwick's "Ginungagap" in *TriQuarterly 49*, Kevin Christensen's "Bellerophon" in the Spring *Destinies*, and Kim Stanley Robinson's "On The North Pole of Pluto" in *Orbit 21*. It seems to me that these stories legitimately fall within — or should fall within — *Analog*'s purview, and that *Analog* would have been the richer for them and others like them.

Davis Publications is scheduled to start a third SF magazine in the summer of 1981, a quarterly called *Science Fiction Digest*, which will feature condensed versions of forthcoming novels.

Once again, *The Magazine of Fantasy and Science Fiction* was easily the best and most consistent in literary quality of all the SF magazines, having even less competition this year than it usually does. Excellent fiction by Edward Bryant, Stephen King, Bob Leman, Harlan Ellison, Thomas M. Disch, Marta Randall, Keith Roberts, Jerrold Mundis, Michael Shea, Bruce McAllister, John Kessel, Lisa Tuttle, James Patrick Kelly, Charles L. Grant, Hilbert Schenck, Ian Watson, Jane Yolen, and others appeared in *F&SF* during 1980. *F&SF* has always been a "marginal" commercial proposition, though, and in these increasingly hard times, I worry about losing her. There are months when it seems as if *F&SF* is singlehandedly keeping excellence in the magazine market, and SF would be a much drearier place without her. I urge everyone reading these words to subscribe to *F&SF*; the magazine is difficult to find on most newsstands anyway, and anyone sincerely interested in reading the best SF published during the year can't afford to miss it (*F&SF*'s subscription address is: Mercury Press, Inc., P.O. Box 56, Cornwall, CT 06753; $15 for one year, twelve issues). If you intend to subscribe to any SF magazine, make it *F&SF*.

As mentioned above, *Fantastic, Asimov's SF Adventure Magazine,* and *Galileo* died in 1980. *Galaxy,* purchased last year by *Galileo,* published one issue under the new management, and then died too, ending three decades as one of SF's top magazines. *Amazing,* which had been following an all-reprint policy, began publishing original fiction again, although to date they have run little of value, seemingly just publishing the top slice of their slush pile. Still, *Amazing* has come startlingly back to life several times in the past after the memorial services had already been read over its grave, and it just might be about to do the Lazarus trick again. *Eternity,* a "semi-prozine" edited by Stephen Gregg and Henry Vogel, features some interesting columns and commentary by top professionals (particularly Orson Scott Card's book review column, one of the best in the field at the moment, and Edward Bryant's film review column) and, to date, rather amateurish fiction, although at least one decent story by Orson Scott Card did appear here. *Eternity*'s intentions seem good, and I wish them well, but in these troubled economic times I am not sanguine about its chances of survival, let alone its chances of upgrading itself to an acceptably professional level of circulation and quality. *(Eternity*: P.O. Box 510, Clemson, SC 29631.) There were no issues of *Shayol* or *Whispers* published during 1980.

A new, slick, large-format SF magazine called *The Twilight Zone Magazine* is scheduled to begin publication in 1981, financed by the publishers of *Gallery,* and I am quite hopeful about it. Edited by writer T.E.D. Klein, it will supposedly feature fantasy, horror fiction, and "soft" SF, which is close enough to *F&SF*'s successful formula (although I expect that in actual practice fantasy will be more heavily emphasized than it is at *F&SF*) that, if handled well, the magazine could be quite good. I have my fingers crossed, anyway, and 1981 should tell the tale.

For the first time in a few years, the original anthology market was moderately strong in 1980, with the "Big Two" anthology series (*Universe* and *New Dimensions*) producing their most solid volumes in some time, the appearance of several excellent one-shot anthologies, and the founding of a promising new anthology series. On the downhill side, we seem to be losing at least one of the more prominent series of recent years, and some of the others produced issues that were lackluster at best.

Actually, the "Big Two" anthology series were momentarily the "Big Three" again this year, with Damon Knight's *Orbit 21* (Harper & Row), the final issue of the long-running *Orbit* series, appearing like a ghost of things past more than two years after the series had already been officially pronounced dead. The mills of the publishing world often grind exceedingly slow, and this volume was already in inventory when Harper & Row axed the series in 1978. Unfortunately, although it was nice to see an *Orbit* again — I miss them — *Orbit 21* does not make a really memorable capstone for the series; 1978's *Orbit 20* was much better suited for that role, containing as it did not only work from most of the major authors associated with *Orbit* (Wilhelm, Wolfe, Lafferty) but one of the best stories ever published in *Orbit,* Gene Wolfe's superb novella "Seven American Nights." *Orbit 21* is devoted instead almost entirely to new writers (often first-sale authors), and they don't manage to come up with anything nearly as monumental as the Wolfe piece, although they do produce some good work. The best thing here is Kim Stanley Robinson's excellent and unusual novella "On the

North Pole of Pluto,'' with Raymond G. Embrak, Richard Kearns, Lelia Rose Foreman, and John Barfoot also contributing interesting though occasionally flawed work.

Another ghost from Harper & Row's past was haunting the bookstores in 1980: Robert Silverberg's *New Dimensions 10,* already in inventory when Harper dropped this series as well, in 1979. Like *Orbit 21, New Dimensions 10* contains one long, strong story, Orson Scott Card's powerful "Holy"; the rest of the volume is filled out with weaker material, although there is also some decent stuff by John Kessel, Gregory Benford, and Peter Santiago C.

Harper & Row dropped the last of its anthology series this year, the reprint *Nebula Award Stories* series, and seems to be pretty well out of that end of the business. *Nebula Award Stories Fifteen,* to be published in 1981, will be that last issue of this series to appear from them (they have been publishing the Nebula Award anthology since *Nebula Award Stories Seven* in 1973).

With *New Dimensions* now a paperback original, Terry Carr's *Universe* is the last of the major anthology series still in hardcover, and I sometimes wonder how long it is going to be able to survive as a hardcover in the face of inflation and the rising cost of paper, printing, and labor, all eventually reflected in a book's cover price. Swimming against the evolutionary current, Roy Torgeson's *Chrysalis,* formerly a paperback original, *became* a hardcover series this year, but I am not sanguine about its chances either. I think that the handwriting is on the wall for the hardcover anthology series, and that their days are numbered.

Carr's *Universe 10* (Doubleday) and Silverberg and Randall's *New Dimensions 11* (Pocket Books) were very close in quality this year, the best issues of any anthology series published in 1980. *Universe 10* is perhaps somewhat more even in overall quality: It contains what is probably the year's single best story — Howard Waldrop's "The Ugly Chickens" — as well as good work by Michael Bishop, James Tiptree, Jr., Lee Killough, Mary Pangborn, and F.M. Busby; nothing here is really bad, although not all of it is exceptional. *New Dimensions 11* (the first issue of this series from Pocket Books, and the first to feature Marta Randall as co-editor) also contains some of the year's best stories — Suzy McKee Charnas's "Unicorn Tapestry" and Michael Swanwick's "The Feast of St. Janis" — in addition to good work by Pat Cadigan, Craig Strete, Alan Ryan, and Mary Pangborn; the rest of the book, however, is uninspired.

Judy-Lynn del Rey's *Stellar 5* (Del Rey) was bland, as most recent *Stellars* have been. This series has published little that has aroused any real enthusiasm since the days when the first two *Stellars* featured memorable work by writers such as Isaac Asimov and Robert Silverberg. There is some workmanlike but uninspired stuff by G.C. Edmondson, Philip K. Dick, James P. Hogan, and others in this particular *Stellar.* Charles L. Grant's *Shadows 3* (Doubleday) also seems to lack some of the strength and pizazz of past *Shadows,* although it remains much more to my taste than *Stellar 5;* the best work here is by Chelsea Quinn Yarbro and Pat Murphy, with interesting but weaker material by Juleen Brantingham, Alan Ryan, Steve Rasnic Tem, Peter Pautz, and others.

Peter Weston's *Andromeda* series seems to have died. James Baen's *Destinies* (Ace) is dying; Ace's new management does not plan to continue with *Destinies,* although several volumes already in preparation will appear in 1981. Although I often did not agree with the thrust or the aesthetic stance of *Destinies,* good work by Gordon R. Dickson, Larry Niven, Kevin Christensen, Dean Ing, Charles Sheffield, and others did appear there in 1980, and I will be sorry to see it go. SF is in dire need of as many diverse short-fiction markets as it can support. There is an as-yet unconfirmed rumor that Baen will eventually start another *Destinies*-type "bookzine" series at Pinnacle/Tor.

George R.R. Martin's *New Voices III* (Berkley) featured good work by Suzy McKee Charnas, Alan Brennert, and John Varley.

Roy Torgeson's *Chrysalis* series produced three issues this year, *Chrysalis 6* and *Chrysalis 7* in paperback from Zebra, *Chrysalis 8* in hardcover from Doubleday. Of all current anthology editors, Torgeson is one of the most receptive to experimentalism and the publishing of diverse types of story material. On the plus side, this means that he has provided a home for some excellent unconventional material that might have otherwise gone a-begging; on the minus side, since a certain percentage of all experiments are failures, the individual *Chrysalis* volumes are often uneven and sometimes weak. Experiments in *Chrysalis* this year that were successful included work by Pat Murphy, Orson Scott Card, Paul H. Cook, Michael Bishop, Barry N. Malzberg, Glenn Chang, and others.

Another series that leans strongly toward the experimental is the newly founded *The Berkley Showcase* (Berkley), edited by Victoria Schochet and John Silbersack (Silbersack resigned his editorial position at Berkley toward the end of the year, and future volumes of *Showcase* will be edited by Schochet alone). Two issues of *Showcase* appeared in 1980. Again, some of the experiments here are failures, but many are not, and so far *Showcase*'s per-issue success ratio seems somewhat higher than that of *Chrysalis.* Good stories by Thomas M. Disch, R.A. Lafferty, Orson Scott Card, Elizabeth A. Lynn, John Kessel, Howard Waldrop, Janet Morris, P.C. Hodgell, and others appeared in *The Berkley Showcase* during 1980.

There were also a number of good one-shot original anthologies published in 1980, several of them also featuring a high percentage of experimental and unconventional work. Perhaps too high a percentage in the case of Ursula K. Le Guin and Virginia Kidd's *Interfaces* (Ace); the anthology is dominated by James Tiptree, Jr.'s, long and brilliant novella "Slow Music," but — with the exception of another long piece by Robert Holdstock — much of the rest seems insubstantial. Perhaps this is because the remainder of the material is so similar in tone, one surreal piece after another, few of them above vignette length. None of the remaining stories is major work, although some of them — notably the pieces by Michael Bishop, Gene Wolfe, John Crowley, and Philippa C. Maddern — are more successful than others. Le Guin and Kidd's *Edges* (Pocket Books) is much more to my taste, although the material here is at least as unconventional as that in *Interfaces,* perhaps more so. Somehow it also seems more substantial, and

Edges is probably the best one-shot original anthology of the year. The center-piece here is M.J. Engh's evocative and brilliantly crafted long novella "The Oracle," which all by itself makes *Edges* worth buying; I think I enjoyed it more than anything else I've read this year under novel length. Although it's straining things a bit even to classify it as fantasy, let alone science fiction, read it anyway, because Engh really is working out on the "edges" here, in heretofore unexplored territory. *Edges* also contains first-rate work by Naomi Mitchison, Damien Broderick, Thomas M. Disch, Gene Wolfe, and Avram Davidson.

Kirby McCauley's *Dark Forces* (Viking) is billed as an attempt to assemble "an anthology with the scope and dynamism of Harlan Ellison's *Dangerous Visions,* but in the supernatural horror field," and in many ways it succeeds. Unlike *Dangerous Visions,* there is little deliberate taboo-breaking here (just about all of the book's contents could have been sold to conventional genre markets, I would imagine), but McCauley *has* managed to put together an anthology that will certainly be perceived as a landmark volume in the still-evolving field of modern horror fiction. There is some first-rate work here by Joe Haldeman, Gene Wolfe, Isaac Bashevis Singer, Edward Bryant, Clifford D. Simak, Lisa Tuttle, T.E.D. Klein, Russell Kirk, and twelve others, as well as a short novel by Stephen King and an illustrated piece by Edward Gorey. In a way, I like Ramsey Campbell's less ambitious *New Terrors 1* (Pan) almost as well as *Dark Forces.* It features excellent stories by Gene Wolfe and Lisa Tuttle, as well as good work by Steve Rasnic, Russell Kirk, Karl Edward Wagner, Cherry Wilder, Campbell himself, and others. A great deal of interesting and vigorous hybrid work is being done in the shadowy borderlands between SF and the "modern horror story," and the SF reader will find these two "horror" anthologies well worth investigating.

Of special interest in this category are two special SF issues of "literary" magazines that function as one-shot anthologies. Considered as such, they are among the best one-shot anthologies of the year. David G. Hartwell, Editor of Timescape Books, edited *TriQuarterly 49,* a special all-SF issue of that well-known literary magazine, containing one of the year's best stories, Michael Swanwick's "Ginungagap," as well as good work by Ursula K. Le Guin, Gene Wolfe, and Thomas M. Disch, a long and intriguing critical essay by Algis Budrys, an excerpt from Samuel R. Delaney's new novel, and more. (*TriQuarterly:* 1735 Benson Avenue, Northwestern University, Evanston, IL 60201; $5.95 for issue 49.) *Their Immortal Hearts,* a special publication of the *West Coast Poetry Review,* is a paperback collection that features three good novellas by Barry N. Malzberg, Michael Bishop, and Bruce McAllister. ($5 from *West Coast Poetry Review,* 1335 Dartmouth Drive, Reno, NV 89509.)

There were also several original anthologies of "high fantasy" (as opposed to horror fantasy) this year, and the best of these in overall quality was probably Orson Scott Card's *Dragons of Light* (Ace). Although there is nothing really earth-shaking here, most of the stories are pleasant and entertaining, and the book as a whole makes an enjoyable read; the best work here is by Michael Bishop,

George R.R. Martin, Roger Zelazny, Jane Yolen, and Richard Kearns. Much the same could be said of Ellen Kushner's *Basilisk* (Ace), which featured good original work by Elizabeth A. Lynn, Michael Bishop, and Joan D. Vinge, and good reprint material by M. John Harrison and Alan Garner. Roy Torgeson's *Other Worlds 2* (Zebra) featured an excellent novella by Avram Davidson, as well as good material by Roger Zelazny, Pat Murphy, Poul Anderson, and others.

Good short stories were generally scarce in 1980 in both the magazine and the original anthology market, although there were many first-rate novellas and novelettes.

The reprint anthology market, moribund only a few years ago, was strong again in 1980, and once again Martin Henry Greenberg was ubiquitous. The two best reprint anthologies of 1980, and among the best in many years, are undoubtedly Robert Silverberg and Martin Henry Greenberg's *An Arbor House Treasury of Great Science Fiction* and *An Arbor House Treasury of Great Science Fiction Short Novels,* both available from Priam Books in $8.95 trade paperback editions. (Considering the combined wordage of these two massive volumes, that's amazingly inexpensive.) They comprise a particularly good introduction to the SF of the sixties and seventies, and will undoubtedly take their place as standard reference anthologies alongside such classics as the two SFWA Hall of Fame volumes or *The Hugo Winners*. Other excellent retrospective reprint anthologies published this year were Frederik Pohl, Martin Harry Greenberg, and Joseph D. Olander's *Galaxy: Thirty Years of Science Fiction* (Playboy Press); Edward L. Ferman's *The Magazine of Fantasy and Science Fiction: A 30-Year Retrospective* (Doubleday); and James Gunn's *The Road to Science Fiction, Vol. 3* (NAL). Among the best of 1980's nonretrospective reprint anthologies were Terry Carr's *Dream's Edge* (Sierra Club Books), a good collection of SF stories about ecology (there were three or four SF ecology anthologies in the mid-seventies, but this is the first one I've seen in a number of years — an omen of times to come?); Brian W. Aldiss's *Perilous Planets* (Avon); and Jack Dann and Gardner Dozois's *Aliens!* (Pocket Books), about which I will say no more, except that *I* liked it.

Also interesting were: Richard A. Lupoff's *What If? Vol. 1* (Pocket Books); Pohl, Greenberg, and Olander's *The Great Science Fiction Series* (Harper & Row); Ben Bova's *The Best From Omni* (Omni Society), an anthology in magazine form which sold over 300,000 copies on newsstands; Jim Baen's *Galaxy: The Best of My Years* (Ace); and Reginald Bretnor's *The Spear of Mars* (Ace).

Nineteen-eighty was a good year for novels, all in all, but there were so *many* of them! Since 1976 the number of new SF and fantasy novels released annually has steadily increased, until now the flood of new titles has become almost impossible for any one reviewer to encompass. I deal with 48 novels in this Summation, most of them at far less length than they deserve, and even so, that's only the tip of the iceberg. There were certainly at least a hundred other new novels released in 1980 that aren't even mentioned here, probably more, and I'm uncomfortably aware that there are undoubtedly some that I've never even *heard* of, in spite of a dogged effort to read everything, a task that is just about impossible now, and becomes more nearly impossible every year.

This year's novels were a very mixed bag. Nineteen-eighty was a year in which some novices and near novices produced some very good work, and some of the biggest names in the field — Heinlein, Bester, Farmer, Niven, King — produced novels that were, to one extent or another, dissappointments. Large-screen, vividly colored, picaresque science-fantasy novels *(The Snow Queen, Lord Valentine's Castle)* were big this year, and many other novels also hung ambiguously on the shadowy aesthetic borderline between SF and fantasy *(The Shadow of the Torturer, The Orphan, The Magic Labyrinth, Wizard, The Northern Girl, Firestarter, The Vampire Tapestry, The Dreaming Dragons, Songmaster, The Number of the Beast, The Wall of Years, Wild Seed,* and a half-dozen others). The extent to which SF has come to be dominated by series and trilogies (some of these "trilogies" now extended to four or five volumes) also became apparent this year. Some of the best books of the year were the beginning volumes of trilogies or series *(The Shadow of the Torturer, The Orphan,* and *Wild Seed,* which was a "prequel" to an already published series), while a large number of other books *(Wizard, Beyond the Blue Event Horizon, The Northern Girl, Ringworld Engineers, The Magic Labyrinth)* suffered in varying degrees from being the middle or concluding books of series.

The two best novels of 1980, and among the best of any year, were Gene Wolfe's *The Shadow of the Torturer* (Simon & Schuster) and Gregory Benford's *Timescape* (Simon & Schuster). *The Shadow of the Torturer* is in many ways a masterpiece, an evocative and marvelously strange book, a magical and passionate book peopled with bizarre and wonderful characters. It is an absolutely unique literary creation, something that counts heavily with me in these days when we flounder in countless Tolkien and *Star Wars* imitations — no one but Wolfe could possibly have written this book. *Timescape* is also a monumental novel, and comes as close as any book I've ever seen to fulfilling that old goal of a book that functions *both* as a valid SF novel and as a fully realized "mainstream" novel of character; it's finely written and characterized, the contrasting *milieu* are perfectly realized, the insider's view into the strange world of the working scientist is compelling and convincing, the conceptual content is awesome and completely original. The "slow pace" that some reviewers complained of did not bother me a bit: This is a book that is meant to be savored, not tossed down like popcorn. With these two novels alone — even ignoring their other work — Wolfe and Benford have insured themselves of a place in genre history. They are simply two of the best SF writers of our times.

Robert Stallman's *The Orphan* (Pocket Books) is also first-rate, a real sleeper, a beautifully crafted and very subtle book that I came to with no expectations (in fact with negative expectations, expecting another dumb werewolf book) but that hooked me at once and moved me more than once before it was over. Stallman, whose first novel this is, was one of those rare and special talents who come along only once in a long while, and his tragic death this year was a major blow to the genre.

Nineteen-eighty also saw the publication of a number of other excellent books that all partook of the atmosphere of fantasy to one degree or another. Suzy McKee Charnas's *The Vampire Tapestry* (Simon & Schuster) is one of the most original handlings of the vampire theme in recent years, and the characterization here is among the strongest and most vivid I can remember. I did think, though, that the material worked better piece by piece, as novellas and novelettes, than it did as a complete novel. Octavia Butler's *Wild Seed* (Doubleday) is another powerful novel with a vivid and original protagonist and a warmth and strength of characterization that permeates the text. In plot, this is an old-fashioned wild talents melodrama, and it's only the *tone* of the writing and characterization (which is closer to that of a good historical novel) that keeps you from realizing it most of the time. I did have trouble suspending disbelief in some of the cosmic mutant huggermugger that goes on here, particularly in the number and range of the protagonist's powers — she sure has a lot of them. Nevertheless, *Wild Seed* and last year's *Kindred* are more than sufficient to establish Butler as one of the best of the new writers. Many of the same compliments already paid to *Wild Seed* and *The Vampire Tapestry* would apply equally as well to Elizabeth A. Lynn's *The Northern Girl* (Putnam), the concluding volume in her "Tornor" trilogy. It is an evocative and lyrically written novel, peopled with strong and compassionately drawn characters; it will be a bit too slowly paced for some tastes, but others will find it fascinating throughout. Ursula K. Le Guin's *The Beginning Place* (Harper & Row) is an economical and deceptively simple little book that seems at first to be a juvenile (disgruntled teenagers visit a fairytale world) but which ultimately reveals unexpected strengths, depths, and complications, an underlying vein of horror, even a smidgen of sex. It is as terse and evocatively stark as anything Le Guin has done in recent years, and very good. All the *parts* of Robert Silverberg's *Lord Valentine's Castle* are there — intelligent writing, atmospheric setting, a plot with mysteries to unfold, strange creatures, a king seeking to regain his throne — but somehow the passion that should animate them is not. I am very glad to see Silverberg writing again after his long silence, but, although I admired *Lord Valentine's Castle* intellectually, as a technical exercise, it somehow failed to stir that adolescent dreamer who lives in the heart of every fantasy fan. Joan D. Vinge's *The Snow Queen* (Dial), on the other hand, somehow has the fire, the naïve enthusiasm and wonder, that *Lord Valentine's Castle* lacks, although in many ways it is technically inferior to Silverberg's book, suffering particularly from some serious underlying flaws in the background and plot-logic; nevertheless, it delivers plenty of color and excitement, and my guess is that it will win at least one of the major awards this year. Chelsea Quinn Yarbro's *Ariosto* (Pocket Books) was another fantasy novel reminiscent in tone of a good historical novel, set in a fascinating alternate world; the Pocket edition also featured the year's most beautiful cover art (by Don Maitz).

Good straight-fantasy novels this year included Paul Hazel's *Yearwood* (Little, Brown), Gillian Bradshaw's *Hawk of May* (Simon & Schuster), and Parke Godwin's *Firelord* (Doubleday).

Frederik Pohl's *Beyond the Blue Event Horizon* (Del Rey), the final part of Pohl's "Heechee" series, is in many ways an excellent book, but (and how tired Pohl must be of hearing this) it is not as strong as Pohl's 1977 *Gateway,* the middle book of the sequence — the final secret of the Heechee, when it is at last revealed, seems (perhaps inevitably) rather anticlimactic, and the whole "Old One" section (besides being uneasily reminiscent of a Star Trek episode called "The Apple") seemed to me to be basically a bit of stage misdirection; the real story here was a confrontation between humans and the Heechee themselves, not the rather easily resolved problem posed by the "Old One," a straw man set up so the characters would have something to knock down. All this having been said, *Beyond the Blue Event Horizon* remains head-and-shoulders above almost anything of this type; only a few truly superb books like Benford's *Timescape* and Pohl's own *Gateway* manage to beat it on its own terms. Much less successful, and also much more damaged by being a sequel to a well-known novel, is Larry Niven's *Ringworld Engineers* (Del Rey). After the Ringworld itself, SF's ultimate artifact, discovered in the earlier novel *Ringworld,* all the marvels the characters come across here on the surface of the Ringworld seem rather flat, and the picaresque plot ultimately becomes dull. This is a book aimed directly at real *Ringworld* fans (who are legion), and in fact depends so heavily on your having read the earlier book that you may find much of it incomprehensible if you have not. John Varley's *Wizard* (Putnam) also suffers from being the middle book of a series, and also contains a lot of picaresque travel-log stuff that becomes dull in spots. Still, I liked it, liked it better in fact than *Titan,* the first book in the series. There is some good writing and conceptualization here, and a lovely kind of DeCampian wackiness and whimsy that is new to Varley's work, as well as a few vivid characters, at least one of whom is more-or-less thrown away. Varley is still having a lot of trouble with pacing at novel length, though, especially with what should or should not be left off-stage (he omits several scenes that really should have been here, and details some unnecessary scenes at considerable length). Still, I am looking forward to the final book of the series, although I hope that he tones down the picaresque element in it — since he certainly has left himself more than enough plot to deal with instead.

Walter Tevis's *Mockingbird* (Doubleday) was one of the most critically acclaimed books of the year, but I was a good deal less enthusiastic about it. It's written well enough, but the plot, background situation, and message seemed not only old hat but actually rather dumb. I also had mixed feelings about Stephen King's *Firestarter* (Viking). On one hand, I enjoyed it; it was a sizzlingly fast read, as are most of King's books. On the other hand, the melodrama here is not even thinly disguised, with King's CIA-like secret organization striking me as particularly unconvincing. At times, particularly toward the end, the book reads like an old James Bond movie (to mix a metaphor), and as the young protagonist's

Cosmic Mutant powers grew and grew they became more and more like something out of a Marvel Comic book. Unusually for King, there were also signs of padding and sloppy writing here, although, as I've said, most of it whizzed by very facilely. I've come to deeply respect King's talent over the last few years, but *Firestarter,* while not a really *bad* book, is not a patch on last year's excellent *The Dead Zone.* Alfred Bester's *Golem 100* (Simon & Schuster) was an even more severe disappointment, taking what was once a good short story and padding it out outrageously into an ultimately rather distasteful novel; nor does the mixture of text and graphics work for me, seeming a heavy-handed elaboration of techniques explored with much more grace over twenty years ago in Bester's own *The Stars My Destination.* Philip Jose Farmer's *The Magic Labyrinth* (Putnam) is a muddled and disappointing end to one of SF's major series; the Riverworld series started well with *To Your Scattered Bodies Go,* but has been running downhill from book to book ever since, the narrative thrust gradually getting lost in a maze of unnecessary characters and subplots. Orson Scott Card's *Songmaster* (Dial) is atmospheric and well written, but I had a lot of difficulty suspending my disbelief in the powers of Card's Singers effectively enough to make the rest of the plot credible. Originally one of the most popular radio shows in Britain, the material in Douglas Adam's *Hitchhiker's Guide to the Galaxy* (Harmony Books) probably comes across a lot funnier on the radio than it does in flat cold print; as a novel, the book is dreadfully padded, although there are some funny lines and situations here, particularly in the opening few chapters. It might have worked better as a short story. John Shirley's *City Come A-Walking* (Dell) is clumsy in places and riddled with logical inconsistencies, but it also has a certain raw power all its own; along with Bruce Sterling's *The Artificial Kid* (Harper & Row), about which most of the same comments could be made, and some recent work by Nicholas Yermakov, it seems to herald the development of a sort of "punk SF," developing upon a set of sensibilities that to date have been represented in SF primarily by the work of Harlan Ellison. Although it is probably the best-selling SF novel of the year, Robert A. Heinlein's *The Number of the Beast* (Fawcett) is dreadful, by far the worst novel Heinlein has ever written. The characters talk interminably in nearly indistinguishable voices, and what plot there is sort of peters out halfway through the book; the rest of the text, monstrously self-indulgent, should have been published in a fanzine, if they could find a fanzine large enough to contain it. Submitted under any other name than Heinlein's, this mishmosh would have — and should have — been rejected out of hand.

Also interesting this year were David Brin's *Sundiver* (Bantam), Charles L. Harness's *The Catalyst* (Pocket Books), Paul F. Pruess's *Gates of Heaven* (Bantam), Marta Randall's *Dangerous Games* (Pocket Books), Pamela Sargent's *Watchstar* (Pocket Books), Hal Clement's *Nitrogen Fix* (Ace), Norman Spinrad's *Songs from the Stars* (Pocket Books), Damien Broderick's *The Dreaming Dragons* (Pocket Books), M. John Harrison's *A Storm of Wings* (Doubleday), Andrew M. Stephenson's *The Wall of Years* (Dell), Poul Anderson's *The Devil's Game* (Pocket Books), Greg Bear's *Beyond Heaven's River* (Dell), G. C. Edmondson's *The Man Who Corrupted Earth* (Ace), Kathleen M. Sidney's *Michael and the Magic Man* (Berkley), Manly Wade Wellman's *After Dark* (Doubleday), C.J. Cherryh's *Serpent's Reach* (DAW), and a number of reprints of long-unavailable novels such as Fritz Leiber's *The Sinful Ones* (Pocket Books), Jack Vance's *The Languages of Pao* (DAW), and Edgar Pangborn's *West of the Sun* and *A Mirror for Observers,* both from Dell. SF readers may also be interested in a number of historical novels by Poul Anderson published by Zebra this year that were reminiscent of fantasy in mood, among them *The Golden Slave, Rogue Sword,* and the three-volume novel *The Last Viking.*

Nineteen-eighty was Gene Wolfe's year in many respects, for the year's best short-story collection, and one of the best ever published, was Gene Wolfe's long-overdue collection *The Island of Doctor Death and Other Stories and Other Stories* (Pocket Books). This magnificent collection contains some of the very best short fiction of the seventies, including superlative pieces such as "The Hero as Werewolf," "Seven American Nights," "The Eyeflash Miracles," "Tracking Song," "Alien Stones," the title story, and others. If you only buy one short-story collection this year, this should be the one. Also excellent is Jack Dann's *Timetipping* (Doubleday). The book is made somewhat uneven by the apprentice work that is included to fill it out, but Dann's mature work, particularly the stories from the last few years, is innovative, eloquent, and exciting, as far ahead of its time as the work of Charles Harness was ahead of the SF world of the fifties, baroque and packed with wild new ideas; particularly noteworthy here are the title story and the novelette "Camps," a Nebula finalist. Another innovative voice, now tragically silenced, belonged to the late Tom Reamy, and Reamy's *San Diego Lightfoot Sue and Other Stories* (Earthlight) which contains almost all of his short fiction, is another first-rate collection; note here the title story, as well as "Twilla" and "Under the Hollywood Sign." Hilbert Schenck's *Wave Rider* (Pocket Books) is an unusually strong debut collection of SF stories that all deal with mankind's interaction with the sea, including the powerful novella "Battle of the Abaco Reefs," a Nebula and Hugo finalist last year. Harlan Ellison's *Shatterday* (Houghton Mifflin) contains, as well as some minor stuff, most of Ellison's major work of the past few years, most notably the title story, "All the Birds Come Home to Roost," and "All the Lies That Are My Life." John Varley's *The Barbie Murders* is a good deal weaker overall than his 1979 collection *The Persistence of Vision,* but still contains good material like "Good-bye, Robinson Crusoe," "Bagatelle," and "Beatnik Bayou."

The year's other interesting collections were: Thomas M. Disch's *Fundamental Disch* (Bantam), *The Best of Walter M. Miller, Jr.* (Pocket Books), Theodore Sturgeon's *The Golden Helix* (Dell), Roger Zelazny's *The Last Defender of Camelot* (Pocket Books), William Tenn's *The Seven Sexes* (Del Rey), Richard Cowper's *Out There Where the Big Ships Go* (Pocket Books), Frederik Pohl and C.M. Kornbluth's *Before the Universe* (Bantam), Spider Robinson's *Antinomy* (Dell), and Robert A. Heinlein's *Expanded Universe* (Grosset & Dunlap).

The SF-oriented nonfiction / SF reference-book field, very strong for the last few years, was somewhat weak in 1980; it appears that the stream of books *about* SF is running dry, at least for the moment.

The major event of the year in this category was probably the publication of the second half of Isaac Asimov's immense autobiography, the 828-page *In Joy Still Felt* (Doubleday), which brings Asimov's account of his life up to 1978. If you liked last year's *In Memory Yet Green,* the first half of this autobiography (I did), then you will enjoy *In Joy Still Felt.* If you were one of those who felt the earlier volume was dull, then stay away: I found *In Joy Still Felt* to be somewhat less interesting than its predecessor, in part because Asimov's descriptions of his Brooklyn boyhood were my favorite part of the earlier book and their welcome hint of color is missing here, and in part because Asimov has, by his own admission, spent the greater part of his mature years sitting in his office turning out book after book after book, something which doesn't describe well. Nevertheless, as in the last volume, Asimov's skill as an anecdotist and the charm he manages to inject into the description of even the most trivial of incidents, keep the book of at least low-key interest throughout. Asimov fans, of course, will find this to be just their cup of meat.

Charles Platt's *Dreammakers* (Berkley) is a book of interviews with an assortment of SF writers, something we've seen before, but Platt's interviews are, in the main, competent, sophisticated, and interesting, something we haven't seen much of in recent years — published interviews with SF writers tend instead to be shallow, clumsy, and jejune. True, some of the interviews here are much better than others. Platt seems to have interviewed writers like Asimov and Herbert only for form's sake, rather superficially, and it's easy to see that his heart isn't in it; on the other hand, his interviews with people such as Ellison, Malzberg, Dick, and Moorcock are excellent, with the Ellison piece in particular as good a job as I've ever seen done on that much-interviewed author. Although I could quibble with some of Platt's selection of interview subjects (E.C. Tubb? Hank Stine? Why not Gene Wolfe? Ursula K. Le Guin? Fritz Leiber? Joanna Russ?), on the whole, *Dreammakers* is excellent, recommended for those who want to know something about the personalities behind the words. Also excellent is Alexis Gilliland's *The Iron Law of Bureaucracy* (Loompanics Unlimited, P.O. Box 264, Mason, MI 48854; $4.95), a collection of brilliant, biting, and erudite cartoons, many of them on SF and fantasy themes, most of them originally published in SF fanzines. Although he recently won a well-deserved Hugo as Best Fan Artist of 1979, Gilliland remains almost totally unknown outside of organized SF fandom. It's a pity, because in wit and originality he is the equal of better-known cartoonists like B. Kliban and Gahan Wilson, and some of his concepts — the "Federal Bureau of Humor," for instance — rank with the best work of comic surrealists like John Sladek and George Alec Effinger. A number of interesting author studies also appeared this year; among the best were *Jack Vance* (Taplinger) and Joan Gordon's *Joe Haldeman* (Starmont).

Nineteen - eighty also the arrival of an event as eagerly awaited by media fans as the Second Coming — the sequel to 1977's *Star Wars,* released at last, not called *Star Wars II,* as venerable Hollywood tradition would seem to dictate it should be, but rather given to the eager world as *The Empire Strikes Back.* There is some good news and some bad news about this long-awaited event. First, the good news: *The Empire Strikes Back* is handsome, inventive, exciting, and professionally slick, and makes all the *Star Wars* imitations that have lumbered down the pike since 1977 (especially TV's execrable *Battlestar Galactica*) look like the silly mush that they are. It is a junk movie, of course, but a well-made junk movie, a *fun* junk movie. There have been good SF/fantasy movies since the original *Star Wars,* of course — notably *Watership Down* and *Alien,* two amazingly different movies — but none, since *Star Wars,* that are nearly as much *fun* as *The Empire Strikes Back.* Now the bad news: It is not, to my taste anyway, nearly as good (or as much fun) as the original *Star Wars.* Somehow, some of the special magic of the original is gone. *The Empire Strikes Back* is heavier textured without being any more profound (some critics have made a great point about the characterization being "deeper and more mature" in *Empire,* but how they can say that with a straight face, I don't know — Dostoevski this is not, guys, even here), the special effects and the set-dressing are nowhere near as good (rather inept in places, in fact), and it ends with a thundering anticlimax, a real letdown. It is all very well to think of the *Star Wars* saga as an old-time Saturday-matinee serial, as Lucas reportedly does, but three years is an unconscionably long wait between episodes, and I can't help but feel that each movie ought to be able to stand on its own feet (as, in fact, *Star Wars* does). We also have to sit through a great deal more of Lucas's three-a-penny mysticism about the Force here (which Lucas apparently takes quite seriously), all delivered as solemnly as Moses handing down the Word from the Mount: Yoda *is* cute, though, even if he does occasionally sound suspiciously like *Sesame Street*'s Grover. All you have to do, though, is think back to last year's unbelievably awful *The Black Hole,* and all these quibbles vanish, and you realize just how much there is here to be thankful for. 1980's other major SF/fantasy movie was *The Shining,* Stanley Kubrick's long-awaited film adaptation of Stephen King's best-selling horror novel. This is a movie that has everything going for it: an intelligent director, a good book to work from, excellent actors to work with, masterful cinematography. And yet *The Shining* is ultimately flat and disappointing. Perhaps Kubrick's dispassionate, distanced eye is too cool and remote for a horror movie: the film is just not *scary.* The famous bathtub scene, for instance, the scariest in the book, is shot under glaring fluorescent lights in a clinical, sterile way that is almost boring. Had Hitchcock shot that scene, he'd have brought you bolt upright in your chair screaming. There is also no character buildup here: In the book, Jack Torrence is a good but weak man slowly succumbing to evil, and we feel his own horror as he slides relentlessly into madness. In the movie, Jack Nicholson, playing a grimacing, eye-rolling Jack Torrence, is clearly crazy as a loon from the very first scene. Nicholson's shameless overacting here is often entertaining, but it is not *effective*. The audience with whom I saw the movie kept breaking into gales of laughter at some of the lines Nicholson delivers while he's chasing his family around with an ax, certainly the wrong emotion to be evoked in a scene that is supposed to be horrifying and breathtakingly tense. In fact, it is impossible to sympathize or identify with any of the main characters, none of whom seem to like each other much from the very start. Shelley Duvall is a vacuous wimp who later screams a lot; the child is chilly and remote; and Scatman Crothers's character, the only warm human being on the screen, is thrown pointlessly away for shock's sake. And so the book's vision of a loving family being torn painfully apart by external forces is lost; you don't much *care* what happens to any of these people, and by the end of the film, all suspense is gone. A major disappointment.

PBS's television version of Ursula K. Le Guin's novel *The Lathe of Heaven* was much more satisfactory. An intelligent and literate movie, it can be ranked among the best recent SF movies, and certainly among the best SF ever created for television, marred only by the murkiness of the ending, which was nearly incomprehensible to people who had not read Le Guin's book. By contrast, NBC's adaptation of Ray Bradbury's *The Martian Chronicles* was heavy-handed and ponderous, keeping the structure of Bradbury's famous book while draining it of all its poetry, subtlety, and substance. Rankin-Bass's animated *Return of the King,* shown on network TV, was horrible enough to make even the strongest-stomached Tolkien fan blanch. Back at the movies, there were a zillion inept hack-'em-up horror and occult films, and Dino De Laurentiis's *Flash Gordon* was the usual dumb-dumb million-dollar camp comic book, unusual only for the bit of class provided by Max von Sydow as Ming the Merciless.

The 38th World Science Fiction Convention, Noreascon II, was held in Boston over the Labor Day weekend, and drew an attendance of almost six thousand, making it the largest worldcon of all time. It was a well-run and well-organized convention that nevertheless came perilously close at times to collapsing under its own weight, making me wonder what the practical limit of worldcon size is, and how soon it will be reached. The 1979 Hugo Awards, presented at Noreascon II, were: Best Novel, *The Fountains of Paradise,* by Arthur C. Clarke; Best Novella, "Enemy Mine," by Barry B. Longyear; Best Novelette, "Sandkings," by George R.R. Martin; Best Short Story, "The Way of Cross and Dragon," by George R.R. Martin; Best Non-Fiction Book, *The Science Fiction Encyclopedia,* by Peter Nicholls; Best Professional Editor, George H. Scithers; Best Professional Artist, Michael Whelan; Best Dramatic Presentation, *Alien;* Best Fan Artist, Alexis Gilliland; Best Fan Writer, Bob Shaw; Best Fanzine, *Locus;* plus the John W. Campbell, Jr., Award to Barry B. Longyear and the Grandmaster of Fantasy Award to Ray Bradbury.

The 1979 Nebula Awards were: Best Novel, *The Fountains of Paradise,* by Arthur C. Clarke; Best Novella, "Enemy Mine," by Barry B. Longyear; Best Novelette, "Sandkings," George R.R. Martin; Best Short Story, "giANTS," by Edward Bryant.

The Sixth World Fantasy Awards were: Best Novel, *Watchtower,* by Elizabeth A. Lynn; Best Collection, *Amazons!* edited by Jessica Amanda Salmonson; Best Short Fiction, "The Woman Who Loved the Moon," by Elizabeth A. Lynn and "Mackintosh Willy," by Ramsey Campbell (tie); Best Artist, Don Maitz; Special Award (professional) Donald M. Grant; Special Award (nonprofessional) Paul Allen; plus a Life Achievement Award to Manly Wade Wellman.

Dead in 1980 were: John Collier, author of the International Fantasy Award-winning collection *Fancies and Goodnights,* and of several other books that contained fantasy elements; Catherine Tarrant, long-time assistant editor of *Astounding/Analog* under the editorship of John W. Campbell, Jr.; J. O. Bailey, author of the pioneering work of SF criticism, *Pilgrims Through Time and Space;* George R. Stewart, author of the reknowned after-the-Holocaust novel *Earth Abides,* which won an International Fantasy Award; Alfred Hitchcock, perhaps the most famous of filmmakers in the horror/suspense genre, whose *Psycho!* provided the model for innumerable films to come; George Pal, producer of *Destination Moon, The Time Machine,* and many other SF films; Robert Stallman, a new author whose fantasy novel *The Orphan,* part of a trilogy completed just before his death, was one of the best novels of 1980; Kris Neville, author of "Bettyann," "New Apples in the Garden," "Cold War," and dozens of other stories; H. Warner Munn, early *Weird Tales* author and a member of the Lovecraft circle, author of *Merlin's Ring* and *The Lost Legion;* Joseph Samachson, who as "William Morrison" wrote the well-known story "Country Doctor"; Romain Gary, French novelist, author of *The Gasp* and *Hissing Tales;* Doris Pitkin Buck, for years a prominent member of the Milford Writer's Conference and the author of dozens of stories that appeared primarily in *F&SF,* a personal friend; Joan Thurston, wife of SF writer Bob Thurston, and a personal friend of mine for many years; Susan Wood, well-known SF critic, academic, fan, and fan writer, winner of a Hugo Award as Best Fan Writer, editor of the recent collection of Le Guin essays *The Language of the Night;* new SF writer Susan C. Petrey; and long-time SF writers Wallace West, George P. Elliot, and Arthur R. Tofte.

Howard Waldrop is known for his wild, soaring imagination and his strong, shaggy humor, but here, in "The Ugly Chickens," a Nebula finalist that may be the year's single best story, he has outdone even himself: only Waldrop could have produced a funny, excellently crafted, and ultimately very touching SF story about —dodos. Dodos? Well, you'll have to read it . . . but I can guarantee that you haven't seen anything quite like it before, and are unlikely to see anything like it ever again, either.

Born in Houston, Mississippi, Waldrop now lives in Austin, Texas, where he collects dodo memorabilia of all sorts. He has sold short fiction to markets as diverse as Analog, Zoo World, Galaxy, Crawdaddy, Universe, Shayol, New Dimensions, Nickelodeon, Orbit, The Berkley Showcase, *and others. His first novel, written in collaboration with fellow Texan Jake Saunders, was* The Texas—Israeli War *(Del Rey); he is reported to be currently at work on a new novel. His story "Mary Margaret Road-Grader" was in our* Sixth Annual Collection, *and two long collaborations with Steven Utley, "Custer's Last Jump" and "Black as the Pit, from Pole to Pole" were in our* Sixth Annual Collection *and* Seventh Annual Collection, *respectively.*

HOWARD WALDROP
The Ugly Chickens

My car was broken, and I had a class to teach at eleven. So I took the city bus, something I rarely do.

I spent last summer crawling through the Big Thicket with cameras and tape recorder, photographing and taping two of the last ivory-billed woodpeckers on the earth. You can see the films at your local Audubon Society showroom.

This year I wanted something just as flashy but a little less taxing. Perhaps a population study on the Bermuda cahow, or the New Zealand *takahe*. A month or so in the warm (not hot) sun would do me a world of good. To say nothing of the advance of science.

I was idly leafing through Greenway's *Extinct and Vanishing Birds of the World*. The city bus was winding its way through the ritzy neighborhoods of Austin, stopping to let off the Chicanas, black women and Vietnamese who tended the kitchens and gardens of the rich.

"I haven't seen any of those ugly chickens in a long time," said a voice close by.

A gray-haired lady was leaning across the aisle toward me.

I looked at her, then around. Maybe she was a shopping-bag lady. Maybe she was just talking. I looked straight at her. No doubt about it, she was talking to me. She was waiting for an answer.

"I used to live near some folks who raised them when I was a girl," she said. She pointed.

I looked down at the page my book was open to.

What I should have said was: That is quite impossible, madam. This is a drawing of an extinct bird of the island of Mauritius. It is perhaps the most famous dead bird in the world. Maybe you are mistaking this drawing for that of some rare Asiatic turkey, peafowl, or pheasant. I am sorry, but you *are* mistaken.

I should have said all that.

What she said was, "Oops, this is my stop." And got up to go.

My name is Paul Lindberl. I am twenty-six years old, a graduate student in ornithology at the University of Texas, a teaching assistant. My name is not unknown in the field. I have several vices and follies, but I don't think foolishness is one of them.

The stupid thing for me to do would have been to follow her.

She stepped off the bus.

I followed her.

I came into the departmental office, truiling scattered papers in the whirlwind behind me. "Martha! Martha!" I yelled.

She was doing something in the supply cabinet.

"Jesus, Paul! What do you want?"

"Where's Courtney?"

"At the conference in Houston. You know that. You missed your class. What's the matter?"

"Petty cash. Let me at it!"

"Payday was only a week ago. If you can't — "

"It's business! It's fame and adventure and the chance of a lifetime! It's a long sea voyage that leaves . . . a plane ticket. To either Jackson, Mississippi, or Memphis. Make it Jackson, it's closer. I'll get receipts! I'll be famous. Courtney will be famous. You'll even be famous! This university will make even more money! I'll pay you back. Give me some paper. I gotta write Courtney a note. When's the next plane out? Could you get Marie and Chuck to take over my classes Tuesday and Wednesday? I'll try to be back Thursday unless something happens. Courtney'll be back tomorrow, right? I'll call him from, well, wherever. Do you have some coffee?"

And so on and so forth. Martha looked at me like I was crazy. But she filled out the requisition anyway.

"What do I tell Kemejian when I ask him to sign these?"

"Martha, babe, sweetheart. Tell him I'll get his picture in *Scientific American*."

"He doesn't read it."

"*Nature,* then!"

"I'll see what I can do." she said.

The lady I had followed off the bus was named Jolyn (Smith) Jimson. The story she told me was so weird that it had to be true. She knew things only an expert, or someone with firsthand experience, could know. I got names from her, and addresses, and directions, and tidbits of information. Plus a year: 1927.

And a place. Northern Mississippi.

I gave her my copy of the Greenway book. I told her I'd call her as soon as I got back into town. I left her standing on the corner near the house of the lady she cleaned up for twice a week. Jolyn Jimson was in her sixties.

Think of the dodo as a baby harp seal with feathers. I know that's not even close, but it saves time.

In 1507, the Portuguese, on their way to India found the (then unnamed) Mascarene Islands in the Indian Ocean — three of them a few hundred miles apart, all east of Madagascar.

It wasn't until 1598, when that old Dutch sea Captain Cornelius van Neck bumped into them, that the islands received their names — names which changed several times through the centuries as the Dutch, French, and English changed them every war or so. They are now known as Rodriguez, Réunion, and Mauritius.

The major feature of these islands was large flightless, stupid, ugly, bad-tasting birds. Van Neck and his men named them *dod-aarsen,* stupid ass, or *dodars*, "silly birds," or solitaires.

There were three species — the dodo of Mauritius, the real gray-brown, hooked-beak clumsy thing that weighed twenty kilos or more; the white, some-what slimmer, dodo of Réunion; and the solitaires of Rodriguez and Réunion, which looked like very fat, very dumb light-colored geese.

The dodos all had thick legs, big squat bodies twice as large as turkeys', naked faces, and big long downcurved beaks ending in a hook like a hollow linoleum knife. Long ago they had lost the ability to fly, and their wings had degenerated to flaps the size of a human hand with only three or four feathers in them. Their tails were curly and fluffy, like a child's afterthought at decoration. They had absolutely no natural enemies. They nested on the open ground. They probably hatched their eggs wherever they happened to lay them.

No natural enemies until van Neck and his kind showed up. The Dutch, French, and Portuguese sailors who stopped at the Mascarenes to replenish stores found that besides looking stupid, dodos *were* stupid. They walked right up to them and hit them on the head with clubs. Better yet, dodos could be herded around like sheep. Ship's logs are full of things like: "Party of ten men ashore. Drove half-a-hundred of the big turkey-like birds into the boat. Brought to ship where they are given the run of the decks. Three will feed a crew of 150."

Even so, most of the dodo, except for the breast, tasted bad. One of the Dutch words for them was *"walghvogel,"* "disgusting bird." But on a ship three months out on a return from Goa to Lisbon, well, food was where you found it. It was said, even so, that prolonged boiling did not improve the flavor.

Even so, the dodos might have lasted, except that the Dutch, and later the French, colonized the Mascarenes. The islands became plantations and dumping places for religious refugees. Sugar cane and other exotic crops were raised there.

With the colonists came cats, dogs, hogs, and the cunning *rattus norvegicus* and the rhesus monkey from Ceylon. What dodos the hungry sailors left were chased down (they were dumb and stupid, but they could run when they felt like it) by dogs in the open. They were killed by cats as they sat on their nests. Their eggs were stolen and eaten by monkeys, rats, and hogs. And they competed with the pigs for all the low-growing goodies of the islands.

The last Mauritius dodo was seen in 1681, less than a hundred years after man first saw them. The last white dodo walked off the history books around 1720. The solitaires of Rodriguez and Réunion, last of the genus as well as the species, may have lasted until 1790. Nobody knows.

Scientists suddenly looked around and found no more of the Didine birds alive, anywhere.

This part of the country was degenerate before the first Snopes ever saw it. This road hadn't been paved until the late fifties, and it was a main road between two county seats. That didn't mean it went through civilized country. I'd traveled for miles and seen nothing but dirt banks red as Billy Carter's neck and an occasional church. I expected to see Burma Shave signs, but realized this road had probably never had them.

I almost missed the turnoff onto the dirt and gravel road the man back at the service station had marked. It led onto the highway from nowhere, a lane out of a field. I turned down it and a rock the size of a golf ball flew up over the hood and put a crack three inches long in the windshield of the rent-a-car I'd gotten in Grenada.

It was a hot, muggy day for this early. The view was obscured in a cloud of dust every time the gravel thinned. About a mile down the road, the gravel gave out completely. The roadway turned into a rutted dirt pathway, just wider than the car, hemmed in on both sides by a sagging three-strand barbed wire fence.

In some places the fenceposts were missing for a few meters. The wire lay on the ground and in some places disappeared under it for long stretches.

The only life I saw was a mockingbird raising hell with something under a thorn bush the barbed wire had been nailed to in place of a post. To one side now was a grassy field which had gone wild, the way everywhere will look after we blow ourselves off the face of the planet. The other was fast becoming woods — pine, oak, some black gum and wild plum, fruit not out this time of the year.

I began to ask myself what I was doing here. What if Ms. Jimson was some imaginative old crank who — but no. Wrong, maybe, but even the wrong was worth checking. But I knew she hadn't lied to me. She had seemed incapable of lies — a good ol' girl, backbone of the South, of the earth. Not a mendacious gland in her being.

I couldn't doubt her, or my judgment either. Here I was, creeping and bouncing down a dirt path in Mississippi, after no sleep for a day, out on the thin ragged edge of a dream. I *had* to take it on faith.

The back of the car sometimes slid where the dirt had loosened and gave way to sand. The back tire stuck once, but I rocked out of it. Getting back out again would be another matter. Didn't anyone ever use this road?

The woods closed in on both sides like the forest primeval, and the fence had long since disappeared. My odometer said ten kilometers and it had been twenty minutes since I'd turned off the highway. In the rearview mirror, I saw beads of sweat and dirt in the wrinkles of my neck. A fine patina of dust covered everything inside the car. Clots of it came through the windows.

The woods reached out and swallowed the road. Branches scraped against the windows and the top. It was like falling down a long dark leafy tunnel. It was dark and green in there. I fought back an atavistic urge to turn on the headlights. The roadbed must be made of a few centuries of leaf mulch. I kept constant pressure on the accelerator and bulled my way through.

Half a log caught and banged and clanged against the car bottom. I saw light ahead. Fearing for the oil pan, I punched the pedal and sped out.

I almost ran through a house.

It was maybe ten meters from the trees. The road ended under one of the windows. I saw somebody waving from the corner of my eye.

I slammed on the brakes.

A whole family was on the porch, looking like a Walker Evans Depression photograph, or a fever dream from the mind of a "Hee-Haw" producer. The house was old. Strips of peeling paint a meter long tapped against the eaves.

"Damned good thing you stopped," said a voice. I looked up. The biggest man I had ever seen in my life leaned down into the driver-side window.

"If we'd have heard you sooner, I'd've sent one of the kids down to the end of the driveway to warn you," he said.

Driveway?

His mouth was stained brown at the corners. I figured he chewed tobacco until I saw the sweet-gum snuff brush sticking from the pencil pocket in the bib of his overalls. His hands were the size of catchers' mitts. They looked like they'd never held anything smaller than an ax handle.

"How y'all?" he said, by way of introduction.

"Just fine," I said. I got out of the car.

"My name's Lindberl," I said, extending my hand. He took it. For an instant, I thought of bear traps, shark's mouths, closing elevator doors. The thought went back to wherever it is they stay.

"This the Gudger place?" I asked.

He looked at me blankly with his gray eyes. He wore a diesel truck cap, and had on a checked lumberjack shirt beneath the coveralls. His rubber boots were the size of the ones Karloff wore in *Frankenstein*.

"Naw. I'm Jim Bob Krait. That's my wife Jenny, and there's Luke and Skeeno and Shirl." He pointed to the porch.

The people on the porch nodded.

"Lessee? Gudger? No Gudgers round here I know of. I'm sorta new here." I took that to mean he hadn't lived here for more than twenty years or so.

"Jennifer!" he yelled. "You know of anybody named Gudger?" To me he said, "My wife's lived around heres all her life."

His wife came down onto the second step of the porch landing. "I think they used to be the ones what lived on the Spradlin place before the Spradlins. But the Spradlins left around the Korean War. I didn't know any of the Gudgers myself. That's while we was living over to Water Valley."

"You an insurance man?" asked Mr. Krait.

"Uh . . . no," I said. I imagined the people on the porch leaning toward me, all ears. "I'm a . . . I teach college."

"Oxford?" asked Krait.

"Uh, no. University of Texas."

"Well, that's a damn long way off. You say you're looking for the Gudgers?"

"Just their house. The area. As your wife said, I understand they left. During the Depression, I believe."

"Well, they musta had money," said the gigantic Mr. Krait. "Nobody around here was rich enough to *leave* during the Depression."

"Luke!" he yelled. The oldest boy on the porch sauntered down. He looked anemic and wore a shirt in vogue with the Twist. He stood with his hands in his pockets.

"Luke, show Mr. Lindbergh — "

"Lindberl."

"Mr. Lindberl here the way up to the old Spradlin place. Take him as far as the old log bridge, he might get lost before then."

"Log bridge broke down, Daddy."

"When?"

"October, Daddy."

"Well, hell, somethin' else to fix! Anyway, to the creek."

He turned to me. "You want him to go along on up there, see you don't get snakebit?"

"No, I'm sure I'll be fine."

"Mind if I ask what you're going up there for?" he asked. He was looking away from me. I could see having to come right out and ask was bothering him. Such things usually came up in the course of conversation.

"I'm a — uh, bird scientist. I study birds. We had a sighting — someone told us the old Gudger place — the area around here — I'm looking for a rare bird. It's hard to explain."

I noticed I was sweating. It was hot.

"You mean like a good God? I saw a good God about twenty-five years ago, over next to Bruce," he said.

"Well, no." (A good God was one of the names for an ivory-billed woodpecker, one of the rarest in the world. Any other time I would have dropped my jaw. Because they were thought to have died out in Mississippi by the teens, and by the fact that Krait knew they *were* rare.)

I went to lock my car up, then thought of the protocol of the situation. "My car be in your way?" I asked.

"Naw. It'll be just fine," said Jim Bob Krait. "We'll look for you back by sundown, that be all right?"

For a minute, I didn't know whether that was a command or an expression of concern.

"Just in case I get snakebit," I said. "I'll try to be careful up there."

"Good luck on findin' them rare birds," he said. He walked up to the porch with his family.

"Les go," said Luke.

Behind the Krait house was a hen house and pigsty where hogs lay after their morning slop like islands in a muddy bay, or some Zen pork sculpture. Next we passed broken farm machinery gone to rust, though there was nothing but uncultivated land as far as the eye could see. How the family made a living I don't know. I'm told you can find places just like this throughout the South.

We walked through woods and across fields, following a sort of path. I tried to memorize the turns I would have to take on my way back. Luke didn't say a word the whole twenty minutes he accompanied me, except to curse once when he stepped into a bull nettle with his tennis shoes.

We came to a creek which skirted the edge of a woodsy hill. There was a rotted log forming a small dam. Above it the water was nearly a meter deep, below it, half that much.

"See that path?" he asked.

"Yes."

"Follow it up around the hill, then across the next field. Then you cross the creek again on the rocks, and over the hill. Take the left-hand path. What's left of the house is about three-quarters the way up the next hill. If you come to a big bare rock cliff, you've gone too far. You got that?"

I nodded.

He turned and left.

The house had once been a dog-run cabin, like Ms. Jimson had said. Now it was fallen in on one side, what they call sigoglin (or was it anti-sigoglin?) I once heard a hymn on the radio called "The Land Where No Cabins Fall." This was the country songs like that were written in.

Weeds grew everywhere. There were signs of fences, a flattened pile of wood that had once been a barn. Farther behind the house were the outhouse remains. Half a rusted pump stood in the backyard. A flatter spot showed where the vegetable garden had been; in it a single wild tomato, pecked by birds, lay rotting. I passed it. There was lumber from three outbuildings, mostly rotten and green with algae and moss. One had been a smokehouse and woodshed combination. Two had been chicken roosts. One was larger than the other. It was there I started to poke around and dig.

Where? Where? I wish I'd been on more archaeological digs, knew the places to look. Refuse piles, midden heaps, kitchen scrap piles, compost boxes. Why hadn't I been born on a farm so I'd know instinctively where to search.

I prodded around the grounds. I moved back and forth like a setter casting for the scent of quail. I wanted more, more. I still wasn't satisfied.

Dusk. Dark, in fact. I trudged into the Krait's front yard. The tote sack I carried was full to bulging. I was hot, tired, streaked with fifty years of chicken shit. The Kraits were on their porch. Jim Bob lumbered down like a friendly mountain.

I asked him a few questions, gave them a Xerox of one of the dodo pictures, left them addresses and phone numbers where they could reach me.

Then into the rent-a-car. Off to Water Valley, acting on information Jennifer Krait gave me. I went to the postmaster's house at Water Valley. She was getting ready for bed. I asked questions. She got on the phone. I bothered people until one in the morning. Then back into the trusty rent-a-car.

On to Memphis as the moon came up on my right. Interstate 55 was a glass ribbon before me. WLS from Chicago was on the radio.

I hummed along with it, I sang at the top of my voice.

The sackful of dodo bones, beaks, feet, and eggshell fragments kept me company on the front seat.

Did you know a museum once traded an entire blue whale skeleton for one of a dodo?

Driving, driving.

THE DANCE OF THE DODOS

I used to have a vision sometimes — I had it long before this madness came up. I can close my eyes and see it by thinking hard. But it comes to me most often, most vividly when I am reading and listening to classical music, especially Pachelbel's *Canon in D*.

It is near dusk in The Hague, and the light is that of Franz Hals, of Rembrandt. The Dutch royal family and their guests eat and talk quietly in the great dining hall. Guards with halberds and pikes stand in the corners of the room. The family is arranged around the table; the king, queen, some princesses, a prince, a couple of other children, an invited noble or two. Servants come out with plates and cups but they do not intrude.

On a raised platform at one end of the room an orchestra plays dinner music — a harpsichord, viola, cello, three violins, and woodwinds. One of the royal dwarfs sits on the edge of the platform, his foot slowly rubbing the back of one of the dogs sleeping near him.

As the music of Pachelbel's *Canon in D* swells and rolls through the hall, one of the dodos walks in clumsily, stops, tilts its head, its eyes bright as a pool of tar. It sways a little, lifts its foot tentatively, one, then another, rocks back and forth in time to the cello.

The violins swirl. The dodo begins to dance, its great ungainly body now graceful. It is joined by the other two dodos who come into the hall, all three turning in sort of a circle.

The harpsichord begins its counterpoint. The fourth dodo, the white one from Réunion, comes from its place under the table and joins the circle with the others.

It is most graceful of all, making complete turns where the others only sway and dip on the edge of the circle they have formed.

The music rises in volume; the first violinist sees the dodos and nods to the king. But he and the others at the table have already seen. They are silent, transfixed — even the servants stand still, bowls, pots, and kettles in their hands forgotten.

Around the dodos dance with bobs and weaves of their ugly heads. The white dodo dips, takes a half-step, pirouettes on one foot, circles again.

Without a word the King of Holland takes the hand of the Queen and they come around the table, children before the spectacle. They join in the dance, waltzing (anachronism) among the dodos while the family, the guests, the soldiers watch and nod in time with the music.

Then the vision fades, and the afterimage of a flickering fireplace and a dodo remains.

The dodo and its kindred came by ships to the ports of civilized men. The first we have record of is that of Captain van Neck, who brought back two in 1599 — one for the King of Holland, and one which found its way through Cologne to the menagerie of Emperor Rudolf II.

This royal aviary was at Schloss Negebau, near Vienna. It was here that the first paintings of the dumb old birds were done by Georg and his son Jacob Hoefnagel, between 1602 and 1610. They painted it among more than ninety species of birds which kept the Emperor amused.

Another Dutch artist named Roelandt Savery, as someone said, ''made a career out of the dodo.'' He drew and painted them many times, and was no doubt personally fascinated by them. Obsessed, even. Early on, the paintings are consistent; the later ones have inaccuracies. This implies he worked from life first, then from memory as his model went to that place soon to be reserved for all its species. One of his drawings has two of the Raphidae scrambling for some goodie on the ground. His works are not without charm.

Another Dutch artist (they seemed to sprout up like mushrooms after a spring rain) named Peter Withoos also stuck dodos in his paintings, sometimes in odd and exciting places — wandering around during their owner's music lessons, or stuck with Adam and Eve in some Edenic idyll.

The most accurate representation, we are assured, comes from half a world away from the religious and political turmoil of the seafaring Europeans. There is an Indian miniature painting of the dodo which now rests in a museum in Russia. The dodo could have been brought by the Dutch or Portuguese in their travels to Goa and the coasts of the Indian subcontinent. Or they could have been brought centuries before by the Arabs who plied the Indian Ocean in their triangular-sailed craft, and who may have discovered the Mascarenes before the Europeans cranked themselves up for the First Crusade.

At one time early in my bird-fascination days (after I stopped killing them with BB guns but before I began to work for a scholarship) I once sat down and figured out where all the dodos had been.

Two with van Neck in 1599, one to Holland, one to Austria. Another was in Count Solms's park in 1600. An account speaks of "One in Italy, one in Germany, several to England, eight or nine to Holland." William Boentekoe van Hoorn knew of "one shipped to Europe in 1640, another in 1685" which he said was "also painted by Dutch artists." Two were mentioned as "being kept in Surrat House in India as pets," perhaps one of which is the one in the painting. Being charitable, and considering "several" to mean at least three, that means twenty dodos in all.

There had to be more, when boatloads had been gathered at the time.

What do we know of the Didine birds? A few ships' logs, some accounts left by travelers and colonists. The English were fascinated by them. Sir Hamon Lestrange, a contemporary of Pepys, saw exhibited "a Dodar from the Island of Mauritius . . . it is not able to flie, being so bigge." One was stuffed when it died, and was put in the Museum Tradescantum in South Lambeth. It eventually found its way into the Ashmolean Museum. It grew ratty and was burned, all but a leg and the head, in 1755. By then there were no more dodos, but nobody had realized that yet.

Francis Willughby got to describe it before its incineration. Earlier, old Carolus Clusius in Holland studied the one in Count Solms's park. He collected everything known about the Raphidae, describing a dodo leg Pieter Pauw kept in his natural history cabinet, in *Exoticarium libri decem* in 1605, seven years after their discovery.

Francois Leguat, a Huguenot who lived on Réunion for some years, published an account of his travels in which he mentioned the dodos. It was published in 1708 (after the Mauritius dodo was extinct) and included the information that "some of the males weigh forty-five pound. One egg, much bigger than that of a goos is laid by the female, and takes seven weeks hatching time."

The Abbé Pingré visited the Mascarenes in 1761. He saw the last of the Rodriguez solitaires, and collected what information he could about the dead Mauritius and Réunion members of the genus.

After that, only memories of the colonists and some scientific debate as to *where* the Raphidae belonged in the great taxonomic scheme of things — some said pigeons, some said rails — were left. Even this nitpicking ended. The dodo was forgotten.

When Lewis Carroll wrote *Alice in Wonderland* in 1865, most people thought he invented the dodo.

The service station I called from in Memphis was busier than a one-legged man in an ass-kicking contest. Between bings and dings of the bell, I finally realized the call had gone through.

The guy who answered was named Selvedge. I got nowhere with him. He mistook me for a real estate agent, then a lawyer. Now he was beginning to think I was some sort of a con man. I wasn't doing too well, either. I hadn't slept in two days. I must have sounded like a speed freak. My only progress was that I found that Ms. Annie Mae Gudger (childhood playmate of Jolyn Jimson) was now, and had been, the respected Ms. Annie Mae Radwin. This guy Selvedge must have been a secretary or toady or something.

We were having a conversation comparable to that between a shrieking macaw and a pile of mammoth bones. Then there was another click on the line.

"Young man?" said the other voice, an old woman's voice, southern, very refined but with a hint of the hills in it.

"Yes? Hello! Hello!"

"Young man, you say you talked to a Jolyn somebody? Do you mean Jolyn Smith?"

"Hello! Yes! Ms. Radwin, Ms. Annie Mae Radwin who used to be Gudger? She lives in Austin now. Texas. She used to live near Water Valley, Mississippi. Austin's where I'm from. I . . ."

"Young man?" asked the voice again, "are you sure you haven't been put up to this by my hateful sister Alma?"

"Who? No, ma'am. I met a woman named Jolyn . . ."

"I'd like to talk to you, young man," said the voice. Then offhandedly, "Give him directions to get here, Selvedge."

Click.

I cleaned out my mouth as best I could in the service station restroom, tried to shave with an old clogged Gillette disposable in my knapsack, and succeeded in gapping up my jawline. I changed into a clean pair of jeans and the only other shirt I had with me, and combed my hair. I stood in front of the mirror.

I still looked like the dog's lunch.

The house reminded me of Presley's mansion, which was somewhere in the neighborhood. From a shack on the side of a Mississippi hill to this, in forty years. There are all sorts of ways of making it. I wondered what Annie Mae Gudger's had been. Luck? Predation? Divine intervention? Hard work? Trover and replevin?

Selvedge led me toward the sun room. I felt like Philip Marlowe going to meet a rich client. The house was filled with that furniture built sometime between the turn of the century and the 1950s — the ageless kind. It never looks great, it never looks ratty, and every chair is comfortable.

I think I was expecting some formidable woman with sleeve blotters and a green eyeshade hunched over a rolltop desk with piles of paper whose acceptance or rejection meant life or death for thousands.

Who I met was a charming lady in a green pantsuit. She was in her sixties, her hair still a straw wheat color. It didn't look dyed. Her eyes were blue as my first-grade teacher's had been. She was wiry and looked as if the word *fat* was not in her vocabulary.

"Good morning, Mr. Lindberl." She shook my hand. "Would you like some coffee? You look as if you could use it."

"Yes, thank you."

"Please sit down." She indicated a white wicker chair at a glass table. A serving tray with coffee pot, cups, tea bags, croissants, napkins, and plates lay on the tabletop.

After I swallowed half a cup of coffee at a gulp, she said, "What you wanted to see me about must be important."

"Sorry about my manners," I said. "I know I don't look it, but I'm a biology assistant at the University of Texas. An ornithologist. Working on my Master's. I met Ms. Jolyn Jimson two days ago. . . "

"How is Jolyn? I haven't seen her in, oh, Lord, it must be on to fifty years. The time gets away."

"She seemed to be fine. I only talked to her half an hour or so. That was . . ."

"And you've come to see me about . . .?"

"Uh. The . . . about some of the poultry your family used to raise, when they lived near Water Valley."

She looked at me a moment. Then she began to smile.

"Oh, you mean the ugly chickens?" she said.

I smiled. I almost laughed. I knew what Oedipus must have gone through.

It is now 4:30 in the afternoon. I am sitting at the downtown Motel 6 in Memphis. I have to make a phone call and get some sleep and catch a plane.

Annie Mae Gudger Radwin talked for four hours, answering my questions, setting me straight on family history, having Selvedge hold all her calls.

The main problem was that Annie Mae ran off in 1928, the year *before* her father got his big break. She went to Yazoo City, and by degrees and stages worked her way northward to Memphis and her destiny as the widow of a rich mercantile broker.

But I get ahead of myself.

Grandfather Gudger used to be the overseer for Colonel Crisby on the main plantation near McComb, Mississippi. There was a long story behind that. Bear with me.

Colonel Crisby himself was the scion of a seafaring family with interests in both the cedars of Lebanon (almost all cut down for masts for His Majesty's and others' navies) and Egyptian cotton. Also teas, spices, and any other salable commodity that came their way.

When Colonel Crisby's grandfather reached his majority in 1802, he waved goodbye to the Atlantic Ocean at Charleston, South Carolina, and stepped westward into the forest. When he stopped, he was in the middle of the Chickasaw Nation, where he opened a trading post and introduced slaves to the Indians.

And he prospered and begat Colonel Crisby's father, who sent back to South Carolina for everything his father owned. Everything — slaves, wagons, horses, cattle, guinea fowl, peacocks, and dodos, which everybody thought of as atrociously ugly poultry of some kind, one of the seafaring uncles having bought them off a French merchant in 1721. (I surmised these were white dodos from Réunion, unless they had been from even earlier stock. The dodo of Mauritius was already extinct by then.)

All this stuff was herded out west to the trading post in the midst of the Chickasaw Nation. (The tribes around there were of the confederation of the Dancing Rabbits.)

And Colonel Crisby's father prospered, and so did the guinea fowl and the dodos. Then Andrew Jackson came along and marched the Dancing Rabbits off up the Trail of Tears to the heaven of Oklahoma. And Colonel Crisby's father begat Colonel Crisby, and put the trading post in the hands of others, and moved his plantation westward still to McComb.

Everything prospered but Colonel Crisby's father, who died. And the dodos, with occasional losses to the avenging weasel and the egg-sucking dog, reproduced themselves also.

Then along came Granddaddy Gudger, a Simon Legree role model, who took care of the plantation while Colonel Crisby raised ten companies of men and marched off to fight the War of the Southern Independence.

Colonel Crisby came back to the McComb plantation earlier than most, he having stopped much of the same volley of Minié balls that caught his commander, General Beauregard Hanlon, on a promontory bluff during the Siege of Vicksburg.

He wasn't dead, but death hung around the place like a gentlemanly bill collector for a month. The Colonel languished, went slap-dab crazy and freed all his slaves the week before he died (the war lasted another two years after that). Not having any slaves, he didn't need an overseer.

Then comes the Faulkner part of the tale, straight out of *As I Lay Dying,* with the Gudger family returning to the area of Water Valley (before there was a Water Valley), moving through the demoralized and tattered displaced persons of the South, driving their dodos before them. For Colonel Crisby had given them to his former overseer for his faithful service. Also followed the story of the bloody murder of Granddaddy Gudger at the hands of the Freedman's militia during the rising of the first Klan, and of the trials and tribulations of Daddy Gudger in the years between 1880 and 1910, when he was between the ages of four and thirty-four.

Alma and Annie Mae were the second and fifth of Daddy Gudger's brood, born three years apart. They seemed to have hated each other from the very first time Alma looked into little Annie Mae's crib. They were kids by Daddy Gudger's second wife (his desperation had killed the first) and their father was already on his sixth career. He had been a lumberman, a stump preacher, a plowman-for-hire (until his mules broke out in farcy buds and died of the glanders), a freight hauler (until his horses died of overwork and the hardware store reposessed the wagon), a politician's roadie (until the politician lost the election). When Alma and Annie Mae were born, he was failing as a sharecropper. Somehow Gudger had made it through the Depression of 1898 as a boy, and was too poor after that to notice more about economics than the price of Beech-Nut tobacco at the store.

Alma and Annie Mae fought, and it helped none at all that Alma, being the oldest daughter, was both her mother's and her father's darling. Annie Mae's life was the usual unwanted poor-white-trash child's hell. She vowed early to run away and realized her ambition at thirteen.

All this I learned this morning. Jolyn (Smith) Jimson was Annie Mae's only friend in those days — from a family even poorer than the Gudgers. But somehow there was food, and an occasional odd job. And the dodos.

"My father hated those old birds," said the cultured Annie Mae Radwin, nee Gudger, in the solarium. "He always swore he was going to get rid of them someday but just never seemed to get around to it. I think there was more to it than that. But they were so much *trouble*. We always had to keep them penned up at night and go check for their eggs. They wandered off to lay them and forgot where they were. Sometimes no new ones were born at all in a year.

"And they got so *ugly*. Once a year. I mean, terrible looking, like they were going to die. All their feathers fell off, and they looked like they had mange or something. Then the whole front of their beaks fell off, or worse, hung halfway on for a week or two. They looked like big old naked pigeons. After that they'd lose weight, down to twenty or thirty pounds, before their new feathers grew back.

"We were always having to kill foxes that got after them in the turkey house. That's what we called their roost, the turkey house. And we found their eggs all sucked out by cats and dogs. They were so stupid we had to drive them into their roost at night. I don't think they could have found it standing ten feet from it."

She looked at me.

"I think much as my father hated them, they meant something to him. As long as he hung on to them, he knew he was as good as Granddaddy Gudger. You may not know it, but there was a certain amount of family pride about Granddaddy Gudger. At least in my father's eyes. His rapid fall in the world had a sort of grandeur to it. He'd gone from a relatively high position in the old order, and maintained some grace and stature after the Emancipation. And though he lost everything, he managed to keep those ugly old chickens the Colonel had given him, as sort of a symbol.

"And as long as he had them, too, my daddy thought himself as good as his father. He kept his dignity, even when he didn't have anything else."

I asked what happened to them. She didn't know, but told me who did and where I could find her.

That's why I'm going to make a phone call.

"Hello. Dr. Courtney. Dr. Courtney? This is Paul. Memphis, Tennessee. It's too long to go into. No, of course not, not yet. But I've got evidence. What? Okay, how do trochanters, coracoids, tarsometatarsi, and beak sheaths sound? From their hen house, where else? Where would you keep *your* dodos, then?

"Sorry. I haven't slept in a couple of days. I need some help. Yes, yes. Money. Lots of money.

"Cash. Three hundred dollars, maybe. Western Union, Memphis, Tennessee. Whichever one's closest to the airport. Airport. I need the department to set up reservations to Mauritius for me. . .

"No. No. Not wild goose chase, wild *dodo* chase. Tame dodo chase. I *know* there aren't any dodos on Mauritius! I know that. I could explain. I know it'll mean a couple of grand . . . if . . . but. . . .

"Look, Dr. Courtney. Do you want *your* picture in *Scientific American,* or don't you?"

I am sitting in the airport café in Port Louis, Mauritius. It is now three days later, five days since that fateful morning my car wouldn't start. God bless the Sears Diehard people. I have slept sitting up in a plane seat, on and off, different planes, different seats, for 24 hours, Kennedy to Paris, Paris to Cairo, Cairo to Madagascar. I felt like a brand-new man when I got here.

Now I feel like an infinitely sadder and wiser brand-new man. I have just returned from the hateful sister Alma's house in the exclusive section of Port Louis, where all the French and British officials used to live.

Courtney will get his picture in *Scientific American,* all right. Me too. There'll be newspaper stories and talk shows for a few weeks for me, and I'm sure Annie Mae Gudger Radwin on one side of the world and Alma Chandler Gudger Moliere on the other will come in for their share of glory.

I am putting away cup after cup of coffee. The plane back to Tananarive leaves in an hour. I plan to sleep all the way back to Cairo, to Paris, to New York, pick up my bag of bones, sleep back to Austin.

Before me on the table is a packet of documents, clippings, and photographs. I have come half the world for this. I gaze from the package, out the window across Port Louis to the bulk of Mont Pieter Both, which overshadows the city and its famous racecourse.

Perhaps I should do something symbolic. Cancel my flight. Climb the mountain and look down on man and all his handiworks. Take a pitcher of martinis with me. Sit in the bright semitropical sunlight (it's early dry winter here). Drink the martinis slowly, toasting Snuffo, God of Extinction. Here's one for the great auk. This is for the Carolina parakeet. Mud in your eye, passenger pigeon. This one's for the heath hen. Most importantly, here's one each for the Mauritius dodo, the white dodo of Réunion, the Réunion solitaire, the Rodriguez solitaire. Here's to the Raphidae, great Didine birds that you were.

Maybe I'll do something just as productive, like climbing Mont Pieter Both and pissing into the wind.

How symbolic. The story of the dodo ends where it began, on this very island. Life imitates cheap art. Like the Xerox of the Xerox of a bad novel. I never expected to find dodos still alive here (this is the one place they would have been noticed). I still can't believe Alma Chandler Gudger Moliere could have lived here twenty-five years and not *know* about the dodo, never set foot inside the Port Louis Museum, where they have skeletons and a stuffed replica the size of your little brother.

After Annie Mae ran off, the Gudger family found itself prospering in a time the rest of the country was going to hell. It was 1929. Gudger delved into politics again, and backed a man who knew a man who worked for Theodore "Sure Two-Handed Sword of God" Bilbo, who had connections everywhere. Who introduced him to Huey "Kingfish" Long just after that gentleman lost the Louisiana governor's election one of the times. Gudger stumped around Mississippi, getting up steam for Long's Share the Wealth plan, even before it had a name.

The upshot was that the Long machine in Louisiana knew a rabble-rouser when it saw one, and invited Gudger to move to the Sportsman's Paradise, with his family, all expenses paid, and start working for the Kingfish at the unbelievable salary of $62.50 a week. Which prospect was like turning a hog loose under a persimmon tree, and before you could say Backwoods Messiah, the Gudger clan was on its way to the land of pelicans, graft, and Mardi Gras.

Almost. But I'll get to that.

Daddy Gudger prospered all out of proportion with his abilities, but many men did that during the Depression. First a little, thence to more, he rose in bureaucratic (and political) circles of the state, dying rich and well hated with his fingers in *all* the pies.

Alma Chandler Gudger became a debutante (she says Robert Penn Warren put her in his book) and met and married Jean Carl Moliere, only heir to rice, indigo, and sugar-cane growers. They had a happy wedded life, moving first to the West Indies, later to Mauritius, where the family sugar-cane holdings were one of the largest on the island. Jean Carl died in 1959. Alma was his only survivor.

So local family makes good. Poor sharecropping Mississippi people turn out to have a father dying with a smile on his face, and two daughters who between them own a large portion of the planet.

I open the envelope before me. Ms. Alma Moliere had listened politely to my story (the University had called ahead and arranged an introduction through the director of the Port Louis Museum, who knew Ms. Moliere socially) and told me what she could remember. Then she sent a servant out to one of the storehouses (large as a duplex) and he and two others came back with boxes of clippings, scrapbooks, and family photos.

"I haven't looked at any of this since we left St. Thomas," she said. "Let's go through it together."

Most of it was about the rise of Citizen Gudger.

"There's not many pictures of us before we came to Louisiana. We were so frightfully poor then, hardly anyone we knew had a camera. Oh, look. Here's one of Annie Mae. I thought I threw all those out after Momma died."

This is the photograph. It must have been taken about 1927. Annie Mae is wearing some unrecognizable piece of clothing that approximates a dress. She leans on a hoe, smiling a snaggle-toothed smile. She looks to be ten or eleven. Her eyes are half-hidden by the shadow of the brim of a gapped straw hat she wears. The earth she is standing in barefoot has been newly turned. Behind her is one corner of the house, and the barn beyond has its upper hay windows open. Out-of-focus people are at work there.

A few feet behind her, a huge male dodo is pecking at something on the ground. The front two-thirds of it shows, back to the stupid wings and the edge of the upcurved tail feathers. One foot is in the photo, having just scratched at something, possibly an earthworm, in the new-plowed clods. Judging by its darkness, it is the gray, or Mauritius, dodo.

The photograph is not very good, one of those 3½ × 5 jobs box cameras used to take. Already I can see this one, and the blowup of the dodo, taking up a double-page spread in *S. A.* Alma told me around then they were down to six or seven of the ugly chickens, two whites, the rest gray-brown.

Besides this photo, two clippings are in the package, one from the Bruce *Banner-Times,* the other from the Oxford newspaper; both are columns by the same woman dealing with "Doings in Water Valley." Both mention the Gudger family moving from the area to seek its fortune in the swampy state to the west, and telling how they will be missed. Then there's a yellowed clipping from the front page of the Oxford paper with a small story about the Gudger Farewell Party in Water Valley the Sunday before (dated October 19, 1929).

There's a handbill in the package, advertising the Gudger Family Farewell Party, Sunday October 15, 1929, Come One Come All. (The people in Louisiana who sent expense money to move Daddy Gudger must have overestimated the costs by an exponential factor. I said as much.)

"No," Alma Moliere said. "There was a lot, but it wouldn't have made any difference. Daddy Gudger was like Thomas Wolfe and knew a shining golden opportunity when he saw one. Win, lose, or draw, he was never coming back *there* again. He would have thrown some kind of soirée whether there had been money for it or not. Besides, people were much more sociable then, you mustn't forget.''

I asked her how many people came.

''Four or five hundred,'' she said. ''There's some pictures here somewhere.'' We searched awhile, then we found them.

Another thirty minutes to my flight. I'm not worried sitting here. I'm the only passenger, and the pilot is sitting at the table next to mine talking to an RAF man. Life is much slower and nicer on these colonial islands. You mustn't forget.

I look at the other two photos in the package. One is of some men playing horseshoes and washer-toss, while kids, dogs, and women look on. It was evidently taken from the east end of the house looking west. Everyone must have had to walk the last mile to the old Gudger place. Other groups of people stand talking. Some men, in shirt-sleeves and suspenders, stand with their heads thrown back, a snappy story, no doubt, just told. One girl looks directly at the camera from close up, shyly, her finger in her mouth. She's about five. It looks like any snapshot of a family reunion which could have been taken anywhere, anytime. Only the clothing marks it as backwoods 1920s.

Courtney will get his money's worth. I'll write the article, make phone calls, plan the talk show tour to coincide with publication. Then I'll get some rest. I'll be a normal person again; get a degree, spend my time wading through jungles after animals which will all be dead in another twenty years, anyway.

Who cares? The whole thing will be just another media event, just this year's Big Deal. It'll be nice getting normal again. I can read books, see movies, wash my clothes at the laundromat, listen to Johnathan Richman on the stereo. I can study and become an authority on some minor matter or other.

I can go to museums and see all the wonderful dead things there.

''That's the memory picture,'' said Alma. ''They always took them at big things like this, back in those days. Everybody who was there would line up and pose for the camera. Only we couldn't fit everybody in. So we had two made. This is the one with us in it.''

The house is dwarfed by people. All sizes, shapes, dress, and age. Kids and dogs in front, women next, then men at the back. The only exceptions are the bearded patriarchs seated toward the front with the children — men whose eyes face the camera but whose heads are still ringing with something Nathan Bedford Forrest said to them one time on a smoke-filled field. This photograph is from another age. You can recognize Daddy and Mrs. Gudger if you've seen their photographs before. Alma pointed herself out to me.

But the reason I took the photograph is in the foreground. Tables have been built out of sawhorses, with doors and boards nailed across them. They extend the entire width of the photograph. They were covered with food, more food than you can imagine.

"We started cooking three days before. So did the neighbors. Everybody brought something," said Alma.

It's like an entire Safeway had been cooked and set out to cool. Hams, quarters of beef, chickens by the tubful, quail in mounds, rabbit, butterbeans by the bushel, yams, Irish potatoes, an acre of corn, eggplants, peas, turnip greens, butter in five-pound moulds, cornbread and biscuits, gallon cans of molasses, redeye gravy by the pot.

And five huge birds — twice as big as turkeys, legs capped like for Thanksgiving, drumsticks the size of Schwarzenegger's biceps, whole-roasted, lying on their backs on platters large as cocktail tables.

The people in the crowd sure look hungry.

"We ate for days," said Alma.

I already have the title for the *Scientific American* article. It's going to be called "The Dodo is *Still* Dead."

Cosmologists have been playing with many exotic theories in recent years concerning the origin of life on Earth, but here Larry Niven — multiple Hugo-and-Nebula award winner, author of Ringworld *(Del Rey),* A World Out of Time *(Del Rey),* World of Ptavvs *(Del Rey), and* Neutron Star *(Del Rey), among many other books — outdoes most of them in one shot, producing a terse and eloquent story whose ultimate implications will linger in your mind long after the last page is turned.*

LARRY NIVEN
The Green Marauder

I was tending bar alone that night. The chirpsithra interstellar liner that had left Earth four days earlier had taken most of my customers. The Draco Tavern was nearly empty.

The man at the bar was drinking gin and tonic. Two glig — gray and compact beings, wearing furs in three tones of green — were at a table with a chirpsithra guide. They drank vodka and consommé, no ice, no flavorings. Four farsilshree had their bulky, heavy environment tanks crowded around a bigger table. They smoked smoldering yellow paste through tubes. Every so often I got them another jar of paste.

The man was talkative. I got the idea he was trying to interview the bartender and owner of Earth's foremost multi-species tavern.

"Hey, not me," he protested. "I'm not a reporter. I'm Greg Noyes, with the *Scientific American* TV show."

"Didn't I see you trying to interview the glig, earlier tonight?"

"Guilty. We're doing a show on the formation of life on Earth. I thought maybe I could check a few things. The gligstith(click)optok — " He said that slowly, but got it right. " — have their own little empire out there, don't they? Earthlike worlds, a couple of hundred. They must know quite a lot about how a world forms an oxygenating atmosphere." He was careful with those polysyllabic words. Not quite sober, then.

"That doesn't mean they want to waste an evening lecturing the natives."

He nodded. "They didn't know anyway. Architects on vacation. They got me talking about my home life. I don't know how they managed that." He pushed his drink away. "I'd better switch to espresso. Why would a thing that *shape* be interested in my sex life? And they kept asking me about territorial imperatives — " He stopped, then turned to see what I was staring at.

Three chirpsithra, just coming in. One was in a floating couch with life support equipment attached.

"I thought they all looked alike," he said.

I said, "I've had chirpsithra in here for close to thirty years, but I can't tell them apart. They're all perfect physical specimens, after all, by their own standards. I never saw one like *that*."

I gave him his espresso, then put three sparkers on a tray and went to the chirpsithra table.

Two were exactly like any other chirpsithra: eleven feet tall, dressed in pouched belts and their own salmon-colored exoskeletons, and very much at their ease. The chirps claim to have settled the entire galaxy long ago — meaning the useful planets, the tidally locked oxygen worlds that happen to circle close around cool red-dwarf suns — and they act like the reigning queens of wherever they happen to be. But the two seemed to defer to the third. She was a foot shorter than they were. Her exoskeleton was as clearly artificial as dentures: alloplastic bone worn on the outside. Tubes ran under the edges from the equipment in her floating couch. Her skin between the plates was more gray than red. Her head turned slowly as I came up. She studied me, bright-eyed with interest.

I asked, "Sparkers?" as if chirpsithra ever ordered anything else.

One of the others said, "Yes, and serve the ethanol mix of your choice to yourself and the other native. Will you join us?"

I waved Noyes over, and he came at the jump. He pulled up one of the floating chairs I keep around to put a human face on a level with a chirpsithra's. I went for another espresso and a Scotch and soda and (catching a soft imperative *hoot* from the farsilshree) a jar of yellow paste. When I returned they were deep in conversation.

"Rick Schumann," Noyes cried, "meet Ftaxanthir and Hrofillis and Chorrikst. Chorrikst tells me she's nearly two *billion* years old!"

I heard the doubt beneath his exuberance. The chirpsithra could be the greatest liars in the universe, and how would we ever know? Earth didn't even have interstellar probes when the chirps came.

Chorrikst spoke slowly, in a throaty whisper, but her translator box was standard: voice a little flat, pronunciation perfect. "I have circled the galaxy numberless times, and taped the tales of my travels for funds to feed my wanderlust. Much of my life has been spent at the edge of light speed, under relativistic time-compression. So you see, I am not nearly so old as all that."

I pulled up another floating chair. "You must have seen wonders beyond counting," I said. Thinking: *My God, a short chirpsithra! Maybe it's true. She's a different color, too, and her fingers are shorter. Maybe the species has actually changed since she was born!*

She nodded slowly. "Life never bores. Always there is change. In the time I have been gone, Saturn's ring has been pulled into separate rings, making it even more magnificent. Tides from the moons? And Earth has changed beyond recognition."

Noyes spilled a little of his coffee. "You were here? When?"

"Earth's air was methane and ammonia and oxides of nitrogen and carbon.

The natives had sent messages across interstellar space . . . directing them toward yellow suns, of course, but one of our ships passed through a beam, and so we established contact. We had to wear life support,'' she rattled on, while Noyes and I sat with our jaws hanging, ''and the gear was less comfortable then. Our spaceport was a floating platform, because quakes were frequent and violent. But it was worth it. Their cities — ''

Noyes said, ''Just a minute. Cities? We've never dug up any trace of, of nonhuman cities?''

Chorrikst looked at him. ''After seven hundred and eighty million years, I should think not. Besides, they lived in the offshore shallows in a not very salty ocean. If the quakes spared them, their tools and their cities still deteriorated rapidly. Their lives were short too, but their memories were inherited. Death and change were accepted facts for them, more than for most intelligent species. Their works of philosophy gained great currency among my people, and spread to other species too.''

Noyes wrestled with his instinct for tact and good manners, and won. ''How? How could anything have evolved that far? The Earth didn't even have any oxygen atmosphere! Life was just getting started; there weren't even trilobites!''

''They had evolved for as long as you have,'' Chorrikst said with composure. ''Life began on Earth one and a half billion years ago. There were organic chemicals in abundance, from passage of lightning through the reducing atmosphere. Intelligence evolved, and eventually built an impressive civilization. They lived slowly, of course. Their biochemistry was less energetic. Communication was difficult. They were not stupid, only slow. I visited Earth three times, and each time they had made more progress.''

Almost against his will, Noyes asked, ''What did they look like?''

''Small and soft and fragile, much more so than yourselves. I cannot say they were pretty, but I grew to like them. I would toast them according to your customs,'' she said. ''They wrought beauty in their cities and beauty in their philosophies, and their works are in our libraries still. They will not be forgotten.''

She touched her sparker, and so did her younger companions. Current flowed between her two claws, through her nervous system. She said, ''Sssss . . .''

I raised my glass, and nudged Noyes with my elbow. We drank to our predecessors. Noyes lowered his cup and asked, ''What happened to them?''

''They sensed world-wide disaster coming,'' Chorrikst said, ''and they prepared; but they thought it would be quakes. They built cities to float on the ocean surface, and lived underneath. They never noticed the green scum growing in certain tidal pools. By the time they knew the danger, the green scum was everywhere. It used photosynthesis to turn carbon dioxide into oxygen, and the raw oxygen killed whatever it touched, leaving fertilizer to feed the green scum. The world was dying when we learned of the problem, and then what could we do? A photosynthesis-using scum growing beneath a yellow-white star? There was nothing in our libraries that would help. We tried, of course, but we were unable to stop it. The sky had turned an admittedly lovely transparent blue, and the tide pools were green, and the offshore cities were crumbling before we gave up the fight. There was an attempt to transplant some of the natives to a suitable world; but biorhythm upset made them sterile. I have not been back since, until now.''

The depressing silence was broken by Chorrikst herself. ''Well, the Earth is greatly changed, and of course your own evolution began with the green plague. I have heard tales of humanity from my companions. Would you tell me something of your lives?''

And we spoke of humankind, but I couldn't seem to find much enthusiasm for it. The anaerobic life that survived the advent of photosynthesis includes gangrene and botulism and not much else. I wondered what Chorrikst would find when next she came, and whether she would have reason to toast our memory.

Meteoric careers are commonplace in SF, and it is not unusual to see an author go from total obscurity to fame in the course of a handful of years. In 1976, in our Sixth Annual Collection, I predicted that an unknown new writer named John Varley would become one of the biggest names in SF — a prediction that has come true with a vengeance in the last few years. Now I'd like to make a similar prediction about an unknown new writer named Michael Swanwick, who made his debut in 1980 with two of the strongest and most compelling stories of recent years, "The Feast of St. Janis" in New Dimensions 11 and "Ginungagap" in TriQuarterly 49 — both stories were critically well-received, both have stirred up a good deal of excitement, and both have gone on to become Nebula Award Finalists this year, an unusual honor for a writer at the very beginning of his career. Already, though, with his first few stories, Swanwick has developed a unique and exciting voice all his own, and clearly marked himself as a writer to watch in the eighties. What I said about Varley in 1976 applies just as well to Swanwick: "Here, obviously, is a talent in the making, as clearly recognizable as Delany and Niven and Zelazny and Tiptree had been."

Born in Schenectady, New York, Swanwick has worked at the usual ragtag assortment of writer's odd jobs, the most interesting of which probably was a stint at the National Solar Heating and Cooling Information Center at the Franklin Institute in Philadelphia. He has stories upcoming in New Dimensions 12, Universe 11, Proteus, and Penthouse, and is currently at work on his first novel. He lives in Philadelphia with his wife Marianne.

In the vivid and evocative story that follows, he takes us on a tour of a ruined future America where the dead hand of the past lies heavy on the living, and nothing is quite what it seems.

MICHAEL SWANWICK
The Feast of St. Janis

Take a load off, Janis
and
You put the load right on me
— "THE WAIT," (trad.)

Wolf stood in the early morning fog watching the *Yankee Clipper* leave Baltimore harbor. His elbows rested against a cool, clammy wall, its surface eroded smooth by the passage of countless hands, almost certainly dating back to before the Collapse. A metallic gray sparkle atop the foremast drew his eye to the dish

24

antenna that linked the ship with the geosynchrous *Trickster* seasats it relied on to plot winds and currents.

To many the wooden *Clipper,* with its computer-designed hydrofoils and hand-sewn sails, was a symbol of the New Africa. Wolf, however, watching it merge into sea and sky, knew only that it was going home without him.

He turned, and walked back into the rick-a-rack of commercial buildings crowded against the waterfront. The clatter of hand-drawn carts mingled with a melange of exotic cries and shouts, the alien music of a dozen American dialects. Workers, clad in coveralls most of them, swarmed about, grunting and cursing in exasperation when an iron wheel lurched in a muddy pothole. Yet there was something furtive and covert about them, as if they were hiding an ancient secret.

Craning to stare into the dark recesses of a warehouse, Wolf collided with a woman clad head to foot in chador. She flinched at his touch, her eyes glaring above the black veil, then whipped away. Not a word was exchanged.

A citizen of Baltimore in its glory days would not have recognized the city. Where the old buildings had not been torn down and buried, shanties crowded the streets, taking advantage of the space automobiles had needed. Sometimes they were built *over* the streets, so that alleys became tunnelways, and sometimes these collapsed, to the cries and consternation of the natives.

It was another day with nothing to do. He could don a filter mask and tour the Washington ruins, but he had already done that, and besides the day looked like it was going to be hot. It was unlikely he'd hear anything about his mission, not after months of waiting on American officials who didn't want to talk with him. Wolf decided to check back at his hostel for messages, then spend the day in the bazaars.

Children were playing in the street outside the hostel. They scattered at his approach. One, he noted, lagged behind the others, hampered by a malformed leg. He mounted the unpainted wooden steps, edging past an old man who sat at the bottom. The old man was laying down tarot cards with a slow and fatalistic disregard for what they said; he did not look up.

The bell over the door jangled notice of Wolf's entry. He stepped into the dark foyer.

Two men in the black uniforms of the political police appeared, one to either side of him. "Wolfgang Hans Mbikana?" one asked. His voice had the dust of ritual on it; he knew the answer. "You will come with us," the other said.

"There is some mistake," Wolf objected.

"No, sir, there is no mistake," one said mildly. The other opened the door. "After you, Mr. Mbikana."

The old man on the stoop squinted up at them, looked away, and slid off the step.

The police walked Wolf to an ancient administrative building. They went up marble steps sagging from centuries of foot-scuffing, and through an empty lobby. Deep within the building they halted before an undistinguished-looking door. "You are expected," the first of the police said.

"I beg your pardon?"

The police walked away, leaving him there. Apprehensive, he knocked on the door. There was no answer, so he opened it and stepped within.

A woman sat at a desk just inside the room. Though she was modernly dressed, she wore a veil. She might have been young; it was impossible to tell. A flick of her eyes, a motion of one hand, directed him to the open door of an inner room. It was like following an onion to its conclusion, a layer of mystery at a time.

A heavy-set man sat at the final desk. He was dressed in the traditional suit and tie of American businessmen. But there was nothing quaint or old-fashioned about his mobile, expressive face or the piercing eyes he turned on Wolf.

"Sit down," he grunted, gesturing toward an old, overstuffed chair. Then, "Charles DiStephano. Comptroller for Northeast Regional. You're Mbikana, right?"

"Yes, sir." Wolf gingerly took the proffered chair, which did not seem all that clean. It was becoming clear to him now; DiStephano was one of the men on whom he had waited these several months, the biggest of the lot, in fact. "I represent — "

"The Southwest Africa Trade Company." DiStephano lifted some documents from his desk. "Now this says you're prepared to offer — among other things — resource data from your North American *Coyote* landsat in exchange for the right to place students in Johns Hopkins. I find that an odd offer for your organization to make."

"Those are my papers," Wolf objected. "As a citizen of Southwest Africa, I'm not used to this sort of cavalier treatment."

"Look kid, I'm a busy man; I have no time to discuss your rights. The papers are in my hands, I've read them, the people that sent you knew I would. Okay? So I know what you want and what you're offering. What I want to know is *why* you're making this offer."

Wolf was disconcerted. He was used to a more civilized, a more leisurely manner of doing business. The oldtimers at SWATC had warned him that the pace would be different here, but he hadn't had the experience to decipher their veiled references and hints. He was painfully aware that he had gotten the mission, with its high salary and the promise of a bonus, only because it was not one that appealed to the older hands.

"America was hit hardest," he said, "but the Collapse was world-wide." He wondered whether he should explain the system of corporate social responsibility that African business was based on. Then decided that if DiStephano didn't know, he didn't want to. "There are still problems. Africa has a high incidence of birth defects." *Because America exported its poisons; its chemicals, and pesticides, and foods containing a witch's brew of preservatives.* "We hope to do away with the problem; if a major thrust is made, we can clean up the gene pool in less than a century. But to do this requires professionals — eugenicists, embryonic surgeons — and while we have these, they are second-rate. The very best still come from your nation's medical schools."

"We can't spare any."

"We don't propose to steal your doctors. We'd provide our own students; fully trained doctors who need only the specialized training."

"There are only so many openings at Hopkins," DiStephano said. "Or at U of P, or the UVM Medical College, for that matter."

"We're prepared to — " Wolf pulled himself up short. "It's in the papers. We'll pay enough that you can expand to meet the needs of twice the number of students we require." The room was dim and oppressive. Sweat built up under Wolf's clothing.

"Maybe so. You can't buy teachers with money, though." Wolf said nothing. "I'm also extremely reluctant to let your people *near* our medics. You can offer them money, estates — things our country cannot afford. And we *need* our doctors. As it is, only the very rich can get the corrective surgery they require."

"If you're worried about our pirating your professionals, there are ways around that. For example, a clause could be written — " Wolf went on, feeling more and more in control. He was getting somewhere. If there wasn't a deal to be made, the discussion would never have gotten this far.

The day wore on. DiStephano called in aides and dismissed them. Twice, he had drinks sent in. Once, they broke for lunch. Slowly the heat built, until it was sweltering. Finally, the light began to fail, and the heat grew less oppressive.

DiStephano swept the documents into two piles, returned one to Wolf, and put the other inside a desk drawer. "I'll look these over, have our legal boys run a study. There shouldn't be any difficulties. I'll get back to you with the final word in — say a month. September 21st. I'll be in Boston then, but you can find me easily enough, if you ask around."

"A month? But I thought . . ."

"A month. You can't hurry City Hall," DiStephano said firmly. "Ms. Corey!"

The veiled woman was at the door, remote, elusive. "Sir."

"Drag Kaplan out of his office. Tell him we got a kid here he should give the VIP treatment to. Maybe a show. It's a Hopkins thing, he should earn his keep."

"Yes, sir." She was gone.

"Thank you," Wolf said, "but I don't really need . . ."

"Take my advice, kid, take all the perks you can get. God knows there aren't many left. I'll have Kaplan pick you up at your hostel in an hour."

Kaplan turned out to be a slight, balding man with nervous gestures, some sort of administrative functionary for Hopkins. Wolf never did get the connection. But Kaplan was equally puzzled by Wolf's status, and Wolf took petty pleasure in not explaining it. It took some of the sting off of having his papers stolen.

Kaplan led Wolf through the evening streets. A bright sunset circled the world, and the crowds were much thinner. "We won't be leaving the area that's zoned for electricity,'' Kaplan said. ''Otherwise I'd advise against going out at night at all. Lot of jennie-deafs out then.''

''Jennie-deafs?''

''Mutes. Culls. The really terminal cases. Some of them can't pass themselves off in daylight even wearing coveralls. Or chador — a lot are women.'' A faintly perverse expression crossed the man's face, leaving not so much as a greasy residue.

''Where are we going?'' Wolf asked. He wanted to change the subject. A vague presentiment assured him he did not want to know the source of Kaplan's expression.

''A place called Peabody's. You've heard of Janis Joplin, our famous national singer?''

Wolf nodded, meaning no.

''The show is a re-creation of her act. Woman name of Maggie Horowitz does the best impersonation of Janis I've ever seen. Tickets are almost impossible to get, but Hopkins has special influence in this case because — ah, here we are.''

Kaplan led him down a set of concrete steps and into the basement of a dull, brick building. Wolf experienced a moment of dislocation. It was a bookstore. Shelves and boxes of books and magazines brooded over him, a packrat's clutter of paper.

Wolf wanted to linger, to scan the ancient tomes, remnants of a time and culture fast sinking into obscurity and myth. But Kaplan brushed past them without a second glance and he had to hurry to keep up.

They passed through a second room full of books, then into a hallway where a gray man held out a gnarled hand and said, ''Tickets, please.''

Kaplan gave the man two crisp pasteboard cards, and they entered a third room.

It was a cabaret. Wooden chairs clustered about small tables with flickering candles at their centers. The room was lofted with wood beams, and a large, unused fireplace dominated one wall. Another wall had obviously been torn out at one time to make room for a small stage. Over a century's accumulation of memorabilia covered the walls or hung from the rafters, like barbarian trinkets from toppled empires.

''Peabody's is a local institution,'' Kaplan said. ''In the twentieth century it was a speakeasy. H.L. Mencken himself used to drink here.'' Wolf nodded, though the name meant nothing to him. ''The bookstore was a front and the drinking went on here in back.''

The place was charged with a feeling of the past. It invoked America's bygone days as a world power. Wolf half-expected to see Theodore Roosevelt or Henry Kissinger come striding in. He said something to this effect and Kaplan smiled complacently.

''You'll like the show, then,'' he said.

A waiter took their orders. There was barely time to begin on the drinks when a pair of spotlights came on, and the stage curtain parted.

A woman stood alone in the center of the stage. Bracelets and bangles hung from her wrists, gaudy necklaces from her throat. She wore large tinted glasses and a flowered granny gown. Her nipples pushed against the thin dress. Wolf stared at them in horrified fascination. She had an extra set, immediately below the first pair.

The woman stood perfectly motionless. Wolf couldn't stop staring at her nipples; it wasn't just the number, it was the fact of their being visible at all. So quickly had he taken on this land's taboos.

The woman threw her head back and laughed. She put one hand on her hip, thrust the hip out at an angle, and lifted the microphone to her lips. She spoke, and her voice was harsh and raspy.

"About a year ago I lived in a rowhouse in Newark, right? Lived on the third floor, and I thought I had my act together. But nothing was going right, I wasn't getting any . . . action. Know what I mean? No talent comin' around. And there was this chick down the street, didn't have much and she was doing okay, so I say to myself: *What's wrong, Janis?* How come she's doing so good and you ain't gettin' any? So I decided to check it out, see what she had that I didn't. And one day I get up early, look out the window, and I see this chick out there *hustling!* I mean, she was doing the streets at NOON! So I said to myself, Janis honey, you ain't even trying. And when ya want action, ya gotta try. Yeah. Try just a little bit harder."

The music swept up out of nowhere, and she was singing: "Try-iiii, Try-iiii, Just a little bit harder . . ."

And unexpectedly, it was good. It was like nothing he had ever heard, but he understood it, almost on an instinctual level. It was world-culture music. It was universal.

Kaplan dug fingers into Wolf's arm, brought his mouth up to Wolf's ear. "You see? You see?" he demanded. Wolf shook him off, impatiently. He wanted to hear the music.

The concert lasted forever, and it was done in no time at all. It left Wolf sweaty and emotionally spent. Onstage, the woman was energy personified. She danced, she strutted, she wailed more power into her songs than seemed humanly possible. Not knowing the original, Wolf was sure it was a perfect re-creation. It had that feel.

The audience loved her. They called her back for three encores, and then a fourth. Finally, she came out, gasped into the mike, "I love ya, honeys, I truly do. But please — no more. I just couldn't do it." She blew a kiss, and was gone from the stage.

The entire audience was standing, Wolf among them, applauding furiously. A hand fell on Wolf's shoulder, and he glanced to his side annoyed. It was Kaplan. His face was flushed, and he said, "Come on." He pulled Wolf free of the crowd and backstage to a small dressing room. Its door was ajar and people were crowded into it.

One of them was the singer, hair stringy and out-of-place, laughing and gesturing widely with a Southern Comfort bottle. It was an antique, its label lacquered to the glass, and three-quarters filled with something amber-colored.

"Janis, this is — " Kaplan began.

"The name is Maggie," she sang gleefully. "Maggie Horowitz. I ain't no *dead* blues singer. And don't you forget it."

"This is a fan of yours, Maggie. From Africa." He gave Wolf a small shove. Wolf hesitantly stumbled forward, grimacing apologetically at the people he displaced.

"Whee-howdy!" Maggie whooped. She downed a slug from her bottle. "Pleased ta meetcha, Ace. Kinda light for an African, aintcha?"

"My mother's people were descended from German settlers." And it was felt that a light-skinned representative could handle the touchy Americans better, but he didn't say that.

"Whatcher name, Ace?"

"Wolf."

"Wolf!" Maggie crowed. "Yeah, you look like a real heartbreaker, honey. Guess I'd better be careful around you, huh? Likely to sweep me off my feet and deflower me." She nudged him with an elbow. "That's a joke, Ace."

Wolf was fascinated. Maggie was *alive*, a dozen times more so than her countrymen. She made them look like zombies. Wolf was also a little afraid of her.

"*Hey*. Whatcha think of my singing, hah?"

"It was excellent," Wolf said. "It was — " he groped for words " — in my land the music is quieter, there is not so much emotion."

"Yeah, well *I* think it was fucking good, Ace. Voice's never been in better shape. Go tell 'em that at Hopkins, Kaplan. Tell 'em I'm giving them their money's worth."

"Of course you are," Kaplan said.

"Well, I *am*, goddammit. Hey, this place is like a morgue! Let's ditch this matchbox dressing room and hit the bars. Hey? Let's party."

She swept them all out of the dressing room, out of the building, and into the street. They formed a small, boisterous group, noisily wandering the city, looking for bars.

"There's one a block thataway," Maggie said. "Let's hit it. Hey, Ace, I'd likeya to meet Cynthia. Sin, this is Wolf. Sin and I are like one person inside two skins. Many's the time we've shared a piece of talent in the same bed. Hey?" She cackled, and grabbed at Cynthia's ass.

"Cut it out, Maggie." Cynthia smiled when she said it. She was a tall, slim, striking woman.

"Hey, this town is DEAD!" Maggie screamed the last word, then gestured them all to silence so they could listen for the echo. "There it is." She pointed and they swooped down on the first bar.

After the third bar, Wolf lost track. At some point he gave up on the party and somehow made his way back to his hotel. The last he remembered of Maggie she was calling after him, "Hey, Ace, don't be a party poop." Then, "At least be sure to come back tomorrow, goddammit."

Wolf spent most of the next day in his room, drinking water and napping. His hangover was all but gone by the time evening took the edge off the day's heat. He thought of Maggie's half-serious invitation, dismissed it and decided to go to the Club.

The Uhuru Club was ablaze with light by the time he wandered in, a beacon in a dark city. Its frequenters, after all, were all African foreign service, with a few commercial reps such as himself forced in by the insular nature of American society, and the need for polite conversation. It was *de facto* exempt from the power-use laws that governed the natives.

"Mbikana! Over here, lad, let me set you up with a drink." Nnamdi of the consulate waved him over to the bar. Wolf complied, feeling conspicuous as he always did in the Club. His skin stood out here. Even the American servants were dark, though whether this was a gesture of deference or arrogance on the part of the local authorities, he could not guess.

"Word is that you spent the day closeted with the comptroller." Nnamdi had a gin-and-tonic setup. Wolf loathed the drink, but it was universal among the service people. "Share the dirt with us." Other faces gathered around; the service ran on gossip.

Wolf gave an abridged version of the encounter and Nnamdi applauded. "A full day with the Spider King and you escaped with your balls intact. An auspicious beginning for you, lad."

"Spider King?"

"Surely you were briefed on regional autonomy — how the country was broken up when it could no longer be managed by a central directorate? There *is* no higher authority than DiStephano in this part of the world, boy."

"Boston," Ajuji sniffed. Like most of the expatriates, she was a failure; unlike many, she couldn't hide the fact from herself. "That's exactly the sort of treatment one comes to expect from these savages."

"Now, Ajuji," Nnamdi said mildly. "These people are hardly savages. Why, before the Collapse they put men on the moon."

"Technology! Hard-core technology, that's all it was, of a piece with the kind that almost destroyed us all. If you want a measure of a people, you look at how they live. These — *yanks*," she hissed the word to emphasize its filthiness, "live in squalor. Their streets are filthy, their cities are filthy, and even the ones who aren't rotten with genetic disease are filthy. A child can be taught to clean up after itself. What does that make them?"

"Human beings, Ajuji."

"Hogwash, Nnamdi."

Wolf followed the argument with acute embarrassment. He had been brought up to expect well from people with social standing. To hear gutter language and low prejudice from them was almost beyond bearing. Suddenly, it *was* beyond bearing. He stood, his stool making a scraping noise as he pushed it back. He turned his back on them all, and left.

"Mbikana! You mustn't — " Nnamdi called after him.

"Oh, let him go" Ajuji cut in, with a satisfied tone, "you mustn't expect better. After all, he's practically one of *them*."

Well, maybe he was.

Wolf wasn't fully aware of where he was going until he found himself at Peabody's. He circled the building, and found a rear door. He tried the knob; it turned loosely in his hand. Then the door swung open and a heavy, bearded man in coveralls leaned out. "Yes?" he said in an unfriendly tone.

"Uh," Wolf said. "Maggie Horowitz told me I could drop by."

"Look, pilgrim, there are a lot of people try to get backstage. My job is to keep them out unless I know them. I don't know you."

Wolf tried to think of some response to this, and failed. He was about to turn away when somebody unseen said, "Oh, let him in, Deke."

It was Cynthia. "Come on," she said in a bored voice. "Don't clog up the doorway." The guard moved aside, and he entered.

"Thank you," he said.

"*Nada,*" she replied. "As Maggie would say. The dressing room is that way, pilgrim."

"Wolf, honey!" Maggie shrieked. "How's it going, Ace? Ya catch the show?"

"No, I — "

"You shoulda. I was good. Really good. Janis herself was never better. Hey, gang! Let's split, hah? Let's go somewhere and get down and boogie."

A group of twenty ended up taking over a methane-lit bar outside the zoned-for-electricity sector. Three of the band members had brought along their instruments, and they talked the owner into letting them play. The music was droning and monotonous. Maggie listened appreciatively, grinning and moving her head to the music.

"Whatcha think of that, Ace? Pretty good, hey? That's what we call Dead music."

Wolf shook his head. "I think it's well-named."

"Hey, guys, you hear that? Wolf here just made a funny. There's hope for you yet, honey." Then she sighed. "Can't get behind it, huh? That's really sad, man. I mean they played *good* music back then; it was real. We're just echoes, man. Just playing away at them old songs. Got none of our own worth singing."

"Is that why you're doing the show, then?" Wolf asked, curious.

Maggie laughed. "Hell no. I do it because I got the chance. DiStephano got in touch with me — "

"DiStephano? The comptroller?"

"One of his guys, anyway. They had this gig all set up and they needed someone to play Janis. So they ran a computer search and came up with my name. And they offered me money, and I spent a month or two in Hopkins being worked over, and here I am. On the road to fame and glory.'' Her voice rose and warbled and mocked itself on the last phrase.

''Why did you have to go to Hopkins?''

''You don't think I was *born* looking like this? They had to change my face around. Changed my voice too, for which God bless. They brought it down lower, widened out my range, gave it the strength to hold onto them high notes and push 'em around.''

''Not to mention the mental implants,'' Cynthia said.

''Oh, yeah, and the 'plants so I could talk in a bluesy sorta way without falling out of character,'' Maggie said. ''But that was minor.''

Wolf was impressed. He had known that Hopkins was good, but this — ! ''What I don't understand is why your government did all this. What possible benefit is there for them?''

''Beats the living hell out of me, lover-boy. Don't know, don't care, and don't ask. That's my motto.''

A long-haired, pale young man sitting nearby said, ''The government is all hacked up on social engineering. They do a lot of weird things, and you never find out why. You learn not to ask questions.''

''Hey, listen, Hawk, bringing Janis back to life isn't weird. It's a beautiful thing to do,'' Maggie objected. ''Yeah, I only wish they could *really* bring her back. Sit her down next to me. Love to talk with that lady.''

''You two would tear each other's eyes out,'' Cynthia said.

''What? Why?''

''Neither one of you'd be willing to give up the spotlight to the other.''

Maggie cackled. ''Ain't it the truth? Still, she's one broad I'd love to have met. A *real* star, see? Not a goddammed echo like me.''

Hawk broke in, said, ''You, Wolf. Where does your pilgrimage take you now? The group goes on tour the day after tomorrow; what are your plans?''

''I don't really have any,'' Wolf said. He explained his situation. ''I'll probably stay in Baltimore until it's time to go up North. Maybe I'll take a side trip or two.''

''Why don't you join the group, then?'' Hawk asked. ''We're planning to make the trip one long party. And we'll slam into Boston in just less than a month. The tour ends there.''

''That,'' said Cynthia, ''is a real bright idea. All we need is another nonproductive person on board the train.''

Maggie bristled. ''So what's wrong with that? Not like we're paying for it, is it? What's wrong with it?''

''Nothing's wrong with it. It's just a dumb idea.''

''Well, *I* like it. How about it, Ace? You on the train or off?''

''I — '' He stopped. Well, why not? ''Yes. I would be pleased to go along.''

"Good." She turned to Cynthia. "*Your* problem, sweets, is that you're just plain jealous."

"Oh Christ, here we go again."

"Well, don't bother. It won't do you any good. Hey, you see that piece of talent at the far end of the bar?"

"Maggie, that 'piece of talent,' as you call him, is eighteen years old. At most."

"Yeah. Nice though." Maggie stared wistfully down the bar. "He's kinda pretty, ya know?"

Wolf spent the next day clearing up his affairs, and arranging for letters of credit. The morning of departure day, he rose early and made his way to Baltimore Station. A brief exchange with the guards let him into the walled trainyard.

The train was an ungainly steam locomotive with a string of rehabilitated cars behind it. The last car had the word *Pearl* painted on it, in antique psychedelic lettering.

"Hey, Wolf! Come lookit this mother." A lone figure waved at him from the far end of the train. Maggie.

Wolf joined her. "What do you think of it, hah?"

He searched for something polite to say. "It is very impressive," he said finally. The word that leaped to mind was *grotesque*.

"Yeah. Runs on garbage, you know that? Just like me."

"Garbage?"

"Yeah, there's a methane processing plant nearby. Hey, lookit me! Up and awake at eight in the morning. Can ya take it? Had to get behind a little speed to do it, though."

The idiom was beyond him. "You mean — you were late waking up?"

"What? Oh, hey, man you can be — look, forget I said a thing. No." She pondered a second. "Look, Wolf. There's this stuff called 'speed,' it can wake you up in the morning, give you a little boost, get you going. Ya know?"

Awareness dawned. "You mean amphetamines."

"Yeah, well this stuff ain't exactly legal, dig? So I'd just as soon you didn't spread the word around. I mean, I trust you, man, but I wanna be sure you know what's happening before you go shooting off your mouth."

"I understand," Wolf said. "I won't say anything. But you know that amphetamines are — "

"Gotcha, Ace. Hey, you gotta meet the piece of talent I picked up last night. Hey, Dave! Get your ass over here, lover."

A young, sleepy-eyed blond shuffled around the edge of the train. He wore white shorts, defiantly it seemed to Wolf, and a loose blouse buttoned up to his neck. Giving Maggie a weak hug around the waist, he nodded to Wolf.

"Davie's got four nipples, just like me. How about that? I mean, it's gotta be a pretty rare mutation, hah?"

Dave hung his head, half-blushing. "Aw, Janis," he mumbled. Wolf waited for Maggie to correct the boy, but she didn't. Instead, she led them around and around the train, chatting away madly, pointing out this, that, and the other thing.

Finally, Wolf excused himself, and returned to his hostel. He left Maggie prowling about the train, dragging her pretty boy after her. Wolf went out for a long lunch, picked up his bags, and showed up at the train earlier than most of the entourage.

The train lurched, and pulled out of the station. Maggie was in constant motion, talking, laughing, directing the placement of luggage. She darted from car to car, never still. Wolf found a seat and stared out the window. Children dressed in rags ran alongside the tracks, holding out hands, and begging for money. One or two of the party threw coins; more laughed and threw bits of garbage.

Then the children were gone, and the train was passing through endless miles of weathered ruins. Hawk sat down beside Wolf. "It'll be a slow trip," he said. "The train has to go around large sections of land it's better not to go through." He stared moodily at the broken-window shells that were once factories and warehouses. "Look out there, pilgrim, *that's* my country," he said in a disgusted voice. "Or the corpse of it."

"Hawk, you're close to Maggie."

"Now if you go out to the center of the continent . . ." Hawk's voice grew distant. "There's a cavern out there, where they housed radioactive waste. It was formed into slugs and covered with solid gold — anything else deteriorates too fast. The way I figure it, a man with a lead suit could go into the cavern and shave off a fortune. There's tons of the stuff there." He sighed. "Someday I'm going to rummage through a few archives and go."

"Hawk, you've got to *listen* to me."

Hawk held up a hand for silence. "It's about the drugs, right? You just found out and you want me to warn her."

"Warning her isn't good enough. Someone has to stop her."

"Yes, well. Try to understand, Maggie was in Hopkins for *three months* while they performed some very drastic surgery on her. She didn't look a thing like she does now, and she could sing but her voice wasn't anything to rave about. Not to mention the mental implants.

"Imagine the pain she went through. Now ask yourself what are the two most effective pain killers in existence?"

"Morphine and heroin. But in my country, when drugs are resorted to, the doctors wean the patients off them before their release."

"That's not the point. Consider this — Maggie could have had Hopkins remove the extra nipples. They could have done it. But she wasn't willing to go through the pain."

"She seems proud of them."

"She talks about them a lot, at least."

The train lurched and stumbled. Three of the musicians had uncrated their quitars and were playing more "Dead" music. Wolf chewed his lip in silence for a time, then said, "So what is the point you're making?"

"Simply that Maggie was willing to undergo the greater pain so that she could become Janis. So, when I tell you she only uses drugs as pain killers, you have to understand that I'm not necessarily talking about physical pain." Hawk got up and left.

Maggie danced into the car. "Big time!" she whooped. "We made it into the big time, boys and girls. Hey, let's party!"

The next ten days were one extended party, interspersed with concerts. The reception in Wilmington was phenomenal. Thousands came to see the show; many were turned away. Maggie was unsteady before the first concert, achingly afraid of failure. But she played a rousing set, and was called back time and time again. Finally, exhausted and limp, her hair sticking to a sweaty forehead, she stood up front and gasped, "That's all there is, boys and girls. I love ya, and I wish there was more ta give ya, but there ain't. You used it all up." And the applause went on and on . . . .

The four shows in Philadelphia began slowly, but built up big. A few seats were unsold at the first concert; people were turned away for the second. The last two were near-riots. The group entrained to Newark for a day's rest and put on a Labor Day concert that made the previous efforts look pale. They stayed in an obscure hostel for an extra day's rest.

Wolf spent his rest day sight-seeing. While in Philadelphia he had hired a native guide and prowled through the rusting refinery buildings at Point Breeze. They rose to the sky forever in tragic magnificence, and it was hard to believe there had ever been enough oil in the world to fill the holding tanks there. In Wilmington, he let the local guide lead him to a small Italian neighborhood to watch a religious festival.

The festival was a parade, led first by a priest trailed by eight altargirls with incense burners and fans. Then came twelve burly men carrying the flower-draped body of an ancient Cadillac. After them came the faithful, in coveralls and chador, singing.

Wolf followed the procession to the river, where the car was placed in a hole in the ground, sprinkled with holy water, and set afire. He asked the guide what story lay behind the ritual, and the boy shrugged. It was old, he was told, very very old.

It was late when Wolf returned to the hostel. He was expecting a party but found it dark and empty. Cynthia stood in the foyer, hands behind her back, staring out a barred window at black nothingness.

"Where is everybody?" Wolf asked. It was hot. Insects buzzed about the coal-oil lamp, batting against it frenziedly.

Cynthia turned, studied him oddly. Her forehead was beaded with sweat. "Maggie's gone home — she's attending a mid-school reunion. She's going to show her old friends what a hacking big star she's become. The others?'' She shrugged. ''Off wherever puppets go when there's no one to bring them to life. Their rooms, probably.''

''Oh.'' Cynthia's dress clung damply to her legs and sides. Dark stains spread out from under her armpits. ''Would you like to play a game of chess or — something?''

Cynthia's eyes were strangely intense. She took a step closer to him. ''Wolf, I've been wondering. You've been celibate on this trip. Is there a problem? No? Maybe a girl friend back home?''

''There was, but she won't wait for me.'' Wolf made a deprecating gesture. ''Maybe that was part of the reason I took this trip.''

She took one of his hands, placed it on her breast. ''But you *are* interested in girls?'' Then, before he could shape his answer into clumsy words, she whispered, ''Come on,'' and led him to her room.

Once inside, Wolf seized Cynthia and kissed her, deeply and long. She responded with passion, then drew away and with a little shove toppled him onto the bed. ''Off with your clothes,'' she said. She shucked her blouse in a complex, fluid motion. Pale breast bobbled, catching vague moonlight from the window.

After an instant's hesitation, Wolf doffed his own clothing. By contrast with Cynthia he felt weak and irresolute, and it irked him to feel that way. Determined to prove he was nothing of the kind, he reached for Cynthia as she dropped onto the bed beside him. She evaded his grasp.

''Just a moment, pilgrim.'' She rummaged through a bag by the headboard. ''Ah. Care for a little treat first? It'll enhance the sensations.''

''Drugs?'' Wolf asked, feeling an involuntary horror.

''Oh, come down off your high horse. Once won't melt your genes. Give a gander at what you're being so critical of.''

''What is it?''

''Vanillla ice cream,'' she snapped. She unstoppered a small vial and meticulously dribbled a few grains of white powder onto a thumbnail. ''This is expensive, so pay attention. You want to breathe it all in with one snort. Got that? So by the numbers: Take a deep breath and breathe out slowly. That's it. Now in. Now out and hold.''

Cynthia laid her thumbnail beneath Wolf's nose, pinched one nostril shut with her free hand. ''Now in fast. Yeah!''

He inhaled convulsively and was flooded with sensations. A crisp, clean taste filled his mouth, and a spray of fine white powder hit the back of his throat. It tingled pleasantly. His head felt spacious. He moved his jaw, suspiciously searching about with his tongue.

Cynthia quickly snorted some of the powder herself, restoppering the vial.

''Now,'' she said. ''Touch me. Slowly, slowly, we've got all night. That's the way. Ahhh.'' She shivered. ''I think you've got the idea.''

They worked the bed for hours. The drug, whatever it was, made Wolf feel strangely clear-headed and rational, more playful and more prone to linger. There was no urgency to their lovemaking; they took their time. Three, perhaps four times they halted for more of the powder, which Cynthia doled out with careful ceremony. Each time they returned to their lovemaking with renewed interest and resolution to take it slowly, to postpone each climax to the last possible instant.

The evening grew old. Finally, they lay on the sheets, not touching, weak and exhausted. Wolf's body was covered with a fine sheen of sweat. He did not care to even think of making love yet another time. He refrained from saying this.

"Not bad," Cynthia said softly. "I must remember to recommend you to Maggie."

"Sin, why do you do that?"

"Do what?"

"We've just — been as intimate as two human beings can be. But as soon as it's over, you say something cold. Is it that you're afraid of contact?"

"Christ." It was an empty syllable, devoid of religious content, and flat. Cynthia fumbled in her bag, found a flat metal case, pulled a cigarette out and lit it. Wolf flinched inwardly. "Look, pilgrim, what are you asking for? You planning to marry me and take me away to your big, clean African cities to meet your momma? Hah?

"Didn't think so. So what do you want from me? Mental souvenirs to take home and tell your friends about? I'll give you one: I spent years saving up enough to go see a doctor, find out if I could have any brats. Went to one last year and what do you think he tells me? I've got red-cell Dyscrasia, too far gone for treatment, there's nothing to do but wait. Lovely, hah? So one of these days it'll catch up with me and I'll die. Nothing to be done. So long as I eat right, I won't start wasting away, so I can keep my looks up to the end. I could buy a little time if I gave up drugs like this — " she waved the cigarette, and an ash fell on Wolf's chest. He brushed it away quickly — "and the white powder, and anything else that make life worth living. But it wouldn't buy me enough time to do anything worth doing." She fell silent. "Hey. What time is it?"

Wolf climbed out of bed, rummaged through his clothing until he found his timepiece. He held it up to the window, squinted. "Um. Twelve . . . fourteen."

"Oh, *nukes.*" Cynthia was up and scrabbling for her clothes. "Come on, get dressed. Don't just stand there."

Wolf dressed himself slowly. "What's the problem?"

"I promised Maggie I'd get some people together to walk her back from that damned reunion. It ended *hours* ago, and I lost track of the time." She ignored his grin. "Ready? Come on, we'll check her room first and then the foyer. God, is she going to be mad!"

They found Maggie in the foyer. She stood in the center of the room, haggard and bedraggled, her handbag hanging loosely from one hand. Her face was livid with rage. The sputtering lamp made her face look old and evil.

"Well!" she snarled. "Where have you two been?"

"In my room, balling," Cynthia said calmly. Wolf stared at her, appalled.

"Well that's just beautiful. That's really beautiful, isn't it? Do you know where I've been while my two best friends were upstairs humping their brains out? Hey? Do you want to know?'' Her voice reached a hysterical peak. ''I was being *raped by two jennie-deafs,* that's where!''

She stormed past them, half-cocking her arm as if she were going to assault them with her purse, then thinking better of it. They heard her run down the hall. Her door slammed.

Bewildered, Wolf said, ''But I — ''

''Don't let her dance on your head,'' Cynthia said. ''She's lying.''

''Are you certain?''

''Look, we've lived together, bedded the same men — I know her. She's all hacked off at not having an escort home. And Little Miss Sunshine has to spread the gloom.''

''We should have been there,'' Wolf said dubiously. ''She could have been killed, walking home alone.''

''Whether Maggie dies a month early or not doesn't make a bit of difference to me, pilgrim. I've got my own problems.''

''A month — ? Is Maggie suffering from a disease too?''

''We're all suffering, we all . . . Ah, the hell with you too.'' Cynthia spat on the floor, spun on her heel and disappeared down the hallway. It had the rhythm and inevitability of a witch's curse.

The half-day trip to New York left the troupe with play time before the first concert, but Maggie stayed in seclusion, drinking. There was talk about her use of drugs, and this alarmed Wolf, for they were all users of drugs themselves.

There was also gossip about the reunion. Some held that Maggie had dazzled her former friends — who had not treated her well in her younger years — had been glamorous and gracious. The predominant view, however, was that she had been soundly snubbed, that she was still a freak and an oddity in the eyes of her former contemporaries. That she had left the reunion alone.

Rumors flew about the liaison between Wolf and Cynthia too. The fact that she avoided him only fed the speculation.

Despite everything the New York City concerts were a roaring success. All four shows were sold out as soon as tickets went on sale. Scalpers made small fortunes that week, and for the first time the concerts were allowed to run into the evening. Power was diverted from a section of the city to allow for the lighting and amplification. And Maggie sang as she had never sung before. Her voice roused the audiences to a frenzy, and her blues were enough to break a hermit's heart.

They left for Hartford on the tenth, Maggie sequestered in her compartment in the last car. Crew members lounged about idly. Some strummed guitars, never quite breaking into a recognizable tune. Others talked quietly. Hawk flipped tarot cards into a heap, one at a time.

''Hey, this place is fucking *dead!*'' Maggie was suddenly in the car, her expression an odd combination of defiance and guilt. "Let's party! Hey? Let's hear some music." She fell into Hawk's lap and nibbled on an ear.

"Welcome back, Maggie," somebody said.

"*Janis!*" she shouted happily. "The lady's name is Janis!"

Like a rusty machine starting up, the party came to life. Music jelled. Voices became animated. Bottles of alcohol appeared and were passed around. And for the remainder of the two days that the train spent making wide, looping detours to avoid the dangerous stretches of Connecticut and New York, the party never died.

There were tense undertones to the party, however, a desperate quality in Maggie's gaiety. For the first time, Wolf began to feel trapped, to count the days that separated him from Boston and the end of the tour.

The dressing room for the first Hartford concert was cramped, small, badly lit — like every other dressing room they'd encountered. "Get your ass over here, Sin," Maggie yelled. "You've gotta make me up so I look strung out, like Janis did."

Cynthia held Maggie's chin, twisted it to the left, to the right. "Maggie, you don't *need* makeup to look strung out."

"Goddammit, yes I *do*. Let's get it on. Come one, come on — I'm a star, I shouldn't have to put up with this shit."

Cynthia hesitated, then began dabbing at Maggie's face, lightly accentuating the lines, the bags under her eyes.

Maggie studied the mirror. "Now *that's* grim," she said. "That's really grotesque."

"That's what you look like, Maggie."

"You cheap bitch! You'd think *I* was the one who nodded out last night before we could get it on." There was an awkward silence. "Hey, Wolf!" She spun to face him. "What do *you* say?"

"Well," Wolf began, embarrassed, "I'm afraid Cynthia's . . . "

"You see? Let's get this show on the road." She grabbed her cherished Southern Comfort bottle and upended it.

"That's not doing you any good either."

Maggie smiled coldly. "Shows what *you* know. Janis always gets smashed before a concert. Helps her voice." She stood, made her way to the curtains. The emcee was winding up his pitch.

"Ladies and gentlemen . . . Janis!"

Screams arose. Maggie sashayed up to the mike, lifted it, laughed into it.

"Heyyy. Good ta see ya." She swayed and squinted at the crowd and was off and into her rap. "Ya know, I went ta see a doctor the other week. Told him I was worried about how much drinking I was doing. Told him I'd been drinkin' heavy since I was twelve. Get up in the morning and have a few Bloody Marys with breakfast. Polish off a fifth before lunch. Have a few drinks at dinner, and really get into it when the partying begins. Told him how much I drank for many years. So I said, 'Look, Doc, none of this ever hurt me any, but I'm kinda worried, ya know? Give it to me straight, have I got a problem? And he said, 'Man, *I* don't think you've got a problem. *I* think you're doing just *fine!*' " Cheers from the audience. Maggie smiled smugly. "Well, honey, *everybody's* got problems, and I'm no exception." The music came up. "But when I got problems, I got an answer, 'cause I can sing dem ole-time blues. Just sing my problems away." She launched into "Ball and Chain" and the audience went wild.

Backstage, Wolf was sitting on a stepladder. He had bought a cup of water from a vendor and was nursing it, taking small sips. Cynthia came up and stood beside him. They both watched Maggie strutting on stage, stamping and sweating, writhing and howling.

"I can never get over the contrast," Wolf said, not looking at Cynthia. "Out there, everybody is excited. Back here, it's calm and peaceful. Sometimes I wonder if we're seeing the same thing the audience does."

"Sometimes it's hard to see what's right in front of your face." Cynthia smiled a sad, cryptic smile and left. Wolf had grown used to such statements and gave it no more thought.

The second and final Hartford show went well. However, the first two concerts in Providence were bad. Maggie's voice and timing were off, and she had to cover with theatrics. At the second show she had to order the audience to dance — something that had never been necessary before. Her onstage raps became bawdier and more graphic. She moved her body as suggestively as a stripper, employing bumps and grinds. The third show was better, but the earthy elements remained.

The cast wound up in a bar in a bad section of town, where guards with guns covered the doorway from fortified booths. Maggie got drunk and ended up crying. "Man, I was so blitzed when I went onstage — you say I was good?"

"Sure, Maggie.," Hawk mumbled. Cynthia snorted.

"You were very good," Wolf assured her.

"I don't remember a goddammed thing," she wailed. "You say I was good? It ain't fair, man. If I was good, I deserve to be able to remember it. I mean, what's the point otherwise? Hey?"

Wolf patted her shoulder clumsily. She grabbed the front of his dashiki and buried her face in his chest. "Wolf, Wolf, what's gonna *happen* to me?" she sobbed.

"Don't cry," he said, patting her hair.

Finally, Wolf and Hawk had to lead her back to the hostel. No one else was willing to quit the bar.

They skirted an area where all the buildings had been torn down but one. It stood alone, with great gaping holes where plate glass had been, and large nonfunctional arches on one side.

"It was a fast-food building," Hawk explained when Wolf asked. He sounded embarrassed.

"Why is it still standing?"

"Because there are ignorant and superstitious people everywhere," Hawk muttered. Wolf dropped the subject.

The streets were dark and empty. They went back into the denser areas of town, and the sound of their footsteps bounced off the buildings. Maggie was leaning half-conscious on Hawk's shoulder, and he almost had to carry her.

There was a stirring in the shadows. Hawk tensed. "Speed up a bit, if you can," he whispered.

Something shuffled out of the darkness. It was large and only vaguely human. It moved toward them. "What — ?" Wolf whispered.

"Jennie-deaf," Hawk whispered back. "If you know any clever tricks, this is the time to use 'em." The thing broke into a shambling run.

Wolf thrust a hand into a pocket and whirled to face Hawk. "Look," he said in a loud, angry voice. "I've taken *enough* from you! I've got a *knife* and I don't care *what* I do!" The jennie-deaf halted. From the corner of his eye, Wolf saw it slide back into the shadows.

Maggie looked up with a sleepy, quizical expression. "Hey, what . . . ."

"Never mind," Hawk muttered. He upped his pace, half-dragging Maggie after him. "That was arrogant," he said approvingly.

Wolf forced his hand from his pocket. He found he was shivering from aftershock. "*Nada,*" he said. Then, "That is the correct term?"

"Yeah."

"I wasn't certain that jennie-deafs really existed."

"Just some poor mute with gland trouble. Don't think about it."

Autumn was just breaking out when the troupe hit Boston. They arrived to find the final touches being put on the stage on Boston Commons. A mammoth concert was planned; dozens of people swarmed about making preparations.

"This must be how America was all the time before the Collapse," Wolf said, impressed. He was ignored.

The morning of the concert, Wolf was watching canvas being hoisted above the stage, against the chance of rain, when a gripper ran up and said, "You, pilgrim, have you seen Janis?"

"Maggie," he corrected automatically. "No, not recently."

"Thanks," the man gasped, and ran off. Not long after, Hawk hurried by and asked, "Seen Maggie lagging about?"

"No. Wait, Hawk, what's going on? You're the second person to ask me that."

Hawk shrugged. "Maggie's disappeared. Nothing to scream about."

"I hope she'll be back in time for the show."

"The local police are hunting for her. Anyway, she's got the implants; if she can move she'll be on stage. Never doubt it." He hurried away.

The final checks were being run, and the first concertgoers beginning to straggle in when Maggie finally appeared. Uniformed men held each arm; she looked sober and angry. Cynthia took charge, dismissed the police, and took Maggie to the trailer that served as a dressing room.

Wolf watched from a distance, decided he could be of no use. He ambled about the Commons aimlessly, watching the crowd grow. The people coming in found places to sit, took them, and waited. There was little talk among them, and what there was was quiet. They were dressed brightly, but not in their best. Some carried winejugs or blankets.

They were an odd crew. They did not look each other in the eye; their mouths were grim, their faces without expression. Their speech was low, but with an undercurrent of tension. Wolf wandered among them, eavesdropping, listening to fragments of their talk.

"Said that her child was going to . . ."

" . . . needed that. Nobody needed that."

"Couldn't have paid it away . . ."

" . . . tasted odd, so I didn't . . ."

"Had to tear down three blocks . . ."

" . . . blood."

Wolf became increasingly uneasy. There was something about their expressions, their tone of voice. He bumped into Hawk, who tried to hurry past.

"Hawk, there is something very wrong happening."

Hawk's face twisted. He gestured toward the light tower. "No time," he said, "the show's beginning. I've got to be at my station." Wolf hesitated, then followed the man up the ladders of the light tower.

All of the Commons was visible from the tower. The ground was thick with people, hordes of ant specks against the brown of trampled earth. Not a child among them, and that felt wrong too. A gold and purple sunset smeared itself three-quarters of the way around the horizon.

Hawk flicked lights on and off, one by one, referring to a sheet of paper he held in one hand. Sometimes he cursed and respliced wires. Wolf waited. A light breeze ruffled his hair, though there was no hint of wind below.

"This is a sick country," Hawk said. He slipped a headset on, played a red spot on the stage, let it wink out. "You there, Patrick? The Kliegs go on in two." He ran a check on all the locals manning lights, addressing them by name. "Average lifespan is something like forty-two—if you get out of the delivery room alive. The birthrate has to be very high to keep the population from dwindling away to nothing." He brought up all the red and blue spots. The stage was bathed in purple light. The canvas above looked black in contrast. An obscure figure strolled to the center mike.

"Hit it, Patrick." A bright pool of light illuminated the emcee. He coughed, went into his spiel. His voice boomed over the crowd, relayed away from the stage by a series of amps with timed delay along each rank, so that his voice reached the distant listeners in synchronization with the further amplification. The crowd moved sluggishly about the foot of the tower, set in motion by latecomers straggling in. "So the question you should ask yourself is why the government is wasting its resources on a goddammed show."

"All right," Wolf said. "Why?" He was very tense, very still. The breeze swept away his sweat, and he wished he had brought along a jacket. He might need one later.

"Because their wizards said to — the damn social engineers and their machines," Hawk answered. "Watch the crowd."

" . . . JANIS!" the loudspeakers boomed. And Maggie was on stage, rapping away, handling the microphone suggestively, obviously at the peak of her form. The crowd exploded into applause. Offerings of flowers were thrown through the air. Bottles of liquor were passed hand over hand and deposited on the stage.

From above it could not be seen how the previous month had taken its toll on Maggie. The lines on her face, the waxy skin, were hidden by the colored light. The Kliegs bounced off her sequined dress dazzlingly.

Halfway through her second song, Maggie came to an instrumental break and squinted out at the audience. "Hey, what the fuck's the matter with you guys? Why ain't you *dancing*?" At her cue, scattered couples rose to their feet. "Ready on the Kliegs," Hawk murmured into his headset. "Three, four, and five on the police." Bright lights pinpointed three widely separated parts of the audience, where uniformed men were struggling with dancers. A single Klieg stayed on Maggie, who pointed an imperious finger at one struggling group and shrieked, "Why are you trying to stop them from dancing? I want them to dance. I *command* them to dance!"

With a roar, half the audience were on their feet. "Shut down three. Hold four and five to the count of three, then off. One — Two — Three! Good." The police faded away, lost among the dancers.

"That was prearranged," Wolf said. Hawk didn't so much as glance at him.

"It's part of the legend. You, Wolf, over to your right." Wolf looked where Hawk was pointing, saw a few couples at the edge of the crowd slip from the light into the deeper shadows.

"What am I seeing?"

"Just the beginning." Hawk bent over his control board.

By slow degrees the audience became drunk and then rowdy. As the concert wore on, an ugly, excited mood grew. Sitting far above it all, Wolf could still feel the hysteria grow, as well as see it. Women shed chador and danced atop it, not fully dressed. Men ripped free of their coveralls. Hawk directed lights onto a few, held them briefly; in most cases the couples went on, unheeding.

Small fights broke out, and were quelled by police. Bits of trash were gathered up and set ablaze, so that small fires dotted the landscape. Wisps of smoke floated up. Hawk played colored spots on the crowd. By the time darkness was total, the lights and the bestial noise of the revelers combined to create the feel of a Witch's Sabbath.

"Pretty nasty down there," Hawk observed. "And all most deliberately engineered by government wizards."

"But there is no true feeling involved," Wolf objected. "It is nothing but animal lust. No — no involvement."

"Yeah." Onstage, Maggie was building herself up into a frenzy. And yet her blues were brilliant — she had never been better. "Not so much different from the other concerts. The only difference is that tonight nobody waits until they go home."

"Your government can't believe that enough births will result from this night to make any difference."

"Not tonight, no. But all these people will have memories to keep them warm over the winter." Then he spat over the edge of the platform. "Ahhhh, why should I spout their lies for them? It's just bread and circuses is all, just a goddammed release for the masses."

Maggie howled with delight. "Whee-ew, man! I'm gettin' horny just looking at you. Yeah, baby, get it on, that's right." She was strutting up and down the stage, a creature of boundless energy, while the band filled the night with music, fast and urgent.

"Love it!" She stuck her tongue out at the audience and received howls of approval. She lifted her Southern Comfort bottle, took a gigantic swig, her hips bouncing to the music. More howls. She caressed the neck of the bottle with her tongue.

"Yeah! Makes me horny as sin, 'deed it does. Ya know," she paused a beat, then continued, "that's something I can really understand, man. 'Cause I'm just a horny little hippie chick myself. Yeah." Wolf suddenly realized that she was competing against the audience itself for its attention, that she was going to try to outdo everybody present.

Maggie stroked her hand down the front of her dress, lingering between her breasts, then between her legs. She shook her hair back from her eyes, the personification of animal lust. "I mean, shit. I mean, hippie chicks don't even wear no underwear." More ribald howls and applause. "Don't believe me, do ya?"

Wolf stared, was unable to look away as Maggie slowly spread her legs wide and squatted, giving the audience a good look up her skirt. Her frog face leered, and it was an ugly, lustful thing. She lowered a hand to the stage behind her for support, and beckoned. "Come to momma," she crooned.

It was like knocking the chocks out from a dam. There was an instant of absolute stillness, and then the crowd roared and surged forward. An ocean of humanity converged on the stage, smashing through the police lines, climbing up on the wooden platform. Wolf had a brief glimpse of Maggie trying to struggle to her feet, before she was overrun. There was a dazed, disbelieving expression on her face.

"Mother of Sin," Wolf whispered. He stared at the mindless, evil mob below. They were in furious motion, pushing, straining, forcing each other in great swirling eddies. He waited for the stage to collapse, but it did not. The audience kept climbing atop it, pushing one another off its edge, and it did not collapse. It would have been a mercy if it had.

A hand waved above the crowd, clutching something that sparkled. Wolf could not make it out at first. Then another hand waved a glittering rag, and then another, and he realized that these were shreds of Maggie's dress.

Wolf wrapped his arms around a support to keep from falling into the horror below. The howling of the crowd was a single, chaotic noise; he squeezed his eyes shut, vainly trying to fend it off. "Right on cue," Hawk muttered. "Right on goddammed cue." He cut off all the lights, and placed a hand on Wolf's shoulder.

"Come on. Our job is done here."

Wolf twisted to face Hawk. The act of opening his eyes brought on a wave of vertigo, and he slumped to the platform floor, still clutching the support desperately. He wanted to vomit, and couldn't. "It's — they — Hawk, did you *see* it? Did you see what they did? Why didn't someone — ?" he choked on his words.

"Don't ask me," Hawk said bitterly. "I just play the part of Judas Iscariot in this little drama." He tugged at Wolf's shoulders. "Let's go, pilgrim. We've got to go down now." Wolf slowly weaned himself of the support, allowed himself to be coaxed down from the tower.

There were men in black uniforms at the foot of the tower. One of them addressed Hawk. "Is this the African national?" Then, to Wolf: "Please come with us, sir. We have orders to see you safely to your hostel."

Tears flooded Wolf's eyes and he could not see the crowd, the Commons, the men before him. He allowed himself to led away, as helpless and as trusting as a small child.

In the morning, Wolf lay in bed staring at the ceiling. A fly buzzed somewhere in the room, and he did not look for it. In the streets iron-wheeled carts rumbled by, and children chanted a counting-out game.

After a time he rose, dressed, and washed his face. He went to the hostel's dining room for breakfast.

There, finishing off a piece of toast, was DiStephano.

"Good morning, Mr. Mbikana. I was beginning to think I'd have to send for you." He gestured to a chair. Wolf looked about, took it. There were at least three of the political police seated nearby.

DiStephano removed some documents from his jacket pocket, handed them to Wolf. "Signed, sealed, and delivered. We made some minor changes in the terms, but nothing your superiors will object to." He placed the last corner of toast in the side of his mouth. "I'd say this was a rather bright beginning to your professional career."

"Thank you," Wolf said automatically. He glanced at the documents, could make no sense of them, dropped them in his lap.

"If you're interested, the *African Genesis* leaves port tomorrow morning. I've made arrangements that a berth be ready for you, should you care to take it.

Of course there will be another passenger ship in three weeks if you wish to see more of our country.''

"No," Wolf said hastily. Then, because that seemed rude, "I'm most anxious to see my home again. I've been away far too long.''

DiStephano dabbed at the corners of his mouth with a napkin, let it fall to the tablecloth. "Then that's that.'' He started to rise.

"Wait," Wolf said. "Mr. DiStephano, I . . . I would very much like an explanation.''

DiStephano sat back down. He did not pretend not to understand the request. "The first thing you must know," he said, "is that Ms. Horowitz was not our first Janis Joplin.''

"No," Wolf said.

"Nor the second.''

Wolf looked up.

"She was the twenty-third, not counting the original. The show is sponsored every year, always ending in Boston on the Equinox. So far, it has always ended in the same fashion.''

Wolf wondered if he should try to stab the man with a fork, if he should rise up and attempt to strangle him. There should be rage, he knew. He felt nothing. "Because of the brain implants.''

"No. You must believe me when I say that I wish she had lived. The implants helped her keep in character, nothing more. It's true that she did not recall the previous women who played the part of Janis. But her death was not planned. It's simply something that — happens.''

"Every year.''

"Yes. Every year Janis offers herself to the crowd. And every year they tear her apart. A sane woman would not make the offer; a sane people would not respond in that fashion. I'll know that my country is on the road to recovery come the day that Janis lives to make a second tour.'' He paused. "Or the day we can't find a woman willing to play the role, knowing how it ends.''

Wolf tried to think. His head felt dull and heavy. He heard the words, and he could not guess whether they made sense or not. "One last question," he said. "Why me?''

DiStephano rose. "One day you may return to our nation," he said. "Or perhaps not. But you will certainly rise to a responsible position within the Southwest Africa Trade Company. Your decisions will affect our economy.'' Four men in uniform also rose from their chairs. "When that happens, I want you to understand one thing about our land: *We have nothing to lose.* Good day, and a long life to you, sir.''

DiStephano's guards followed him out.

It was evening. Wolf's ship rode in Boston harbor, waiting to carry him home. Away from this magic nightmare land, with its ghosts and walking dead. He stared at it and he could not make it real; he had lost all capacity for belief.

The ship's dinghy was approaching. Wolf picked up his bags.

Although Isaac Asimov is one of the most famous SF writers of all time — author of The Foundation Trilogy *(Avon),* The Caves of Steel *(Fawcett),* I, Robot *(Fawcett), and literally dozens of nonfiction books on all conceivable subjects, mainstay of the lecture circuit and the television talk show, the only SF writer ever to have an SF magazine named after him* (Isaac Asimov's Science Fiction Magazine), *multiple Hugo-and-Nebula award winner, and so on — he is* not *usually thought of as an expert on theological matters (although, come to think of it, there* is *Asimov's Guide to the Bible). Here though, in an incisive and thoughtful little story, he takes us beyond the veil of death for a conversation with a certain Entity, and provides a new and unique answer for that perennial question about the purpose of life.*

Asimov's story "Found!" was in our Eighth Annual Collection. *He lives in New York City with his wife Janet.*

ISAAC ASIMOV
The Last Answer

Murray Templeton was forty-five years old, in his prime, and with all parts of his body in perfect working order except for certain key portions of his coronary arteries, but that was enough.

The pain had come suddenly, had mounted to an unbearable peak, and had then ebbed steadily. He could feel his breath slowing and a kind of gathering peace washing over him.

There is no pleasure like the absence of pain — immediately after pain. Murray felt an almost giddy lightness as though he were lifting in the air and hovering.

He opened his eyes and noted with distant amusement that the others in the room were still agitated. He had been in the laboratory when the pain had struck, quite without warning, and when he had staggered, he had heard surprised outcries from the others before everything vanished into overwhelming agony.

Now, with the pain gone, the others were still hovering, still anxious, still gathered about his fallen body —

— Which, he suddenly realized, he was looking down on.

He was down there, sprawled, face contorted. He was up here, at peace and watching.

He thought: "Miracle of miracles! The life-after-life nuts were right."

And although that was a humiliating way for an atheistic physicist to die, he felt only the mildest surprise, and no alteration of the peace in which he was immersed.

He thought: "There should be an angel, or something, coming for me."

The Earthly scene was fading. Darkness was invading his consciousness and off in a distance, as a last glimmer of sight, there was a figure of light, vaguely human in form, and radiating warmth.

Murray thought: "What a joke on me. I'm going to heaven."

Even as he thought that, the light faded, but the warmth remained. There was no lessening of the peace even though in all the Universe only he remained — and the Voice.

The Voice said, "I have done this so often, and yet I still have the capacity to be pleased at success."

It was in Murray's mind to say something, but he was not conscious of possessing a mouth, tongue; or vocal cords. Nevertheless, he tried to make a sound. He tried, mouthlessly, to hum words or breathe them or just push them out by a contraction of — something.

And they came out. He heard his own voice, quite recognizable, and his own words, infinitely clear.

Murray said, "Is this Heaven?"

The Voice said, "This is no place as you understand place."

Murray was embarrassed, but the next question had to be asked. "Pardon me if I sound like a jackass. Are you God?"

Without changing intonation or in any way marring the perfection of the sound, the Voice sounded amused. "It is strange that I am always asked that in, of course, an infinite number of ways. There is no answer I can give that you would comprehend. I *am* — which is all that I can say significantly and you may cover that with any word or concept you please."

Murray said, "And what am I? A soul? Or am I only personified existence, too?" He tried not to sound sarcastic, but it seemed to him that he had failed. He thought then, fleetingly, of adding a "Your Grace" or "Holy One" or *something* to counteract the sarcasm, and could not bring himself to do so even though for the first time in his existence he speculated on the possibility of being punished for his insolence — or sin? — with Hell, and whatever that might be like.

The Voice did not sound offended. "You are easy to explain — even to you. You may call yourself a soul if that pleases you, but what you are is a nexus of electromagnetic forces, so arranged that all the interconnections and interrelationships are exactly imitative of those of your brain in your Universe-existence — down to the smallest detail. Therefore you have your capacity for thought, your memories, your personality. It still seems to you that you are you."

Murray found himself incredulous. "You mean the essence of my brain was permanent."

"Not at all. There is nothing about you that is permanent except what I choose to make so. I formed the nexus. I constructed it while you had physical existence and adjusted it to the moment when the existence failed."

The Voice seemed distinctly pleased with itself, and went on after a moment's pause. "An intricate but entirely precise construction. I could, of course, do it for every human being on your world but I am pleased that I do not. There is pleasure in the selection."

"You choose very few then."

"Very few."

"And what happens to the rest?"

"Oblivion! — Oh, of course, you imagine a Hell."

Murray would have flushed if he had the capacity to do so. He said, "I do not. It is spoken of. Still, I would scarcely have thought I was virtuous enough to have attracted your attention as one of the Elect."

"Virtuous? — Ah, I see what you mean. It is troublesome to have to force my thinking small enough to permeate yours. No, I have chosen you for your capacity for thought, as I choose others, in quadrillions, from all the intelligent species of the Universe."

Murray found himself suddenly curious, the habit of a lifetime. He said, "Do you choose them all yourself or are there others like you?"

For a fleeting moment, Murray thought there was an impatient reaction to that, but when the Voice came, it was unmoved. "Whether or not there are others is irrelevant to you. This Universe is mine, and mine alone. It is my intention, my construction, intended for my purpose alone."

"And yet with quadrillions of nexi you have formed, you spend time with me? Am I that important?"

The Voice said, "You are not important at all. I am also with others in a way which, to your perception, would seem simultaneous."

"And yet you are one?"

Again amusement. The Voice said, "You seek to trap me into an inconsistency. If you were an amoeba who could consider individuality only in connection with single cells and if you were to ask a sperm whale, made up of 30 quadrillion cells, whether it was one of many, how could the sperm whale answer in a way that would be comprehensible to the amoeba?"

Murray said dryly, "I'll think about it. It may become comprehensible."

"Exactly. That is your function. You will think."

"To what end. You already know everything, I suppose."

The Voice said, "Even if I knew everything, I could not know that I know everything."

Murray said, "That sounds like a bit of Eastern philosophy — something that sounds profound precisely because it has no meaning."

The Voice said, "You have promise. You answer my paradox with a paradox — except that mine is not a paradox. Consider. I have existed eternally, but what does that mean? It means I cannot remember having come into existence. If I could, I would not have existed eternally. If I cannot remember having come into existence, then there is at least one thing — the nature of my coming into existence — that I do not know.

"Then, too, although what I know is infinite, it is also true that what there is to know is infinite, and how can I be sure that both infinities are equal. The infinity of potential knowledge may be infinitely greater than the infinity of my actual knowledge. Here is a simple example: If I knew every one of the even integers, I would know an infinite number of items, and yet I would still not know a single odd integer.''

Murray said, ''But the odd integers can be derived. If you divide every even integer in the entire infinite series by two, you will get another infinite series which will contain within it the infinite series of odd integers.''

The Voice said, ''You have the idea. I am pleased. It will be your task to find other such ways, far more difficult ones, from the known to the not-yet-known. You have your memories. You will remember all the data you have ever collected or learned, or that you have or will deduce from that data. If necessary, you will be allowed to learn what additional data you will consider relevant to the problems you set yourself.''

''Could you not do all that for yourself?''

The Voice said, ''I can, but it is more interesting this way. I constructed the Universe in order to have more facts to deal with. I inserted the uncertainty principle, entropy, and other randomization factors to make the whole not instantly obvious. It has worked well for it has amused me for its entire existence.

''I then allowed complexities that produced first life and then intelligence, and used it as a source for a research team, not because I need the aid, but because it would introduce a new random factor. I found I could not predict the next interesting piece of knowledge gained, where it would come from, by what means derived.''

''Does that ever happen?''

''Certainly. A century doesn't pass in which some interesting item doesn't appear somewhere,'' the Voice said.

''Something that you could have thought of yourself, but had not done so yet?''

''Yes.''

Murray said, ''Do you actually think there's a chance of my obliging you in this manner?''

''In the next century? Virtually none. In the long run, though, your success is certain, since you will be engaged eternally.''

Murray said, ''I will be thinking through eternity? Forever?''

''Yes.''

''To what end?''

''I have told you. To find new knowledge.''

''But beyond that. For what purpose am I to find new knowledge?''

''It was what you did in your Universe-bound life. What was its purpose then?''

Murray said, ''To gain new knowledge that only I could gain. To receive the praise of my fellows. To feel the satisfaction of accomplishment knowing that I had only a short time allotted me for the purpose. — Now I would gain only what you could gain yourself if you wished to take a small bit of trouble. You cannot praise me; you can only be amused. And there is no credit or satisfaction in accomplishment when I have all eternity to do it in.''

The Voice said, ''And you do not find thought and discovery worthwhile in itself? You do not find it requiring no further purpose?''

''For a finite time, yes. Not for all eternity.''

''I see your point. Nevertheless, you have no choice.''

''You say I am to think. You cannot make me do so.''

The Voice said, ''I do not wish to constrain you directly. I will not need to. Since you can do nothing but think, you will think. You do not know how not to think.''

''Then I will give myself a goal. I will invent a purpose.''

The Voice said tolerantly, ''That you can certainly do.''

''I have already found a purpose.''

''May I know what it is?''

''You know already. I know we are not speaking in the ordinary fashion. You adjust my nexus in such a way that I believe I hear you and I believe I speak, but you transfer thoughts to me and from me directly. And when my nexus changes with my thoughts you are at once aware of them and do not need my voluntary transmission.''

The Voice said, ''You are surprisingly correct. I am pleased — But it also pleases me to have you tell me your thoughts voluntarily.''

''Then I will tell you. The purpose of my thinking will be to discover a way to disrupt this nexus of me that you have created. I do not want to think for no purpose but to amuse you. I do not want to think forever to amuse you. I do not want to exist forever to amuse you. All my thinking will be directed toward ending the nexus. *That* would amuse *me*.''

The Voice said, ''I have no objection to that. Even concentrated thought on ending your own existence may, despite you, come up with something new and interesting. And, of course, if you succeed in this suicide attempt you will have accomplished nothing, for I would instantly reconstruct you and in such a way as to make your method of suicide impossible. And if you found another and still more subtle fashion of disrupting yourself, I would reconstruct you with that possibility eliminated and so on. It could be an interesting game, but you will nevertheless exist eternally. It is my will.''

Murray felt a quaver but the words came out with a perfect calm. ''Am I in Hell then, after all? You have implied there is none, but if this were Hell you would lie as part of the game of Hell.''

The Voice said, ''In that case, of what use to assure you that you are not in Hell? Nevertheless, I assure you. There is here neither Heaven nor Hell. There is only myself.''

Murray said, ''Consider, then, that my thoughts may be useless to you. If I come up with nothing useful, will it not be worth your while to — disassemble me and take no further trouble with me.''

''As a reward? You want Nirvana as the prize of failure and you intend to assure me failure? There is no bargain there. You will not fail. With all Eternity before you, you cannot avoid having at least one interesting thought, however you try against it.''

"Then I will create another purpose for myself. I will not try to destroy myself. I will set as my goal the humiliation of you. I will think of something you have not only never thought of but never could think of. I will think of the last answer, beyond which there is no knowledge further.''

The Voice said, ''You do not understand the nature of the infinite. There may be things I have not yet troubled to know. There cannot be anything I cannot know.''

Murray said thoughtfully, ''You cannot know your beginning. You have said so. Therefore you cannot know your end. Very well, then. That will be my purpose and that will be the last answer. I will not destroy myself. I will destroy *you* — if you do not destroy me first.''

The Voice said, ''Ah! You come to that in rather less than average time. I would have thought it would have taken you longer. There is not one of those I have with me in this existence of perfect and eternal thought that does not have the ambition of destroying me. It cannot be done.''

Murray said, ''I have all eternity to think of a way of destroying you.''

The Voice said, equably, ''Then try to think of it.'' And it was gone.

But Murray had his purpose now and was content.

But what could *any* Entity, conscious of eternal existence, want — but an end?

For what else had the Voice been searching for countless billions of years? And for what other reason had intelligence been created and certain specimens salvaged and put to work, but to aid in that great search? And Murray intended that it would be he, and he alone, who would succeed.

Carefully, and with the thrill of purpose, Murray began to think.

He had plenty of time.

GEORGE R.R. MARTIN
Nightflyers

When Jesus of Nazareth hung dying on his cross, the *volcryn* passed within a light-year of his agony, headed outward. When the Fire Wars raged on Earth, the *volcryn* sailed near Old Poseidon, where the seas were still unnamed and unfished. By the time the stardrive had transformed the Federated Nations of Earth into the Federal Empire, the *volcryn* had moved into the fringes of Hrangan space. The Hrangans never knew it. Like us they were children of the small bright worlds that circled their scattered suns, with little interest and less knowledge of the things that moved in the gulfs between.

War flamed for a thousand years and the *volcryn* passed through it, unknowing and untouched, safe in a place where no fires could ever burn. Afterward the Federal Empire was shattered and gone, and the Hrangans vanished in the dark of the Collapse, but it was no darker for the *volcryn*.

When Kleronomas took his survey ship out from Avalon, the *volcryn* came within ten light-years of him. Kleronomas found many things, but he did not find the *volcryn*. Not then did he and not on his return to Avalon a lifetime later.

When I was a child of three, Kleronomas was dust, as distant and dead as Jesus of Nazareth and the *volcryn* passed close to Daronne. That season all the

Crey sensitives grew strange and sat staring at the stars with luminous, flickering eyes.

When I was grown, the *volcryn* had sailed beyond Tara, past the range of even the Crey, still heading outward.

And now I am old and the *volcryn* will soon pierce the Tempter's Veil where it hangs like a black mist between the stars. And we follow, we follow. Through the dark gulfs where no one goes, through the emptiness, through the silence that goes on and on, my *Nightflyer* and I give chase.

From the hour the *Nightflyer* slipped into stardrive, Royd Eris watched his passengers.

Nine riders had boarded at the orbital docks above Avalon; five women and four men, each an Academy scholar, their backgrounds as diverse as their fields of study. Yet, to Royd, they dressed alike, looked alike, even sounded alike. On Avalon, most cosmopolitan of worlds, they had become as one in their quest for knowledge.

The *Nightflyer* was a trader, not a passenger vessel. It offered one double cabin, one closet-sized single. The other academicians rigged sleepwebs in the four great cargo holds, some in close confinement with the instruments and computer systems they had packed on board. When restive, they could wander two short corridors, one leading from the drive-room and the main airlock up past the cabins to a well-appointed lounge-library-kitchen, the other looping down to the cargo holds. Ultimately it did not matter where they wandered. Even in the sanitary stations, Royd had eyes and ears.

And always and everywhere, Royd watched.

Concepts like a right of privacy did not concern him, but he knew they might concern his passengers, if they knew of his activities. He made certain that they did not.

Royd's own quarters, three spacious chambers forward of the passenger lounge, were sealed and inviolate; he never left them. To his riders, he was a disembodied voice over the communicators that sometimes called them for long conversations, and a holographic specter that joined them for meals in the lounge. His ghost was a lithe, pale-eyed young man with white hair who dressed in filmy pastel clothing twenty years out of date, and it had the disconcerting habit of looking past the person Royd was addressing or in the wrong direction altogether, but after a few days the academicians grew accustomed to it. The holograph walked only in the lounge, in any event.

But Royd, secretly, silently, lived everywhere, and ferreted out all of their little secrets.

The cyberneticist talked to her computers, and seemed to prefer their company to that of humans.

The xenobiologist was surly, argumentative, and a solitary drinker.

The two linguists, lovers in public, seldom had sex and snapped bitterly at each other in private.

The psipsych was a hypochondriac given to black depressions, which worsened in the close confines of the *Nightflyer*.

Royd watched them work, eat, sleep, copulate; he listened untiringly to their talk. Within a week, the nine of them no longer seemed the same to him at all. Each of them was strange and unique, he had concluded.

By the time the *Nightflyer* had been under drive for two weeks, two of the passengers had come to engage even more of his attention. He neglected none of them, watched all, but now, specially, he focused on Karoly d'Branin and Melantha Jhirl.

"Most of all, I want to know the *why* of them," Karoly d'Branin told him one false night the second week out from Avalon. Royd's luminescent ghost sat close to d'Branin in the darkened lounge, watching him drink bittersweet chocolate. The others were all asleep. Night and day are meaningless on a starship, but the *Nightflyer* kept the usual cycles, and most of the passengers followed them. Only Karoly d'Branin, administrator and generalist, kept his own solitary time.

"The *if* of them is important as well, Karoly," Royd replied, his soft voice coming from the communicator panels in the walls. "Can you be truly certain if these aliens of yours exist?"

"*I* can be certain," Karoly d'Branin replied. "That is enough. If everyone else were certain as well, we would have a fleet of research ships instead of your little *Nightflyer*." He sipped at his chocolate, and gave a satisfied sigh. "Do you know the Nor T'alush, Royd?"

The name was strange to him, but it took Royd only a moment to consult his library computer. "An alien race on the other side of human space, past the Fyndii worlds and the Damoosh. Possibly legendary."

D'Branin chuckled. "Your library is out of date. You must supplement it the next time you are on Avalon. Not legends, no, real enough, though far away. We have little information about the Nor T'alush, but we are sure they exist, though you and I may never meet one. They were the start of it all.

"I was coding some information into the computers, a packet newly arrived from Dam Tullian after twenty standard years in transit. Part of it was Nor T'alush folklore. I had no idea how long that had taken to get to Dam Tullian, or by what route it had come, but it was fascinating material. Did you know that my first degree was in xenomythology?"

"I did not," Royd said. "Please continue."

"The *volcryn* story was among the Nor T'alush myths. It awed me; a race of sentients moving out from some mysterious origin in the core of the galaxy, sailing toward the galactic edge and, it was alleged, eventually bound for intergalactic space itself, meanwhile keeping always to the interstellar depths, no planetfalls, seldom coming within a light-year of a star. And doing it all *without a stardrive,* in ships moving only a fraction of the speed of light! That was the detail that obsessed me! Think how *old* they must be, those ships!"

"Old," Royd agreed. "Karoly, you said *ships*. More than one?"

"Oh, yes, there are," d'Branin said. "According to the Nor T'alush, one or two appeared first, on the innermost edges of their trading sphere, but others followed. Hundreds of them, each solitary, moving by itself, bound outward, always outward. The direction was always the same. For fifteen thousand standard years they moved between the Nor T'alush stars, and then they began to pass out from among them. The myth said that the last *volcryn* ship was gone three thousand years ago."

"Eighteen thousand years," Royd said, adding, "are your Nor T'alush that old?"

D'Branin smiled. "Not as star-travelers, no. According to their own histories, the Nor T'alush have only been civilized for about half that long. That stopped me for a while. It seemed to make the *volcryn* story clearly a legend. A wonderful legend, true, but nothing more.

"Ultimately, however, I could not let it alone. In my spare time, I investigated, cross-checking with other alien cosmologies to see whether this particular myth was shared by any races other than the Nor T'alush. I thought perhaps I would get a thesis out of it. It was a fruitful line of inquiry.

"I was startled by what I found. Nothing from the Hrangans, or the Hrangan slave-races, but that made sense, you see. They were *out* from human space, the *volcryn* would not reach them until after they had passed through our own sphere. When I looked *in*, however, the *volcryn* story was everwhere. The Fyndii had it, the Damoosh appeared to accept it as literal truth — and the Damoosh, you know, are the oldest race we have ever encountered — and there was a remarkably similar story told among the gethsoids of Aath. I checked what little was known about the races said to flourish farther in still, beyond even the Nor T'alush, and they had the *volcryn* story too."

"The legend of the legends," Royd suggested. The specter's wide mouth turned up in a smile.

"Exactly, exactly," d'Branin agreed. "At that point, I called in the experts, specialists from the Institute for the Study of Nonhuman Intelligence. We researched for two years. It was all there, in the files and the libraries at the Academy. No one had ever looked before, or bothered to put it together.

"The *volcryn* have been moving through the man-realm for most of human history, since before the dawn of spaceflight. While we twist the fabric of space itself to cheat relativity, they have been sailing their great ships right through the heart of our alleged civilization, past our most populous worlds, at stately slow sublight speeds, bound for the Fringe and the dark between the galaxies. Marvelous, Royd, marvelous!"

"Marvelous," Royd agreed.

Karoly d'Branin set down his chocolate cup and leaned forward eagerly toward Royd's projection, but his hand passed through empty light when he tried to grasp his companion by the forearm. He seemed disconcerted for a moment, before he began to laugh at himself. "Ah, my *volcryn*. I grow overenthused, Royd. I am so close now. They have preyed on my mind for a dozen years, and within a month I will have them. Then, *then,* if only I can open communication, if only my people can reach them, then at last I will know the *why* of it!''

The ghost of Royd Eris, master of the *Nightflyer,* smiled for him and looked on through calm unseeing eyes.

Passengers soon grow restless on a starship under drive, sooner on one as small and spare as the *Nightflyer.* Late in the second week, the speculation began. Royd heard it all.

"Who is this Royd Eris, really?" the xenobiologist complained one night when four of them were playing cards. "Why doesn't he come out? What's the purpose of keeping himself sealed off from the rest of us?"

"Ask him," the linguist suggested.

No one did.

When he was not talking to Karoly d'Branin, Royd watched Melantha Jhirl. She was good to watch. Young, healthy, active, Melantha Jhirl had a vibrancy about her that the others could not touch. She was big in every way; a head taller than anyone else on board, large-framed, large-breasted, long-legged, strong, muscles moving fluidly beneath shiny coal-black skin. Her appetites were big as well. She ate twice as much as any of her colleagues, drank heavily without ever seeming drunk, exercised for hours every day on equipment she had brought with her and set up in one of the cargo holds. By the third week out she had sexed with all four of the men on board and two of the women. Even in bed she was always active, exhausting most of her partners. Royd watched her with consuming interest.

"I am an improved model," she told him once as she worked out on her parallel bars, sweat glistening on her bare skin, her long black hair confined in a net.

"Improved?" Royd said. He could not send his holographic ghost down to the holds, but Melantha had summoned him with the communicator to talk while she exercised, not knowing he would have been there anyway.

She paused in her routine, holding her body aloft with the strength of her arms. "Altered, Captain," she said. She had taken to calling him that. "Born on Prometheus among the elite, child of two genetic wizards. Improved, Captain. I require twice the energy you do, but I use it all. A more efficient metabolism, a stronger and more durable body, an expected lifespan half again the normal human's. My people have made some terrible mistakes when they try to radically redesign the lessers, but the small improvements they do well."

She resumed her exercises, moving quickly and easily, silent until she had finished. Then, breathing heavily, she crossed her arms and cocked her head and grinned. "Now you know my life story, Captain, unless you care to hear the part about my defection to Avalon, my extraordinary work in nonhuman anthropology, and my tumultuous and passionate lovelife. Do you?"

"Perhaps some other time," Royd said, politely.

"Good," Melantha Jhirl replied. She snatched up a towel and began to dry the sweat from her body. "I'd rather hear your life story, anyway. Among my modest attributes is an insatiable curiosity. Who are you, Captain? Really?"

"One as improved as you," Royd replied, "should certainly be able to guess."

Melantha laughed, and tossed her towel at the communicator grille.

By that time all of them were guessing, when they did not think Royd was listening. He enjoyed the rumors.

"He talks to us, but he can't be seen," the cyberneticist said. "This ship is uncrewed, seemingly all automated except for him. Why not entirely automated, then? I'd wager Royd Eris is a fairly sophisticated computer system, perhaps an artificial intelligence. Even a modest program can carry on a blind conversation indistinguishable from a human's."

The telepath was a frail young thing, nervous, sensitive, with limp flaxen hair and watery blue eyes. He sought out Karoly d'Branin in his cabin, the cramped single, for a private conversation. "I feel it," he said excitedly. "Something is wrong, Karoly, something is very wrong. I'm beginning to get frightened."

D'Branin was startled. "Frightened? I don't understand, my friend. What is there for you to fear?"

The young man shook his head. "I don't know, I don't know. Yet it's there, I feel it. Karoly, I'm picking up something. You know I'm good, I am, that's why you picked me. Class one, tested, and I tell you I'm afraid. I sense it. Something dangerous. Something volatile — and alien."

"My *volcryn*?" d'Branin said.

"No, no, impossible. We're in drive, they're light-years away." The telepath's laugh was desperate. "I'm not *that* good, Karoly. I've heard your Crey story, but I'm only a human. No, this is close. On the ship."

"One of us?"

"Maybe," the telepath said. "I can't sort it out."

D'Branin sighed and put a fatherly hand on the young man's shoulder. "I thank you for coming to me, but I cannot act unless you have something more definite. This feeling of yours — could it be that you are just tired? We have all of us been under strain. Inactivity can be taxing."

"This is real," the telepath insisted, but he left peacefully.

Afterward d'Branin went to the psipsych, who was lying in her sleepweb surrounded by medicines, complaining bitterly of aches. "Interesting," she said when d'Branin told her. "I've felt something too, a sense of threat, very vague, diffuse. I thought it was me, the confinement, the boredom, the way I feel. My moods betray me at times. Did he say anything more specific?"

"No."

"I'll make an effort to move around, read him, read the others, see what I can pick up. Although, if this is real, he should know it first. He's a one, I'm only a three.''

D'Branin nodded, reassured. Later, when the rest had gone to sleep, he made some chocolate and talked to Royd through the false night. But he never mentioned the telepath once.

"Have you noticed the clothes on that holograph he sends us?'' the xenobiologist said to the others. ''A decade out of style, at least. I don't think he really looks like that. What if he's deformed, sick, ashamed to be seen the way he really looks? Perhaps he has some disease. The Slow Plague can waste a person terribly, but it takes decades to kill, and there are other contagions, manthrax and new leprosy and Langamen's Disease. Could it be that Royd's self-imposed quarantine is just that? A quarantine. Think about it.''

In the fifth week out, Melantha Jhirl pushed her pawn to the sixth rank and Royd saw it was unstoppable and resigned. It was his eighth straight defeat at her hands in as many days. She was sitting cross-legged on the floor of the lounge, the chessmen spread out before her on a viewscreen, its receiver dark. Laughing, she swept them away. ''Don't feel bad, Royd,'' she told him. ''I'm an improved model. Always three moves ahead.''

''I should tie in my computer,'' he replied. ''You'd never know.'' His holographic ghost materialized suddenly, standing in front of the viewscreen, and smiled at her.

''I'd know within three moves,'' Melantha Jhirl said. ''Try it.'' She stood up and walked right through his projection on her way to the kitchen, where she found herself a bulb of beer. ''When are you going to break down and let me behind your wall for a visit, Captain?'' she asked, talking up to a communicator grille. She refused to treat his ghost as real. ''Don't you get lonely there? Sexually frustrated? Claustrophobic?''

''I've flown the *Nightflyer* all my life, Melantha,'' Royd said. His projection ignored, winked out. ''If I were subject to claustrophobia, sexual frustration, or loneliness, such a life would have been impossible. Surely that should be obvious to you, being as improved a model as you are?''

She took a squeeze of her beer and laughed her mellow, musical laugh at him. ''I'll solve you yet, Captain,'' she warned.

''Fine,'' he said. ''Meanwhile, tell me some more lies about your life.''

''Have you ever heard of Jupiter?'' the xenotech demanded of the others. She was drunk, lolling in her sleepweb in the cargo hold.

''Something to do with Earth,'' one of the linguists said. ''The same myth system originated both names, I believe.''

''Jupiter,'' the xenotech announced loudly, ''is a gas giant in the same solar system as Old Earth. Didn't know that, did you? They were on the verge of exploring it when the stardrive was discovered, oh, way back. After that, nobody bothered with gas giants. Just slip into drive and find the habitable worlds, settle them, ignore the comets and the rocks and the gas giants — there's another star just a few light-years away, and it has more habitable planets. But there were people who thought those Jupiters might have life, you know. Do you see?''

The xenobiologist looked annoyed. "If there is intelligent life on the gas giants, it shows no interest in leaving them," he snapped. "All of the sentient species we have met up to now have originated on worlds similar to Earth, and most of them are oxygen breathers. Unless you suggest that the *volcryn* are from a gas giant?''

The xenotech pushed herself up to a sitting position and smiled conspiratorially. "Not the *volcryn*," she said. "Royd Eris. Crack that forward bulkhead in the lounge, and watch the methane and ammonia come smoking out." Her hand made a sensuous waving motion through the air, and she convulsed with giddy laughter.

"I dampened him," the psipsych reported to Karoly d'Branin during the sixth week. "Psionine-4. It will blunt his receptivity for several days, and I have more if he needs it.''

D'Branin wore a stricken look. "We talked several times, he and I. I could see that he was becoming ever more fearful, but he could never tell me the why of it. Did you absolutely have to shut him off?''

The psipsych shrugged. "He was edging into the irrational. You should never have taken a class one telepath, d'Branin. Too unstable.''

"We must communicate with an alien race. I remind you that is no easy task. The *volcryn* are perhaps more alien than any sentients we have yet encountered. Because of that we needed class one skills.''

"Glib," she said, "but you might have no working skills at all, given the condition of your class one. Half the time he's catatonic and half the time crazy with fear. He insists that we're all in real physical danger, but he doesn't know why or from what. The worst of it is I can't tell if he's really sensing something or simply having an acute attack of paranoia. He certainly displays some classic paranoid symptoms. Among other things, he believes he's being watched. Perhaps his condition is completely unrelated to us, the *volcryn*, and his talent. I can't be sure at this point in time.''

"What of your own talent?" d'Branin said. "You are an empath, are you not?''

"Don't tell me my job," she said sharply. "I sexed with him last week. You don't get more proximity or better rapport for esping than that. Even under those conditions, I couldn't be sure of anything. His mind is a chaos, and his fear is so rank it stank up the sheets. I don't read anything from the others either, besides the ordinary tensions and frustrations. But I'm only a three, so that doesn't mean much. My abilities are limited. You know I haven't been feeling well, d'Branin. I can barely breathe on this ship. My head throbs. Ought to stay in bed.''

"Yes, of course," d'Branin said hastily. "I did not mean to criticize. You have been doing all you can under difficult circumstances. Yet, I must ask, is it vital he be dampened? Is there no other way? Royd will take us out of drive soon, and we will make contact with the *volcryn*. We will need him.''

The psipsych rubbed her temple wearily. ''My other option was an injection of esperon. It would have opened him up completely, tripled his psionic receptivity for a few hours. Then, hopefully, he could home in this danger he's feeling. Exorcise it if it's false, deal with it if it's real. But psionine-4 is a lot safer. The physical side effects of esperon are debilitating, and emotionally I don't think he's stable enough to deal with that kind of power. The psionine should tell us something. If his paranoia continues to persist, I'll know it has nothing to do with his telepathy.''

''And if it does not persist?'' Karoly d'Branin said.

She smiled wickedly. ''Then we'll know that he really was picking up some sort of threat, won't we?''

False night came, and Royd's wraith materialized while Karoly d'Branin sat brooding over his chocolate. ''Karoly,'' the apparition said, ''would it be possible to tie in the computer your team brought on board with my shipboard system? Those *volcryn* stories fascinate me, and I'd like to be able to study them at my leisure.''

''Certainly,'' d'Branin replied in an offhand, distracted manner. ''It is time we got our system up and running in any case. Soon, now, we will be dropping out of drive.''

''Soon,'' Royd agreed. ''Approximately seventy hours from now.''

At dinner the following day, Royd's projection did not appear. The academicians ate uneasily, expecting their host to materialize at any moment, take his accustomed place, and join in the mealtime conversation. Their expectations were still unfulfilled when the afterdinner pots of chocolate and spiced tea and coffee were set on the table before them.

''Our captain seems to be occupied,'' Melantha Jhirl observed, leaning back in her chair and swirling a snifter of brandy.

''We will be shifting out of drive soon,'' Karoly d'Branin said. ''There are preparations to make.''

Some of the others looked at one another. All nine of them were present, although the young telepath seemed lost in his own head. The xenobiologist broke the silence. ''He doesn't eat. He's a damned holograph. What does it matter if he misses a meal? Maybe it's just as well. Karoly, a lot of us have been getting uneasy about Royd. What do you know about this mystery man anyway?''

D'Branin looked at him with wide, puzzled eyes. ''Know, my friend?'' he said, leaning forward to refill his cup with the thick, bittersweet chocolate. ''What is there to know?''

''Surely you've noticed that he never comes out to play with us,'' the female linguist said drily. ''Before you engaged his ship, did anyone remark on this quirk of his?''

''I'd like to know the answer to that too,'' her partner said. ''A lot of traffic comes and goes through Avalon. How did you come to choose Eris? What were you told about him?''

D'Branin hesitated. ''Told about him? Very little, I must admit. I spoke to a few port officials and charter companies, but none of them were acquainted with Royd. He had not traded out of Avalon originally, you see.''

''Where *is* he from?'' the linguists demanded in unison. They looked at each other, and the woman continued. ''We've listened to him. He has no discernible accent, no idiosyncrasies of speech to betray his origins. Tell us, where did this *Nightflyer* come from?''

''I — I don't know, actually,'' d'Branin admitted, hesitating. ''I never thought to ask him about it.''

The members of his research team glanced at each other incredulously. ''You never thought to *ask*?'' the xenotech said. ''How did you select this ship, then?''

''It was available. The administrative council approved my project and assigned me personnel, but they could not spare an Academy ship. There were budgetary constraints as well.'' All eyes were on him.

''What d 'Branin is saying,'' the psipsych interrupted, ''is that the Academy was pleased with his studies in xenomyth, with the discovery of the *volcryn* legend, but less than enthusiastic about his plan to prove the *volcryn* real. So they gave him a small budget to keep him happy and productive, assuming that this little mission would be fruitless, and they assigned him workers who wouldn't be missed back on Avalon.'' She looked around at each person. ''Except for d'Branin,'' she said, ''not a one of us is a first-rate scholar.''

''Well, you can speak for yourself,'' Melantha Jhirl said. ''I volunteered for this mission.''

''I won't argue the point,'' the psipsych said. ''The crux is that the choice of the *Nightflyer* is no large enigma. You engaged the cheapest charter you could find, didn't you, d'Branin?''

''Some of the available ships would not even consider my proposition,'' d'Branin said. ''The sound of it is odd, we must admit. And many ship masters seemed to have a superstitious fear of dropping out of drive in interstellar space, without a planet near. Of those who agreed to the conditions, Royd Eris offered the best terms, and he was able to leave at once.''

''And we *had* to leave at once,'' said the female linguist. ''Otherwise the *volcryn* might get away. They've only been passing through this region for ten thousand years, give or take a few thousand,'' she said sarcastically.

Someone laughed. D'Branin was nonplussed. ''Friends, no doubt I could have postponed departure. I admit I was eager to meet my *volcryn,* to ask them the questions that have haunted me, to discover the why of them, but I must also admit that a delay would have been no great hardship. But *why?* Royd is a gracious host, a skilled pilot, he has treated us well.''

"He has made himself a cipher,'' someone said.

"What is he hiding?'' another voice demanded.

Melantha Jhirl laughed. When all eyes had moved to her, she grinned and shook her head. ''Captain Royd is perfect, a strange man for a strange mission. Don't any of you love a mystery? Here we are flying light-years to intercept a hypothetical alien starship from the core of the galaxy that has been outward bound for longer than humanity has been having wars, and all of you are upset because you can't count the warts of Royd's nose.'' She leaned across the table to refill her brandy snifter. ''My mother was right,'' she said lightly. ''Normals are subnormal.''

''Melantha is correct,'' Karoly d'Branin said quietly. ''Royd's foibles and neuroses are his business, if he does not impose them on us.''

''It makes me uncomfortable,'' someone complained weakly.

''For all we know, Karoly,'' said the xenotech, ''we might be traveling with a criminal or an alien.''

''Jupiter,'' someone muttered. The xenotech flushed red, and there was sniggering around the long table.

But the young, pale-haired telepath looked up suddenly and stared at them all with wild, nervous eyes. ''An *alien*,'' he said.

The psipsych swore. ''The drug is wearing off,'' she said quickly to d'Branin. ''I'll have to go back to my room to get some more.''

All of the others looked baffled; d'Branin had kept his telepath's condition a careful secret. ''What drug?'' the xenotech demanded. ''What's going on here?''

''Danger,'' the telepath muttered. He turned to the cyberneticist sitting next to him, and grasped her forearm in a trembling hand. ''We're in danger, I tell you, I'm reading it. Something *alien*. And it means us ill.''

The psipsych rose. ''He's not well,'' she announced to the others. ''I've been dampening him with psionine, trying to hold his delusions in check. I'll get some more.'' She started toward the door.

''Wait,'' Melantha Jhirl said. ''Not psionine. Try esperon.''

''Don't tell me my job, woman.''

''Sorry,'' Melantha said. She gave a modest shrug. ''I'm one step ahead of you, though. Esperon might exorcise his delusions, no?''

''Yes, but — ''

''And it might let him focus on this threat he claims to detect, correct?''

''I know the characteristics of esperon,'' the psipsych said testily.

Melantha smiled over the rim of her brandy glass. ''I'm sure you do,'' she said. ''Now listen to me. All of you are anxious about Royd, it seems. You can't stand not knowing what he's concealing about himself. You suspect him of being a criminal. Fears like that won't help us work together as a team. Let's end them. Easy enough.'' She pointed. ''Here sits a class one telepath. Boost his power with esperon and he'll be able to recite our captain's life history to us, until we're all suitably bored with it. Meanwhile he'll also be vanquishing his personal demons.''

"He's watching us," the telepath said in a low, urgent voice.

"Karoly," the xenobiologist said, "this has gone too far. Several of us are nervous, and this boy is terrified. I think we all need an end to the mystery of Royd Eris. Melantha is right."

D'Branin was troubled. "We have no right — "

"We have the *need*," the cyberneticist said.

D'Branin's eyes met those of the psipsych, and he sighed. "Do it," he said. "Get him the esperon."

"He's going to kill me," the telepath screamed and leaped to his feet. When the cyberneticist tried to calm him with a hand on his arm, he seized a cup of coffee and threw it square in her face. It took three of them to hold him down. "Hurry," one commanded, as the youth struggled.

The psipsych shuddered and quickly left the lounge.

Royd was watching.

When the psipsych returned, they lifted the telepath to the table and forced him down, pulling aside his hair to bare the arteries in his neck.

Royd's ghost materialized in its empty chair at the foot of the long dinner table. "Stop that," it said calmly. "There is no need."

The psipsych froze in the act of slipping an ampule of esperon into her injection gun, and the xenotech started visibly and released one of the telepath's arms. But the captive did not pull free. He lay on the table, breathing heavily, too frightened to move, his pale blue eyes fixed glassily on Royd's projection.

Melantha Jhirl lifted her brandy glass in salute. "Boo," she said. "You've missed dinner, Captain."

"Royd," said Karoly d'Branin, "I am sorry."

The ghost stared unseeing at the far wall. "Release him," said the voice from the communicators. "I will tell you my great secret, if my privacy intimidates you so."

"He *has* been watching us," the male linguist said.

"Tell, then," the xenotech said suspiciously. "What are you?"

"I liked your guess about the gas giants," Royd said. "Sadly, the truth is less dramatic. I am an ordinary *Homo sapiens* in late middle age. Sixty-eight standard, if you require precision. The holograph you see before you was the real Royd Eris, although some years ago. I am older now."

"Oh?" The cyberneticist's face was red where the coffee had scalded her. "Then why the secrecy?"

"I will begin with my mother," Royd replied. "The *Nightflyer* was her ship originally, custom built to her design in the Newholme spaceyards. My mother was a free-trader, a notably successful one. She made a fortune through a willingness to accept the unusual consignment, fly off the major trade routes, take her cargo a month or a year or two years beyond where it was customarily transferred. Such practices are riskier but more profitable than flying the mail runs. My mother did not worry about how often she and her crews returned home. Her ships were her home. She seldom visited the same world twice if she could avoid it.''

"Adventurous," Melantha said.

"No," said Royd. "Sociopathic. My mother did not like people, you see. Not at all. Her one great dream was to free herself from the necessity of a crew. When she grew rich enough, she had it done. The *Nightflyer* was the result. After she boarded it at Newholme, she never touched a human being again, or walked a planet's surface. She did all her business from the compartments that are now mine. She was insane, but she did have an interesting life, even after that. The worlds she saw, Karoly! The things she might have told you! Your heart would break. She destroyed most of her records, however, for fear that other people might get some use or pleasure from her experience after her death. She was like that.''

"And you?" the xenotech said.

"I should not call her my mother," Royd continued. "I am her cross-sex clone. After thirty years of flying this ship alone, she was bored. I was to be her companion and lover. She could shape me to be a perfect diversion. She had no patience with children, however, and no desire to raise me herself. As an embryo, I was placed in a nurturant tank. The computer was my teacher. I was to be released when I had attained the age of puberty, at which time she guessed I would be fit company.

"Her death, a few months after the cloning, ruined the plan. She had programmed the ship for such an eventuality, however. It dropped out of drive and shut down, drifted in interstellar space for eleven years while the computer made a human being out of me. That was how I inherited the *Nightflyer*. When I was freed, it took me some years to puzzle out the operation of the ship and my own origins.''

"Fascinating," said d'Branin.

"Yes," said the female linguist, "but it doesn't explain why you keep yourself in isolation.''

"Ah, but it does," Melantha Jhirl said. "Captain, perhaps you should explain further for the less improved models?''

"My mother hated planets," Royd said. "She hated stinks and dirt and bacteria, the irregularity of the weather, the sight of other people. She engineered for us a flawless environment, as sterile as she could possibly make it. She disliked gravity as well. She was accustomed to weightlessness, and preferred it. These were the conditions under which I was born and raised.

"My body has no natural immunities to anything. Contact with any of you would probably kill me, and would certainly make me very sick. My muscles are feeble, atrophied. The gravity the *Nightflyer* is now generating is for your comfort, not mine. To me it is agony. At the moment I am seated in a floating chair that supports my weight. I still hurt, and my internal organs may be suffering damage. It is one reason why I do not often take on passengers.''

"You share your mother's opinion of the run of humanity, then?" the psipsych said.

"I do not. I like people. I accept what I am, but I did not choose it. I experience human life in the only way I can, vicariously, through the infrequent passengers I dare to carry. At those times, I drink in as much of their lives as I can."

"If you kept your ship under weightlessness at all times, you could take on more riders, could you not?" suggested the xenobiologist.

"True," Royd said politely. "I have found, however, that most people choose not to travel with a captain who does not use his gravity grid. Prolonged free-fall makes them ill and uncomfortable. I could also mingle with my guests, I know, if I kept to my chair and wore a sealed environment suit. I have done so. I find it lessens my participation instead of increasing it. I become a freak, a maimed thing, one who must be treated differently and kept at a distance. I prefer isolation. As often as I dare, I study the aliens I take on as riders."

"Aliens?" the xenotech said, in a confused voice.

"You are all aliens to me," Royd answered.

Silence then filled the *Nightflyer*'s lounge.

"I am sorry this had to happen, my friend," Karoly d'Branin said to the ghost.

"Sorry," the psipsych said. She frowned and pushed the ampule of esperon into the injection chamber. "Well, it's glib enough, but is it the truth? We still have no proof, just a bedtime story. The holograph could have claimed it was a creature from Jupiter, a computer, or a diseased war criminal just as easily." She took two quick steps forward to where the young telepath still lay on the table. "He still needs treatment, and we still need confirmation. I don't care to live with all this anxiety, when we can end it all now." Her hand pushed the unresisting head to one side, she found the artery, and pressed the gun to it.

"No," the voice from the communicator said sternly. "Stop. I order it. This is my ship. Stop."

The gun hissed loudly, and there was a red mark when she lifted it from the telepath's neck.

He raised himself to a half-sitting position, supported by his elbows, and the psipsych moved close to him. "Now," she said in her best professional tones, "focus on Royd. You can do it, we all know how good you are. Wait just a moment, the esperon will open it all up for you."

His pale blue eyes were clouded. "Not close enough," he muttered. "One, I'm one, tested. Good, you know I'm good, but I got to be *close*." He trembled.

She put an arm around him, stroked him, coaxed him. "The esperon will give you range," she said. "Feel it, feel yourself grow stronger. Can you feel it? Everything's getting clear, isn't it?" Her voice was a reassuring drone. "Remember the danger now, remember, go find it. Look beyond the wall, tell us about it. Tell us about Royd. Was he telling the truth? Tell us. You're good, we all know that, you can tell us.'' The phrases were almost an incantation.

He shrugged off her support and sat upright by himself. ''I can feel it,'' he said. His eyes were suddenly clearer. ''Something — my head hurts — I'm *afraid!''*

''Don't be afraid,'' the psipsych said. ''The esperon won't make your head hurt, it just makes you better. Nothing to fear.'' She stroked his brow. ''Tell us what you see.''

The telepath looked at Royd's ghost with terrified little-boy eyes, and his tongue flicked across his lower lip. ''He's — ''

Then his skull exploded.

It was three hours later when the survivors met again to talk.

In the hysteria and confusion of the aftermath, Melantha Jhirl had taken charge. She gave orders, pushing her brandy aside and snapping out commands with the ease of one born to it, and the others seemed to find a numbing solace in doing as they were told. Three of them fetched a sheet, and wrapped the headless body of the young telepath within, and shoved it through the drive-room airlock at the end of the ship. Two others, on Melantha's order, found water and cloth and began to clean up the lounge. They did not get far. Mopping the blood from the tabletop, the cyberneticist suddenly began to retch violently. Karoly d'Branin, who had sat still and shocked since it happened, woke and took the blook-soaked rag from her hand and led her away, back to his cabin.

Melantha Jhirl was helping the psipsych, who had been standing very close to the telepath when he died. A sliver of bone had penetrated her cheek just below her right eye, she was covered with blood and pieces of flesh and bone and brain, and she had gone into shock. Melantha removed the bone splinter, led her below, cleaned her, and put her to sleep with a shot of one of her own drugs.

And, at length, she got the rest of them together in the largest of the cargo holds, where three of them slept. Seven of the surviving eight attended. The psipsych was still asleep, but the cyberneticist seemed to have recovered. She sat cross-legged on the floor, her features pale and drawn, waiting for Melantha to begin.

It was Karoly d'Branin who spoke first, however. ''I do not understand,'' he said. ''I do not understand what has happened. What could . . . ''

''Royd killed him, is all,'' the xenotech said bitterly. ''His secret was endangered, so he just — just blew him apart.''

''I cannot believe that,'' Karoly d'Branin said, anguished. ''I cannot. Royd and I, we have talked, talked many a night when the rest of you were sleeping. He is gentle, inquisitive, sensitive. A dreamer. He understands about the *volcryn*. He would not do such a thing.''

''His holograph certainly winked out quick enough when it happened,'' the female linguist said. ''And you'll notice he hasn't had much to say since.''

''The rest of you haven't been unusually talkative either,'' Melantha Jhirl said. "I don't know what to think, but my impulse is to side with Karoly. We have no proof that the captain was responsible for what happened."

The xenotech made a loud rude noise. "Proof."

"In fact," Melantha continued unperturbed, "I'm not even sure anyone is responsible. Nothing happened until he was given the esperon. Could the drug be at fault?"

"Hell of a side effect," the female linguist muttered.

The xenobiologist frowned. "This is not my field, but I know esperon is an extremely potent drug, with severe physical effects as well as psionic. The instrument of death was probably his own talent, augmented by the drug. Besides boosting his principal power, his telepathic sensitivity, esperon would also tend to bring out other psi-talents that might have been latent in him."

"Such as?" someone demanded.

"Biocontrol. Telekinesis."

Melantha Jhirl was way ahead of him. "Increase the pressure inside his skull sharply, by rushing all the blood in his body to his brain. Decrease the air pressure around his head simultaneously, using teke to induce a short-lived vacuum. Think about it."

They thought about it, and none of them liked it.

"It could have been self-induced," Karoly d'Branin said.

"Or a stronger talent could have turned his power against him," the xenotech said stubbornly.

"No human telepath has talent on that order, to seize control of someone else, body and mind and soul, even for an instant."

"Exactly," the xenotech said. "No *human* telepath."

"Gas giant people?" The cyberneticist's tone was mocking.

The xenotech stared her down. "I could talk about Crey sensitives or *githyanki* soulsucks, name a half-dozen others off the top of my head, but I don't need to. I'll only name one. A Hrangan Mind."

That was a disquieting thought. All of them fell silent and moved uneasily, thinking of the vast, inimical power of a Hrangan Mind hidden in the command chambers of the *Nightflyer,* until Melantha Jhirl broke the spell. "That is ridiculous," she said. "Think of what you're saying, if that isn't too much to ask. You're supposed to be xenologists, the lot of you, experts in alien languages, psychology, biology, technology. You don't act the part. We warred with Old Hranga for a thousand years, but we *never* communicated successfully with a Hrangan Mind. If Royd Eris is a Hrangan, they've certainly improved their conversational skills in the centuries since the Collapse."

The xenotech flushed. "You're right," she mumbled. "I'm jumpy."

"Friends," Karoly d'Branin said, "we must not panic or grow hysterical. A terrible thing has happened. One of our colleagues is dead, and we do not know why. Until we do, we can only go on. This is no time for rash actions against the innocent. Perhaps, when we return to Avalon, an investigation will tell us what happened. The body is safe, is it not?"

"We cycled it through the airlock into the drive-room," said the male linguist. "Vacuum in there. It'll keep."

"And it can be reclaimed on our return," d'Branin said, satisfied.

"That return should be immediate," the xenotech said. "Tell Eris to turn this ship around."

D'Branin looked stricken. "But the *volcryn!* A week more, and we will know them, if my figures are correct. Surely it is worth one week additional to know that they exist?"

The xenotech was stubborn. "A man is dead. Before he died, he talked about aliens and danger. Maybe we're in danger too. Maybe these *volcryn* are the cause, maybe they're more potent than even a Hrangan Mind. Do you care to risk it? And for what? Your sources may be fictional or exaggerated or wrong, your interpretations and computations may be incorrect, or they may have changed course — the *volcryn* may not even be within light-years of where we'll drop out!"

"Ah," Melantha Jhirl said, "I understand. Then we shouldn't go on because they won't be there, and besides, they might be dangerous."

D'Branin smiled and the female linguist laughed. "Not funny," said the xenotech, but she argued no more.

"No," Melantha continued, "any danger we are in will not increase significantly in the time it will take us to drop out of drive and look about for *volcryn*. We would have to drop out anyway, to reprogram. Besides, we have come a long way for these *volcryn,* and I admit to being curious." She looked at each of them in turn, but none of them disagreed. "We continue, then."

"And what do we do with Royd?" d'Branin asked.

"Treat the captain as before, if we can," Melantha said decisively. "Open lines to him and talk. He's probably as shocked and dismayed as we are, and possibly fearful that we might blame him, try to hurt him, something like that. So we reassure him. I'll do it, if no one else wants to talk to him." There were no volunteers. "All right. But the rest of you had better try to act normally."

"Also," said d'Branin, "we must continue with our preparations. Our sensory instruments must be ready for deployment as soon as we shift out of drive and reenter normal space, our computer must be functioning."

"It's up and running," the cyberneticist said quietly. "I finished this morning, as you requested." She had a thoughtful look in her eyes, but d'Branin did not notice. He turned to the linguists and began discussing some of the preliminaries he expected from them, and in a short time the talk had turned to the *volcryn,* and little by little the fear drained out of the group.

Royd, listening, was glad.

She returned to the lounge alone.

Someone had turned out the lights. "Captain?" she said, and he appeared to her, pale, glowing softly, with eyes that did not really see. His clothes, filmy and out of date, were all shades of white and faded blue. "Did you hear, Captain?"

His voice over the communicator betrayed a faint hint of surprise. "Yes. I hear and see everything on my *Nightflyer*, Melantha. Not only in the lounge. Not only when the communicators and viewscreens are on. How long have you known?''

"Known?'' She laughed. "Since you praised the gas giant solution to the Roydian mystery.''

"I was under stress. I have never made a mistake before.''

"I believe you, Captain,'' she said. "No matter. I'm the improved model, remember? I'd guessed weeks ago.''

For a time Royd said nothing. Then: "When do you begin to reassure me?''

"I'm doing so right now. Don't you feel reassured yet?''

The apparition gave a ghostly shrug. "I am pleased that you and Karoly do not think I murdered that man.''

She smiled. Her eyes were growing accustomed to the room. By the faint light of the holograph, she could see the table where it had happened, dark stains across its top. Blood. She heard a faint dripping, and shivered. "I don't like it in here.''

"If you would like to leave, I can be with you wherever you go.''

"No,'' she said. "I'll stay. Royd, if I asked you to, would you shut off your eyes and ears throughout the ship? Except for the lounge? It would make the others feel better, I'm sure.''

"They don't know.''

"They will. You made that remark about gas giants in everyone's hearing. Some of them have probably figured it out by now.''

"If I told you I had cut myself off, you would have no way of knowing whether it was the truth.''

"I could trust you,'' Melantha said.

Silence. The specter looked thoughtful. "As you wish,'' Royd's voice said finally. "Everything off. Now I see and hear only in here.''

"I believe you.''

"Did you believe my story?'' Royd asked.

"Ah,'' she said. "A strange and wondrous story, Captain. If it's a lie, I'll swap lies with you any time. You do it well. If it's true, then you are a strange and wondrous man.''

"It's true,'' the ghost said quietly. "Melantha — '' His voice hesitated.

"Yes.''

"I watched you copulating.''

She smiled. "Ah,'' she said. "I'm good at it.''

"I wouldn't know,'' Royd said. "You're good to watch.''

Silence. She tried not to hear the dripping. "Yes,'' she said after a long hesitation.

"Yes? What?''

"Yes, Royd, I would probably sex with you if it were possible.''

"How did you know what I was thinking?''

"I'm an improved model,'' she said. "And no, I'm not a telepath. It wasn't so difficult to figure out. I told you, I'm three moves ahead of you.''

Royd considered that for a long time. "I believe I'm reassured," he said at last.

"Good," said Melantha Jhirl. "Now reassure me."

"Of what?"

"What happened in here? Really?"

Royd said nothing.

"I think you know something," Melantha said. "You gave up your secret to stop us from injecting him with esperon. Even after your secret was forfeit, you ordered us not to go ahead. Why?"

"Esperon is a dangerous drug," Royd said.

"More than that, Captain," Melantha said. "What killed him?"

"*I* didn't."

"One of us? The *volcryn*?"

Royd said nothing.

"Is there an alien aboard your ship, Captain?" she asked. "Is that it?"

Silence.

"Are we in danger? Am *I* in danger, Captain? I'm not afraid. Does that make me a fool?"

"I like people," Royd said at last. "When I can stand it, I like to have passengers. I watch them, yes. It's not so terrible. I like you and Karoly especially. You have nothing to fear. I won't let anything happen to you."

"What might happen?" she asked.

Royd said nothing.

"And what about the others, Royd? Are you taking care of them, too? Or only Karoly and me?"

No reply.

"You're not very talkative tonight," Melantha observed.

"I'm under strain," his voice replied. "Go to bed, Melantha Jhirl. We've talked long enough."

"All right, Captain," she said. She smiled at his ghost and lifted her hand. His own rose to meet it. Warm dark flesh and pale radiance brushed, melded, were one. Melantha Jhirl turned to go. It was not until she was out in the corridor, safe in the light once more, that she began to tremble.

False midnight. The talks had broken up, the nightmares had faded, and the academicians were lost in sleep. Even Karoly d'Branin slept, his appetite for chocolate quelled by his memories of the lounge.

In the darkness of the largest cargo hold, three sleepwebs hung, sleepers snoring softly in two. The cyberneticist lay awake, thinking, in the third. Finally she rose, dropped lightly to the floor, pulled on her jumpsuit and boots, and shook the xenotech from her slumber. "Come," she whispered, beckoning. They stole off into the corridor, leaving Melantha Jhirl to her dreams.

"What the hell," the xenotech muttered when they were safely beyond the door. She was half-dressed, disarrayed, unhappy.

"There's a way to find out if Royd's story was true," the cyberneticist said carefully. "Melantha won't like it, though. Are you game to try?"

"What?" the other asked. Her face betrayed her interest.

"Come," the cyberneticist said.

One of the three lesser cargo holds had been converted into a computer room. They entered quietly; all empty. The system was up, but dormant. Currents of light ran silkily down crystalline channels in the data grids, meeting, joining, splitting apart again; rivers of wan multihued radiance crisscrossing a black landscape. The chamber was dim, the only noise a low buzz at the edge of human hearing, until the cyberneticist moved through it, touching keys, tripping switches, directing the silent luminescent currents. Slowly the machine woke.

"What are you *doing?*" the xenotech said.

"Karoly told me to tie in our system with the ship," the cyberneticist replied as she worked. "I was told Royd wanted to study the *volcryn* data. Fine, I did it. Do you understand what that means?"

Now the xenotech was eager. "The two systems are tied together!"

"Exactly. So Royd can find out about the *volcryn*, and we can find out about Royd." She frowned. "I wish I knew more about the *Nightflyer*'s hardware, but I think I can feel my way through. This is a pretty sophisticated system d'Branin requisitioned."

"Can you take over?" the xenotech asked excitedly.

"Take over?" The cyberneticist sounded puzzled. "You been drinking again?"

"No, I'm serious. Use your system to break into the ship's control, overwhelm Eris, countermand his orders, make the *Nightflyer* respond to us, down here."

"Maybe," the cyberneticist said doubtfully, slowly. "I could try, but why do that?"

"Just in case. We don't have to use the capacity. Just so we have it, if an emergency arises."

The cyberneticist shrugged. "Emergencies and gas giants. I only want to put my mind at rest about Royd." She moved over to a readout panel, where a half-dozen meter-square viewscreens curved around a console, and brought one of them to life. Long fingers brushed across holographic keys that appeared and disappeared as she touched them, the keyboard changing shape even as she used it. Characters began to flow across the viewscreen, red flickerings encased in glassy black depths. The cyberneticist watched, and finally froze them. "Here," she said, "here's my answer about the hardware. You can dismiss your takeover idea, unless those gas giant people of yours are going to help. The *Nightflyer*'s bigger and smarter than our little system here. Makes sense, when you stop to think about it. Ship's all automated, except for Royd." She whistled and coaxed her search program with soft words of encouragement. "It looks as though there *is* a Royd, though. Configurations are all wrong for a robot ship. Damn, I would have bet anything." The characters began to flow again, the cyberneticist watching the figures as they drifted by. "Here's life-support specs, might tell us something." A finger jabbed, and the screen froze once more.

"Nothing unusual," the xenotech said in disappointment.

"Standard waste disposal. Water recycling. Food processor, with protein and vitamin supplements in stores." She began to whistle. "Tanks of Renny's moss and neograss to eat up the CO_2. Oxygen cycle, then. No methane or ammonia. Sorry about that."

"Go sex with a computer."

The cyberneticist smiled. "Ever tried it?" Her fingers moved again. "What else should I look for? Give me some ideas."

"Check the specs for nurturant tanks, cloning equipment, that sort of thing. Find Royd's life history. His mother's. Get a readout on the business they've done, all this alleged trading." Her voice grew excited, and she took the cyberneticist by her shoulder. "A log, a ship's log! There's got to be a log. Find it! You must."

"All right." She whistled, happy, one with her systems, riding the data winds, in control, curious. The readout screen turned a bright red and began to blink at her, but she only smiled. "Security," she said, her fingers a blur. As suddenly as it had come, the blinking red field was gone. "Nothing like slipping past another system's security. Like slipping onto a man."

Down the corridor, an alarm sounded a whooping call. "Damn," the cyberneticist said, "that'll wake everyone." She glanced up when the xenotech's fingers dug painfully into her shoulder, squeezing, hurting.

A gray steel panel slid almost silently across the access to the corridor. "Wha — ?" the cyberneticist said.

"That's an emergency airseal," the xenotech said in a dead voice. She knew starships. "It closes when they're about to load or unload cargo in vacuum."

Their eyes went to the huge curving outer airlock above their heads. The inner lock was almost completely open, and as they watched it clicked into place, and the seal on the outer door cracked, and now it was open half a meter, sliding, and beyond was twisted nothingness so bright it burned the eyes.

"Oh," the cyberneticist said. She had stopped whistling.

Alarms were hooting everywhere. The passengers began to stir. Melantha Jhirl leaped from her sleepweb and darted into the corridor, nude, concerned, alert. Karoly d'Branin sat up drowsily. The psipsych muttered fitfully in her drug-induced sleep. The xenobiologist cried out in alarm

Far away metal crunched and tore, and a violent shudder ran through the ship, throwing the linguists out of their sleepwebs, knocking Melantha from her feet.

In the command quarters of the *Nightflyer* was a spherical room with featureless white walls, a lesser sphere — a control console — suspended in its center. The walls were always blank when the ship was in drive; the warped and glaring underside of space-time was painful to behold.

But now darkness woke in the room, a holoscape coming to life, cold black and stars everywhere, points of icy unwinking brilliance, the floating control sphere the only feature in the simulated sea of night.

The *Nightflyer* had shifted out of drive.

Melantha Jhirl found her feet again and thumbed on a communicator. The alarms were still hooting, and it was hard to hear. "Captain," she shouted, "what's happening?"

"I don't know," Royd's voice replied. "I'm trying to find out. Wait here. Gather the others to you."

She did as he had said, and only when they were all together in the corridor did she slip back to her web to don some clothing. She found only six of them. The psipsych was still unconscious and could not be roused, and they had to carry her. And the xenotech and cyberneticist were missing. The rest looked uneasily at the seal that blocked cargo hold three.

The communicator came back to life as the alarms died. "We have returned to normal space," Royd's voice said, "but the ship is damaged. Hold three, your computer room, was breached while we were under drive. It was ripped apart by the flux. The computer automatically dropped us out of drive, or the drive forces might have torn my entire ship apart."

"Royd," d'Branin said, "two of my team are . . . "

"It appears that your computer was in use when the hold was breached," Royd said carefully. "We can only assume that they are dead. I cannot be sure. At Melantha's request, I have deactivated most of my eyes and ears, retaining only the lounge inputs. I do not know what happened. But this is a small ship, Karoly, and if they are not with you, we must assume the worst." He paused briefly. "If it is any consolation, they died quickly and painlessly."

The two linguists exchanged a long, meaningful look. The xenobiologist's face was red and angry, and he started to say something. Melantha Jhirl slipped her hand over his mouth firmly. "Do we know how it happened, Captain?" she asked.

"Yes," he said, reluctantly.

The xenobiologist had taken the hint, and Melantha took away her hand to let him breathe. "Royd?" she prompted.

"It sounds insane, Melantha," his voice replied, "but it appears your colleagues opened the hold's loading lock. I doubt that they did so deliberately, of course. They were apparently using the system interface to gain entry to the *Nightflyer*'s data storage and controls."

"I see," Melantha said. "A terrible tragedy."

"Yes," Royd agreed. "Perhaps more terrible than you think. I have yet to assess the damage to my ship."

"We should not keep you, Captain, if you have duties to perform," Melantha said. "All of us are shocked, and it is difficult to talk now. Investigate the condition of your ship, and we'll continue our discussion in the morning. All right?''

"Yes," Royd said.

Melantha thumbed the communicator plate. Now officially, the device was off. Royd could not hear them.

Karoly d'Branin shook his large, grizzled head. The linguists sat close to one another, hands touching. The psipsych slept. Only the xenobiologist met her gaze. "Do you believe him?" he snapped abruptly.

"I don't know," Melantha Jhirl said, "but I do know that the other three cargo holds can all be flushed just as hold three was. I'm moving my sleepweb into a cabin. I suggest those who are living in hold two do the same."

"Good idea," the female linguist said. "We can crowd in. It won't be comfortable, but I don't think I'd sleep the sleep of angels in the holds anymore."

"We should also take our suits out of storage in four and keep them close at hand," her partner suggested.

"If you wish," Melantha said. "It's possible that all the locks might pop open simultaneously. Royd can't fault us for taking precautions." She flashed a grim smile. "After today, we've earned the right to act irrationally."

"This is no time for your damned jokes, Melantha," the xenobiologist said, fury in his voice. "Three dead, a fourth maybe deranged or comatose, the rest of us endangered — "

"We still have no idea what is happening," she pointed out.

"Royd Eris is killing us!" he shouted, pounding his fist into an open palm to emphasize his point. "I don't know who or what he is, and I don't know if that story he gave us is true, and I don't *care*. Maybe he's a Hrangan Mind or the avenging angel of the *volcryn* or the second coming of Jesus Christ. What the hell difference does it make? *He's killing us!*"

"You realize," Melantha said gently, "that we cannot actually know whether the good captain has turned off his inputs down here. He could be watching and listening to us right now. He isn't, of course. He told me he wouldn't and I believe him. But we have only his word on that. Now, *you* don't appear to trust Royd. If that's so, you can hardly put any faith in his promises. It follows that from your point of view it might not be wise to say the things that you're saying," She smiled slyly.

The xenobiologist was silent.

"The computer is gone, then," Karoly d'Branin said in a low voice before Melantha could resume.

She nodded. "I'm afraid so."

He rose unsteadily to his feet. "I have a small unit in my cabin," he said. "A wrist model, perhaps it will suffice. I must get the figures from Royd, learn where we have dropped out. The *volcryn* — " He shuffled off down the corridor and disappeared into his cabin.

"Think how distraught he'd be if *all* of us were dead," the female linguist said bitterly. "Then he'd have no one to help him look for *volcryn*."

"Let him go," Melantha said. "He is as hurt as any of us, maybe more so. He wears it differently. His obsessions are his defense."

"What's *our* defense?"

"Ah," said Melantha. "Patience, maybe. All of the dead were trying breach Royd's secret when they died. We haven't tried. Here we sit discussing their deaths."

"You don't find that suspicious?"

"Very," Melantha Jhirl said. "I even have a method of testing my suspicions. One of us can make yet another attempt to find out whether our captain told us the truth. If he or she dies, we'll know." She stood up abruptly. "Forgive me, however, if I'm not the one who tries. But don't let me stop you if you have the urge. I'll note the results with interest. Until then, I'm going to move out of the cargo area and get some sleep."

"Arrogant bitch," the male linguist observed almost conversationally after Melantha had left.

"Do you think he can hear us?" the xenobiologist whispered quietly.

"Every pithy word," the female linguist said, rising. They all stood up. "Let's move our things and put her — " she jerked a thumb at the psipsych — "back to bed." Her partner nodded.

"Aren't we going to *do* anything?" the xenobiologist said. "Make plans. Defenses."

The linguist gave him a withering look, and pulled her companion off in the other direction.

"Melantha? Karoly?"

She woke quickly, alert at the mere whisper of her name, and sat up in the narrow bunk. Next to her, Karoly d'Branin moaned softly and rolled over, yawning.

"Royd?" she asked. "Is it morning now?"

"Yes," replied the voice from the walls. "We are drifting in interstellar space three light-years from the nearest star, however. In such a context, does morning have meaning?"

Melantha laughed. "Debate it with Karoly, when he wakes up enough to listen. Royd, you said *drifting?* How bad . . . ?"

"Serious," he said, "but not dangerous. Hold three is a complete ruin, hanging from my ship like a broken metal eggshell, but the damage was confined. The drives themselves are intact, and the *Nightflyer's* computers did not seem to suffer from your machine's destruction. I feared they might. Electronic death trauma."

D'Branin said, "Eh? Royd?"

Melantha patted him. "I'll tell you later, Karoly," she said. "Royd, you sound serious. Is there more?"

"I am worried about our return flight, Melantha," he said. "When I take the *Nightflyer* back into drive, the flux will be playing directly on portions of the ship that were never engineered to withstand it. The airseal across hold three is a particular concern. I've run some projections, and I don't know if it can take the stress. If it bursts, my whole ship will split apart in the middle. My engines will go shunting off by themselves, and the rest . . . ''

"I see. Is there anything we can do?"

"Yes. The exposed areas would be easy enough to reinforce. The outer hull is armored to withstand the warping forces, of course. We could mount it in place, a crude shield, but it would suffice. Large portions of the hull were torn loose when the locks opened, but they are still out there, floating within a kilometer or two, and could be used.''

At some point, Karoly d'Branin had come awake. "My team has four vacuum sleds. We can retrieve these pieces for you.''

"Fine, Karoly, but that is not my primary concern. My ship is self-repairing within certain limits, but this exceeds those limits. I will have to do this myself.''

"You?" d'Branin said. "Friend, you said — that is, your muscles, your weakness — cannot we help with this?"

"I am only a cripple in a gravity field, Karoly," Royd said. "Weightless, I am in my element, and I will be killing our gravity grid momentarily, to try to gather my own strength for the repair work. No, you misunderstand. I am capable of the work. I have the tools, and my own heavy-duty sled.''

"I think I know what you are concerned about," Melantha said.

"I'm glad," Royd said. "Perhaps, then, you can answer my question. If I emerge from the safety of my chambers, can you keep your friends from killing me?"

Karoly d'Branin was shocked. "Royd, Royd, we are scholars, we are not soldiers or criminals, we do not — we are human, how can you think that we would threaten you?"

"Human," Royd repeated, "but alien to me, suspicious of me. Give me no false assurances, Karoly.''

The administrator sputtered. Melantha took his hand and bid him quiet. "Royd," she said, "I won't lie to you. You'd be in some danger. But I'd hope that, by coming out, you'd make the rest of them joyously happy. They'd be able to see that you hold the truth, wouldn't they?"

"They would," Royd said, "but would it be enough to offset their suspicions? They believe I killed your friends, do they not?"

"Some, perhaps. Half believe it, half fear it. They are frightened, Captain. *I* am frightened.''

"No more than I."

"I would be less frightened if I knew what *did* happen. Do you know?''
Silence.

"Royd, if . . . ''

"I tried to stop the esperon injection," he said. "I might have saved the other two, if I had seen them, heard them, known what they were about. But you made me turn off my monitors, Melantha. I cannot help what I cannot see.''

Hesitation. "I would feel safer if I could turn them back on. I am blind and deaf. It is frustrating. I cannot help if I am blind and deaf."

"Turn them on, then," Melantha said suddenly. "I was wrong. I did not understand. Now I do, though."

"Understand what?" Karoly said.

"You do not understand," Royd said. "You do *not*. Don't pretend that you do, Melantha Jhirl. *Don't!*" The calm voice from the communicator was shrill with emotion.

"What?" Karoly said. "Melantha, I do not understand."

Her eyes were thoughtful. "Neither do I," she said. "Neither do I, Karoly." She kissed him lightly. "Royd," she resumed, "it seems to me you must make this repair, regardless of what promises we can give you. You won't risk your ship by slipping back into drive in your present condition. The only other option is to drift here until we all die. What choice do we have?"

"I have a choice," Royd said with deadly seriousness. "I could kill all of you, if that were the only way to save my ship."

"You could try," Melantha said.

"Let us have no more talk of death," d'Branin said.

"You are right, Karoly," Royd said. "I do not wish to kill any of you. But I must be protected."

"You will be," Melantha said. "Karoly can set the others to chasing your hull fragments. I'll never leave your side. I'll assist you; the work will be done three times as fast."

Royd was polite. "In my experience, most planet-bounds are clumsy and easily tired in weightlessness. It would be more efficient if I worked alone."

"It would not," she replied. "I remind you that I'm the improved model, Captain. Good in free-fall as well as in bed. I'll help."

"As you will. In a few moments, I shall depower the gravity grid. Karoly, go and prepare your people. Unship your sled and suit up. I will exit *Nightflyer* in three hours, after I have recovered from the pains of your gravity. I want all of you outside the ship when I leave."

It was as though some vast animal had taken a bite out of the universe.

Melantha Jhirl waited on her sled close by the *Nightflyer,* and looked at stars. It was not so very different out here, in the depths of interstellar space. The stars were cold, frozen points of light; unwinking, austere, more chill and uncaring somehow than the same suns made to dance and twinkle by an atmosphere. Only the absence of a landmark primary reminded her of where she was: in the places between, where men do not stop, where the *volcryn* sail ships impossibly ancient. She tried to pick out Avalon's sun, but she did not know where to search. The configurations were strange to her, and she had no idea of how she was oriented. Behind her, before her, above, all around, the starfields stretched endlessly. She glanced down beneath her sled and the *Nightflyer,* expecting still more alien stars, and the bite hit her with an almost physical force.

Melantha fought off a wave of vertigo. She was suspended above a pit, a yawning chasm in the universe, black starless, vast.

Empty.

She remembered then: the Tempter's Veil. Just a cloud of dark gas, nothing really, galactic pollution that obscured the light from the stars of the Fringe. But this close at hand, it looked immense, terrifying. She had to break her gaze when she began to feel as if she were falling. It was a gulf beneath her and the frail silver-white shell of the *Nightflyer*, a gulf about to swallow them.

Melantha touched one of the controls on the sled's forked handle, swinging around so the Veil was to her side instead of beneath her. That seemed to help, somehow. She concentrated on the *Nightflyer*. It was the largest object in her universe, brightly lit, ungainly; three small eggs side by side, two larger spheres beneath and at right angles, lengths of tube connecting it all. One of the eggs was shattered now, giving the craft an unbalanced cast.

She could see the other sleds as they angled through the black, tracking the missing pieces of eggshell, grappling with them, bringing them back. The linguistic team worked together, as always, sharing a sled. The xenobiologist was alone. Karoly d'Branin had a silent passenger; the psipsych, freshly drugged, asleep in the suit they had dressed her in. Royd had insisted that the ship be cleared completely, and it would have taken time and care to rouse the psipsych to consciousness; this was the safer course.

While her colleagues labored, Melantha Jhirl waited for Royd Eris, talking to the others occasionally over the comm link. The two linguists, unaccustomed to weightlessness, were complaining a lot. Karoly tried to soothe them. The xenobiologist worked in silence, argued out. He had been vehement earlier in his opposition to going outside, but Melantha and Karoly had finally worn him down and it seemed as if he had nothing more to say. Melantha now watched him flit across her field of vision, a stick figure in form-fitting black armor standing stiff and erect at the controls of his sled.

At last the circular airlock atop the foremost of the *Nightflyer*'s major spheres dilated, and Royd Eris emerged. She watched him approach, wondering what he would look like. She had so many different pictures. His genteel, cultured, too-formal voice sometimes reminded her of the dark aristocrats of her native Prometheus, the wizards who toyed with human genes. At other times his naïveté made her think of him as an inexperienced youth. His ghost was a tired looking, thin young man, and he was supposed to be considerably older than that pale shadow, but Melantha found it difficult to hear an old man talking when he spoke.

Royd's sled was larger than theirs and of a different design; a long oval plate with eight jointed, grappling arms bristling from its underside like the legs of a metal spider, and the snout of a heavy-duty cutting laster mounted above. His suit was odd too, more massive than the Academy worksuits, with a bulge between its shoulder blades that was probably a powerpack, and rakish radiant fins atop shoulders and helmet.

But when he was finally near enough for Melantha to see his face, it was just a face. White, very white, that was the predominant impression she got; white hair cropped very short, a white stubble around the sharply chiseled lines of his jaw, almost invisible eyebrows beneath which blue eyes moved restlessly. His skin was pale and unlined, scarcely touched by time.

He looked wary, she thought. And perhaps a bit frightened.

He stopped his sled close to hers, amid the twisted ruin that had been cargo hold three, and surveyed the damage, the pieces of floating wreckage that once had been flesh and blood, glass, metal, plastic. Hard to distinguish now, all of them fused and burned and frozen together. "We have a good deal of work to do, Melantha," he said.

"First let's talk," she replied. She shifted her sled closer and reached out to him, but the distance was still too great, the width of the two vacuum sleds keeping them apart. Melantha backed off, and turned herself over completely, so that Royd hung upside down in her world and she upside down in his. Then she moved toward him again, positioning her sled directly over/under his. Their gloved hands met, brushed, parted. Melantha adjusted her altitude. Their helmets touched.

"I don't — " Royd began to say uncertainly.

"Turn off your comm," she commanded. "The sound will carry through the helmets."

He blinked and used his tongue controls and it was done.

"Now we can talk," she said.

"I do not like this, Melantha," he said. "This is too obvious. This is dangerous."

"There's no other way," she said. "Royd, I *do* know."

"Yes," he said. "I knew you did. Three moves ahead, Melantha. I remember the way you play chess. You are safer if you feign ignorance, however."

"I understand that, Captain. Other things I'm less sure about. Can we talk about it?"

"No. Don't ask me to. Just do as I tell you. You are in danger, all of you, but I can protect you. The less you know, the better I can protect you." Through the transparent faceplates, his expression was grim.

She stared into his upside-down eyes. "Your ship is killing us, Captain. That's my suspicion, anyway. Not you. It. Only that doesn't make sense. You command the *Nightflyer*. How can it act independently? And why? What motive? How was that psionic murder accomplished? It can't be the ship. Yet it can't be anything else. Help me, Captain."

He blinked; there was anguish behind his eyes. "I should never have accepted Karoly's charter. Not with a telepath among you. It was risky. But I wanted to see the *volcryn*.

"You understand too much already, Melantha," Royd continued. "I can't tell you more. The ship is malfunctioninng, that is all you need know. It is not safe to push too hard. As long as I am at the controls, however, you and your colleagues are in small danger. Trust me."

"Trust is a two-way bond," Melantha said steadily.

Royd lifted his hand and pushed her away, then tongued his comm back to life. "Enough gossip," he briskly announced. "We have repairs to make. Come. I want to see just how improved you are."

In the solitude of her helmet, Melantha Jhirl swore softly.

The xenobiologist watched Royd Eris emerge on his oversized work sled, watched Melantha Jhirl move to him, watched as she turned over and pressed her faceplate to his. He could scarcely contain his rage. Somehow they were all in it together, Royd and Melantha and possibly old d'Branin as well, he thought sourly. She had protected him from the first, when they might have taken action together, stopped him, found out who or what he was. And now three were dead, killed by the cipher in the misshapen spacesuit, and Melantha hung upside down, her face pressed to his like lovers kissing.

He tongued off his comm and cursed. The others were out of sight, off chasing spinning wedges of half-slagged metal. Royd and Melantha were engrossed in each other, the ship abandoned and vulnerable. This was his chance. No wonder Eris had insisted that all of them precede him into the void; outside, isolated from the controls of the *Nightflyer*, he was only a man. A weak one at that.

Smiling a thin hard smile, the xenobiologist brought his sled around in a wide circle and vanished into the gaping maw of the drive-room. His lights flickered past the ring of nukes and sent long bright streaks along the sides of the closed cylinders of the stardrives, the huge engines that bent the stuff of space-time, encased in webs of metal and crystal. Everything was open to the vacuum. It was better that way; atmosphere corroded and destroyed.

He set the sled down, dismounted, moved to the airlock. This was the hardest part, he thought. The headless body of the young telepath was tethered loosely to a massive support strut, a grisly guardian by the door. The xenobiologist had to stare at it while he waited for the lock to cycle. Whenever he glanced away, somehow he would find his eyes creeping back to it. The body looked almost natural, as if it had never had a head. The xenobiologist tried to remember the young man's face, and failed, but then the lock door slid open and he gratefully pushed the thought away and entered.

He was alone in the *Nightflyer*.

A cautious man, he kept his suit on, though he collapsed the helmet and yanked loose the suddenly limp metallic fabric so it fell behind his back like a hood. He could snap it in place quickly enough if the need arose. In cargo hold four, where they had stored their equipment, the xenobiologist found what he was looking for; a portable cutting laser, charged and ready. Low power, but it would do.

Slow and clumsy in weightlessness, he pulled himself through the corridor into the darkened lounge.

It was chilly inside, the air cold on his cheeks. He tried not to notice. He braced himself at the door and pushed off across the width of the room, sailing above the furniture, which was all safely bolted into place.

As he drifted toward his objective, something wet and cold touched his face. It startled him, but it was gone before he could make out what it was.

When it happened again, he snatched at it, caught it, and felt briefly sick. He had forgotten. No one had cleaned the lounge yet. The — *remains* were still there, floating now, blood and flesh and bits of bone and brain. All around him.

He reached the far wall, stopped himself with his arms, pulled himself down to where he wanted to go. The bulkhead. The wall. No doorway was visible, but the metal couldn't be very thick. Beyond was the control room, the computer access, safety, power. The xenobiologist did not think of himself as a vindictive man. He did not intend to harm Royd Eris, that judgment was not his to make. He would take control of the *Nightflyer,* warn Eris away, make certain the man stayed sealed in his suit. He would take them all back without any more mysteries, any more killings. The Academy arbiters could listen to the story, and probe Eris, and decide the right and wrong of it, guilt and innocence, what should be done.

The cutting laser emitted a thin pencil of scarlet light. The xenobiologist smiled and applied it to the bulkhead. It was slow work, but he had patience. They would not have missed him, quiet as he'd been, and if they did they would assume he was off sledding after some hunk of salvage. Eris's repairs would take hours, maybe days, to finish. The bright blade of the laser smoked where it touched the metal. He applied himself diligently.

Something moved on the periphery of his vision, just a little flicker, barely seen. A floating bit of brain, he thought. A sliver of bone. A bloody piece of flesh, hair still hanging from it. Horrible things, but nothing to worry about. He was a biologist, he was used to blood and brains and flesh. And worse, and worse; he had dissected many an alien in his day.

Again the motion caught his eye, teased at it. Not wanting to, he found himself drawn to look. He could not *not* look, somehow, just as he had been unable to ignore the headles telepath in the airlock. He looked.

It was an eye.

The xenobiologist trembled and the laser slipped sharply off to one side, so he had to wrestle with it to bring it back to the channel he was cutting. His heart raced. He tried to calm himself. Nothing to be frightened of. No one was home, and if Royd should return, well, he had the laser as a weapon and he had his suit on if an airlock blew.

He looked at the eye again, willing away his fear. It was just an eye, the eye of the young telepath, intact, bloody but intact, the same watery blue eye the boy had when alive, nothing supernatural. A piece of dead flesh, floating in the lounge amid other pieces of dead flesh. Someone should have cleaned up the lounge, he thought angrily. It was indecent to leave it like this, it was uncivilized.

The eye did not move. The other grisly bits were drifting on the air currents that flowed across the room, but the eye was still. Fixed on him. Staring.

He cursed himself and concentrated on the laser, on his cutting. He had burned an almost straight line up the bulkhead for about a meter. He began another at right angles.

The eye watched dispassionately. The xenobiologist suddenly found he could not stand it. One hand released its grip on the laser, reached out, caught the eye, flung it across the room. The action made him lose balance. He tumbled backward, the laser slipping from his grasp, his arms flapping like the wings on some absurd heavy bird. Finally he caught an edge of the table and stopped himself.

The laser hung in the center of the room, still firing, turning slowly where it floated. That did not make sense. It should have ceased fire when he released it. A malfunction, he thought. Smoke rose from where the thin line of the laser traced a path across the carpet.

With a shiver of fear, the xenobiologist realized that the laser was turning toward him.

He raised himself, put both hands flat against the table, pushed off out of the way.

The laser was turning more swiftly now.

He slammed into a wall, grunted in pain, bounced off the floor, kicked. The laser was spinning quickly, chasing him. He soared, braced himself for a ricochet off the ceiling. The beam swung around, but not fast enough. He'd get it while it was still firing off in the other direction.

He moved close, reached, and saw the eye.

It hung just above the laser. Staring.

The xenobiologist made a small whimpering sound low in his throat, and his hand hesitated — not long, but long enough — and the scarlet beam came up and around.

Its touch was a light, hot caress across his neck.

It was more than an hour later before they missed him. Karoly d'Branin noticed his absence first, called for him over the comm net, and got no answer. He discussed it with the others.

Royd Eris moved his sled back from the armor plate he had just mounted, and through his helmet Melantha Jhirl could see the lines around his mouth grow hard. His eyes were sharply alert.

It was just then that the screaming began.

A shrill bleat of pain and fear, followed by choked, anguished sobbing. They all heard it. It came over the comm net and filled their helmets.

"It's him," a woman's voice said. The linguist.

"He's hurt," her partner added. "He's crying for help. Can't you hear it?"

"Where — ?" someone started.

"The ship," the female linguist said. "He must have returned to the ship."

Royd Eris said, "No. I warned — "

"We're going to go check," the linguist said. Her partner cut free the hull fragment they had been towing, and it spun away, tumbling. Their sled angled down towards the *Nightflyer*.

"Stop," Royd said. "I'll return to my chambers and check from there, if you wish. Stay outside until I give you clearance."

"Go to hell," the linguist snapped at him over the open circuit.

"Royd, my friend, what can you mean?" Karoly d'Branin said. His sled was in motion too, hastening after the linguists, but he had been farther out and it was a long way back to the ship. "He is hurt, perhaps seriously. We must help."

"No," Royd said. "Karoly, *stop*. If your colleague went back to the ship alone, he is dead."

"How do you know that?" the male linguist demanded. "Did you arrange it? Set traps?"

"Listen to me," Royd continued. "You can't help him now. Only I could have helped him, and he did not listen to me. Trust me. Stop."

In the distance, d'Branin's sled slowed. The linguists did not. "We've already listened to you too damn much, I'd say," the woman said. She almost had to shout to be heard above the sobs and whimpers, the agonized sounds that filled their universe. "Melantha," she said, "keep Eris right where he is. We'll go carefully, find out what is happening inside, but I don't want him getting back to his controls. Understood?"

Melantha Jhirl hesitated. Sounds of terror and agony beat against her ears; it was hard to think.

Royd swung his sled around to face her, and she could feel the weight of his stare. "Stop them," he said. "Melantha, Karoly, order it. They do not know what they are doing." His voice was edged with despair.

In his face, Melantha found decision. "Go back inside quickly, Royd. Do what you can. I'm going to try to intercept them."

He nodded to her across the gulf, but Melantha was already in motion. Her sled backed clear of the work area, congested with hull fragments and other debris, then accelerated briskly as she raced toward the rear of the *Nightflyer*.

But even as she approached, she knew it was too late. The linguists were too close, and already moving much faster than she was.

"*Don't,*" she said, authority in her tone. "The ship isn't safe, damn it."

"Bitch," was all the answer she got.

Karoly's sled pursued vainly. "Friends, you must stop, please, I beg it of you, let us talk this out together."

The unending whimpers were his only reply.

"I am your superior," he said. "I order you to wait outside. Do you hear me? I order it, I invoke the authority of the Academy. Please, my friends, please listen to me."

Melantha watched as the linguists vanished down the long tunnel of the drive-room.

A moment later she halted her sled near the waiting black mouth, debating whether she should follow them into the *Nightflyer*. She might be able to catch them before the airlock opened.

Royd's voice, hoarse counterpoint to the crying, answered her unvoiced question. "Stay, Melantha. Proceed no further."

She looked behind her. Royd's sled was approaching.

"What are you doing?" she demanded. "Royd, use your own lock. You have to get back inside!"

"Melantha," he said calmly, "I cannot. The ship will not respond to me. The control lock will not dilate. I don't want you or Karoly inside the ship until I can return to my controls."

Melantha Jhirl looked down the shadowed barrel of the drive-room, where the linguists had vanished.

"What will — ?"

"Beg them to come back, Melantha. Plead with them. Perhaps there is still time, if they will listen to you."

She tried. Karoly d'Branin tried too. The crying, the moaning, the twisted symphony went on and on. But they could not raise the two linguists at all.

"They've cut out their comm," Melantha said furiously. "They don't want to listen to us. Or that . . . that *sound*."

Royd's sled and Karoly d'Branin's reached her at the same time. "I do not understand," Karoly said. "What is happening?"

"It is simple, Karoly," Royd replied. "I am being kept outside until — until Mother is done with them."

The linguists left their vacuum sled next to the one the xenobiologist had abandoned and cycled through the airlock in unseemly haste, with hardly a glance for the grim headless doorman.

Inside they paused briefly to collapse their helmets. "I can still hear him," the man said.

The woman nodded. "The sound is coming from the lounge. Hurry."

They kicked and pulled their way down the corridor in less than a minute. The sounds grew steadily louder, nearer. "He's in there," the woman said when they reached the chamber door.

"Yes," her partner said, "but is he alone? We need a weapon. What if . . . Royd had to be lying. There *is* someone else on board. We need to defend ourselves."

The woman would not wait. "There are two of us," she said. "Come *on!*" With that she launched herself through the doorway and into the lounge.

It was dark inside. What little light there was spilled through the door from the corridor. Her eyes took a long moment to adjust. "Where are you?" she cried in confusion. The lounge seemed empty, but maybe it was only the light.

"Follow the sound," the man suggested. He stood in the door, glancing warily about for a minute, before he began to feel his way down a wall, groping with his hands.

The woman, impatient, propelled herself across the room, searching. She brushed against a wall in the kitchen area, and that made her think of weapons.

She knew where the utensils were stored. "Here," she said. "Here, I've got a knife, that should thrill you." She waved it, and brushed against a floating bubble of blood as big as her fist. It burst and reformed into a hundred smaller globules.

"Oh, merciful God," the man said in a voice thick with fear.

"What?" she demanded. "Did you find him? Is he — ?"

He was fumbling his way back toward the door, creeping along the wall the way he had come. "Get out of here," he warned. "Oh, *hurry.*"

"Why?" She trembled despite herself.

"I found the source," he said. "The screams, the crying. Come *on!*"

"Wha — "

He whimpered. "It was the grille. Oh, don't you see? It's coming from the communicator!" He reached for the door, and sighed audibly, and he did not wait for her. He bolted down the corridor and was gone.

She braced herself and positioned herself in order to follow him.

The sounds stopped. Just like that: turned off.

She kicked, floated toward the coor, knife in hand.

Something dark crawled from beneath the dinner table and rose to block her path. She saw it clearly for a moment, outlined in the light from the corridor. The xenobiologist, still in his vacuum suit, but with his helmet pulled off. He had something in his hands that he raised to point at her. It was a laser, she saw, a simple cutting laser.

She was moving straight toward him. She flailed and tried to stop herself, but she could not.

When she got quite close, she saw that he had a second mouth below his chin, and it was grinning at her, and little droplets of blood flew from it, wetly, as he moved.

The man rushed down the corridor in a frenzy of fear, bruising himself as he smashed into walls. Panic and weightlessness made him clumsy. He kept glancing over his shoulder as he fled, hoping to see his lover coming after him, but terrified of what he might see in her stead.

It took a long, *long* time for the airlock to open. As he waited, trembling, his pulse began to slow. He steadied himself with an effort. Once inside the chamber, with the inner door sealed between him and the lounge, he began to feel safe.

Suddenly he could barely remember why he had been so terrified.

And he was ashamed; he had run, abandoned her. And for what? What had frightened him so? An empty lounge? Noises from a communicator? Why, that only meant the xenobiologist was alive somewhere else in the ship, in pain, spilling his agony into a comm unit.

Resolute, he reached out and killed the cycle on the airlock, then reversed it. The air that had been partially sucked out came gusting back into the chamber.

The man shook his head ruefully. He'd hear no end of this, he knew. She would never let him forget it. But at least he would return, and apologize. That would count for something.

As the inner door rolled back, he felt a brief flash of fear again, an instant of stark terror when he wondered what might have emerged from the lounge to wait for him in the corridors of the *Nightflyer*. He willed it away.

When he stepped out, she was waiting for him.

He could see neither anger nor disdain in her curiously calm features, but he pushed himself toward her and tried to frame a plea for forgiveness anyway. "I don't know why I — "

With languid grace, her hand came out from behind her back. The knife was in it. That was when he finally noticed the hole burned in her suit, just between her breasts.

"Your *mother?*" Melantha Jhirl said incredulously as they hung helpless in the emptiness beyond the ship.

"She can hear everything we say," Royd replied. "But at this point, it no longer makes any difference. Your friend must have done something very foolish, very threatening. Now she is determined to kill you all."

"She, she, what do you mean?" D'Branin's voice was puzzled. "Royd, surely you do not tell us that your mother is still alive. You said she died even before you were born."

"She did, Karoly," Royd said. "I did not lie to you."

"No," Melantha said. "I didn't think so. But you did not tell use the whole truth, either."

Royd nodded. "Mother is dead, but her — ghost still lives, and animates my *Nightflyer*." He chuckled grimly. "Perhaps it would be more fitting to say her *Nightflyer*. My control is tenuous at best."

"Royd," d'Branin said, "my *volcryn* are more real than any ghosts." His voice chided gently.

"I don't believe in ghosts either," Melantha Jhirl said with a frown.

"Call it what you will, then," Royd said. "My term is as good as any. The reality is unchanged. My mother, or some part of my mother, lives in the *Nightflyer*, and she is killing you all as she has killed others before."

"Royd, you do not make sense," d'Branin said. "I — "

"Karoly, let the captain explain."

"Yes," Royd said. "The *Nightflyer* is very — very *advanced*, you know. Automated, self-repairing, large. It had to be, if Mother were to be freed from the necessity of crew. It was built on Newholme, you will recall. I have never been there, but I understand that Newholme's technology is quite sophisticated. Avalon could not duplicate this ship, I suspect. There are few worlds that could."

"The point, Captain?"

"The point — the point is the computers, Melantha. They had to be extraordinary. They are, believe me, they are. Crystal-matrix cores, laser-grid data retrieval, and other — other features."

"Are you telling us that the *Nightflyer* is an Artificial Intelligence?"

"No," Royd said, "not as I understand it. But it is something close. Mother had a capacity for personality impress built in. She filled the central crystal with her own memories, desires, quirks, her loves and her — hates. That was why she trusted the computer with my education, you see? She knew it would raise me as she herself would, had she the patience. She programmed it in certain other ways as well.''

''And you cannot deprogram, my friend?'' Karoly asked.

Royd's voice was despairing. ''I have *tried*, Karoly. But I am a weak hand at systems work, and the programs are very complicated, the machines very sophisticated. At least three times I have eradicated her, only to have her surface again. She is a phantom program, and I cannot track her. She comes and goes as she will. A ghost, do you see? Her memories and her personality are so intertwined with the programs that run the *Nightflyer* that I cannot get rid of her without wiping the entire system. But that would leave me helpless. I could never reprogram, and with the computers down the entire ship would fail, drives, life support, everything. I would have to leave the *Nightflyer,* and that would kill me.''

''You should have told us, my friend,'' Karoly d'Branin said. ''On Avalon, we have many cyberneticists, some very great minds. We might have aided you. We could have provided expert help.''

''Karoly, I have *had* expert help. Twice I have brought systems specialists on board. The first one told me what I have just told you; that it was impossible without wiping the programs completely. The second had trained on Newholme. She thought she could help me. Mother killed her.''

''You are still omitting something,'' Melantha Jhirl said. 'I understand how your cybernetic ghost can open and close airlocks at will and arrange other accidents of that nature. But that first death, our telepath, how do you explain that?''

''Ultimately I must bear the guilt,'' Royd replied. ''My loneliness led me to a grievous error. I thought I could safeguard you, even with a telepath among you. I have carried other riders safely. I watch them constantly, warn them away from dangerous acts. If Mother attempts to interfere, I countermand her directly from the control room. That usually works. Not always. Usually. Before you she had killed only five times, and the first three died when I was quite young. That was how I learned about her. That party included a telepath too.

''I should have known better, Karoly. My hunger for life has doomed you all to death. I overestimated my own abilities, and underestimated her fear of exposure. She strikes out when she is threatened, and telepaths are always a threat. They sense her, you see. A malign, looming presence, they tell me, something cool and hostile and inhuman.''

''Yes,'' Karoly d'Branin said, ''yes, that was what he said. An alien, he was certain of it.''

''No doubt she feels alien to a telepath used to the familiar contours of organic minds. Hers is not a human brain, after all. What it is I cannot say — a complex of crystalline memories, a hellish network of interlocking programs, a meld of circuitry and spirit. Yes, I can understand why she might feel alien.''

"You still haven't explained how a computer program could explode a man's skull," Melantha said patiently.

"Have you ever held a whisper-jewel?" Royd Eris asked her.

"Yes," she replied. She had even owned one once; a dark blue crystal, packed with the memories of a particularly satisfying bout of lovemaking. It had been esper-etched on Avalon, her feelings impressed onto the jewel, and for more than a year she had only to touch it to grow randy. It had finally faded, though, and afterward she had lost it.

"Then you know that psionic power can be stored," Royd said. "The central core of my computer system is resonant crystal. I think Mother impressed it as she lay dying."

"Only an esper can etch a whisper-jewel," Melantha said.

"You never asked me the *why* of it, Karoly," Royd said. "Nor you, Melantha. You never asked why Mother hated people so. She was born gifted, you see. On Avalon, she might have been a class one, tested and trained and honored, her talent nurtured and rewarded. I think she might have been very famous. She might have been stronger than a class one, but perhaps it is only after death that she acquired such power, linked as she is to the *Nightflyer*.

"The point is moot. She was not born on Avalon. On her birth world, her ability was seen as a curse, something alien and fearful. So they cured her of it. They used drugs and electroshock and hypno-training that made her violently ill whenever she tried to use her talent. She never lost her power, of course, only the ability to use it effectively, to control it with her conscious mind. It remained part of her, suppressed, erratic, a source of shame and pain. And half a decade of institutional cure almost drove her insane. No wonder she hated people."

"What was her talent? Telepathy?"

"No. Oh, some rudimentary ability perhaps. I have read that all psi talents have several latent abilities in addition to their one developed strength. But Mother could not read minds. She had some empathy, although her cure had twisted it curiously, so that the emotions she felt literally sickened her. But her major strength, the talent they took five years to shatter and destroy, was teke."

Melantha Jhirl swore. "No wonder she hated gravity. Telekinesis under weightlessness is — "

"Yes," Royd finished. "'Keeping the *Nightflyer* under gravity tortures me, but it limits Mother."

In the silence that followed that comment, each of them looked down the dark cylinder of the drive-room. Karoly d'Branin moved awkwardly on his sled. "They have not returned," he said finally.

"They are probably dead," Royd said dispassionately.

"What will we do, friend Royd? We must plan. We cannot wait here indefinitely."

"The first question is what can *I* do," Royd Eris replied. "I have talked freely, you'll note. You deserved to know. We have passed the point where ignorance was a protection. Obviously things have gone too far. There have been too many deaths and you have been witness to all of them. Mother cannot allow you to return to Avalon alive."

"Ah," said Melantha, "true. But what shall she do with *you*? Is your own status in doubt, Captain?"

"The crux of the problem," Royd admitted. "You are still three moves ahead, Melantha. I wonder if it will suffice. Your opponent is four ahead this game, and most of your pawns are already captured. I fear checkmate is imminent."

"Unless I can persuade my opponent's king to desert, no?"

She could see Royd smile at her wanly. "She would probably kill me too if I chose to side with you."

Karoly d'Branin was slow to grasp the point. "But — but what else could you — "

"My sled has a laser. Yours do not. I could kill you both, right now, and thereby earn my way into the *Nightflyer*'s good graces."

Across the three meters that lay between their sleds, Melantha's eyes met Royd's. Her hands rested easily on the thruster controls. "You could try, Captain. Remember, the improved model isn't easy to kill."

"I would not kill you, Melantha Jhirl," Royd said seriously. "I have lived sixty-eight standard years, and I have never lived at all. I am tired, and you tell grand, gorgeous lies. If we lose, we will all die together. If we win, well, I shall die anyway, when they destroy the *Nightflyer* — either that or live as a freak in an orbital hospital, and I would prefer death — "

"We will build you a new ship, Captain," Melantha said.

"Liar," Royd replied. But his tone was cheerful. "No matter. I have not had much of a life anyway. Death does not frighten me. If we win, you must tell me about your *volcryn* once again, Karoly. And you, Melantha, you must play chess with me once more, and . . ." His voice trailed off.

"And sex with you?" she finished, smiling.

"If you would," he said quietly. "I have never — *touched*, you know. Mother died before I was born." He shrugged. "Well, Mother has heard all of this. Doubtless she will listen carefully to any plans we might make, so there is no sense making them. There is no chance now that the control lock will admit me, since it is keyed directly into the ship's computer. So we must follow your colleagues through the drive-room, and enter through the manual lock, and take what chances we are given. If I can reach consoles and restore gravity, perhaps we — "

He was interrupted by a low groan.

For an instant Melantha thought the *Nightflyer* was wailing at them again, and she was surprised that it was so stupid as to try the same tactic twice. Then the groan sounded a second time, and in the back of Karoly d'Branin's sled the forgotten fourth survivor struggled against the bonds that held her down. D'Branin hastened to free her, and the psipsych tried to rise to her feet and almost floated off the sled until he caught her hand and pulled her back. "Are you well?" he asked. "Can you hear me? Have you pain?"

Imprisoned beneath a transparent faceplate, wide frightened eyes flicked rapidly from Karoly to Melantha to Royd, and then to the broken *Nightflyer*. Melantha wondered whether the woman was insane, and started to caution d'Branin, when the psipsych spoke suddenly.

"The *volcryn*," was all she said, "the *volcryn*. Oh, oh, the *volcryn!*"

Around the mouth of the drive-room, the ring of nuclear engines took on a faint glow. Melantha Jhirl heard Royd suck in his breath sharply. She gave the thruster controls of her sled a violent twist. "Hurry," she said, "the *Nightflyer* is preparing to move."

A third of the way down the long barrel of the drive-room, Royd pulled abreast of her, stiff and menacing in his black, bulky armor. Side by side they sailed past the cylindrical stardrives and the cyberwebs; ahead, dimly lit, was the main airlock and its ghastly sentinel.

"When we reach the lock, jump over to my sled," Royd said. "I want to stay armed and mounted, and the chamber is not large enough for two sleds."

Melantha Jhirl risked a quick glance behind her. "Karoly," she called. "Where are you?"

"I am outside, Melantha," the answer came. "I cannot come, my friend. Forgive me."

"But we have to stay together," she said.

"No," d'Branin's voice replied, "no, I could not risk it, not when we are so close. It would be so tragic, so futile, Melantha, to come so close and fail. Death I do not mind, but I must see them first, finally, after all these years." His voice was firm and calm.

Royd Eris cut in. "Karoly, my mother is going to move the ship. Don't you understand? You will be left behind, lost."

"I will wait," d'Branin replied. "My *volcryn* are coming, and I will wait for them."

Then there was no more time for conversation, for the airlock was almost upon them. Both sleds slowed and stopped, and Royd Eris reached out and began the cycle while Melantha moved to the rear of the huge oval worksled. When the outer door moved aside, they glided through into the lock chamber.

"When the inner door opens, it will begin," Royd told her evenly. "Most of the permanent furnishings are either built in or welded or bolted into place, but the things that your team brought on board are not. Mother will use those things as weapons. And beware of doors, airlocks, any equipment tied in to the *Nightflyer*'s computer. Need I warn you not to unseal your suit?"

"Hardly," she replied.

Royd lowered the sled a little, and its grapplers made a metallic sound as they touched against the chamber floor.

The inner door opened, and Royd applied his thrusters.

Inside the linguists were waiting, swimming in a haze of blood. The man had been slit from crotch to throat and his intestines moved like a nest of pale, angry snakes. The woman still held the knife. They swam closer with a grace they had never possessed in life.

Royd lifted his foremost grapplers and smashed them to the side. The man caromed off a bulkhead, leaving a wide wet mark where he struck, and more of his guts came sliding out. The woman lost control of the knife. Royd accelerated past them, driving up the corridor, through the cloud of blood.

"I'll watch behind," Melantha said, and she turned and put her back to his. Already the two corpses were safely behind them. The knife was floating uselessly in the air. She started to tell Royd that they were all right when the blade abruptly shifted and came after them, as if some invisible force had taken hold of it.

"*Swerve!*" she shouted.

The sled shot wildly to one side. The knife missed by a full meter, and glanced ringingly off a bulkhead.

But it did not drop. It came at them again.

The lounge loomed ahead. Dark.

"The door is too narrow," Royd said. "We will have to abandon the sled, Melantha." Even as he spoke, they hit: he wedged the sled squarely into the doorframe, and the sudden impact jarred them loose.

For a moment Melantha floated clumsily in the corridor, trying to get her balance. The knife slashed at her, opening her suit and her shoulder. She felt sharp pain and the warm flush of bleeding. "*Damn,*" she shrieked. The knife came around again, spraying droplets of blood.

Melantha's hand darted out and caught it.

She muttered something under her breath, and wrenched the blade free of the force that had been gripping it.

Royd had regained the controls of his sled and seemed intent on some manipulation. Beyond, in the dimness of the lounge, Melantha saw a dark semi-human shape float into view.

"*Royd!*" she warned, but as she did the thing activated its laser. The pencil beam caught Royd square in the chest.

He touched his own firing stud. The sled's heavy-duty laser cindered the xenobiologist's weapon and burned off his right arm and part of his chest. Its pulsing shaft hung in the air, and smoked against the far bulkhead.

Royd made some adjustments and began cutting a hold. "We'll be through in five minutes or less," he said curtly, without stopping or looking up.

"Are you all right?" Melantha asked.

"I'm uninjured," he replied. "My suit is better armored than yours, and his laser was a low-powered toy."

Melantha turned her attention back to the corridor.

The linguists were pulling themselves toward her, one on each side of the passage, to come at her from two directions at once. She flexed her muscles. Her shoulder throbbed where she had been cut. Otherwise she felt strong, almost reckless. "The corpses are coming after us again," she told Royd. "I'm going to take them."

"Is that wise?" he asked. "There are two of them."

"I'm an improved model," Melantha said, "and they're dead." She kicked herself free of the sled and sailed toward the man. He raised his hands to block her. She slapped them aside, bent one arm back and heard it snap, and drove her knife deep into his throat before she realized what a useless gesture that was. The man continued to flail at her. His teeth snapped grotesquely.

Melantha withdrew her blade, seized him, and with all her considerable strength threw him bodily down the corridor. He tumbled, spinning wildly, and vanished into the haze of his own blood.

Melantha then flew in the opposite direction.

The woman's hands went around her from behind.

Nails scrabbled against her faceplate until they began to bleed, leaving red streaks on the plastic.

Melantha spun to face her attacker, grabbed a thrashing arm, and flung the woman down the passageway to crash into her struggling companion.

"I'm through," Royd announced.

She turned to see. A smoking meter-square opening had been cut through one wall of the lounge. Royd killed the laser, gripped both sides of the doorframe, and pushed himself toward it.

A piercing blast of sound drilled through her head. She doubled over in agony. Her tongue flicked out and clicked off the comm; then there was blessed silence.

In the lounge it was raining. Kitchen utensils, glasses and plates, pieces of human bodies, all lashed violently across the room, and glanced harmlessly off Royd's armored form. Melantha — eager to follow — drew back helplessly. That rain of death would cut her up to pieces in her lighter, thinner vacuum suit. Royd reached the far wall and vanished into the secret control section of the ship. She was alone.

The *Nightflyer* lurched, and sudden acceleration provided a brief semblance of gravity. She was thrown to one side. Her left shoulder smashed painfully against the sled.

All up and down the corridor doors were opening.

The linguists were moving toward her once again.

The *Nightflyer* was a distant star sparked by its nuclear engines. Blackness and cold enveloped them, and below was the unending emptiness of the Tempter's Veil, but Karoly d'Branin did not feel afraid. He felt strangely transformed.

The void was alive with promise.

"They *are* coming," he whispered. "Even I, who have no psi at all, even I can feel it. The Crey story must be so, even from light-years off they can be sensed. Marvelous!"

The psipsych seemed very small. "The *volcryn*," she muttered. "What good can they do us? I hurt. The ship is gone. D'Branin, my head aches.'' She made a small frightened noise. ''The boy said that, just after I injected him, before . . . before . . . you know. He said that his head hurt.''

''Quiet, my friend. Do not be afraid. I am here with you. Wait. Think only of what we shall witness, think only of that!''

''I can sense them,'' the psipsych said.

D'Branin was eager. ''Tell me, then. We have the sled. We shall go to them. Direct me.''

''Yes,'' she agreed. ''Yes. Oh, yes.''

Gravity returned: in a flicker, the universe became almost normal.

Melantha fell to the deck, landed easily and rolled, and was on her feet cat-quick.

The objects that had been floating ominously through the open doors along the corridor all came clattering down.

The blood was transformed from a fine mist to a slick covering on the corridor floor.

The two corpses dropped heavily from the air, and lay still.

Royd spoke to her. His voice came from the communicator grills built into the walls, not over her suit comm. ''I made it,'' he said.

''I noticed,'' she replied.

''I'm at the main control console,'' he continued. ''I have restored the gravity with a manual override, and I'm cutting off as many computer functions as possible. We're still not safe, though. She will try to find a way around me. I'm countermanding her by sheer force, as it were. I cannot afford to overlook anything, and if my attention should lapse for even a moment . . . Melantha, was your suit breached?''

''Yes. Cut at the shoulder.''

''Change into another one. *Immediately*. I think the counterprogramming I'm doing will keep the locks sealed, but I can't take any chances.''

Melantha was already running down the corridor, toward the cargo hold where the suits and equipment were stored.

''When you have changed,'' Royd continued, ''dump the corpses into the mass conversion unit. You'll find the appropriate hatch near the drive-room, just to the left of the main lock. Convert any other loose objects that are not indispensable as well; scientific instruments, books, tapes, tableware — ''

''Knives,'' suggested Melantha.

''By all means.''

''Is teke still a threat, Captain?''

''Mother is vastly weaker in a gravity field,'' Royd said. ''She has to fight it. Even boosted by the *Nightflyer*'s power, she can only move one object at a time, and she has only a fraction of the lifting force she wields under weightless conditions. But the power is still there, remember. Also, it is possible she will find a way to circumvent me and cut out the gravity again. From here I can restore it in an instant, but I don't want any weapons lying around even for that brief period of time."

Melantha had reached the cargo area. She stripped off her vacuum suit and slipped into another one in record time. Then she gathered up the discarded suit and a double armful of instruments and dumped them into the conversion chamber. Afterward she turned her attention to the bodies. The man was no problem. The woman crawled down the hall after her as she pushed him through, and thrashed weakly when it was her own turn, a grim reminder that the *Nightflyer*'s powers were not all gone. Melantha easily overcame her feeble struggles and forced her through.

The corpse of the xenobiologist was less trouble, but while she was cleaning out the lounge a kitchen knife came spinning at her head. It came slowly, though, and Melantha just batted it aside, then picked it up and added it to the pile for conversion.

She was working through the second cabin, carrying the psipsych's abandoned drugs and injection gun under her arm, when she heard Royd cry out.

A moment later, a force like a giant invisible hand wrapped itself around her chest and squeezed and pulled her, struggling to the floor.

Something was moving across the stars.

Dimly and far off, d'Branin could see it, though he could not yet make out details. But it was there, that was unmistakable, some vast shape that blocked off a section of the starscape. It was coming at them dead on.

How he wished he had his team with him now, his telepath, his experts, his instruments.

He pressed harder on the thrusters.

Pinned to the floor, hurting, Melantha Jhirl risked opening her suit's comm. She had to talk to Royd. "Are you there?" she asked. "What's happening?" The pressure was awful, and it was growing steadily worse. She could barely move.

The answer was pained and slow in responding. ". . . outwitted . . . me," Royd's voice managed. ". . . hurts . . . to . . . talk."

"Royd —"

". . . she . . . teked . . . dial . . . up . . . two . . . gees . . . three . . . higher . . . right . . . here . . . on . . . the . . . board . . . all . . . I . . . have to . . . to do . . . turn it . . . back . . . back . . . let me . . ."

Silence. Then, finally, when Melantha was near despair, Royd's voice again. One word: ". . . can't . . ."

Melantha's chest felt as if it were supporting ten times her own weight. She could imagine the agony Royd must be in; Royd, for whom even one gravity was painful and dangerous. Even if the dial was an arm's length away, she knew his feeble musculature would never let him reach it. "Why," she started, having somewhat less trouble talking than Royd, "why would she turn *up* the . . . gravity . . . it . . . weakens her too, yes?"

". . . yes . . . but . . . in a . . . time . . . hour . . . minute . . . my . . . my heart . . . will burst . . . and . . . and then . . . you alone . . . she . . . will . . . kill gravity . . . kill you . . ."

Painfully, Melantha reached out her arm and dragged herself half a length down the corridor. "Royd . . . hold on . . . I'm coming . . ." She dragged herself forward again. The psipsych's drug kit was still under her arm, impossibly heavy. She eased it down and started to shove it aside, then reconsidered. Instead she opened its lid.

The ampules were all neatly labeled. She glanced over them quickly, searching for adrenaline or synthastim, anything that might give her the strength she needed to reach Royd. She found several stimulants, selected the strongest, and was loading it into the injection gun with awkward, agonized slowness when her eyes chanced on the supply of esperon.

Melantha did not know why she hesitated. Esperon was only one of a half-dozen psionic drugs in the kit, but something about seeing it bothered her, reminded her of something she could not quite lay her finger on. She was trying to sort it out when she heard the noise.

"Royd," she said, "your mother . . . could she move . . . she couldn't move anything . . . teke it . . . in this high a gravity . . . could she?"

"Maybe," he answered, ". . . if . . . concentrate . . . all her . . . power . . . hard . . . maybe possible . . . why?"

"Because," Melantha Jhirl said grimly, "because something . . . some*one* . . . is cycling through the airlock."

The *volcryn* ship filled the universe.

"It is not truly a ship, not as I thought it would be," Karoly d'Branin was saying. His suit, Academy designed, had a built-in encoding device, and he was recording his comments for posterity, strangely secure in the certainty of his impending death. "The scale of it is difficult to imagine, difficult to estimate. Vast, vast. I have nothing but my wrist computer, no instruments, I cannot make accurate measurements, but I would say, oh, a hundred kilometers, perhaps as much as three hundred, across. Not solid mass, of course, not at all. It is delicate, airy, no ship as we know ships. It is — oh, beautiful — it is crystal and gossamer, alive with its own dim lights, a vast intricate kind of spiderwebby craft — it reminds me a bit of the old starsail ships they used once, in the days before drive, but this great construct, it is not solid, it cannot be driven by light. It is no ship at all, really. It is all open to vacuum, it has no sealed cabins or life-support spheres, none visible to me, unless blocked from my line of sight in some fashion, and no, I cannot believe that, it is too open, too fragile. It moves quite rapidly. I would wish for the instrumentation to measure its speed, but it is enough to be here. I am taking our sled at right angles to it, to get clear of its path, but I cannot say that I will make it. It moves so much faster than we. Not at light speed, no, far below it, but still faster than the *Nightflyer* and its nuclear engines, I would guess. Only a guess.

"The *volcryn* craft has no visible means of propulsion. In fact, I wonder how — perhaps it *is* a light-sail, laser-launched millennia ago, now torn and rotted by some unimaginable catastrophe — but no, it is too symmetrical, too beautiful, the webbings, the great shimmering veils near the nexus, the beauty of it.

"I must describe it, I must be more accurate, I know. It is difficult, I grow too excited. It is large, as I have said, kilometers across. Roughly — let me count — yes roughly octagonal in shape. The nexus, the center is a bright area, a small darkness surrounded by a much greater area of light, but only the dark portion seems entirely solid — the lighted areas are translucent, I can see stars through them, though discolored, shifted toward the purple. Veils, I call those the veils. From the nexus and the veils eight long — oh, vastly long — spurs project, not quite spaced evenly, so it is not a true geometric octagon — ah, I see better now, one of the spurs is shifted, oh, very slowly, the veils are rippling — they are mobile then, those projections, and the webbing runs from one spur to the next, around and around, but there are — patterns, odd patterns, it is not at all the simple webbing of a spider. I cannot quite see order in the patterns, in the traceries of the webs, but I feel sure that the order is there, the meaning is waiting to be found.

"There are lights. Have I mentioned the lights? The lights are brightest around the center nexus, but they are nowhere very bright, a dim violet. Some visible radiation, then, but not much. I would like to take an ultraviolet reading of this craft, but I do not have the instrumentation. The lights move. The veils seem to ripple, and lights run constantly up and down the length of the spurs, at differing rates of speed, and sometimes other lights can be seen traversing the webbing, moving across the patterns. I do not know what the lights are or whether they emanate from inside the craft or outside.

"The *volcryn* myths, this is really not much like the legends, not truly. Though, as I think, now I recall a Nor T'alush report that the *volcryn* ships were impossibly large, but I took that for exaggeration. And lights, the *volcryn* have often been linked to lights, but those reports were so vague, they might have meant anything, described anything from a laser propulsion system to simple exterior lighting; I could not know it meant this. Ah, what mysteries! The ship is still too far away for me to see the finer detail. I think perhaps the darker area in the center *is* a craft, a life capsule. The *volcryn* must be inside it. I wish my team was with me, my telepath. He was a class one, we might have made contact, might have communicated with them. The things we would learn! To think how old this craft is, how ancient this race, how long they have been outbound! It fills me with awe. Communication would be such a gift, such an impossible gift, but they are so alien."

"*D'Branin,*" The psipsych said in a low, urgent voice. "Can't you feel?"

Karoly d'Branin looked at his companion as if seeing her for the first time. "Can *you* feel them? You are a three, can you sense them now, strongly?"

"Long ago," the psipsych said. "Long ago."

"Can you project? Talk to them. Where are they? In the center area?"

"Yes," she replied, and she laughed. Her laugh was shrill and hysterical, and d'Branin had to recall that she was a very sick woman. "Yes, in the center, d'Branin, that's where the pulses come from. Only you're wrong about them. It's not a *them* at all, your legends are all lies, lies. I wouldn't be surprised if we were the first to ever see your *volcryn,* to ever come this close. The others, those aliens of yours, they merely *felt,* deep and distantly, sensed a bit of the nature of the *volcryn* in their dreams and visions, and fashioned the rest to suit themselves. Ships, and wars, and a race of eternal travelers, it is all — all — "

"What do you mean, my friend?" Karoly said, baffled. "You do not make sense. I do not understand."

"No," the psipsych said, her voice suddenly gentle. "You do not, do you? You cannot feel it, as I can. So clear now. This must be how a one feels, all the time. A one full of esperon."

"*What* do you feel? *What?* "

"It's not a *them,* Karoly," the psipsych said. "It's an *it.* Alive, Karoly, and quite mindless, I assure you."

"Mindless?" d'Branin said. "No, you must be wrong, you are not reading correctly. I will accept that it is a single creature if you say so, a single great marvelous star-traveler, but how can it be mindless? You sensed it, its mind, its telepathic emanations. You and the whole of the Crey sensitives and all the others. Perhaps its thoughts are too alien for you to read."

"Perhaps," the psipsych admitted, "but what I do read is not so terribly alien at all. Only animal. Its thoughts are slow and dark and strange, hardly thoughts at all, faint. The brain must be huge, I grant you that, but it can't be devoted to conscious thought."

"What do you mean?"

"The propulsion system, d'Branin. Don't you *feel?* The pulses? They are threatening to rip off the top of my skull. Can't you guess what is driving your damned *volcryn* across the galaxy? Why they avoid gravity wells? Can't you guess how it is moving?"

"No," d'Branin said, but even as he denied a dawn of comprehension broke across his face, and he looked away from his companion, back at the swelling immensity of the *volcryn,* its lights moving, its veils a-ripple, as it came on and on, across light-years, light-centuries, across eons.

When he looked back at her, he mouthed only a single word: "Teke," he said. Silence filled their world.

She nodded.

Melantha Jhirl struggled to lift the injection gun and press it against an artery. It gave a single loud hiss, and the drug flooded her system. She lay back and gathered her strength, tried to think. Esperon, esperon, why was that important? It had killed the telepath, made him a victim of his own abilities, tripled his power and his vulnerability. Psi. It all came back to psi.

The inner door of the airlock opened. The headless corpse came through.

It moved with jerks, unnatural shufflings, never lifting its legs from the floor.

It sagged as it moved, half-crushed by the weight upon it. Each shuffle was crude and sudden; some grim force was literally yanking one leg forward, then the next. It moved in slow motion, arms stiff by its sides.

But it moved.

Melantha summoned her own reserves and began to crawl away from it, never taking her eyes off its advance.

Her thoughts went round and round, searching for the piece out of place, the solution to the chess problem, finding nothing.

The corpse was moving faster than she was. Clearly, visibly, it was gaining.

Melantha tried to stand. She got to her knees, her heart pounding. Then one knee. She tried to force herself up, to lift the impossible burden on her shoulders. She was strong, she told herself. She was the improved model.

But when she put all her weight on one leg, her muscles would not hold her. She collapsed, awkwardly, and when she smashed against the floor it was as if she had fallen from a building. She heard a sharp *snap,* and a stab of agony flashed up the arm she had tried to use to break her fall. She blinked back tears and choked on her own scream.

The corpse was halfway up the corridor. It must be walking on two broken legs, she realized. It didn't care.

"Melantha . . . heard you . . . are . . . you . . . Melantha?"

"*Quiet,*" she snapped at Royd. She had no breath to waste on talk.

Now she had only one arm. She used the disciplines she had taught herself, willed away the pain. She kicked feebly, her boots scraping for purchase, and she pulled herself forward with her good arm.

The corpse came on and on.

She dragged herself across the threshold of the lounge, worming her way under the crashed sled, hoping it would delay the cadaver.

It was a meter behind her.

In the darkness, in the lounge, there where it had all begun, Melantha Jhirl ran out of strength.

Her body shuddered, and she collapsed on the damp carpet, and she knew that she could go no farther.

On the far side of the door, the corpse stood stiffly. The sled began to shake. Then, with the scrape of metal against metal, it slid backward, moving in tiny sudden increments, jerking itself free and out of the way.

Psi. Melantha wanted to curse it, and cry. Vainly she wished for a psi power of her own, a weapon to blast apart the teke-driven corpse that stalked her. She was improved, she thought angrily, but not improved enough. Her parents had given her all the genetic gifts they could arrange, but psi was beyond them. The gene was astronomically rare, recessive, and —

— and suddenly it came to her.

"*Royd!*" she yelled, put all of her remaining will into her words. "The dial . . . *teke it*. Royd, teke it!"

His reply was very faint, troubled. ". . . can't . . . I don't . . . Mother . . . only . . . her . . . not me . . . no . . ."

"Not mother," she said, desperate. "'You always . . . say . . . *mother*. I forgot . . . forgot. Not your mother . . . listen . . . you're a *clone* . . . same genes . . . you have it, too. The power."

"Don't," he said. "Never . . . must be . . . sex-linked."

"*No!* It *isn't*. I know . . . Promethean, Royd . . . don't tell a Promethean . . . about genes . . . turn it!"

The sled jumped a third of a meter, and listed to the side. A path was clear. The corpse came forward.

". . . trying," Royd said. "Nothing . . . I *can't!*"

"She *cured* you," Melantha said bitterly. "Better than . . . she was . . . cured . . . pre-natal . . . but it's only . . . suppressed . . . you *can!*"

"I . . . don't . . . know . . . how."

The corpse now stood above her. Stopped. Pale-fleshed hands trembled spastically. Began to rise.

Melantha swore, and wept, and made a futile fist.

And all at once the gravity was gone. Far, far away, she heard Royd cry out and then fall silent.

The corpse bobbed awkwardly into the air, its hands hanging limply before it. Melantha, reeling in the weightlessness, tried to ready herself for its furious assault.

But the body did not move again. It floated dead and still. Melantha moved to it, pushed it, and it sailed across the room.

"Royd?" she said uncertainly.

There was no answer.

She pulled herself through the hole into the control chamber.

And found Royd Eris, master of the *Nightflyer*, prone on his back in his armored suit, dead. His heart had given out.

But the dial on the gravity grid was set at zero.

I have held the *Nightflyer*'s crystalline soul within my hands.

It is deep and red and multifaceted, large as my head, and icy to the touch. In its scarlet depths, two small sparks of light burn fiercely and sometimes seem to whirl.

I have crawled through the consoles, wound my way carefully past safeguards and cybernets, taking care to damage nothing, and I have laid rough hands on that great crystal, knowing it is where *she* lives.

And I cannot bring myself to wipe it.

Royd's ghost has asked me not to.

Last night we talked about it once again, over brandy and chess in the lounge. Royd cannot drink, of course, but he sends his specter to smile at me, and he tells me where he wants his pieces moved.

For the thousandth time, he offered to take me back to Avalon, or any world of my choice, if only I would go outside and complete the repairs we abandoned so many years ago, so that the *Nightflyer* might safely slip into stardrive.

For the thousandth time I refused.

He is stronger now, no doubt. Their genes are the same, after all. Their power is the same. Dying, he too found the strength to impress himself upon the great crystal. The ship is alive with both of them, and frequently they fight. Sometimes she outwits him for a moment, and the *Nightflyer* does odd, erratic things. The gravity goes up or down or off completely. Blankets wrap themselves around my throat when I sleep. Objects come hurtling out of dark corners.

Those times have come less frequently of late, though. When they do come, Royd stops her, or I do. Together, the *Nightflyer* is ours.

Royd claims he is strong enough alone, that he does not really need me, that he can keep her under check. I wonder. Over the chessboard, I still beat him nine games out of ten.

And there are other considerations. Our work, for one. Karoly would be proud of us.

The *volcryn* will soon enter the mists of the Tempter's Veil, and we follow close behind. Studying, recording, doing all that old d'Branin would have wanted us to do. It is all in the computer. It is also on tape and on paper, should the computer ever be wiped. It will be interesting to see how the *volcryn* thrives in the Veil. Matter is so thick there, compared to the thin diet of interstellar hydrogen on which the creature has fed for endless eons.

We have tried to communicate with it, with no success. I do not believe it is sentient at all.

And lately Royd has tried to imitate its ways, gathering all his energies in an attempt to move the *Nightflyer* by teke. Sometimes, oddly, his mother even joins him in those efforts. So far they have failed, but we will keep trying.

So the work goes on, and it *is* important work, though not the field I trained for, back in Avalon. We know that our results will reach humanity. Royd and I have discussed it. Before I die, I will destroy the central crystal and clear the computers, and afterward I will set course manually for the close vicinity of an inhabited world. I know I can do it. I have all the time I need, and I am an improved model.

I will not consider the other option, though it means much to me that Royd suggests it again and again. No doubt I could finish the repairs. Perhaps Royd could control the ship without me, and continue the work. But that is not important.

When I finally touched him, for the first and last and only time, his body was still warm. But *he* was gone already. He never felt my touch. I could not keep that promise.

But I can keep my other.

I will not leave him alone with her.

Ever.

Born in White Plains, New York, Edward Bryant now lives in Denver, Colorado, where he manages the famous Milford Writer's Conference. A full-time writer since 1969, Bryant became one of the most popular and prolific SF writers of the seventies, and has won two Nebula Awards, for his short-stories "Stone" and "giANTS." Bryant's stories have appeared everywhere from Orbit *to* National Lampoon *to* Penthouse, *and his books include* Phoenix Without Ashes *(Fawcett Gold Medal), a novelization of a television script by Harlan Ellison, three acclaimed short-story collections,* Among the Dead *(Collier),* Cinnabar *(Bantam), and* Wyoming Sun *(Jelm Mountain Press), and, as editor, the anthology* 2076: The American Tricentennial *(Pyramid). Upcoming is another short-story collection,* Particle Theory *(Timescape Books), which promises to be one of the major collections of 1981. His story "Particle Theory" was in our* Seventh Annual Collection, *and his story "giANTS." was in our* Ninth Annual Collection.*

In the brilliant story that follows, a Nebula Finalist this year, Bryant shows us how the strange *may slowly and subtly intrude into both the physical and psychological landscapes of the daytime world, so that its chilling shadow may fall over you even in the brightest noon, so that you may look up to see dark wings passing overhead.*

EDWARD BRYANT
Strata

Six hundred million years in thirty-two miles. Six hundred million years in fifty-one minutes. Steve Mavrakis traveled in time — courtesy of the Wyoming Highway Department. The epochs raveled between Thermopolis and Shoshoni. The Wind River rambled down its canyon with the Burlington Northern tracks cut into the west walls, and the two-lane blacktop, U.S. 20, sliced into the east. Official signs driven into the verge of the highway proclaimed the traveler's progress:

DINWOODY FORMATION
TRIASSIC
185 – 225 MILLION YEARS

BIG HORN FORMATION
ORDOVICIAN
440 – 500 MILLION YEARS

103

FLATHEAD FORMATION
CAMBRIAN
500 – 600 MILLION YEARS

The mileposts might have been staked into the canyon rock under the pressure of millennia. They were there for those who could not read the stone.

Tonight Steve ignored the signs. He had made this run many times before. Darkness hemmed him. November clawed when he cracked the window to exhaust Camel smoke from the Chevy's cab. The CB crackled occasionally and picked up exactly nothing.

The wind blew — that was nothing unusual. Steve felt himself hypnotized by the skift of snow skating across the pavement in the glare of his brights. The snow swirled only inches above the blacktop, rushing across like surf sliding over the black packed sand of a beach.

Time's predator hunts.

Years scatter before her like a school of minnows surprised. The rush of her passage causes eons to eddy. Wind sweeps down the canyon with the roar of combers breaking on the sand. The moon, full and newly risen, exerts its tidal force.

Moonlight flashes on the slash of teeth.

And Steve snapped alert, realized he had traversed the thirty-two miles, crossed the flats leading into Shoshoni, and was approaching the junction with U.S. 26. Road hypnosis? he thought. Safe in Shoshoni, but it was scary. He didn't remember a goddammed minute of the trip through the canyon! Steve rubbed his eyes with his left hand and looked for an open café with coffee.

It hadn't been the first time.

All those years before, the four of them had thought they were beating the odds. On a chill night in June, high on a mountain edge in the Wind River Range, high on more than mountain air, the four of them celebrated graduation. They were young and clear-eyed: ready for the world. That night they knew there were no other people for miles. Having learned in class that there were 3.8 human beings per square mile in Wyoming, and as *four,* they thought the odds outnumbered.

Paul Onoda, eighteen. He was Sansei — third generation Japanese-American. In 1942, before he was conceived, his parents were removed with eleven thousand other Japanese-Americans from California to the Heart Mountain Relocation Center in northern Wyoming. Twelve members and three generations of the Onodas shared one of four hundred and sixty-five crowded, tar-papered barracks for the next four years. Two died. Three more were born. With their fellows, the Onodas helped farm eighteen hundred acres of virgin agricultural land. Not all of them had been Japanese gardeners or truck farmers in California, so the pharmacists and the teachers and the carpenters learned agriculture. They used irrigation to bring in water. The crops flourished. The Nisei not directly involved with farming were dispatched from camp to be seasonal farm laborers. A historian later laconically noted that "Wyoming benefited by their presence."

Paul remembered the Heart Mountain camps only through the memories of his elders, but those recollections were vivid. After the war, most of the Onodas stayed on in Wyoming. With some difficulty, they bought farms. The family invested thrice the effort of their neighbors, and prospered.

Paul Onoda excelled in the classrooms and starred on the football field of Fremont High School. Once he overheard the president of the school board tell the coach, "By God but that little Nip can run!" He thought about that; and kept on running ever faster.

More than a few of his classmates secretly thought he had it all. When prom time came in his senior year, it did not go unnoticed that Paul had an extraordinarily handsome appearance to go with his brains and athlete's body. In and around Fremont, a great many concerned parents admonished their white daughters to find a good excuse if Paul asked them to the prom.

Carroll Dale, eighteen. It became second nature early on to explain to people first hearing her given name that it had two r's and two l's. Both sides of her family went back four generations in this part of the country and one of her bequests had been a proud mother. Cordelia Carroll had pride, one daughter, and the desire to see the Hereford Carrolls retain *some* parity with the Angus Dales. After all, the Carrolls had been ranching on Bad Water Creek before John Broderick Okie illuminated his Lost Cabin castle with carbide lights. That was when Teddy Roosevelt had been president and it was when all the rest of the cattlemen in Wyoming, including the Dales, had been doing their accounts at night by kerosene lanterns.

Carroll grew up to be a good roper and a better rider. Her apprenticeship intensified after her older brother, her only brother, fatally shot himself during deer season. She wounded her parents when she neither married a man who would take over the ranch nor decided to take over the ranch herself.

She grew up slim and tall, with ebony hair and large, dark, slightly oblique eyes. Her father's father, at family Christmas dinners, would overdo the whiskey in the eggnog and make jokes about Indians in the woodpile until her paternal grandmother would tell him to shut the hell up before she gave him a goodnight the hard way, with a rusty sickle and knitting needles. It was years before Carroll knew what her grandmother meant.

In junior high, Carroll was positive she was eight feet tall in Lilliput. The jokes hurt. But her mother told her to be patient, that the other girls would catch up. Most of the girls didn't; but in high school the boys did, though they tended to be tongue-tied in the extreme when they talked to her.

She was the first girl president of her school's National Honor Society. She was a cheerleader. She was the valedictorian of her class and earnestly quoted John F. Kennedy in her graduation address. Within weeks of graduation, she eloped with the captain of the football team.

It nearly caused a lynching.

Steve Mavrakis, eighteen. Courtesy allowed him to be called a native despite his birth eighteen hundred miles to the east. His parents, on the other hand, had settled in the state after the war when he was less than a year old. Given another decade, the younger native-born might grudgingly concede their adopted roots; the old-timers, never.

Steve's parents had read Zane Grey and *The Virginian,* and had spent many summers on dude ranches in upstate New York. So they found a perfect ranch on the Big Horn River and started a herd of registered Hereford. They went broke. They refinanced and aimed at a breed of inferior beef cattle. The snows of '49 killed those. Steve's father determined that sheep were the way to go — all those double and triple births. Very investment-effective. The sheep sickened, or stumbled and fell into creeks where they drowned, or panicked like turkeys and smothered in heaps in fenced corners. It occurred then to the Mavrakis family that wheat doesn't stampede. All the fields were promptly hailed out before what looked to be a bounty harvest. Steve's father gave up and moved into town where he put his Columbia degree to work by getting a job managing the district office for the Bureau of Land Management.

All of that taught Steve to be wary of sure things.

And occasionally he wondered at the dreams. He had been very young when the blizzards killed the cattle. But though he didn't remember the National Guard dropping hay bales from silver C-47s to cattle in twelve-feet deep snow, he did recall for years after, the nightmares of herds of nonplussed animals futilely grazing barren ground before towering, slowly grinding, bluffs of ice.

The night after the crop duster terrified the sheep and seventeen had expired in paroxysms, Steve dreamed of brown men shrilling and shaking sticks and stampeding tusked, hairy monsters off a precipice and down hundreds of feet to a shallow stream.

Summer nights Steve woke sweating, having dreamed of reptiles slithering and warm waves beating on a ragged beach in the lower pasture. He sat straight, staring out the bedroom window, watching the giant ferns waver and solidify back into cottonwood and box elder.

The dreams came less frequently and vividly as he grew older. He willed that. They altered when the family moved into Fremont. After a while Steve still remembered he had had the dreams, but most of the details were forgotten.

At first the teachers in Fremont High School thought he was stupid. Steve was administered tests and thereafter was labeled an underachiever. He did what he had to do to get by. He barely qualified for the college-bound program, but then his normally easygoing father made threats. People asked him what he wanted to do, to be, and he answered honestly that he didn't know. Then he took a speech class. Drama fascinated him and he developed a passion for what theater the school offered. He played well in *Our Town* and *Arsenic and Old Lace* and *Harvey.* The drama coach looked at Steve's average height and average looks and average brown hair and eyes, and suggested at a hilarious cast party that he become either a character actor or an FBI agent.

By this time, the only dreams Steve remembered were sexual fantasies about girls he didn't dare ask on dates.

Ginger McClelland, seventeen. Who could blame her for feeling out of place? Having been born on the cusp of the school district's regulations, she was very nearly a year younger than her classmates. She was short. She thought of herself as a dwarf in a world of Snow Whites. It didn't help that her mother studiously offered words like "petite" and submitted that the most gorgeous clothes would fit a wearer under five feet, two inches. Secretly she hoped that in one mysterious night she would bloom and grow great, long legs like Carroll Dale. That never happened.

Being an exile in an alien land didn't help either. Though Carroll had befriended her, she had listened to the president of the pep club, the queen of Job's Daughters, and half the girls in her math class refer to her as "the foreign exchange student." Except that she would never be repatriated home; at least not until she graduated. Her parents had tired of living in Cupertino, California, and thought that running a Coast to Coast hardware franchise in Fremont would be an adventurous change of pace. They loved the open spaces, the mountains and free-flowing streams. Ginger wasn't so sure. Every day felt like she had stepped into a time machine. All the music on the radio was old. The movies that turned up at the town's one theater — forget it. The dancing at the hops was grotesque.

Ginger McClelland was the first person in Fremont — and perhaps in all of Wyoming — to use the adjective "bitchin'." It got her sent home from study hall and caused a bemused and confusing interview between her parents and the principal.

Ginger learned not to trust most of the boys who invited her out on dates. They all seemed to feel some sort of perverse mystique about California girls. But she did accept Steve Mavrakis's last-minute invitation to prom. He seemed safe enough.

Because Carroll and Ginger were friends, the four of them ended up double-dating in Paul's father's old maroon DeSoto that was customarily used for hauling fence posts and wire out to the pastures. After the dance, when nearly everyone else was heading to one of the sanctioned after-prom parties, Steve affably obtained from an older intermediary an entire case of chilled Hamms. Ginger and Carroll had brought along jeans and Pendleton shirts in their overnight bags and changed in the restroom at the Chevron station. Paul and Steve took off their white jackets and donned windbreakers. Then they all drove up into the Wind River Range. After they ran out of road, they hiked. It was very late and very dark. But they found a high mountain place where they huddled and drank beer and talked and necked.

They heard the voice of the wind and nothing else beyond that. They saw no lights of cars or outlying cabins. The isolation exhilarated them. They *knew* there was no one else for miles.

That was correct so far as it went.

Foam hissed and sprayed as Paul applied the church key to the cans. Above and below them, the wind broke like waves on the rocks.

"Mavrakis, you're going to the university, right?" said Paul.

Steve nodded in the dim moonlight, added, "I guess so."

"What're you going to take?" said Ginger, snuggling close and burping slightly on her beer.

"I don't know; engineering, I guess. If you're a guy and in the college-bound program, you end up taking engineering. So I figure that's it."

Paul said, "What kind?"

"Don't know. Maybe aerospace. I'll move to Seattle and make space-ships."

"That's neat," said Ginger. "Like in *The Outer Limits*. I wish we could get that here."

"You ought to be getting into hydraulic engineering," said Paul. "Water's going to be really big business not too long from now."

"I don't think I want to stick around Wyoming."

Carroll had been silently staring out over the valley. She turned back toward Steve and her eyes were pools of darkness. "You're really going to leave?"

"Yeah."

"And never come back?"

"Why should I?" said Steve. "I've had all the fresh air and wide open spaces I can use for a lifetime. You know something? I've never even seen the ocean." *And yet he had* felt *the ocean.* He blinked. "I'm getting out."

"Me too," said Ginger. "I'm going to stay with my aunt and uncle in L.A. I think I can probably get into the University of Southern California journalism school."

"Got the money?" said Paul.

"I'll get a scholarship."

"Aren't you leaving?" Steve said to Carroll.

"Maybe," she said. "Sometimes I think so, and then I'm not so sure."

"You'll come back even if you do leave," said Paul. "All of you'll come back."

"Says who?" Steve and Ginger said it almost simultaneously.

"The land gets into you," said Carroll. "Paul's dad says so."

"That's what he says." They all heard anger in Paul's voice. He opened another round of cans. Ginger tossed her empty away and it clattered down the rocks, a noise jarringly out of place.

"Don't," said Carroll. "We'll take the empties down in the sack."

"What's wrong?" said Ginger. "I mean, I . . ." Her voice trailed off and everyone was silent for a minute, two minutes, three.

"What about you, Paul?" said Carroll. "Where do you want to go? What do you want to do?"

"We talked about — " His voice sounded suddenly tightly controlled. "Damn it, I don't know now. If I come back, it'll be with an atomic bomb — "

"What?" said Ginger.

Paul smiled. At least Steve could see white teeth gleaming in the night. "As for what I want to do — " He leaned forward and whispered in Carroll's ear.

She said, "Jesus, Paul! We've got witnesses."

"What?" Ginger said again.

"Don't even ask you don't want to know." She made it one continuous sentence. Her teeth also were visible in the near-darkness. "Try that and I've got a mind to goodnight you the hard way."

"What're you talking about?" said Ginger.

Paul laughed. "Her grandmother."

"Charlie Goodnight was a big rancher around the end of the century," Carroll said. "He trailed a lot of cattle up from Texas. Trouble was, a lot of his expensive bulls weren't making out so well. Their testicles — "

"Balls," said Paul.

" — kept dragging on the ground," she continued. "The bulls got torn up and infected. So Charlie Goodnight started getting his bulls ready for the overland trip with some amateur surgery. He'd cut into the scrotum and shove the balls up into the bull. Then he'd stitch up the sack and there'd be no problem with high-centering. That's called goodnighting."

"See," said Paul. "There are ways to beat the land."

Carroll said, " 'You do what you've got to.' That's a quote from my father. Good pioneer stock."

"But not to me." Paul pulled her close and kissed her.

"Maybe we ought to explore the mountain a little," said Ginger to Steve. "You want to come with me?" She stared at Steve who was gawking at the sky as the moonlight suddenly vanished like a light switching off.

"Oh my God."

"What's wrong?" she said to the shrouded figure.

"I don't know — I mean, nothing, I guess." The moon appeared again. "Was that a cloud?"

"I don't see a cloud," said Paul, gesturing at the broad belt of stars. "The night's clear."

"Maybe you saw a UFO," said Carroll, her voice light.

"You okay?" Ginger touched his face. "Jesus, you're shivering." She held him tightly.

Steve's words were almost too low to hear. "It swam across the moon."

"What did?"

"I'm cold too," said Carroll. "Let's go back down." Nobody argued. Ginger remembered to put the metal cans into a paper sack and tied it to her belt with a hair ribbon. Steve didn't say anything more for a while, but the others all could hear his teeth chatter. When they were halfway down, the moon finally set beyond the valley rim. Farther on, Paul stepped on a loose patch of shale, slipped, cursed, began to slide beyond the lip of the sheer rock face. Carroll grabbed his arm and pulled him back.

"Thanks, Irene." His voice shook slightly, belying the tone of the words.

"Funny," she said.

"I don't get it," said Ginger.

Paul whistled a few bars of the song.

"Good night," said Carroll. "You do what you've got to."

"And I'm grateful for that." Paul took a deep breath. "Let's get down to the car."

When they were on the winding road and driving back toward Fremont, Ginger said, "What did you see up there, Steve?"

"Nothing. I guess I just remembered a dream."

"Some dream." She touched his shoulder. "You're still cold."

Carroll said, "So am I."

Paul took his right hand off the wheel to cover her hand. "We all are."

"I feel all right." Ginger sounded puzzled.

All the way into town, Steve felt he had drowned.

The Amble Inn in Thermopolis was built in the shadow of Round Top Mountain. On the slope above the Inn, huge letters formed from whitewashed stones proclaimed: WORLD'S LARGEST MINERAL HOT SPRING. Whether at night or noon, the inscription invariably reminded Steve of the Hollywood Sign. Early in his return from California, he realized the futility of jumping off the second letter *O*. The stones were laid flush with the steep pitch of the ground. Would-be suicides would only roll down the hill until they collided with the log side of the Inn.

On Friday and Saturday nights, the parking lot of the Amble Inn was filled almost exclusively with four-wheel-drive vehicles and conventional pickups. Most of them had black-enameled gun racks up in the rear window behind the seat. Steve's Chevy had a rack, but that was because he had bought the truck used. He had considered buying a toy rifle, one that shot caps or rubber darts, at a Penney's Christmas catalog sale. But like so many other projects, he never seemed to get around to it.

Tonight was the first Saturday night in June and Steve had money in his pocket from the paycheck he had cashed at Safeway. He had no reason to celebrate; but then he had no reason not to celebrate. So a little after nine he went to the Amble Inn to drink tequila hookers and listen to the music.

The Inn was uncharacteristically crowded for so early in the evening, but Steve secured a small table close to the dance floor when a guy threw up and his girl had to take him home. Dancing couples covered the floor though the headline act, Mountain Flyer, wouldn't be on until eleven. The warm-up group was a Montana band called the Great Falls Dead. They had more enthusiasm than talent, but they had the crowd dancing.

Steve threw down the shots, sucked limes, licked the salt, intermittently tapped his hand on the table to the music, and felt vaguely melancholy. Smoke drifted around him, almost as thick as the special-effects fog in a bad horror movie. The Inn's dance floor was in a dim, domed room lined with rough pine.

He suddenly stared, puzzled by a flash of near-recognition. He had been watching one dancer in particular, a tall woman with curly raven hair, who had danced with a succession of cowboys. When he looked at her face, he thought he saw someone familiar. When he looked at her body, he wondered whether she wore underwear beneath the wide-weave red knit dress.

The Great Falls Dead launched into *Good-hearted Woman* and the floor was instantly filled with dancers. Across the room, someone squealed, "Willieee!" This time the woman in red danced very close to Steve's table. Her high cheekbones looked hauntingly familiar. Her hair, he thought. If it were longer . . . She met his eyes and smiled at him.

The set ended, her partner drifted off toward the bar, but she remained standing beside his table. "Carroll?" he said. *"Carroll?"*

She stood there smiling, with right hand on hip. "I wondered when you'd figure it out."

Steve shoved his chair back and got up from the table. She moved very easily into his arms for a hug. "It's been a long time."

"It has."

"Fourteen years? Fifteen?"

"Something like that."

He asked her to sit at his table, and she did. She sipped a Campari-and-tonic as they talked. He switched to beer. The years unreeled. The Great Falls Dead pounded out a medley of country standards behind them.

" . . . I never should have married, Steve. I was wrong for Paul. He was wrong for me."

" . . . all the wrong reasons . . ."

" . . . did end up in a few made-for-TV movies. Bad stuff. I was always cast as the assistant manager in a holdup scene, or got killed by the werewolf right near the beginning. I think there's something like ninety percent of all actors who are unemployed at any given moment, so I said . . ."

"You really came back here? How long ago?"

" . . . to hell with it . . ."

"How long ago?"

" . . . and sort of slunk back to Wyoming. I don't know. Several years ago. How long were you married, anyway?"

" . . . a year more or less. What do you do here?"

" . . . beer's getting warm. Think I'll get a pitcher . . ."

"What do you do here?"

" . . . better cold. Not much. I get along. You . . ."

" . . . lived in Taos for a time. Then Santa Fe. Bummed around the Southwest a lot. A friend got me into photography. Then I was sick for a while and that's when I tried painting . . ."

" . . . landscapes of the Tetons to sell to tourists?"

"Hardly. A lot of landscapes, but trailer camps and oil fields and perspective vistas of I-80 across the Red Desert . . ."

"I tried taking pictures once . . . kept forgetting to load the camera."

" . . . and then I ended up half-owner of a gallery called Good Stuff. My partner throws pots."

" . . . must be dangerous . . ."

" . . . located on Main Street in Lander . . ."

" . . . going through. Think maybe I've seen it . . ."

"What do you do here?"

The comparative silence seemed to echo as the band ended its set. "Very little," said Steve. "I worked a while as a hand on the Two Bar. Spent some time being a roughneck in the fields up around Buffalo. I've got a pickup — do some short-hauling for local businessmen who don't want to hire a trucker. I ran a little pot. Basically I do whatever I can find. You know."

Carroll said, "Yes, I do know." The silence lengthened between them. Finally she said, "Why did you come back here? Was it because — "

" — because I'd failed?" Steve said, answering her hesitation. He looked at her steadily. "I thought about that a long time. I decided that I could fail anywhere, so I came back here." He shrugged. "I love it. I love the space."

"A lot of us have come back," Carroll said. "Ginger and Paul are here."

Steve was startled. He looked at the tables around them.

"Not tonight," said Carroll. "We'll see them tomorrow. They want to see you."

"Are you and Paul back — " he started to say.

She held up her palm. "Hardly. We're not exactly on the same wavelength. That's one thing that hasn't changed. He ended up being the sort of thing you thought you'd become."

Steve didn't remember what that was.

"Paul went to the School of Mines in Colorado. Now he's the chief exploratory geologist for Enerco."

"Not bad," said Steve.

"Not good," said Carroll. "He spent a decade in South America and the Middle East. Now he's come back home. He wants to gut the state like a fish."

"Coal?"

"And oil. And uranium. And gas. Enerco's got its thumb in a lot of holes." Her voice had lowered, sounded angry. "Anyway, we *are* having a reunion tomorrow, of sorts. And Ginger will be there."

Steve poured out the last of the beer. "I thought for sure she'd be in California."

"Never made it," said Carroll. "Scholarships fell through. Parents said they wouldn't support her if she went back to the West Coast — you know how one hundred and five percent converted immigrants are. So Ginger went to school in Laramie and ended up with a degree in elementary education. She did marry a

grad student in journalism. After the divorce five or six years later, she let him
keep the kid.''

Steve said, "So Ginger never got to be an ace reporter."

"Oh, she did. Now she's the best writer the *Salt Creek Gazette's* got.
Ginger's the darling of the environmental groups and the bane of the energy
corporations.''

"I'll be damned," he said. He accidentally knocked his glass off the table
with his forearm. Reaching to retrieve the glass, he knocked over the empty
pitcher.

"I think you're tired," Carroll said.

"I think you're right."

"You ought to go home and sack out." He nodded. "I don't want to drive all
the way back to Lander tonight," Carroll said. "Have you got room for me?"

When they reached the small house Steve rented off Highway 170, Carroll
grimaced at the heaps of dirty clothes making soft moraines in the living room.
"I'll clear off the couch," she said. "I've got a sleeping bag in my car."

Steve hesitated a long several seconds and lightly touched her shoulders.
"You don't have to sleep on the couch unless you want to. All those years ago
. . . You know, all through high school I had a crush on you? I was too shy to say
anything.''

She smiled and allowed his hands to remain. "I thought you were pretty nice
too. A little shy, but cute. Definitely an underachiever.''

They remained standing, faces a few inches apart, for a while longer.
"Well?" he said.

"It's been a lot of years," Carroll said. "I'll sleep on the couch."

Steve said disappointedly, "Not even out of charity?"

"Especially not for charity." She smiled. "But don't discount the future."
She kissed him gently on the lips.

Steve slept soundly that night. He dreamed of sliding endlessly through a
warm, fluid current. It was not a nightmare. Not even when he realized he had fins
rather than hands and feet.

Morning brought rain.

When he awoke, the first thing Steve heard was the drumming of steady
drizzle on the roof. The daylight outside the window was filtered gray by the
sheets of water running down the pane. Steve leaned off the bed, picked up his
watch from the floor, but it had stopped. He heard the sounds of someone moving
in the living room and called, "Carroll? You up?"

Her voice was a soft contralto. "I am."

"What time is it?"

"Just after eight."

Steve started to get out of bed, but groaned and clasped the crown of his head
with both hands. Carroll stood framed in the doorway and looked sympathetic.
"What time's the reunion?" he said.

"When we get there. I called Paul a little earlier. He's tied up with some sort of meeting in Casper until late afternoon. He wants us to meet him in Shoshoni."

"What about Ginger?"

They both heard the knock on the front door. Carroll turned her head away from the bedroom, then looked back at Steve. "Right on cue," she said. "Ginger didn't want to wait until tonight." She started for the door, said back over her shoulder, "You might want to put on some clothes."

Steve pulled on his least filthy jeans and a sweatshirt labeled AMAX TOWN LEAGUE VOLLEYBALL across the chest. He heard the front door open and close, and words murmured in his living room. When he exited the bedroom he found Carroll talking on the couch with a short blonde stranger who only slightly resembled the long-ago image he'd packed in his mind. Her hair was long and tied in a braid. Her gaze was direct and more inquisitive than he remembered.

She looked up at him and said, "I like the mustache. You look a hell of a lot better now than you ever did then."

"Except for the mustache," Steve said, "I could say the same."

The two women seemed amazed when Steve negotiated the disaster area that was the kitchen and extracted eggs and Chinese vegetables from the refrigerator. He served the huge omelet with toast and freshly brewed coffee in the living room. They all balanced plates on laps.

"Do you ever read the Gazoo?" said Ginger.

"Gazoo?"

"The *Salt Creek Gazette,*" said Carroll.

Steve said, "I don't read any papers."

"I just finished a piece on Paul's company," said Ginger.

"Enerco?" Steve refilled all their cups.

Ginger shook her head. "A wholly owned subsidiary called Native American Resources. Pretty clever, huh?" Steve looked blank. "Not a poor damned Indian in the whole operation. The name's strictly sham while the company's been picking up an incredible number of mineral leases on the reservation. Paul's been concentrating on an enormous new coal field his teams have mapped out. It makes up a substantial proportion of the reservation's best lands."

"Including some sacred sites," said Carroll.

"Nearly a million acres," said Ginger. "That's more than a thousand square miles."

"The land's never the same," said Carroll, "no matter how much goes into reclamation, no matter how tight the EPA says they are."

Steve looked from one to the other. "I may not read the papers," he said, "But no one's holding a gun to anyone else's head."

"Might as well be," said Ginger. "If the Native American Resources deal goes through, the mineral royalty payments to the tribes'll go up precipitously."

Steve spread his palms. "Isn't that good?"

Ginger shook her head vehemently. "It's economic blackmail to keep the tribes from developing their own resources at their own pace."

"Slogans," said Steve. "The country needs the energy. If the tribes don't have the investment capital — "

"They *would* if they weren't bought off with individual royalty payments."

"The tribes have a choice — "

" — with the prospect of immediate gain dangled in front of them by NAR."

"I can tell it's Sunday," said Steve, "even if I haven't been inside a church door in fifteen years. I'm being preached at."

"If you'd get off your ass and think," said Ginger, "nobody'd have to lecture you."

Steve grinned. "I don't think with my ass."

"Look," said Carroll. "It's stopped raining."

Ginger glared at Steve. He took advantage of Carroll's diversion and said, "Anyone for a walk?"

The air outside was cool and rain-washed. It soothed tempers. The trio walked through the fresh morning along the cottonwood-lined creek. Meadowlarks sang. The rain front had moved far to the east; the rest of the sky was bright blue.

"Hell of a country, isn't it?" said Steve.

"Not for much longer if — " Ginger began.

"Gin," Carroll said warningly.

They strolled for another hour, angling south where they could see the hills as soft as blanket folds. The tree-lined draws snaked like green veins down the hillsides. The earth, Steve thought, seemed gathered, somehow expectant.

"How's Danny?" Carroll said to Ginger.

"He's terrific. Kid wants to become an astronaut." A grin split her face. "Bob's letting me have him for August."

"Look at that," said Steve, pointing.

The women looked. "I don't see anything," said Ginger.

"Southeast," Steve said. "Right above the head of the canyon."

"There — I'm not sure." Carroll shaded her eyes. "I thought I saw something, but it was just a shadow."

"Nothing there," said Ginger.

"Are you both blind?" said Steve, astonished. "There was something in the air. It was dark and cigar-shaped. It was there when I pointed."

"Sorry," said Ginger, "didn't see a thing."

"Well, it *was* there," Steve said, disgruntled.

Carroll continued to stare off toward the pass. "I saw it too, but just for a second. I didn't see where it went."

"Damnedest thing. I don't think it was a plane. It just sort of cruised along, and then it was gone."

"All I saw was something blurry," Carroll said. "Maybe it was a UFO."

"Oh, you guys," Ginger said with an air of dawning comprehension. "Just like prom night, right? Just a joke."

Steve slowly shook his head. "I really saw something then, and I saw this now. This time Carroll saw it too." She nodded in agreement.

The wind started to rise from the north, kicking up early spring weeds that had already died and begun to dry.

"I'm getting cold," said Ginger. "Let's go back to the house."

"Steve," said Carroll, "you're shaking."

They hurried him back across the land.

PHOSPHORIC FORMATION
PERMIAN
225 – 270 MILLION YEARS

They rested for a while at the house; drank coffee and talked of the past, of what had happened and what had not. Then Carroll suggested they leave for the reunion. After a small confusion, Ginger rolled up the windows and locked her Saab and Carroll locked her Pinto.

"I hate having to do this," said Carroll.

"There's no choice any more," Steve said. "Too many people around now who don't know the rules."

The three of them got into Steve's pickup. In fifteen minutes they had traversed the doglegs of U.S. 20 through Thermopolis and crossed the Big Horn River. They passed the massive mobile-home park with its trailers and RV's sprawling in carapaced glitter.

The flood of hot June sunshine washed over them as they passed between the twin bluffs, red with iron, and descended into the miles and years of canyon.

TENSLEEP FORMATION
PENNSYLVANIAN
270 – 310 MILLION YEARS

On both sides of the canyon, the rock layers lay stacked like sections from a giant meat slicer. In the pickup cab, the passengers had been listening to the news on KTWO. As the canyon deepened, the reception faded until only a trickle of static came from the speaker. Carroll clicked the radio off.

"They're screwed," said Ginger.

"Not necessarily." Carroll, riding shotgun, stared out the window at the slopes of flowers the same color as the bluffs. "The BIA's still got hearings. There'll be another tribal vote."

Ginger said again, "They're screwed. Money doesn't just talk — it makes obscene phone calls, you know? Paul's got this one bagged. You know Paul — I know him just about as well. Son of a bitch."

"Sorry there's no music," said Steve. "Tape player busted a while back and I've never fixed it."

They ignored him. "Damn it," said Ginger. "It took almost fifteen years, but I've learned to love this country."

"I know that," said Carroll.

No one said anything for a while. Steve glanced to his right and saw tears running down Ginger's cheeks. She glared back at him defiantly. "There's Kleenexes in the glove box," he said.

MADISON FORMATION
MISSISSIPPIAN
310– 350 MILLION YEARS

The slopes of the canyon became more heavily forested. The walls were all shades of green, deeper green where the runoff had found channels. Steve felt time collect in the great gash in the earth, press inward.

"I don't feel so hot," said Ginger.

"Want to stop for a minute?"

She nodded and put her hand over her mouth.

Steve pulled the pickup over across both lanes. The Chevy skidded slightly as it stopped on the graveled turnout. Steve turned off the key and in the sudden silence they heard only the light wind and the tickings as the Chevy's engine cooled.

"Excuse me," said Ginger. They all got out of the cab. Ginger quickly moved through the Canadian thistle and the currant bushes and into the trees beyond. Steve and Carroll heard her throwing up.

"She had an affair with Paul," Carroll said casually. "Not too long ago. He's an extremely attractive man." Steve said nothing. "Ginger ended it. She still feels the tension." Carroll strolled over to the side of the thistle patch and hunkered down. "Look at this."

Steve realized how complex the ground cover was. Like the rock cliffs, it was layered. At first he saw among the sunflowers and dead dandelions only the wild sweetpeas with their blue blossoms like spades with the edges curled inward.

"Look closer," said Carroll.

Steve saw the hundreds of tiny purple moths swooping and swarming only inches from the earth. The creatures were the same color as the low purple blooms he couldn't identify. Intermixed were white, bell-shaped blossoms with leaves that looked like primeval ferns.

"It's like going back in time," said Carroll. "It's a whole nearly invisible world we never see."

The shadow crossed them with an almost subliminal flash, but they both looked up. Between them and the sun had been the wings of a large bird. It circled in a tight orbit, banking steeply when it approached the canyon wall. The creature's belly was dirty white, muting to an almost black on its back. It seemed to Steve that the bird's eye was fixed on them. The eye was a dull black, like unpolished obsidian.

"That's one I've never seen," said Carroll. "What is it?"

"I don't know. The wingspread's got to be close to ten feet. The markings are strange. Maybe it's a hawk? An eagle?"

The bird's beak was heavy and blunt, curved slightly. As it circled, wings barely flexing to ride the thermals, the bird was eerily silent.

"What's it doing?" said Carroll.

"Watching us?" said Steve. He jumped as a hand touched his shoulder.

"Sorry," said Ginger. "I feel better now." She tilted her head back at the great circling bird. "I have a feeling our friend wants us to leave."

They left. The highway wound around a massive curtain of stone in which red splashed down through the strata like dinosaur blood. Around the curve, Steve swerved to miss a deer dead on the pavement — half a deer, rather. The animal's body had been truncated cleanly just in front of its haunches.

"Jesus," said Ginger. "What did that?"

"Must have been a truck," said Steve. "An eighteen-wheeler can really tear things up when it's barreling."

Carroll looked back toward the carcass and the sky beyond. "Maybe that's what our friend was protecting."

GROS VENTRE FORMATION

CAMBRIAN

500 – 600 MILLION YEARS

"You know, this was all under water once," said Steve. He was answered only with silence. "Just about all of Wyoming was covered with an ancient sea. That accounts for a lot of the coal." No one said anything. "I think it was called the Sundance Sea. You know, like in the Sundance Kid. Some Exxon geologist told me that in a bar."

He turned and looked at the two women. And stared. And turned back to the road blindly. And then stared at them again. It seemed to Steve that he was looking at a double exposure, or a triple exposure, or — he couldn't count all the overlays. He started to say something, but could not. He existed in a silence that was also stasis, the death of all motion. He could only see.

Carroll and Ginger faced straight ahead. They looked as they had earlier in the afternoon. They also looked as they had fifteen years before. Steve saw them *in process,* lines blurred. And Steve saw skin merge with feathers, and then scales. He saw gill openings appear, vanish, reappear on textured necks.

And then both of them turned to look at him. Their heads swiveled slowly, smoothly. Four reptilian eyes watched him, unblinking and incurious.

Steve wanted to look away.

The Chevy's tires whined on the level blacktop. The sign read:

SPEED ZONE AHEAD

35 MPH

"Are you awake?" said Ginger.

Steve shook his head to clear it. "Sure," he said. "You know that reverie you sometimes get into when you're driving? When you can drive miles without consciously thinking about it, and then suddenly you realize what's happened?"

Ginger nodded.

"That's what happened."

The highway passed between modest frame houses, gas stations, motels. They entered Shoshoni.

There was a brand-new WELCOME TO SHOSHONI sign, as yet without bullet holes. The population figure had again been revised upward. "Want to bet on when they break another thousand?" said Carroll.

Ginger shook her head silently.

Steve pulled up to the stop sign. "Which way?"

Carroll said, "Go left."

"I think I've got it." Steve saw the half-ton truck with the Enerco decal and NATIVE AMERICAN RESOURCES DIVISION labeled below that on the door. It was parked in front of the Yellowstone Drugstore. "Home of the world's greatest shakes and malts," said Steve. "Let's go."

The interior of the Yellowstone had always reminded him of nothing so much as an old-fashioned pharmacy blended with the interior of the café in *Bad Day at Black Rock*. They found Paul at a table near the fountain counter in the back. He was nursing a chocolate malted.

He looked up, smiled, said, "I've gained four pounds this afternoon. If you'd been any later, I'd probably have become diabetic."

Paul looked far older than Steve had expected. Ginger and Carroll both appeared older than they had been a decade and a half before, but Paul seemed to have aged thirty years in fifteen. The star quarterback's physique had gone a bit to pot. His face was creased with lines emphasized by the leathery curing of skin that has been exposed years to wind and hot sun. Paul's hair, black as coal, was streaked with firn lines of glacial white. His eyes, Steve thought, looked tremendously old.

He greeted Steve with a warm handclasp. Carroll received a gentle hug and a kiss on the cheek. Ginger got a warm smile and a hello. The four of them sat down and the fountain-man came over. "Chocolate all around?" Paul said.

"Vanilla shake," said Ginger.

Steve sensed a tension at the table that seemed to go beyond dissolved marriages and terminated affairs. He wasn't sure what to say after all the years, but Paul saved him the trouble. Smiling and soft-spoken, Paul gently interrogated him.

So what have you been doing with yourself?

Really?

How did that work out?

That's too bad; then what?

What about afterward?

And you came back?

How about since?

What do you do now?

Paul sat back in the scrolled-wire ice-cream-parlor chair, still smiling, playing with the plastic straw. He tied knots in the straw and then untied them.

"Do you know," said Paul, "that this whole complicated reunion of the four of us is not a matter of chance?"

Steve studied the other man. Paul's smile faded to impassivity. "I'm not that paranoid," Steve said. "It didn't occur to me."

"It's a setup."

Steve considered that silently.

"It didn't take place until after I had tossed the yarrow stalks a considerable number of times," said Paul. His voice was wry. "I don't know what the official company policy on such irrational behavior is, but it all seemed right under extraordinary circumstances. I told Carroll where she could likely find you and left the means of contact up to her."

The two women waited and watched silently. Carroll's expression was, Steve thought, one of concern. Ginger looked apprehensive. "So what is it?" he said. "What kind of game am I in?"

"It's no game," said Carroll quickly. "We need you."

"You know what I thought ever since I met you in Miss Gorman's class?" said Paul. "You're not a loser. You've just needed some — direction."

Steve said impatiently, "Come on."

"It's true." Paul set down the straw. "Why we need you is because you seem to see things most others can't see."

Time's predator hunts.

Years scatter before her like a school of minnows surprised. The rush of her passage causes eons to eddy. Wind sweeps down the canyon with the roar of combers breaking on the sand. The moon, full and newly risen, exerts its tidal force.

Moonlight flashes on the slash of teeth.

She drives for the surface not out of rational decision. All blunt power embodied in smooth motion, she simply is what she is.

Steve sat without speaking. Finally he said vaguely, "Things."

"That's right. You see things. It's an ability."

"I don't know . . ."

"We think *we* do. We all remember that night after prom. And there were other times, back in school. None of us has seen you since we all played scatter-geese, but I've had the resources, through the corporation, to do some checking. The issue didn't come up until recently. In the last month, I've read your school records, Steve. I've read your psychiatric history."

"That must have taken some trouble," said Steve. "Should I feel flattered?"

"Tell him," said Ginger. "Tell him what this is all about."

"Yeah," said Steve. "Tell me."

For the first time in the conversation, Paul hesitated. "Okay," he finally said. "We're hunting a ghost on the Wind River."

"Say again?"

"That's perhaps poor terminology." Paul looked uncomfortable. "But what we're looking for is a presence, some sort of extranatural phenomenon."

" 'Ghost' is a perfectly good word," said Carroll.

"Better start from the beginning," said Steve.

When Paul didn't answer immediately, Carroll said, "I know you don't read the papers. Ever listen to the radio?"

Steve shook his head. "Not much."

"About a month ago, an Enerco mineral survey party on the Wind River got the living daylights scared out of them."

"Leave out what they saw," said Paul. "I'd like to leave a control factor in."

"It wasn't just the Enerco people. Others have seen it, both Indians and Anglos. The consistency of the witnesses has been remarkable. If you haven't heard about this at the bars, Steve, you must have been asleep."

"I haven't been all that social for a while," said Steve. "I did hear that someone's trying to scare the oil and coal people off the reservation."

"Not someone," said Paul. "Some*thing*. I'm convinced of that now."

"A ghost," said Steve.

"A presence."

"There're rumors," said Carroll, "that the tribes have revived the Ghost Dance — "

"Just a few extremists," said Paul.

" — to conjure back an avenger from the past who will drive every white out of the country."

Steve knew of the Ghost Dance, had read of the Paiute mystic Wovoka who, in 1888, had claimed that in a vision the spirits had promised the return of the buffalo and the restoration to the Indians of their ancestral lands. The Plains tribes had danced assiduously the Ghost Dance to ensure this. Then in 1890 the United States government suppressed the final Sioux uprising and, except for a few scattered incidents, that was that. Discredited, Wovoka survived to die in the midst of the Great Depression.

"I have it on good authority," said Paul, "that the Ghost Dance was revived *after* the presence terrified the survey crew."

"That really doesn't matter," Carroll said. "Remember prom night? I've checked the newspaper morgues in Fremont and Lander and Riverton. There've been strange sightings for more than a century."

"That was then," said Paul. "The problem now is that the tribes are infinitely more restive, and my people are actually getting frightened to go out into the field." His voice took on a bemused tone. "Arab terrorists couldn't do it, civil wars didn't bother them, but a damned ghost is scaring the wits out of them — literally.''

"Too bad," said Ginger. She did not sound regretful.

Steve looked at the three gathered around the table. He knew he did not understand all the details and nuances of the love and hate and trust and broken affections. "I can understand Paul's concern," he said. "But why the rest of you?"

The women exchanged glances. "One way or another," said Carroll, "we're all tied together. I think it includes you, Steve."

"Maybe," said Ginger soberly. "Maybe not. She's an artist. I'm a journalist. We've all got our reasons for wanting to know more about what's up there."

"In the past few years," said Carroll, "I've caught a tremendous amount of Wyoming in my paintings. Now I want to capture this too."

Conversation languished. The soda-fountain-man looked as though he were unsure whether to solicit a new round of malteds.

"What now?" Steve said.

"If you'll agree," said Paul, "we're going to go back up into the Wind River Canyon to search."

"So what am I? Some sort of damned occult Geiger counter?"

Ginger said, "It's a nicer phrase than calling yourself bait."

"Jesus," Steve said. "That doesn't reassure me much." He looked from one to the next. "Control factor or not, give me some clue what we're going to look for."

Everyone looked at Paul. Eventually he shrugged and said, "You know the Highway Department signs in the canyon? The geological time chart you travel when you're driving U.S. 20?"

Steve nodded.

"We're looking for a relic of the ancient inland sea."

After the sun sank in blood in the west, they drove north and watched dusk unfold into the splendor of the night sky.

"I'll always marvel at it," said Paul. "Do you know, you can see three times as many stars in the sky here as you can from any city?"

"It scares the tourists sometimes," said Carroll.

Ginger said, "It won't after a few more of those coal-fired generating plants are built."

Paul chuckled. "I thought they were preferable to your nemesis, the nukes."

Ginger was sitting with Steve in the back seat of the Enerco truck. Her words were controlled and even, "There are alternatives to both those."

"Try supplying power to the rest of the country with them before the next century," Paul said. He braked suddenly as a jackrabbit darted into the bright cones of light. The rabbit made it across the road.

"Nobody actually *needs* air conditioners," said Ginger.

"I won't argue that point," Paul said. "You'll just have to argue with the reality of all the people who think they do."

Ginger lapsed into silence. Carroll said, "I suppose you should be congratulated for the tribal council vote today. We heard about it on the news."

"It's not binding," said Paul. "When it finally goes through, we hope it will whittle the fifty percent jobless rate on the reservation."

"It sure as hell won't!" Ginger burst out. "Higher mineral royalties mean more incentive not to have a career."

Paul laughed. "Are you blaming me for being the chicken, or the egg?"

No one answered him.

"I'm not a monster," he said.

"I don't think you are," said Steve.

"I know it puts me in a logical trap, but I think I'm doing the right thing."

"All right," said Ginger. "I won't take any easy shots. At least, I'll try."

From the back seat, Steve looked around his uneasy allies and hoped to hell that someone had brought aspirin. Carroll had aspirin in her handbag and Steve washed it down with beer from Paul's cooler.

GRANITE

PRE-CAMBRIAN

600+ MILLION YEARS

The moon had risen by now, a full, icy disc. The highway curved around a formation that looked like a vast, layered birthday cake. Cedar provided spectral candles.

"I've never believed in ghosts," said Steve. He caught the flicker of Paul's eyes in the rearview mirror and knew the geologist was looking at him.

"There are ghosts," said Paul, "and there are ghosts. In spectroscopy, ghosts are false readings. In television, ghost images — "

"What about the kind that haunt houses?"

"In television," Paul continued, "a ghost is a reflected electronic image arriving at the antenna some interval after the desired wave."

"And are they into groans and chains?"

"Some people are better antennas than others, Steve."

Steve fell silent.

"There is a theory," said Paul, "that molecular structures, no matter how altered by process, still retain some sort of 'memory' of their original form."

"Ghosts."

"If you like." He stared ahead at the highway and said, as if musing, "When an ancient organism becomes fossilized, even the DNA patterns that determine its structure are preserved in the stone."

GALLATIN FORMATION

CAMBRIAN

500 – 600 MILLION YEARS

Paul shifted into a lower gear as the half-ton began to climb one of the long, gradual grades. Streaming black smoke and bellowing like a great saurian lumbering into extinction, an eighteen-wheel semi with oil field gear on its back passed them, forcing Paul part of the way onto the right shoulder. Trailing a dopplered call from its airhorn, the rig disappeared into the first of three short highway tunnels quarried out of the rock.

"One of yours?" said Ginger.

"Nope."

"Maybe he'll crash and burn."

"I'm sure he's just trying to make a living," said Paul mildly.

"Raping the land's a living?" said Ginger. "Cannibalizing the past is a living?"

"Shut up, Gin." Quietly, Carroll said, "Wyoming didn't do anything to your family, Paul. Whatever was done, people did it."

"The land gets into the people," said Paul.

"That isn't the only thing that defines them."

"This always has been a fruitless argument," said Paul. "It's a dead past."

"If the past is dead," Steve said, "then why are we driving up this cockamamie canyon?"

AMSDEN FORMATION

PENNSYLVANIAN

270 – 310 MILLION YEARS

Boysen Reservoir spread to their left, rippled surface glittering in the moonlight. The road hugged the eastern edge. Once the crimson taillights of the oil field truck had disappeared in the distance, they encountered no other vehicle.

"Are we just going to drive up and down Twenty all night?" said Steve. "Who brought the plan?" He did not feel flippant, but he had to say something. He felt the burden of time.

"We'll go where the survey crew saw the presence," Paul said. "It's just a few more miles."

"And then?"

"Then we walk. It should be at least as interesting as our hike prom night."

Steve sensed that a lot of things were almost said by each of them at that point.

I didn't know then . . .

Nor do I know for sure yet.

I'm seeking . . .

What?

Time's flowed. I want to know where now, finally, to direct it.

"Who would have thought . . ." said Ginger.

Whatever was thought, nothing more was said.

The headlights picked out the reflective green-and-white Highway Department sign. "We're there," said Paul. "Somewhere on the right there ought to be a dirt access road."

SHARKTOOTH FORMATION
CRETACEOUS
100 MILLION YEARS

"Are we going to use a net?" said Steve. "Tranquilizer darts? What?"

"I don't think we can catch a ghost in a net," said Carroll. "You catch a ghost in your soul."

A small smile curved Paul's lips. "Think of this as the Old West. We're only a scouting party. Once we observe whatever's up here, we'll figure out how to get rid of it."

"That won't be possible," said Carroll.

"Why do you say that?"

"I don't know," she said. "I jsut feel it."

"Women's intuition?" He said it lightly.

"My intuition."

"Anything's possible," said Paul.

"If we really thought you could destroy it," said Ginger, "I doubt either of us would be up here with you."

Paul had stopped the truck to lock the front hubs into four-wheel drive. Now the vehicle clanked and lurched over rocks and across potholes eroded by the spring rain. The road twisted tortuously around series of barely-graded switchbacks. Already they had climbed hundreds of feet above the canyon floor. They could see no lights anywhere below.

"Very scenic," said Steve. If he had wanted to, he could have reached out the right passenger's side window and touched the porous rock. Pine branches whispered along the paint on the left side.

"Thanks to Native American Resources," said Ginger, "this is the sort of country that'll go."

"For Christ's sake," said Paul, finally sounding angry. "I'm *not* the anti-Christ."

"I know that." Ginger's voice softened. "I've loved you, remember? Probably I still do. Is there no way?"

The geologist didn't answer.

"Paul?"

"We're just about there," he said. The grade moderated and he shifted to a higher gear.

"Paul — " Steve wasn't sure whether he actually said the word or not. He closed his eyes and saw glowing fires, opened them again and wasn't sure what he saw. He felt the past, vast and primeval, rush over him like a tide. It filled his nose and mouth, his lungs, his brain. It —

"Oh my God!"

Someone screamed.

"Let go!"

The headlight beams twitched crazily as the truck skidded toward the edge of a sheer dark drop. Both Paul and Carroll wrestled for the wheel. For an instant, Steve wondered whether both of them or, indeed, either of them were trying to turn the truck back from the dark.

Then he saw the great, bulky, streamlined form coasting over the slope toward them. He had the impression of smooth power, immense and inexorable. The dead stare from flat black eyes, each one inches across, fixed them like insects in amber.

"Paul!" Steve heard his own voice. He heard the word echo and then it was swallowed up by the crashing waves. He felt unreasoning terror, but more than that, he felt — awe. What he beheld was juxtaposed on this western canyon, but yet it was not out of place. *Genius loci,* guardian, the words hissed like the surf.

It swam toward them, impossibly gliding on powerful gray-black fins.

Brakes screamed, a tire blew out like a gunshot.

Steve watched its jaws open in front of the windshield; the snout pulling up and back, the lower jaw thrusting forward. The maw could have taken in a heifer. The teeth glared white in reflected light, white with serrated razor-edges. Its teeth were as large as shovel blades.

"Paul!"

The Enerco truck fish-tailed a final time; then toppled sideways into the dark. It fell, caromed off something massive and unseen, and began to roll.

Steve had time for one thought. *Is it going to hurt?*

When the truck came to rest, it was upright. Steve groped toward the window and felt rough bark rather than glass. They were wedged against a pine.

The silence astonished him. That there was no fire astonished him. That he was alive — "Carroll?" he said. "Ginger? Paul?" For a moment, no one spoke.

"I'm here," said Carroll, muffled, from the front of the truck. "Paul's on top of me. Or somebody is. I can't tell."

"Oh God, I hurt," said Ginger from beside Steve. "My shoulder hurts."

"Can you move your arm?" said Steve.

"A little, but it hurts."

"Okay," Steve leaned forward across the front seat. He didn't feel anything like grating, broken bone-ends in himself. His fingers touched flesh. Some of it was sticky with fluid. Gently he pulled whom he assumed was Paul from Carroll beneath. She moaned and struggled upright.

"There should be a flashlight in the glove box," he said.

The darkness was almost complete. Steve could see only vague shapes inside the truck. When Carroll switched on the flashlight, they realized the truck was buried in thick, resilient brush. Carroll and Ginger stared back at him. Ginger looked as if she might be in shock. Paul slumped on the front seat. The angle of his neck was all wrong.

His eyes opened and he tried to focus. Then he said something. They couldn't understand him. Paul tried again. They made out, "Goodnight, Irene." Then he said, "Do what you have . . ." His eyes remained open, but all the life went out of them.

Steve and the women stared at one another as though they were accomplices. The moment crystallized and shattered. He braced himself as best he could and kicked with both feet at the rear door. The brush allowed the door to swing open one foot, then another. Carroll had her door open at almost the same time. It took another few minutes to get Ginger out. They left Paul in the truck.

They huddled on a naturally terraced ledge about halfway between the summit and the canyon floor. There was a roar and bright lights for a few minutes when a Burlington Northern freight came down the tracks on the other side of the river. It would have done no good to shout and wave their arms, so they didn't.

No one seemed to have broken any bones. Ginger's shoulder was apparently separated. Carroll had a nosebleed. Steve's head felt as though he'd been walloped with a two-by-four.

"It's not cold," he said. "If we have to, we can stay in the truck. No way we're going to get down at night. In the morning we can signal people on the road."

Ginger started to cry and they both held her. "I saw something," she said. "I couldn't tell — what was it?"

Steve hesitated. He had a hard time separating his dreams from Paul's theories. The two did not now seem mutually exclusive. He still heard the echoing thunder of ancient gulfs. "I'm guessing it's something that lived here a hundred million years ago," he finally said. "It lived in the inland sea and died here. The sea left, but it never did."

"A native . . . " Ginger said and trailed off. Steve touched her forehead; it felt feverish. "I finally saw," she said. "Now I'm a part of it." In a smaller voice, "Paul." Starting awake like a child from a nightmare, "Paul?"

"He's — all right now," said Carroll, her even tone plainly forced.

"No, he's not," said Ginger. "He's not." She was silent for as time. "He's dead." Tears streamed down her face. "It won't really stop the coal leases, will it?"

"Probably not."

"Politics," Ginger said wanly. "Politics and death. What the hell difference does any of it make now?"

No one answered her.

Steve turned toward the truck in the brush. He suddenly remembered from his childhood how he had hoped everyone he knew, everyone he loved, would live forever. He hadn't wanted change. He hadn't wanted to recognize time. He remembered the split-second image of Paul and Carroll struggling to control the wheel. "The land," he said, feeling the sorrow. "It doesn't forgive."

"That's not true." Carroll slowly shook her head. "The land just *is*. The land doesn't care."

"I care," said Steve.

Amazingly, Ginger started to go to sleep. They laid her down gently on the precipice, covered her with Steve's jacket, and cradled her head, stroking her hair. "Look," she said. "Look." As the moon illuminated the glowing sea.

Far below them, a fin broke the dark surface of the forest.

By now, probably everyone knows that that mysterious figure James Tiptree, Jr. – for many years isolate and closemouthed enough to qualify as the B. Traven of science fiction – is really a pseudonym of Dr. Alice Sheldon, a semiretired experimental psychologist who also writes under the name Raccoona Sheldon. As Tiptree, Dr. Sheldon won two Nebula and two Hugo awards (she also won a Nebula Award as Raccoona Sheldon), and established a reputation as one of the very best short-story writers of the seventies. She has published four books as Tiptree: the well-received collections Ten Thousand Light Years from Home *(Ace),* Warmworlds and Otherwise *(Ballantine), and* Star Songs of an Old Primate *(Del Rey), and a novel,* Up the Walls of the World *(Berkley). As Raccoona Sheldon, her Nebula-winning story "The Screwfly Solution" was in our* Seventh Annual Collection.

Here she shows us a melancholy vision of the end of the human race as we know it, as humanity is seduced into abandoning corporeal existence and merging into a metaphysical alien River that sweeps them away from the Earth forever, and relates the haunting story of those few people who choose to remain behind.

JAMES TIPTREE, JR.
Slow Music

Caoilte tossing his burning hair
And Niamh calling "Away, come away;
Empty your heart of its mortal dream.
. . . We come between man and the deed of his hand,
We come between him and the hope of his heart."

— W. B. YEATS

Lights came on as Jakko walked down the lawn past the house; elegantly concealed spots and floods which made the night into a great intimate room. Overhead the big conifers formed a furry nave drooping toward the black lake below the bluff ahead. This had been a beloved home, he saw; every luxurious device was subdued to preserve the beauty of the forested shore. He walked on a carpet of violets and mosses, in his hand the map that had guided him here from the city.

It was the stillness before dawn. A long-winged night bird swirled in to catch a last moth in the dome of light. Before him shone a bright spearpoint. Jakko saw it was the phosphorescent tip of a mast against the stars. He went down

129

velvety steps to find a small sailboat floating at the dock like a silver leaf reflected on a dark mirror.

In silence he stepped on board, touched the mast.

A gossamer sail spread its fan, the mooring parted soundlessly. The dawn breeze barely filled the sail, but the craft moved smoothly out, leaving a glassy line of wake. Jakko half-poised to jump; he knew nothing of such playtoys, he should go back and find another boat. As he did so, the shore lights went out, leaving him in darkness. He turned and saw Regulus rising ahead where the channel must be. Still, this was not the craft for him. He tugged at the tiller and sail, meaning to turn it back.

But the little boat ran smoothly on, and then he noticed the lights of a small computer glowing by the mast. He relaxed; this was no toy, the boat was fully programmed and he could guess what the course must be. He stood examining the sky, a statue-man gliding across reflected night.

The eastern horizon changed, veiled its stars as he neared it. He could see the channel now, a silvery cut straight ahead between dark banks. The boat ran over glittering shallows where something splashed hugely, and headed into the shining lane. As it did so, all silver changed to lead and the stars were gone. Day was coming. A great pearl-colored blush spread upward before him, developed bands of lavender and rays of coral-gold fire melting to green iridescence overhead. The boat was now gliding on a ribbon of fiery light between black silhouetted banks. Jakko looked back and saw dazzling cloud-cities heaped behind him in the west. The vast imminence of sunrise. He sighed aloud.

He understood that all this demonstration of glory was nothing but the effects of dust and vapor in the thin skin of air around a small planet, whereon he crawled wingless. No vastness brooded; the planet was merely turning with him into the rays of its mediocre primary. His family, everyone, knew that on the River he would encounter the galaxy itself in glory. Suns beyond count, magnificence to which this was nothing. And yet — and yet to him this was not nothing. It was intimately his, man-sized. He made an ambiguous sound in his throat. He resented the trivialization of this beauty, and he resented being moved by it. So he passed along, idly holding the sailrope like a man leashing the living wind, his face troubled and very young.

The little craft ran on unerringly, threading the winding sheen of the canal. As the sun rose, Jakko began to hear a faint drone ahead. The sea surf. He thought of the persons who must have made this voyage before him: the ship's family, savoring their final days of mortality. A happy voyage, a picnic. The thought reminded him that he was hungry; the last ground-car's synthesizer had been faulty.

He tied the rope and searched. The boat had replenished its water, but there was only one food-bar. Jakko lay down in the cushioned well and ate and drank comfortably, while the sky turned turquoise and then cobalt. Presently they emerged into an enormous lagoon and began to run south between low islands. Jakko trailed his hand and tasted brackish salt. When the boat turned east again and made for a seaward opening, he became doubly certain. The craft was programmed for the River, like almost everything else on the world he knew.

Sure enough, the tiny bark ran through an inlet and straight out into the chop beyond a long beach, extruded outriggers, and passed like a cork over the reef-foam onto the deep green swells beyond. Here it pitched once and steadied; Jakko guessed it had thrust down a keel. Then it turned south and began to run along outside the reef, steady as a knife-cut with the wind on its quarter. Going Riverward for sure. The nearest River-place was here called Vidalita or Beata, or sometimes Falaz, meaning Illusion. It was far south and inland. Jakko guessed they were making for a landing where a moveway met the sea. He had still time to think, to struggle with the trouble under his mind.

But as the sun turned the boat into a trim white-gold bird flying over green transparency, Jakko's eyes closed and he slept, protected by invisible deflectors from the bow-spray. Once he opened his eyes and saw a painted fish tearing along magically in the standing wave below his head. He smiled and slept again, dreaming of a great wave dying, a wave that was a many-headed beast. His face became sad and his lips moved soundlessly, as if repeating, "No . . . no . . . "

When he woke they were sailing quite close by a long bluff on his right. In the cliff ahead was a big white building or tower, only a little ruined. Suddenly he caught sight of a figure moving on the beach before it. A living human? He jumped up to look. He had not seen a strange human person in many years.

Yes — it was a live person, strangely colored gold and black. He waved wildly.

The person on the beach slowly raised an arm.

Alight with excitement, Jakko switched off the computer and grabbed the rudder and sail. The line of reef-surf seemed open here. He turned the boat shoreward, riding on a big swell. But the wave left him. He veered erratically, and the surf behind broached into the boat, overturning it and throwing him out. He knew how to swim; he surfaced and struck out strongly for the shore, spluttering brine. Presently he was wading out onto the white beach, a short, strongly-built, reddened young male person with pale hair and water-blue eyes.

The stranger was walking hesitantly toward him. Jakko saw it was a thin, dark-skinned girl wearing a curious netted hat. Her body was wrapped in orange silk and she carried heavy gloves in one hand. Three nervous moondogs followed her. He began turning water out of his shorts pockets as she came up.

"Your . . . boat, " she said in the language of that time. Her voice was low and uncertain.

They both turned to look at the confused place by the reef where the sailboat floated half-submerged.

"I turned it off. The computer." His words came jerkily, too, they were both unused to speech.

"It will come ashore down there." She pointed, still studying him in a wary, preoccupied way. She was much smaller than he. "Why did you turn? Aren't you going to the River?"

"No." He coughed. "Well, yes, in a way. My father wants me to say good-bye. They left while I was traveling."

"You're not . . . ready?"

"No. I don't — " He broke off. "Are you staying alone here?"

"Yes. I'm not going either."

They stood awkwardly in the sea-wind. Jakko noticed that the three moondogs were lined up single file, tiptoeing upwind toward him with their eyes closed, sniffing. They were not, of course, from the moon, but they looked it, being white and oddly shaped.

"It's a treat for them," the girl said. "Something different." Her voice was stronger now. After a pause she added, "You can stay here for a while if you want. I'll show you but I have to finish my work first."

"Thank you," he remembered to say.

As they climbed steps cut in the bluff Jakko asked, "What are you working at?"

"Oh, everything. Right now it's bees."

"Bees!" he marveled. "They made what — honey? I thought they were all gone."

"I have a lot of old things." She kept glancing at him intently as they climbed. "Are you quite healthy?"

"Oh yes. Why not? I'm all alpha so far as I know. Everybody is."

"Was," she corrected. "Here are my bee skeps."

They came around a low wall and stopped by five small wicker huts. A buzzing insect whizzed by Jakko's face, coming from some feathery shrubs. He saw that the bloom-tipped foliage was alive with the golden humming things. Recalling that they could sting, he stepped back.

"You better go around the other way." She pointed. "They might hurt a stranger." She pulled her veil down, hiding her face. Just as he turned away, she added, "I though you might impregnate me."

He wheeled back, not really able to react because of the distracting bees. "But isn't that terribly complicated?"

"I don't think so. I have the pills." She pulled on her gloves.

"Yes, the pills. I know." He frowned. "But you'd have to stay, I mean one just can't — "

"I know that. I have to do my bees now. We can talk later."

"Of course." He started away and suddenly turned back.

"Look!" He didn't know her name. "You, look!"

"What?" She was a strange little figure, black and orange with huge hands and a big veil-muffled head. "What?"

"I felt it. Just then, desire. Can't you see?"

They both gazed at his wet shorts.

"I guess not," he said finally. "'But I felt it, I swear. Sexual desire."

She pushed back her veil, frowning. "It will stay, won't it? Or come back? This isn't a very good place, I mean, the bees. And it's no use without the pills."

"That's so."

He went away then, walking carefully because of the tension around his pubic bone. Like a keel, snug and tight. His whole body felt reorganized. It had been years since he'd felt flashes like that, not since he was fifteen at least. Most people never did. It was variously thought to be because of the River, or from their parents' surviving the Poison Centuries, or because the general alpha strain was so forebrain dominant. It gave him an archaic, secret pride. Maybe he was a throwback.

He passed under cool archways, and found himself in a green, protected place behind the seaward wall. A garden, he saw, looking round surprised at clumps of large tied-up fruiting plants, peculiar trees with green balls at their tops, disorderly rows of rather unesthetic greenery. Tentatively he identified tomatoes, peppers, a feathery leaf which he thought had an edible root. A utilitarian planting. His uncle had once amused the family by doing something of the sort, but not on this scale. Jakko shook his head.

In the center of the garden stood a round stone coping with a primitive apparatus on top. He walked over and looked down. Water, a bucket on a rope. Then he saw that there was also an ordinary tap. He opened it and drank, looking at the odd implements leaning on the coping. Earth-tools. He did not really want to think about what the strange woman had said.

A shadow moved by his foot. The largest moondog had come quite close, inhaling dreamily. "Hello," he said to it. Some of these dogs could talk a little. This one opened its eyes wide but said nothing.

He stared about, wiping his mouth, feeling his clothes almost dry now in the hot sun. On three sides the garden was surrounded by arcades; above him the ruined side was a square cracked masonry tower with no roof. A large place, whatever it was. He walked into the shade of the nearest arcade, which turned out to be littered with a myriad disassembled or partly assembled objects: tools, containers, who knew what. Her "work"? The place felt strange, vibrant and busy. He realized he had entered only empty houses on his year-long journey. This one was alive, lived-in. Messy. It hummed like the bee skeps. He turned down a cool corridor, looking into rooms piled with more stuff. In one, three white animals he couldn't identify were asleep in a heap of cloth on a bed. They moved their ears at him like big pale shells but did not awaken.

He heard staccato noises and came out into another courtyard where plump birds walked with jerking heads. "Chickens!" he decided, delighted by the irrational variety of this place. He went from there into a large room with windows on the sea and heard a door close.

It was the woman, or girl, coming to him, holding her hat and gloves. Her hair was a dark curly cap, her head elegantly small; an effect he had always admired. He remembered something to say.

"I'm called Jakko. What's your name?"

"Jakko." She tasted the sound. "Hello, Jakko. I'm Peachthief." She smiled very briefly, entirely changing her face.

"Peachthief." On impulse he moved toward her, holding out his hands. She tucked her bundle under her arm and took both of his. They stood like that a moment, not quite looking at each other. Jakko felt excited. Not sexually, but more as if the air was electrically charged.

"Well." She took her hands away and began unwrapping a leafy wad. "I brought a honeycomb even if it isn't quite ready." She showed him a sticky looking frame with two dead bees on it. "Come on."

She walked rapidly out into another corridor and entered a shiny room he thought might be a laboratory.

"My food room," she told him. Again Jakko was amazed. There stood a synthesizer, to be sure, but beside it were shelves full of pots and bags and jars and containers of all descriptions. Unknown implements lay about and there was a fireplace which had been partly sealed up. Bunches of plant parts hung from racks overhead. He identified some brownish ovoids in a bowl as eggs. From the chickens?

Peachthief was cleaning the honeycomb with a manually operated knife. "I use the wax for my loom, and for candles. Light."

"What's wrong with the lights?"

"Nothing." She turned around, gesturing emphatically with the knife. "Don't you understand? All these machines, they'll go. They won't run forever. They'll break or wear out or run down. There won't *be* any, anymore. Then we'll have to use natural things."

"But that won't be for centuries!" he protested. "Decades, anyhow. They're all still going, they'll last for us."

"For you," she said scornfully. "Not for me. I intend to stay. With my children." She turned her back on him and added in a friendlier voice, "Besides, the old things are esthetic. I'll show you, when it gets dark."

"But you haven't any children! Have you?" He was purely astonished.

"Not yet." Her back was still turned.

"I'm hungry," he said, and went to work the syntheizer. He made it give him a bar with a hard filler; for some reason he wanted to crunch it in his teeth.

She finished with the honey and turned around. "Have you ever had a natural meal?"

"Oh yes," he said, chewing. "One of my uncles tried that. It was very nice," he added politely.

She looked at him sharply and smiled again, on — off. They went out of the food room. The afternoon was fading into great gold and orange streamers above the courtyard, colored like Peachthief's garment.

"You can sleep here." She opened a slatted door. The room was small and bare, with a window on the sea.

"There isn't any bed," he objected.

She opened a chest and took out a big wad of string. "Hang this end on that hook over there."

When she hung up the other end he saw it was a large mesh hammock.

"That's what I sleep in. They're comfortable. Try it."

He climbed in awkwardly. The thing came up around him like a bag. She gave a short sweet laugh as brief as her smile.

"No, you lie on the diagonal. Like this." She tugged his legs, sending a peculiar shudder through him. "That straightens it, see?"

It would probably be all right, he decided, struggling out. Peachthief was pointing to a covered pail.

"That's for your wastes. It goes on the garden in the end."

He was appalled, but said nothing, letting her lead him out through a room with glass tanks in the walls to a big screened-in porch fronting the ocean. It was badly in need of cleaners. The sky was glorious with opalescent domes and spires, reflections of the sunset behind them, painting amazing colors on the sea.

"This is where I eat."

"What is this place?"

"It was a sea-station last, I think. Station Juliet. They monitored the fish and the ocean traffic, and rescued people and so on."

He was distracted by noticing long convergent dove-blue rays like mysterious paths into the horizon; cloud-shadows cast across the world. Beauty of the dust. Why must it move him so?

" — even a medical section," she was saying. "I really could have babies, I mean in case of trouble."

"You don't mean it." He felt only irritation now. "I don't feel any more desire," he told her.

She shrugged. "I don't, either. We'll talk about it later on."

"Have you always lived here?"

"Oh, no." She began taking pots and dishes out of an insulated case. The three moondogs had joined them silently; she set bowls before them. They lapped, stealing glances at Jakko. They were, he knew, very strong despite their stick-like appearance.

"Let's sit here." She plumped down on one end of the lounge and began biting forcefully into a crusty thing like a slab of drybar. He noticed she had magnificent teeth. Her dark skin set them off beautifully, as it enhanced her eyes. He had never met anyone so different in every way from himself and his family. He vacillated between interest and a vague alarm.

"Try some of the honey." She handed him a container and a spoon. It looked quite clean. He tasted it eagerly; honey was much spoken of in antique writings. At first he sensed nothing but a waxy sliding, but then an overpowering sweetness enveloped his tongue, quite unlike the sweets he was used to. It did not die away but seemed to run up his nose and almost into his ears, in a peculiur way. An *animal* food. He took some more, gingerly.

"I didn't offer you my bread. It needs some chemical, I don't know what. To make it lighter."

"Don't you have an access terminal?"

"Something's wrong with part of it," she said with her mouth full. "Maybe

I don't work it right. We never had a big one like this, my tribe were travelers. They believed in sensory experiences.'' She nodded, licking her fingers. ''They went to the River when I was fourteen.''

''That's very young to be alone. My people waited till this year, my eighteenth birthday.''

''I wasn't alone. I had two older cousins. But they wanted to take an aircar up north, to the part of the River called Rideout. I stayed here. I mean, we never stopped traveling, we never *lived* anywhere. I wanted to do like the plants, make roots.''

''I could look at your program,'' he offered. ''I've seen a lot of different models, I spent nearly a year in cities.''

''What I need is a cow. Or a goat.''

''Why?''

''For the milk. I need a pair, I guess.''

Another animal thing; he winced a little. But it was pleasant, sitting here in the deep blue light beside her, hearing the surf plash quietly below.

''I saw quite a number of horses,'' he told her. ''Don't they use milk?''

''I don't think horses are much good for milk.'' She sighed in an alert, busy way. He had the impression that her head was tremendously energetic, humming with plans and intentions. Suddenly she looked up and began making a high squeaky noise between her front teeth, ''Sssswwt! Sssswwwt!''

Startled, he saw a white flying thing swooping above them, and then two more. They whirled so wildly he ducked.

''That's right,'' she said to them. ''Get busy.''

''What are they?''

''My bats. They eat mosquitoes and insects.'' She squeaked again and the biggest bat was suddenly clinging to her hand, licking honey. It had a small, fiercely complicated face.

Jakko relaxed again. This palce and its strange inhabitant were giving him remarkable memories for the River, anyway. He noticed a faint glow moving where the dark sky joined the darker sea.

''What's that?''

''Oh, the seatrain. It goes to the River landing.''

''Are there people on it?''

''Not anymore. Look, I'll show you.'' She jumped up and was opening a console in the corner, when a sweet computer voice spoke into the air.

''Seatrain Foxtrot Niner calling Station Juliet! Come in, Station Juliet!''

''It hasn't done that for years,'' Peachthief said. She tripped tumblers. ''Seatrain, this is Station Juliet, I hear you. Do you have a problem?''

''Affirmative. Passenger is engaging in nonstandard activities. He-slash-she does not conform to parameters. Request instructions.''

Peachthief thought a minute. Then she grinned. ''Is your passenger moving on four legs?''

''Affirmative! Affirmative!'' Seatrain Foxtrot sounded relieved.

"Supply it with bowls of meat-food and water on the floor and do not interfere with it. Juliet out."

She clicked off, and they watched the far web of lights go by on the horizon, carrying an animal.

"Probably a dog following the smell of people," Peachthief said. "I hope it gets off all right . . . We're quite a wide genetic spread," she went on in a different voice. "I mean, you're so light, and body-type and all."

"I noticed that."

"It would give good heterosis. Vigor."

She was talking about being impregnated, about the fantasy-child. He felt angry.

"Look, you don't know what you're saying. Don't you realize you'd have to stay and raise it for years? You'd be ethically and morally bound. And the River places are shrinking fast, you must know that. Maybe you'd be too late."

"Yes," she said somberly. "Now it's sucked everybody out it's going. But I still mean to stay."

"But you'd hate it, even if there's still time. My mother hated it, toward the end. She felt she had begun to deteriorate energetically, that her life would be lessened. And me — what about me? I mean, I should stay too."

"You'd only have to stay a month. For my ovulation. The male parent isn't ethically bound."

"Yes, but I think that's wrong. My father stayed. He never said he minded it, but he must have."

"You only have to do a month," she said sullenly. "I thought you weren't going on the River right now."

"I'm not. I just don't want to feel bound, I want to travel. To see more of the world, first. After I say goodbye."

She made an angry sound. "You have no insight. You're going, all right. You just don't want to admit it. You're going just like Mungo and Ferrocil."

"Who are they?"

"People who came by. Males, like you. Mungo was last year, I guess. He had an aircar. He said he was going to stay, he talked and talked. But two days later he went right on again. To the River. Ferrocil was earlier, he was walking through. Until he stole my bicycle."

A sudden note of fury in her voice startled him; she seemed to have some peculiar primitive relation to her bicycle, to her *things*.

"Did you want them to impregnate you, too?" Jakko noticed an odd intensity in his own voice as well.

"Oh, I was thinking about it, with Mungo." Suddenly she turned on him, her eyes wide open in the dimness like white-ringed jewels. "Look! Once and for all, I'm not going! I'm alive, I'm a human woman. I am going to stay on this earth and do human things. I'm going to make young ones to carry on the race, even if I have to die here. You can go on out, you — you pitiful shadows!"

Her voice rang in the dark room, jarring him down to his sleeping marrow. He sat silent as though some deep buried bell had tolled.

She was breathing hard. Then she moved, and to his surprise a small live flame sprang up between her cupped hands, making the room a cave.

"That's a candle. That's me. Now go ahead, make fun like Mungo did."

"I'm not making fun," he said, shocked. "It's just that I don't know what to think. Maybe you're right. I really . . . I really don't want to go, in one way," he said haltingly. "I love this earth too. But it's all so fast. Let me . . ."

His voice trailed off.

"Tell me about your family," she said, quietly now.

"Oh, they studied. They tried every access you can imagine. Ancient languages, history, lore. My aunt made poems in English . . . The layers of the earth, the names of body cells and tissues, jewels, everything. Especially stars. They made us memorize star maps. So we'll know where we are, you know, for a while. At least the earth-names. My father kept saying, when you go on the River you can't come back and look anything up. All you have is what you remember. Of course you could ask others, but there'll be so much more, so much new . . ."

He fell silent, wondering for the millionth time; is it possible that I shall go out forever between the stars, in the great streaming company of strange sentiences?

"How many children were in your tribe?" Peachthief was asking.

"Six. I was the youngest."

"The others all went on the River?"

"I don't know. When I came back from the cities the whole family had gone on, but maybe they'll wait a while too. My father left a letter asking me to come and say good-bye, and to bring him anything new I learned. They say you go slowly, you know. If I hurry there'll still be enough of his mind left there to tell him what I saw."

"What did you see? We were at a city once," Peachthief said dreamily. "But I was too young, I don't remember anything but people."

"The people are all gone now. Empty, every one. But everything works, the lights change, the moveways run. I didn't believe everybody was gone until I checked the central control offices. Oh, there were so many wonderful devices." He sighed. "The beauty, the complexity. Fantastic what people made." He sighed again, thinking of the wonderful technology, the creations abandoned, running down. "One strange thing. In the biggest city I saw, old Chio, almost every entertainment-screen had the same tape running."

"What was it?"

"A girl, a young girl with long hair. Almost to her feet, I've never seen such hair. She was laying it out on a sort of table, with her head down. But no sound, I think the audio was broken. Then she poured a liquid all over very slowly. And then she lit it, she set fire to herself. It flamed and exploded and burned her all up. I think it was real." He shuddered. "I could see inside her mouth, her tongue going all black and twisted. It was horrible. Running over and over, everywhere. Stuck.''

She made a revolted sound. ''So you want to tell that to your father, to his ghost, or whatever?''

''Yes. It's all new data, it could be important.''

''Oh yes,'' she said scornfully. Then she grinned at him. ''What about me? Am I new data too? A woman who isn't going to the River? A woman who is going to stay here and make babies? Maybe I'm the last.''

''That's very important,'' he said slowly, feeling a deep confusion in his gut. ''But I can't believe it, I mean, you — ''

''*I mean it.*'' She spoke with infinite conviction. ''I'm going to live here and have babies by you or some other man if you won't stay, and teach them to live on the earth naturally.''

Suddenly he believed her. A totally new emotion was rising up in him, carrying with it sunrises and nameless bonds with earth that hurt in a painless way, as thought a rusted door was opening within him. Maybe this was what he had been groping for.

''I think — I think maybe I'll help you. Maybe I'll stay with you, for a while at least. Our — our children.''

''You'll stay a month?'' she asked wonderingly. ''Really?''

''No, I mean I could stay longer. To make more and see them and help raise them, like my father did. After I come back from saying good-bye I'll really stay.''

Her face changed. She bent to him and took his face between her slim dark hands.

''Jakko, listen. If you go to the River you'll never come back. No one ever does. I'll never see you again. We have to do it now, before you go.''

''But a month is too long!'' he protested. ''My father's mind won't be there, I'm already terribly late.''

She glared into his eyes a minute and then released him, stepping back with her brief sweet laugh. ''Yes, and it's already late for bed. Come on.''

She led him back to the room, carrying the candle, and he marveled anew at the clutter of strange activities she had assembled. ''What's that?''

''My weaving-room.'' Yawning, she reached in and held up a small, rough-looking cloth. ''I made this.''

It was ugly, he thought; ugly and pathetic. Why make such useless things? But he was too tired to argue.

She left him to cleanse himself perfunctorily by the well in the moonlit courtyard, after showing him another waste-place right in the garden. Other peoples' wastes smell bad, he noticed sleepily. Maybe that was the cause of all the ancient wars.

In his room he tumbled into his hammock and fell asleep instantly. His dreams that night were chaotic; crowds, storms, jostling and echoing through strange dimensions. His last image was of a great whirlwind that bore in its forehead a jewel that was a sleeping woman, curled like an embryo.

He waked in the pink light of dawn to find her brown face bending over him, smiling impishly. He had the impression she had been watching him, and jumped quickly out of the hammock.

"Lazy," she said. "I've found the sailboat. Hurry up and eat."

She handed him a wooden plate of bright natural fruits and led him out into the sunrise garden.

When they got down to the beach she led him south, and there was the little craft sliding to and fro, overturned in the shallows amid its tangle of sail. The keel was still protruding. They furled the sail in clumsily and towed it out to deeper water to right it.

"I want this for the children," Peachthief kept repeating excitedly. "They can get fish, too. Oh, how they'll love it!"

"Stand your weight in the keel and grab the siderail," Jakko told her, doing the same. He noticed that her silks had come loose from her breasts, which were high and wide-pointed, quite unlike those of his tribe. The sight distracted him, his thighs felt unwieldy, and he missed his handhold as the craft righted itself and ducked him. When he came up he saw Peachthief scrambling aboard like a cat, clinging tight to the mast.

"The sail! Pull the sail up!" he shouted, and got another faceful of water. But she had heard him, the sail was trembling open like a great wing, silhouetting her shining slim dark body. For the first time Jakko noticed the boat's name, on the stern: Gojack. He smiled. An omen.

Gojack was starting to move smoothly away, toward the reef.

"The rudder!" he bellowed. "Turn the rudder and come back."

Peachthief moved to the tiller and pulled at it; he could see her strain. But Gojack continued to move away from him into the wind, faster and faster toward the surf. He remembered she had been handling the mast where the computer was.

"Stop the computer! Turn it off, turn it off!"

She couldn't possibly hear him. Jakko saw her in frantic activity, wrenching at the tiller, grabbing ropes, trying physically to push down the sail. Then she seemed to notice the computer, but evidently could not decipher it. Meanwhile Gojack fled steadily on and out, resuming its interrupted journey to the River. Jakko realized with horror that she would soon be in dangerous water; the surf was thundering on coral-heads.

"Jump! Come back, jump off!" He was swimming after her as fast as he could, his progress agonizingly slow. He glimpsed her still wrestling with the boat, screaming something he couldn't hear.

"JUMP!"

And finally she did, but only to try jerking Gojack around by its mooring lines. The boat faltered and jibbed, but then went strongly on, towing the threshing girl.

"Let go! Let go!" A wave broke over his head.

When he could see again he found she had at last let go and was swimming aimlessly, watching *Gojack* crest the surf and wing away. At last she turned back toward shore, and Jakko swam to intercept her. He was gripped by an unknown emotion so strong it discoordinated him. As his feet touched bottom he realized it was rage.

She waded to him, her face contorted by weeping. "The children's boat," she wailed. "I lost the children's boat — "

"You're crazy," he shouted. "There aren't any children."

"I lost it — " She flung herself on his chest, crying. He thumped her back, her sides, repeating furiously, "Crazy! You're insane!"

She wailed louder, squirming against him, small and naked and frail. Suddenly he found himself flinging her down onto the wet sand, falling on top of her with his swollen sex crushed between their bellies. For a moment all was confusion, and then the shock of it sobered him. He raised to look under himself and Peachthief stared too, round-eyed.

"Do you w-want to, now?"

In that instant he wanted nothing more than to thrust himself into her, but a sandy wavelet splashed over them and he was suddenly aware of chafing wet cloth and Peachthief gagging brine. The magic waned. He got awkwardly to his knees.

"I thought you were going to be drowned," he told her, angry again.

"I wanted it so, for — for them . . ." She was still crying softly, looking up desolately at him. He understood she wasn't really meaning just the sailboat. A feeling of inexorable involvement spread through him. This mad little being had created some kind of energy-vortex around her, into which he was being sucked along with animals, vegetables, chickens, crowds of unknown things; only *Gojack* had escaped her.

"I'll find it," she was muttering, wringing out her silks, staring beyond the reef at the tiny dwindling gleam. He looked down at her, so fanatic and so vulnerable, and his inner landscape tilted frighteningly, revealing some ancient-new dimension.

"I'll stay with you," he said hoarsely. He cleared his throat, hearing his voice shake. "I mean I'll really stay, I won't go the the River at all. We'll make the, our babies now."

She stared up at him open-mouthed. "But your father! You promised!"

"My father stayed," he said painfully. "It's — it's right, I think."

She came close and grabbed his arms in her small hands.

"Oh, Jakko! But no, listen — *I'll go with you*. We can start a baby as we go, I'm sure of that. Then you can talk to your father and keep your promise and I'll be there to make sure you come back!"

"But you'd be, you'd be pregnant!" he cried in alarm. "You'd be in danger of taking an embryo on the River!"

She laughed proudly. "Can't you get it through your head that I will *not* go on the River? I'll just watch you and pull you out. I'll see you get back here. For a while, anyway," she added soberly. Then she brightened. "Hey, we'll see all kinds of things. Maybe I can find a cow or some goats on the way! Yes, yes! It's a perfect idea.''

She faced him, glowing. Tentatively she brought her lips up to his, and they kissed inexpertly, tasting salt. He felt no desire, but only some deep resonance, like a confirmation in the earth. The three moondogs were watching mournfully.

''Now let's eat!'' she began towing him toward the cliff-steps. ''we can start the pills right now. Oh, I have so much to do! But I'll fix everything, we'll leave tomorrow.''

⁻She was like a whirlwind. In the foodroom she pounced on a small gold-colored pillbox and opened it to show a mound of glowing green and red capsules.

''The red ones with the male symbol are for you.''

She took a green one, and they swallowed solemnly, sharing a water-mug. He noticed that the seal on the box had been broken, and thought of that stranger, Mungo, she had mentioned. How far had her plans gone with him? An unpleasant emotion he had never felt before rose in Jakko's stomach. He sensed that he was heading into more dubious realms of experience than he had quite comtemplated, and took his foodbar and walked away through the arcades to cool down.

When he came upon her again she seemd to be incredibly busy, folding and filling and wrapping things, closing windows and tying doors open. Her intense relations with things again . . . He felt obscurely irritated and was pleased to have had a superior idea.

''We need a map,'' he told her. ''Mine was in the boat.''

''Oh, great idea. Look in the old control room, it's down those stairs. It's kind of scary.'' She began putting oil in her loom.

He went down a white ramp that became a tunnel stairway, and came finally through a heavily armored portal to a circular room deep inside the rock, dimly illumined by portholes sunk in long shafts. From here he could hear the hum of the station energy source. As his eyes adjusted he made out a bank of sensor screens and one big console standing alone. It seemed to have been smashed open; some kind of sealant had been poured over the works.

He had seen a place like this before; he understood at once that from here had been controlled terrible ancient weapons that flew. Probably they still stood waiting in their hidden holes behind the station. But the master control was long dead. As he approached the console he saw that someone had scratched in the cooling sealant. He could make out only the words, '' — WAR NO MORE.'' Undoubtedly this was a shrine of the very old days.

He found a light switch that filled the place with cool glare and began exploring side alleys. Antique gear, suits, cupboards full of masks and crumbling packets he couldn't identify. Among them was something useful — two cloth containers to carry stuff on one's back, only a little mildewed. But where were the maps?

Finally he found one on the control-room wall, right where he had come in. Someone had updated it with scrawled notations. With a tremor he realized how very old this must be; it dated from before the Rivers had touched earth. He could hardly grasp it.

Studying it he saw that there was indeed a big landing-dock not far south, and from there a moveway ran inland about a hundred kilometers to an airpark. If Peachthief could walk twenty-five kilometers they could make the landing by evening, and if the cars were still running the rest would be quick. All the moveways he'd seen had live cars on them. From the airpark a dotted line ran southwest across mountains to a big red circle with a cross in it, marked "VIDA!" That would be the River. They would just have to hope something on the airpark would fly, otherwise it would be a long climb.

His compass was still on his belt. He memorized the directions and went back upstairs. The courtyard was already saffron under great sunset flags.

Peachthief was squatting by the well, apparently having a conference with her animals. Jakko noticed some more white creatures he hadn't seen before, who seemed to live in an open hutch. They had long pinkish ears and mobile noses. Rabbits, or hares perhaps?

Two of the strange white animals he had seen sleeping were now under a bench, chirruping irritably at Peachthief.

"My raccoons," she told Jakko. "They're mad because I woke them up too soon." She said something in a high voice Jakko didn't understand, and the biggest raccoon shook his head up and down in a supercilious way.

"The chickens will be all right," Peachthief said. "Lotor knows how to feed them, to get the eggs. And they can all work the water-lever." The other raccoon nodded crossly, too.

"The rabbits are a terrible problem." Peachthief frowned. "You just haven't much sense, Eusebia," she said fondly, stroking the doe. "I'll have to fix something."

The big raccoon was warbling at her; Jakko thought he caught the word "dog-g-g."

"He wants to know who will settle their disputes with the dogs," Peachthief reported. At this one of the moondogs came forward and said thickly, "We go-o." It was the first word Jakko had heard him speak.

"Oh, good!" Peachthief cried. "Well, that's that!" She bounced up and began pouring something from a bucket on a line of plants. The white raccoons ran off silently with a humping gait.

"I'm so glad you're coming, Tycho," she told the dog. "Especially if I have to come back alone with a baby inside. But they say you're very vigorous, at first anyway."

"You aren't coming back alone," Jakko told her. She smiled a brilliant, noncommittal flash. He noticed she was dressed differently; her body didn't show so much, and she kept her gaze away from him in an almost timid way. But she became very excited when he showed her the backpacks.

"Oh, good. Now we won't have to roll the blankets around our waists. It gets cool at night, you know."

"Does it ever rain?"

"Not this time of year. What we mainly need is lighters and food and water. And a good knife each. Did you find the map?"

He showed it. "Can you walk, I mean really hike if we have to? Do you have shoes?"

"Oh yes. I walk a lot. Especially since Ferrocil stole my bike."

The venom in her tone amused him. The ferocity with which she provisioned her small habitat!

"Men build monuments, women build nests," he quoted from somewhere.

"I don't know what kind of monument Ferrocil built with my bicycle," she said tartly.

"You're a savage," he said, feeling a peculiar ache that came out as a chuckle.

"The race can use some savages. We better eat now and go to sleep so we can start early."

At supper in the sunset-filled porch they scarcely talked. Dreamily Jakko watched the white bats embroidering flight in the air. When he looked down at Peachthief he caught her gazing at him before she quickly lowered her eyes. It came to him that they might eat hundreds, thousands of meals here; maybe all his life. And there could be a child, children, running about. He had never seen small humans younger than himself. It was all too much to take in, unreal. He went back to watching the bats.

That night she accompanied him to his hammock and stood by, shy but stubborn, while he got settled. Then he suddenly felt her hands sliding on his body, toward his groin. At first he thought it was something clinical, but then he realized she meant sex. His blood began to pound.

"May I come in beside you? The hammock is quite strong."

"Yes," he said thickly, reaching for her arm.

But as her weight came in by him she said in a practical voice, "I have to start knotting a small hammock, first thing. Child-size."

It broke his mood.

"Look. I'm sorry, but I've changed my mind. You go on back to yours, we should get sleep now."

"All right." The weight lifted away.

With a peculiar mix of sadness and satisfaction he heard her light footsteps leaving him alone. That night he dreamed strange sensory crescendoes, a tumescent earth and air; a woman who lay with her smiling lips in pale green water, awaiting him, while thin black birds of sunrise stalked to the edge of the sea.

Next morning they ate by candles, and set out as the eastern sky was just turning rose-gray. The ancient white coral roadway was good walking. Peachthief swung right along beside him, her backpack riding smooth.

The moondogs pattered soberly behind. Jakko found himself absorbed in gazing at the brightening landscape. Jungle-covered hills rose away on their right, the sea lay below on their left, sheened and glittering with the coming sunrise.

When a diamond chip of sun broke out of the horizon he almost shouted aloud for the brilliance of it; the palm trees beyond the road lit up like golden torches, the edges of every frond and stone were startlingly clear and jewellike. For a moment he wondered if he could have taken some hallucinogen.

They paced on steadily in a dream of growing light and heat. The day-wind came up, and torn white clouds began to blow over them, bringing momentary coolnesses. Their walking fell into the rhythm Jakko loved, broken only occasionally by crumbled places in the road. At such spots they would often be surprised to find the moondogs sitting waiting for them, having quietly left the road and circled ahead through the scrub on business of their own. Peachthief kept up sturdily, only once stopping to look back at the far white spark of Station Juliet, almost melted in the shimmering horizon.

"This is as far as I've gone south," she told him.

He drank some water and made her drink too, and they went on. The road began to wind, rising and falling gently. When he next glanced back the station was gone. The extraordinary luminous clarity of the world was still delighting him.

When noon came he judged they were well over halfway to the landing. They sat down on some rubble under the palms to eat and drink, and Peachthief fed the moondogs. Then she took out the fertility pillbox. They each took theirs in silence, oddly solemn. Then she grinned.

"I'll give you something for dessert."

She unhitched a crooked knife from her belt and went searching around in the rocks, to come back with a big yellow-brown palm nut. Jakko watched her attack it with rather alarming vigor; she husked it and then used a rock to drive the point home.

"Here." She handed it to him. "Drink out of that hole." He felt a sloshing inside; when he lifted it and drank it tasted hairy and gritty and nothing in particular. But sharp, too, like the day. Peachthief was methodically striking the thing around and around its middle. Suddenly it fell apart, revealing vividly white meat. She pried out a piece.

"Eat this. It's full of protein."

The nutmeat was sweet and sharply organic.

"This is a coconut!" he suddenly remembered.

"Yes. I won't starve, coming back."

He refused to argue, but only got up to go on. Peachthief holstered her knife and followed, munching on a coconut piece. They went on so in silence a long time, letting the rhythm carry them. Once when a lizard waddled across the road Peachthief said to the moondog at her heels, "Tycho, you'll have to learn to catch and eat those one day soon." The moondogs all looked dubiously at the lizard but said nothing. Jakko felt shocked and pushed the thought away.

They were now walking with the sun westering slowly to their right. A flight of big orange birds with blue beaks flapped squawking out of a roadside tree, where they were apparently building some structure. Cloud-shadows fled across the world, making blue and bronze reflections in the sea. Jakko still felt his sensory impressions almost painfully keen; a sunray made the surf-line into a chain of diamonds, and the translucent green of the near shallows below them seemed to enchant his eyes. Every vista ached with light, as if to utter some silent meaning.

He was walking in a trance, only aware that the road had been sound and level for some time, when Peachthief uttered a sharp cry.

"My bicycle! There's my bicycle!" She began to run; Jakko saw shiny metal sticking out of a narrow gulch in the roadway. When he came up to her she was pulling a machine out from beside the roadwall.

"The front wheel — Oh, he bent it! He must have been going too fast and wrecked it here. That Ferrocil! But I'll fix it, I'm sure I can fix it at the Station. I'll push it back with me on the way home."

While she was mourning her machine Jakko looked around and over the low coping of the roadwall. Sheer cliff down there, with the sun just touching a rocky beach below. Something was stuck among the rocks — a tangle of whitish sticks, cloth, a round thing. Feeling his stomach knot, Jakko stared down at it, unwillingly discovering that the round thing had eye-holes, a U-shaped open mouth, blowing strands of hair. He had never seen a dead body before, nobody had, but he had seen pictures of human bones. Shakenly he realized who this had to be: Ferrocil. He must have been thrown over the coping when he hit that crack. Now he was dead, long dead. He would never go on the River. All that had been in that head was perished, gone forever.

Scarcely knowing what he was doing, Jakko grabbed Peachthief by the shoulders, saying roughly, "Come on! Come on!" When she resisted, confusedly he took her by the arm and began forcibly pulling her away from where she might look down. Her flesh felt burning hot and vibrant, the whole world was blasting colors and sounds and smells at him. Images of dead Ferrocil mingled with the piercing scent of some flowers on the roadway. Suddenly an idea struck him; he stopped.

"Listen. Are you sure those pills aren't hallucinaids? I've only had two and everything feels crazy."

"Three," Peachthief said abstractedly. She took his hand and pressed it on her back. "Do that again, run your hand down my back."

Bewildered, he obeyed. As his hand passed her silk shirt onto her thin shorts he felt her body move under it in a way that made him jerk away.

"Feel? Did you feel it? The lordotic reflex," she said proudly. "Female sexuality. It's starting."

"What do you mean, three?"

"You had three pills. I gave you one that first night, in the honey."

"What? But — but — " He struggled to voice the enormity of her violation, pure fury welling up in him. Choking, he lifted his hand and struck her buttocks the hardest blow he could, sending her staggering. It was the first time he had ever struck a person. A moondog growled, but he didn't care.

"Don't you ever — never — play a trick like — " He yanked at her shoulders, meaning to slap her face. His hand clutched a breast instead, he saw her hair blowing like dead Ferrocil's. A frightening sense of mortality combined with pride surged through him, lighting a fire in his loins. The deadness of Ferrocil suddenly seemed violently exciting. He, Jakko, was alive! Ignoring all sanity he flung himself on Peachthief, bearing her down on the road among the flowers. As he struggled to tear open their shorts he was dimly aware that she was helping him. His engorged penis was all reality; he fought past obstructions and then was suddenly, crookedly *in* her, fierce pleasure building. It exploded through him and then had burst out into her vitals, leaving him spent.

Blinking, fighting for clarity, he raised himself up and off her body. She lay wide-legged and disheveled, sobbing or gasping in a strange way, but smiling too. Revulsion sent a sick taste in his throat.

"There's your baby," he said roughly. He found his canteen and drank. The three moondogs had retreated and were sitting in a row, staring solemnly.

"May I have some, please?" Her voice was very low; she sat up, began fixing her clothes. He passed her the water and they got up.

"It's sundown," she said. "Should we camp here?"

"No!" Savagely he started on, not caring that she had to run to catch up. Was this the way the ancients lived? Whirled by violent passions, indecent, uncaring? His doing sex so close to the poor dead person seemed unbelievable. And the world was still assaulting all his senses; when she stumbled against him he could feel again the thrilling pull of her flesh, and shuddered. They walked in silence awhile; he sensed that she was more tired than he, but he wanted only to get as far as possible away.

"I'm not taking any more of those pills," he broke silence at last.

"But you have to! It takes a month to be sure."

"I don't care."

"But, ohhh —"

He said nothing more. They were walking across a twilit headland now. Suddenly the road turned, and they came out above a great bay.

The waters below were crowded with boats of all kinds, bobbing emptily where they had been abandoned. Some still had lights that made faint jewels in the opalescent air. Somewhere among them must be *Gojack*. The last light from the west gleamed on the rails of a moveway running down to the landing.

"Look, there's the seatrain." Peachthief pointed. "I hope the dog or whatever got ashore . . . I can find a sailboat down there, there's lots."

Jakko shrugged. Then he noticed movement among the shadows of the landing-station and forgot his anger long enough to say, "See there! Is that a live man?"

They peered hard. Presently the figure crossed a light place, and they could see it was a person going slowly among the stalled waycars. He would stop with one awhile and then waver on.

"There's something wrong with him," Peachthief said.

Presently the stranger's shadow merged with a car, and they saw it begin to move. It went slowly at first, and then accelerated out to the center lanes, slid up the gleaming rails and passed beyond them to disappear into the western hills.

"The way's working!" Jakko exclaimed. "We'll camp up here and go over to the way-station in the morning, it's closer."

He was feeling so pleased with the moveway that he talked easily with Peachthief over the foodbar dinner, telling her about the cities and asking her what places her tribe had seen. But when she wanted to put their blankets down together he said No, and took his away to a ledge farther up. The three moondogs lay down by her with their noses on their paws, facing him.

His mood turned to self-disgust again; remorse mingled with queasy surges of half-enjoyable animality. He put his arm over his head to shut out the brilliant moonlight and longed to forget everything, wishing the sky held only cold quiet stars. When he finally slept he didn't dream at all, but woke with ominous tollings in his inner ear. *The Horse is hungry,* deep voices chanted. *The Woman is bad!*

He roused Peachthief before sunrise. They ate and set off overland to the hill station; it was rough going until they stumbled onto an old limerock path. The moondogs ranged wide around them, appearing pleased. When they came out at the station shunt they found it crowded with cars.

The power-pack of the first one was dead. So was the next, and the next. Jakko understood what the stranger at the landing had been doing; looking for a live car. The dead cars here stretched away out of sight up the siding; a miserable sight.

"We should go back to the landing," Peachthief said. "He found a good one there."

Jakko privately agreed, but irrationality smouldered in him. He squinted into the hazy distance.

"I'm going up to the switch end."

"But it's so far, we'll have to come all the way back — "

He only strode off; she followed. It was a long way, round a curve and over a rise, dead cars beside them all the way. They were almost at the main tracks when Jakko saw what he had been hoping for; a slight jolting motion in the line. New cars were still coming in ahead, butting the dead ones.

"Oh fine!"

They went on down to the newest-arrived car and all climbed in, the moondogs taking up position on the opposite seat. When Jakko began to work the controls that would take them out to the main line, the car bleated an automatic alarm. A voder voice threatened to report him to Central. Despite its protests, Jakko swerved the car across the switches, where it fell silent and began to accelerate smoothly onto the outbound express lane.

"You really do know how to work these things," Peachthief said admiringly.

"You should learn."

"Why? They'll all be dead soon. I know how to bicycle."

He clamped his lips, thinking of Ferrocil's white bones. They fled on silently into the hills, passing a few more station jams. Jakko's perceptions still seemed too sharp, the sensory world too meaning-filled.

Presently they felt hungry, and found that the car's automatics were all working well. They had a protein drink and a pleasantly fruity bar, and Peachthief found bars for the dogs. The track was rising into mountains now; the car whistled smoothly through tunnels and came out in passes, offering wonderful views. Now and then they had glimpses of a great plain far ahead. The familiar knot of sadness gathered inside Jakko, stronger than usual. To think that all this wonderful system would run down and die in a jumble of rust . . . He had a fantasy of himself somehow maintaining it, but the memory of Peachthief's pathetic woven cloth mocked at him. Everything was a mistake, a terrible mistake. He wanted only to leave, to escape to rationality and peace. If she had drugged him he wasn't responsible for what he'd promised. He wasn't bound. Yet the sadness redoubled, wouldn't let him go.

When she got out the pill-box and offered it he shook his head violently. "No!"

"But you *promised* — "

"No. I hate what it does."

She stared at him in silence, swallowing hers defiantly. "Maybe there'll be some other men by the River," she said after awhile. "We saw one."

He shrugged and pretended to fall asleep.

Just as he was really drowsing the car's warning alarm trilled and they braked smoothly to a halt.

"Oh, look ahead — the way's gone! What is it?"

"A rockslide. An avalanche from the mountains, I think."

They got out among other empty cars that were waiting their prescribed pause before returning. Beyond the last one the way ended in an endless tumble of rocks and shale. Jakko made out a faint footpath leading on.

"Well, we walk. Let's get the packs, and some food and water."

While they were back in the car working the synthesizer, Peachthief looked out the window and frowned. After Jakko finished she punched a different code and some brownish lumps rolled into her hand.

"What's that?"

"You'll see." She winked at him.

As they started on the trail a small herd of horses appeared, coming toward them. The two humans politely scrambled up out of their way. The lead horse was a large yellow male. When he came to Peachthief he stopped and thrust his big head up at her.

"Zhu-gar, zhu-gar," he said sloppily. At this all the other horses crowded up and began saying "zhu-ga, zu-cah," in varying degrees of clarity.

"This *I* know," said Peachthief to Jakko. She turned to the yellow stallion. "Take us on your backs around these rocks. Then we'll give you sugar."

"Zhu-gar," insisted the horse, looking mean.

"Yes, sugar. *After* you take us around the rocks to the rails."

The horse rolled his eyes unpleasantly, but he turned back down. There was some commotion, and two mares were pushed forward.

"Riding horseback is done by means of a saddle and bridle," protested Jakko.

"Also this way. Come on." Peachthief vaulted nimbly onto the back of the smaller mare.

Jakko reluctantly struggled onto the fat round back of the other mare. To his horror, as he got himself astride she put up her head and screamed shrilly.

"You'll get sugar too," Peachthief told her. The animal subsided, and they started off along the rocky trail, single file. Jakko had to admit it was much faster than afoot, but he kept sliding backward.

"Hang onto her mane, that hairy place there," Peachthief called back to him, laughing. "I know how to run a few things too, see?"

When the path widened the yellow stallion trotted up alongside Peachthief.

"I thinking," he said importantly.

"Yes, what?"

"I push you down and eat zhugar now."

"All horses think that," Peachthief told him. "No good. It doesn't work."

The yellow horse dropped back, and Jakko heard him making horse-talk with an old gray-roan animal at the rear. Then he shouldered by to Peachthief again and said, "Why no good I push you down?"

"Two reasons," said Peachthief. "First, if you knock me down you'll never get any more sugar. All the humans will know you're bad and they won't ride on you any more. So no more sugar, never again."

"No more hoomans," the big yellow horse said scornfully. "Hoomans finish."

"You're wrong there too. There'll be a lot more humans. I am making them, see?" She patted her stomach.

The trail narrowed again and the yellow horse dropped back. When he could come alongside he sidled by Jakko's mare.

"I think I push you down now."

Peachthief turned around.

"You didn't hear my other reason," she called to him.

The horse grunted evilly.

"The other reason is that my three friends there will bite your stomach open if you try." She pointed up to where the three moondogs had appeared on a rock as if by magic, grinning toothily.

Jakko's mare screamed again even louder, and the gray roan in back made a haw-haw sound. The yellow horse lifted his tail and trotted forward to the head of the line, extruding manure as he passed Peachthief.

They went on around the great rockslide without further talk. Jakko was becoming increasingly uncomfortable; he would gladly have got off and gone slower on his own two legs. Now and then they broke into a jog trot, which was so painful he longed to yell at Peachthief to make them stop. But he kept silent. As they rounded some huge boulders he was rewarded by a distant view of the unmistakable towers of an airpark to their left on the plain below.

At long last the rockslide ended quite near a station. They stopped among a line of stalled cars. Jakko slid off gratefully, remembering to say "Thank you" to the mare. Walking proved to be uncomfortable too.

"See if there's a good car before I get off!" Peachthief yelled.

The second one he came to was live. He shouted at her.

Next moment he saw trouble among the horses. The big yellow beast charged in, neighing and kicking. Peachthief came darting out of the melee with the moondogs, and fell into the car beside him, laughing.

"I gave our mares all the sugar," she chuckled. Then she sobered. "I think mares *are* good for milk. I told them to come to the station with me when I come back. If that big bully will let them."

"How will they get in a car?" he asked stupidly.

"Why, I'll be walking, I can't run these things."

"But I'll be with you." He didn't feel convinced.

"What for, if you don't want to make babies? You won't be here."

"Well then, why are you coming with me?"

"I'm looking for a cow," she said scornfully. "Or a goat. Or a man."

They said no more until the car turned into the airpark station. Jakko counted over twenty apparently live ships floating at their towers. Many more hung sagging, and some towers had toppled. The field moveways were obviously dead.

"I think we have to find hats," he told Peachthief.

"Why?"

"So the service alarms won't go off when we walk around. Most places are like that."

"Oh."

In the office by the gates they found a pile of crew hats laid out, a thoughtful action by the last of the airpark people. A big hand-lettered sign said, ALL SHIPS ON STAND-BY, MANUAL OVERRIDE. READ DIRECTIONS. Under it was a stack of dusty leaflets. They took one, put on their hats, and began to walk toward a pylon base with several ships floating at its tower. They had to duck under and around the web of dead moveways, and when they reached the station base there seemed to be no way in from the ground.

"We'll have to climb onto that moveway."

They found a narrow ladder and went up, helping the moondogs. The moveway portal was open, and they were soon in the normal passenger lounge. It was still lighted.

"Now if the lift only works."

Just as they were making for the lift shaft they were startled by a voice ringing out.

"Ho! Ho, Roland!"

"That's no voder," Peachthief whispered. "There's a live human here."

They turned back and saw that a strange person was lying half on and half off one of the lounges. As they came close their eyes opened wide: he looked frightful. His thin dirty white hair hung around a horribly creased, caved-in face, and what they could see of his neck and arms was all mottled and decayed-looking. His jerkin and pants were frayed and stained and sagged in where flesh should be. Jakko thought of the cloth shreds around dead Ferrocil and shuddered.

The stranger was staring haggardly at them. In a faint voice he said, "When the chevalier Roland died he predicted that his body would be found a spear's throw ahead of all others and facing the enemy . . . If you happen to be real, could you perhaps give me some water?"

"Of course." Jakko unhooked his canteen and tried to hand it over, but the man's hands shook and fumbled so that Jakko had to hold it to his mouth, noticing a foul odor. The stranger sucked thirstily, spilling some. Behind him the moondogs inched closer, sniffing gingerly.

"What's *wrong* with him?" Peachthief whispered as Jakko stood back.

Jakko had been remembering his lessons. "He's just very, very old, I think."

"That's right." The stranger's voice was stronger. He stared at them with curious avidity. "I waited too long. Fibrillation." He put one feeble hand to his chest. "Fibrillating . . . rather a beautiful word, don't you think? My medicine ran out or I lost it . . . A small hot animal desynchronizing in my ribs."

"We'll help you get to the River right away!" Peachthief told him.

"Too late, my lords, too late. Besides, I can't walk and you can't possibly carry me."

"You can sit up, can't you?" Jakko asked. "There have to be some roll-chairs around here, they had them for injured people." He went off to search the lounge office and found one almost at once.

When he brought it back the stranger was staring up at Peachthief, mumbling to himself in an archaic tongue of which Jakko only understood: ". . . *The breast of a grave girl makes a hill against sunrise.*" He tried to heave himself up to the chair but fell back gasping. They had to lift and drag him in, Peachthief wrinkling her nose.

"Now if the lift only works."

It did. They were soon on the high departure deck, and the fourth portal-berth held a waiting ship. It was a small local ferry. They went through into the windowed main cabin, wheeling the old man, who had collapsed upon himself and was breathing very badly. The moondogs trooped from window to window, looking down. Jakko seated himself in the pilot chair.

"Read me out the instructions," he told Peachthief.

"One, place ship on internal guidance," she read. "Whatever that means. Oh, look, here's a diagram."

"Good."

It proved simple. They went together down the list, sealing the port, disengaging umbilicals, checking vane function, reading off the standby pressures in the gasbags above them, setting the reactor to warm up the drive-motor and provide hot air for operational buoyancy.

While they were waiting, Peachthief asked the old man if he would like to be moved onto a window couch. He nodded urgently. When they got him to it he whispered, "See out!" They propped him up with chair pillows.

The ready-light was flashing. Jakko moved the controls, and the ship glided smoothly out and up. The computer was showing him wind speed, attitude, climb, and someone had marked all the verniers with the words *Course-set — RIVER*. Jakko lined everything up.

"Now it says, put it on automatic," Peachthief read. He did so.

The takeoff had excited the old man. He was straining to look down, muttering incomprehensibly. Jakko caught, *"The cool green hills of Earth . . . Crap!"* Suddenly he sang out loudly, *"There's a hell of a good universe next door — let's go!"* and fell back exhausted.

Peachthief stood over him worriedly. "I wish I could at least clean him up, but he's so weak."

The old man's eyes opened.

"Nothing shall be whole and sound that has not been rent; for love hath built his mansion in the place of excrement." He began to sing crackedly, "Take me to the River, the bee-yew-tiful River, and wash all my sins a-away! . . . You think I'm crazy, girl, don't you?" he went on conversationally. "Never heard of William Yeats. Very high bit-rate, Yeats."

"I think I understand a little," Jakko told him. "One of my aunts did English literature."

"Did literature, eh?" The stranger wheezed, snorted. "And you two — going on the River to spend eternity together as energy matrices or something equally impressive and sexless . . . *Forever wilt thou love and she be fair."* He grunted. "Always mistrusted Keats. No balls. He'd be right at home."

"We're not going on the River," Peachthief said. "At least, I'm not. I'm going to stay and make children."

The old man's ruined mouth fell open, he gazed up at her wildly.

"No!" he breathed. "Is it true? Have I stumbled on the lover and mother of man, the last?"

Peachthief nodded solemnly.

"What is your name, Oh, Queen?"

"Peachthief."

"My god. Somebody still knows of Blake." He smiled tremulously, and his eyelids suddenly slid downward; he was asleep.

"He's breathing better. Let's explore."

The small ship held little but cargo space at the rear. When they came to the food-synthesizer cubby Jakko saw Peachthief pocket something.

"What's that?"

"A little spoon. It'll be just right for a child." She didn't look at him.

Back in the main cabin the sunset was flooding the earth below with level roseate light. They were crossing huge, oddly pockmarked meadows, the airship whispering along in silence, except when a jet whistled briefly now and then for a course correction.

"Look — cows! Those must be cows," Peachthief exclaimed. "See the shadows."

Jakko made out small tan specks that were animals, with grotesque horned shadows stretching away.

"I'll have to find them when I come back. What *is* this place?"

"A big deathyard, I think. Where they put dead bodies. I never saw one this size. In some cities they had buildings just for dead people. Won't all that poison the cows?"

"Oh no, it makes good grass, I believe. The dogs will help me find them. Won't you, Tycho?" she asked the biggest moondog, who was looking down beside them.

On the eastern side of the cabin the full moon was rising into view. The old man's eyes opened, looking at it.

"More water, if you please," he croaked.

Peachthief gave him some, and then got him to swallow broth from the synthesizer. He seemed stronger, smiling at her with his mouthful of rotted teeth.

"Tell me, girl. If you're going to stay and make children, why are you going ot the River?"

"He's going because he promised to talk to his father and I'm going along to see he comes back. And make the baby. Only now he won't take any more pills, I have to try to find another man."

"Ah yes, the pills. We used to call them Wake-ups . . . . They were necessary, after the population-chemicals got around. Maybe they still are, for women. But I think it's mostly in the head. Why won't you take any more, boy? What's wrong with the old Adam?"

Peachthief started to answer but Jakko cut her off. "I can speak for myself. They upset me. They made me do bad, uncontrolled things, and feel, agh — " He broke off with a grimace.

"You seem curiously feisty, for one who values his calm above the continuance of the race."

"It's the pills, I tell you. They're — they're dehumanizing."

"Dee-humanizing," the old man mocked. "And what do you know of humanity, young one? . . . That's what I went to find, that's why I stayed so long among the old, old things from before the River came. I wanted to bring the knowledge of what humanity really was . . . I wanted to bring it all. It's simple, boy. *They died.*" He drew a rasping breath. "Every one of them died. They lived knowing that nothing but loss and suffering and extinction lay ahead. And they cared, terribly. . . . Oh, they made myths, but not many really believed them. *Death* was behind everything, waiting everywhere. Aging and death. No escape . . . Some of them went crazy, they fought and killed and enslaved each other by the millions, as if they could gain more life. Some of them gave up their precious lives for each other. They loved — and had to watch the ones they loved age and die. And in their pain and despair they built, they struggled, some of them sang. But above all, boy, they copulated! Fornicated, fucked, made love!"

He fell back, coughing, glaring at Jakko. Then, seeing that they scarcely understood his antique words, he went on more clearly. "Did sex, do you understand? Made children. It was their only weapon, you see. To send something of themselves into the future beyond their own deaths. Death was the engine of their lives, death fueled their sexuality. Death drove them at each other's throats and into each other's arms. Dying, they triumphed . . . *That* was human life. And now that mighty engine is long stilled, and you call this polite parade of immortal lemmings *humanity*? . . . Even the faintest warmth of that immemorial holocaust makes you flinch away?''

He collapsed, gasping horribly; spittle ran down his chin. One slit of eye still raked them.

Jakko stood silent, shaken by resonances from the old man's words, remembering dead Ferrocil, feeling some deep conduit of reality reaching for him out of the long-gone past. Peachthief's hand fell on his shoulder, sending a shudder through him. Slowly his own hand seemed to lift by itself and cover hers, holding her to him. They watched the old man so for a long moment. His face slowly composed, he spoke in a soft dry tone.

"I don't trust that River, you know . . . You think you're going to remain yourselves, don't you? Communicate with each other and with the essences of beings from other stars . . . The latest news from Betelgeuse.'' He chuckled raspingly.

"That's the last thing people say when they're going,'' Jakko replied. "Everyone learns that. You float out, able to talk with real other beings. Free to move.''

"Yes. What could better match our dreams?'' He chuckled again. "I wonder . . . could that be the lure, just the input end of some cosmic sausage machine? . . .''

"What's that?'' asked Peachthief.

"An old machine that ground different meats together until they came out as one substance . . . Maybe you'll find yourselves gradually mixed and minced and blended into some, some energetic plasma . . . and then maybe squirted out again to impose the terrible gift of consciousness on some innocent race of crocodiles, or poached eggs . . . And so it begins all over again. Another random engine of the universe, giving and taking obliviously . . .'' He coughed, no longer looking at them, and began to murmur in the archaic tongue, "*Ah, when the ghost begins to quicken, confusion of the death-bed over, is it sent . . . Out naked on the roads as the books say, and stricken with the injustice of the stars for punishment?* The injustice of the stars . . .'' He fell silent, and then whispered faintly, "Yet I too long to go.''

"You will,'' Peachthief told him strongly.

"How . . . much longer?''

"We'll be there by dawn,'' Jakko said. "We'll carry you. I swear.''

"A great gift,'' he said weakly. "But I fear . . . I shall give you a better.'' He mumbled on, a word Jakko didn't know; it sounded like "afrodisiack.''

He seemd to lapse into sleep then. Peachthief went and got a damp, fragrant cloth from the clean-up and wiped his face gently. He opened one eye and grinned up at her.

"Madame Tasselass,'' he rasped. "Madame Tasselass, are you really going to save us?''

She smiled down, nodding her head determinedly, Yes. He closed his eyes, looking more peaceful.

The ship was now fleeing through full moonlight, the cabin was so lit with azure and silver that they didn't think to turn on lights. Now and again the luminous mists of a low cloud veiled the windows and vanished again. Just as Jakko was about to propose eating, the old man took several gulping breaths and opened his eyes. His intestines made a bubbling sound.

Peachthief looked at him sharply and picked up one of his wrists. Then she frowned and bent over him, opening his filthy jerkin. She laid her ear to his chest, staring up at Jakko.

"He's not breathing, there's no heartbeat!" She groped inside his jerkin as if she could locate life, two tears rolling down her cheeks.

"He's *dead* — ohhh!" She groped deeper, then suddenly straightened up and gingerly clutched the cloth at the old man's crotch.

"What?"

"He's a woman!" She gave a sob and wheeled around to clutch Jakko, putting her forehead in his neck. "We never even knew her name . . ."

Jakko held her, looking at the dead man-woman, thinking, she never knew mine either. At that moment the airship jolted, and gave a noise like a cable grinding or slipping before it flew smoothly on again.

Jakko had never in his life distrusted machinery, but now a sudden terror contracted his guts. This thing could fall! They could be made dead like Ferrocil, like this stranger, like the myriads in the deathyards below. Echoes of the old voice ranting about death boomed in his head, he had a sudden vision of Peachthief grown old and dying like that. After the Rivers went, dying alone. His eyes filled, and a deep turmoil erupted under his mind. He hugged Peachthief tighter. Suddenly he knew in a dreamlike way exactly what was about to happen. Only this time there was no frenzy; his body felt like warm living rock.

He stroked Peachthief to quiet her sobs, and led her over to the moonlit couch on the far side of the cabin. She was still sniffling, hugging him hard. He ran his hands firmly down her back, caressing her buttocks, feeling her body respond.

"Give me that pill," he said to her. "Now."

Looking at him huge-eyed in the blue moonlight, she pulled out the little box. He took out his and swallowed it deliberately, willing her to understand.

"Take off your clothes." He began stripping off his jerkin, proud of the hot, steady power in his sex. When she stripped and he saw again the glistening black bush at the base of her slim belly, and the silver-edge curve of her body, urgency took him, but still in a magical calm.

"Lie down."

"Wait a minute — " She was out of his hands like a fish, running across the cabin to where the dead body lay in darkness. Jakko saw she was trying to close the dead eyes that still gleamed from the shadows. He could wait; he had never imagined his body could feel like this. She laid the cloth over the stranger's face and came back to him, half-shyly holding out her arms, sinking down spread-legged on the shining couch before him. The moonlight was so brilliant he could see the pink color of her sexual parts. He came onto her gently, controlledly, breathing in an exciting animal odor from her flesh. This time his penis entered easily, an intense feeling of all-rightness.

But a moment later the fires of terror, pity, and defiance deep within him burst up into a flame of passionate brilliance in his coupled groin. The small body under his seemed no longer vulnerable but appetitive. He clutched, mouthed, drove deep into her, exulting. Death didn't die alone, he thought obscurely, as the ancient patterns lurking in his vitals awoke. Death flew with them and flowed by beneath, but he asserted life upon the body of the woman, caught up in a great crescendo of unknown sensations, until a culminant spasm of almost painful pleasure rolled through him into her, relieving him from head to feet.

When he could talk, he thought to ask her, "Did you — " he didn't know the word. "Did it sort of explode you, like me?"

"Well, no." Her lips were by his ear. "Female sexuality is a little different. Maybe I'll show you, later . . . But I think it was good, for the baby."

He felt only a tiny irritation at her words, and let himself drift into sleep with his face in her warm-smelling hair. Dimly the understanding came to him that the great beast of his dreams, the race itself maybe, had roused and used them. So be it.

A cold thing pushing into his ear awakened him, and a hoarse voice said "Foo-ood!" It was the moondogs.

"Oh my, I forgot to feed them!" Peachthief struggled nimbly out from under him.

Jakko found he was ravenous too. The cabin was dark now, as the moon rose overhead. Peachthief located the switches, and made a soft light on their side of the cabin. They ate and drank heartily, looking down at the moonlit world. The deathyards were gone from below them now, they were flying over dark wooded foothills. When they lay down to sleep again they could feel the cabin slightly angle upward as the ship rose higher.

He was roused in the night by her body moving against him. She seemed to be rubbing her crotch.

"Give me your hand," she whispered in a panting voice. She began to make his hands do things to her, sometimes touching him too, her body arching and writhing, sleek with sweat. He found himself abruptly tumescent again, excited and pleased in a confused way. "Now, now!" she commmanded, and he entered her, finding her interior violently alive. She seemed to be half fighting him, half devouring him. Pleasure built all through him, this time without the terror. He pressed in against her shuddering convulsions. "Yes — Oh, yes!" she gasped, and a series of paroxysms swept through her, carrying him with her to explosive peace.

He held himself on and in her until her body and breathing calmed to relaxation, and they slipped naturally apart. It came to him that this sex activity seemed to have more possibilities, as a thing to do, than he had realized. His family had imparted to him nothing of all this. Perhaps they didn't know it. Or perhaps it was too alien to their calm philosophy.

"How do you know about all this?" he asked Peachthief sleepily.

"One of my aunts did literature, too." She chuckled in the darkness. "Different literature, I guess."

They slept almost as movelessly as the body flying with them on the other couch a world away.

A series of noisy bumpings wakened them. The windows were filled with pink mist flying by. The airship seemed to be sliding into a berth. Jakko looked down and saw shrubs and grass close below; it was a ground-berth on a hillside.

The computer panel lit up: RESET PROGRAM FOR BASE.

"No," said Jakko. "We'll need it going back." Peachthief looked at him in a new, companionable way; he sensed that she believed him now. He turned all the drive controls to standby while she worked the food synthesizer. Presently he heard the hiss of the deflating lift-bags, and went to where she was standing by the dead stranger.

"We'll take her, her body, out before we go back," Peachthief said. "Maybe the River will touch her somehow."

Jakko doubted it, but ate and drank his breakfast protein in silence.

When they went to use the wash-and-waste cubby he found he didn't want to clean all the residues of their contact off himself. Peachthief seemed to feel the same way; she washed only her face and hands. He looked at her slender, silk-clad belly. Was a child, his child, starting there? Desire flicked him again, but he remembered he had work to do. His promise to his father; get on with it. Sooner done, sooner back here.

"I love you," he said experimentally, and found the strange words had a startling trueness.

She smiled brilliantly at him, not just off-on. 'I love you, too, I think."

The floor-portal light was on. They pulled it up and uncovered a step-way leading to the ground. The moondogs poured down. They followed, coming out into a blowing world of rosy mists. Clouds were streaming around them; the air was all in motion up the hillside toward the crest some distance ahead of the ship berth. The ground here was uneven and covered with short soft grass, as though animals had cropped it.

"All winds blow to the River," Jakko quoted.

They set off up the hill, followed by the moondogs, who stalked uneasily with pricked ears. Probably they didn't like not being able to smell what was ahead, Jakko thought. Peachthief was holding his hand very firmly as they went, as if determined to keep him out of any danger.

As they walked up onto the flat crest of the hilltop the mists suddenly cleared, and they found themselves looking down into a great, shallow, glittering sunlit valley. They both halted involuntarily to stare at the fantastic sight.

Before them lay a huge midden heap, kilometers of things upon things upon things, almost filling the valley floor. Objects of every description lay heaped there; Jakko could make out clothing, books, toys, jewelry, a myriad artifacts and implements abandoned. These must be, he realized, the last things people had taken with them when they went on the River. In an outer ring not too far below them were tents, ground- and air-cars, even wagons. Everything shone clean and gleaming as if the influence of the River had kept off decay.

He noticed that the nearest ring of encampments intersected other, apparently older and larger rings. There seemed to be no center to the pile.

"The River has moved, or shrunk," he said.

"Both, I think," Peachthief pointed to the right. "Look, there's an old war-place."

A big grass-covered mound dominated the hill crest beside them. Jakko saw it had metal-rimmed slits in its sides. He remembered history: how there were still rulers of people when the River's tendrils first touched earth. Some of the rulers had tried to keep their subjects from the going-out places, posting guards around them and even putting killing devices in the ground. But the guards had gone themselves out on the River, or the River had swelled and taken them. And the people had driven beasts across the mined ground and surged after them into the stream of immortal life. In the end the rulers had gone too, or died out. Looking more carefully, Jakko could see that the green hill slopes were torn and pocked, as though ancient explosions had made craters everywhere.

Suddenly he remembered that he had to find his father in all this vast confusion.

"Where's the River now? My father's mind should reach there still, if I'm not too late."

"See that glittery slick look in the air down there? I'm sure that's a danger place."

Down to their right, fairly close to the rim, was a strangely bright place. As he stared it became clearer: a great column of slightly golden or shining air. He scanned about, but saw nothing else like it all across the valley.

"If that's the only focus left, it's going away fast."

She nodded and then swallowed, her small face suddenly grim. She meant to live on here and die without the River, Jakko could see that. But he would be with her; he resolved it with all his heart. He squeezed her hand hard.

"If you have to talk to your father, we better walk around up here on the rim where it's safe," Peachthief said.

"No-oo," spoke up a moondog from behind them. The two humans turned and saw the three sitting in a row on the crest, staring slit-eyed at the valley.

"All right," Peachthief said. "You wait here. We'll be back soon."

She gripped Jakko's hand even tighter, and they started walking past the old war mound, past the remains of ancient vehicles, past an antique pylon that leaned crazily. There were faint little trails in the short grass. Another war mound loomed ahead; when they passed around it they found themselves suddenly among a small herd of white animals with long necks and no horns. The animals went on grazing quietly as the humans walked by. Jakko thought they might be mutated deer.

"Oh, look!" Peachthief let go his hand. "That's milk — see, her baby is sucking!"

Jakko saw that one of the animals had a knobby bag between its hind legs. A small one half-knelt down beside it, with its head up nuzzling the bag. A mother and her young.

Peachthief was walking cautiously toward them, making gentle greeting sounds. The mother animal looked at her calmly, evidently tame. The baby went on sucking, rolling its eyes. Peachthief reached them, petted the mother, and then bent down under to feel the bag. The animal sidestepped a pace, but stayed still. When Peachthief straightened up she was licking her hand.

"That's good milk! And they're just the right size, we can take them on the airship! On the way-cars, even." She was beaming, glowing. Jakko felt an odd warm constriction in his chest. The intensity with which she furnished her little world, her future nest! *Their* nest . . .

"Come with us, come on," Peachthief was urging. She had her belt around the creature's neck to lead it. It came equably, the young one following in awkward galloping lunges.

"That baby is a male. Oh, this is *perfect*," Peachthief exclaimed. "Here, hold her a minute while I look at that one."

She handed Jakko the end of the belt and ran off. The beast eyed him levelly. Suddenly it drew its upper lip back and shot spittle at his face. He ducked, yelling for Peachthief to come back.

"I have to find my father first!"

"All right," she said, returning. "Oh, look at that!"

Downslope from them was an apparition — one of the white animals, but partly transparent, ghostly thin. It drifted vaguely, putting its head down now and then, but did not eat.

"It must have got partly caught in the River, it's half gone. Oh, Jakko, you can see how dangerous it is! I'm afraid, I'm afraid it'll catch you."

"It won't. I'll be very careful."

"I'm so afraid." But she let him lead her on, towing the animal alongside. As they passed the ghost-creature Peachthief called to it, "You can't live like that. You better go on out. Shoo, shoo!"

It turned and moved slowly out across the piles of litter toward the shining place in the air.

They were coming closer to it now, stepping over more and more abandoned things. Peachthief looked sharply at everything; once she stooped to pick up a beautiful fleecy white square and stuff it in her pack. The hill crest was merging with a long grassy slope, comparatively free of debris, that ran out toward the airy glittering column. They turned down it.

The River-focus became more and more awesome as they approached. They could trace it towering up and up now, twisting gently as it passed beyond the sky. A tendril of the immaterial stream of sidereal sentience that had embraced earth, a pathway to immortal life. The air inside looked no longer golden, but pale silver-gilt, like a great shaft of moonlight coming down through the morning sun. Objects at its base appeared very clear but shimmering, as if seen through cool crystal water.

Off to one side were tents. Jakko suddenly recognized one, and quickened his steps. Peachthief pulled back on his arm.

"Jakko, be careful!"

They slowed to a stop a hundred yards from the tenuous fringes of the River's effect. It was very still. Jakko peered intently. In the verges of the shimmer a staff was standing upright. From it hung a scarf of green and yellow silk.

"Look — that's my father's sign!"

"Oh Jakko, you *can't* go in there."

At the familiar colored sign all the memories of his life with his family had come flooding back on Jakko. The gentle rationality, the solemn sense of preparation for going out from earth forever. Two different realities strove briefly within him. They had loved him, he realized that now. Especially his father . . . But not as he loved Peachthief, his awakened spirit shouted silently. I am of earth! Let the stars take care of their own. His resolve took deeper hold and won.

Gently he released himself from her grip.

"You wait here. Don't worry, it takes a long while for the change, you know that. Hours, days. I'll only be a minute, I'll come right back."

"Ohhh, it's crazy."

But she let him go and stood holding to the milk-animal while he went down the ridge and picked his way out across the midden-heap toward the staff. As he neared it he could feel the air change around him, becoming alive and yet more still.

"Father! Paul! It's Jakko, your son. Can you still hear me?"

Nothing answered him. He took a step or two past the staff, repeating his call.

A resonant susurrus came in his head, as if unearthly reaches had opened to him. From infinity he heard without hearing his father's quiet voice.

You came.

A sense of calm welcome.

"The cities are all empty, Father. All the people have gone, everywhere."

Come.

"No!" He swallowed, fending off memory, fending off the lure of strangeness. "I think it's sad. It's wrong. I've found a woman. We're going to stay and make children."

The River is leaving, Jakko my son.

It was as if a star had called his name, but he said stubbornly, "I don't care. I'm staying with her. Good-bye, father. Good-bye."

Grave regret touched him, and from beyond a host of silent voices murmured down the sky: *Come! Come away.*

"No!" he shouted, or tried to shout, but he could not still the rapt voices. And suddenly, gazing up, he felt the serenity of the River, the overwhelming opening of the door to life everlasting among the stars. All his mortal fears, all his most secret dread of the waiting maw of death, slid out of him and fell away, leaving him almost unbearably light and calmly joyful. He knew that he was being touched, that he could float out upon that immortal stream forever. But even as the longing took him, his human mind remembered that this was the start of the first stage, for which the River was called Beata. He thought of the ghost-animal that had lingered too long. He must leave now, and quickly. With enormous effort he took one step backward, but could not turn.

"Jakko! Jakko! Come back!"

Someone was calling, screaming his name. He did turn then and saw her on the little ridge. Nearby, yet so far. The ordinary sun of earth was brilliant on her and the two white beasts.

"Jakko! Jakko!" Her arms were outstretched, she was running toward him.

It was as if the whole beautiful earth was crying to him, calling to him to come back and take up the burden of life and death. He did not want it. But she must not come here, he knew that without remembering why. He began uncertainly to stumble toward her, seeing her now as his beloved woman, again as an unknown creature uttering strange cries.

"Lady Death," he muttered, not realizing he had ceased to move. She ran faster, tripped, almost fell in the heaps of stuff. The wrongness of her coming here roused him again; he took a few more steps, feeling his head clear a little.

"Jakko!" She reached him, clutched him, dragging him bodily forward from the verge.

At her touch the reality of his human life came back to him, his heart pounded human blood, all stars fled away. He started to run clumsily, half-carrying her with him up to the safety of the ridge. Finally they sank down gasping beside the animals, holding and kissing each other, their eyes wet.

"I thought you were lost, I thought I'd lost you," Peachthief sobbed.

"You saved me."

"H-here," she said. "We b-better have some food." She rummaged in her pack, nodding firmly as if the simple human act could defend against unearthly powers. Jakko discovered that he was quite hungry.

They ate and drank peacefully in the soft, flower-studded grass, while the white animals grazed around them. Peachthief studied the huge strewn valley floor, frowning as she munched.

"So many good useful things here. I'll come back some day, when the River's gone, and look around."

"I thought you only wanted natural things," he teased her.

"Some of these things will last. Look." She picked up a small implement. "It's an awl, for punching and sewing leather. You could make children's sandals."

Many of the people who came here must have lived quite simply, Jakko thought. It was true that there could be useful tools. And metal. Books, too. Directions for making things. He lay back dreamily, seeing a vision of himself in the far future, an accomplished artisan, teaching his children skills. It seemed deeply good.

"Oh, my milk-beast!" Peachthief broke in on his reverie. "Oh, no, you musn't!" She jumped up.

Jakko sat up and saw that the white mother-animal had strayed quite far down the grassy ridge. Peachthief trotted down after her, calling, "Come here! Stop!"

Perversely, the animal moved away, snatching mouthfuls of grass. Peachthief ran faster. The animal threw up its head and paced down off the ridge, among the litter piles.

"'No! Oh, my milk! Come back here, come.''

She went down after it, trying to move quietly and call more calmly.

Jakko had got up, alarmed.

"Come back! Don't go down there!''

"The babies' milk,'' she wailed at him, and made a dash at the beast. But she missed, and it drifted away just out of reach before her.

To his horror Jakko saw that the glittering column of the River had changed shape slightly, eddying out a veil of shimmering light close ahead of the beast.

"Turn back! Let it go!'' he shouted, and began to run with all his might. "Peachthief — Come back!''

But she would not turn, and his pounding legs could not catch up. The white beast was in the shimmer now; he saw it bound up onto a great sun-and-moonlit heap of stuff. Peachthief's dark form went flying after it, uncaring, and the creature leaped away again. He saw her follow, and bitter fear grabbed at his heart. The very strength of her human life is betraying her to death, he thought; I have to get her physically, I will pull her out. He forced his legs faster, faster yet, not noticing that the air had changed around him too.

She disappeared momentarily in a veil of glittering air, and then reappeared, still following the beast. Thankfully he saw her pause and stoop to pick something up. She was only walking now, he could catch her. But his own body was moving sluggishly, it took all his will to keep his legs thrusting him ahead.

"Peachthief! Love, come back!''

His voice seemed muffled in the silvery air. Dismayed, he realized that he too had slowed to a walk, and she was veiled again from his sight.

When he struggled through the radiance he saw her, moving very slowly after the wandering white beast. Her face was turned up, unearthly light was on her beauty. He knew she was feeling the rapture, the call of immortal life was on her. On him, too; he found he was barely stumbling forward, a terrible serenity flooding his heart. They must be passing into the very focus of the River, where it ran strongest.

"Love — '' Mortal grief fought the invading transcendence. Ahead of him the girl faded slowly into the glimmering veils, still following her last earthly desire. He saw that humanity, all that he had loved of the glorious earth, was disappearing forever from reality. Why had it awakened, only to be lost? Spectral voices were near him, but he did not want specters. An agonizing lament for human life welled up in him, a last pang that he would carry with him through eternity. But its urgency fell away. Life incorporeal, immortal, was on him now; it had him as it had her. His flesh, his body was beginning to attenuate, to dematerialize out into the great current of sentience that flowed on its mysterious purposes among the stars.

Still the sense of his earthly self moved slowly after hers into the closing mists of infinity, carrying upon the River a configuration that had been a man striving forever after a loved dark girl, who followed a ghostly white milch deer.

Here Naomi Mitchison – author of the critically acclaimed novel Memories of a
Spacewoman, *as well as several books about Africa, where she was once a tribal
advisor to the Bakgatla of Southeast Botswana – tells a stark and chilling little
tale about witchcraft, evil, and the vulnerability – and strength – of innocence.*

NAOMI MITCHISON
The Finger

Kobedi had a mother but no father. When he was old enough to understand such
things someone said that his father was the Good Man. By that they meant the Bad
Man, because, so often, words, once they are fully known, have meanings other
or opposite to their first appearance. Kobedi, however, hoped that his father was
the fat man at the store. Sometimes his mother went there and brought back many
things, not only the needful meal and oil, but tea and sugar and beautiful tins with
pictures, and almost always sweets for himself. Once, when he was a quite little
boy, he had asked his mother where she kept the money for this and she answered,
"Between my legs." So, when she had drunk too much beer and was asleep on
her back and snoring, he lifted her dress to see if he could find this money and take
a little. But there was nothing there except a smell which he did not like. He had
two small sisters, both fat and flat nosed like the man at the store. But his own nose
was thin, and the Good Man also had a thin nose as though he could cut with it.

Kobedi went to school and he thought he now understood what his mother
had meant though he did not wish to think of it; at least she paid the school fees,
though she grumbled about them. He was in Standard Three and there were
pictures on the wall which he liked; now he wrote sentences in his jotter and they
were ticked in red because they were correct. That was good. But in a while he
bacame aware that things were happening around him which were not good. First
it was the way his mother looked at him, and sometimes felt his arms and legs, and
some of her friends who came and whispered. Then came the time he woke in the
blackest of the night, for there was a smell which made him feel sick and the Good
Man was there, sitting on the stuffed and partly torn sofa under the framed picture
of white Baby Jesus. He was wearing skins of animals over his trousers, and his
toes, which had large nails, clutched and burrowed in the rag rug Kobedi's mother
had made. The Good Man saw that Kobedi was awake because his eyes were open
and staring; he pointed one finger at him. That was the more frightening because
his other hand was under the skirt of a young girl who was sitting next to him,
snuggling. The pointing finger twitched and beckoned and slowly Kobedi unrol-
led himself from his blanket and came over naked and shaking.

The Good Man now withdrew his other hand and his dampish fingers crawled over Kobedi. He took out two sinews from a bundle, rubbing them in the sweat of his own skin until they became thin and hard and twisted and dipped them into a reddish medicine powder he had and spat on them and he pointed the finger again and Kobedi slunk back and pulled the blanket over his head.

The next day the tied-on sinews began to make his skin itch. He tried to pull them off but his mother slapped him, saying they were strong medicine and he must keep them on. He could not do any arithmetic that day. The numbers had lost their meaning and his teacher beat him.

The next time he became aware of that smell in the night he carefully did not move nor open his eyes, but pulled the blanket slowly from his ears so that he could hear the whispering. Again it was the Good Man and his mother and perhaps another woman or even two women. They were speaking of a place and a time, and at that place and time, a happening. The words were so dressed as to mean something else, as when speaking of a knife they called it a little twig, when they spoke of the heart it was the cooking pot, when they spoke of the liver it was the red blanket, and when they spoke of the fat it was the beer froth. And it became clear to Kobedi that when they spoke of the meal sack it was of himself they were speaking. Death, death, the whispers said, and the itching under the sinews grew worse.

The next morning all was as always. The little sisters toddled and played and their mother pounded meal for the porridge and called morning greetings to her neighbors acrosss the wall of the *lapa*. Then she said to him: "After the school is finished you are to go to the store and get me one packet tea. Perhaps he will give you sweets. Here is money for tea."

It was not much money, but it was a little and he knew he had to go and fast. He passed by the school and did not heed the school bell calling to him and he walked to the next village and on to the big road. He waited among people for a truck and fear began to catch upon him; by now he was hungry and bought fatty cakes for five cents. Then he climbed in at the back of the truck with the rest of the people. Off went the truck, north, south, he did not know. Only there was a piece of metal in the bottom of the truck, some kind of rasp, and he worked with this until he had got the sinew off his ankle and he dropped it over the side so that it would be run over by many other trucks. It was harder to get at the arm one and he only managed to scrape his own skin before the truck stopped in a big town.

Now it must be said that Kobedi was lucky; after a short time of hunger and fear he got a job sweeping out a small shop and going with heavy parcels. He was also allowed to sleep on a pile of sacks under the counter, though he must be careful to let nobody know, especially not the police. But under the sacks was a loose board and below it he had a tin, and into this he put money out of his wages, a few cents at a time. He heard about a school that was held in the evenings after work; he did not speak to anyone about it, and indeed he had no friends in the big town because it seemed to him that friends meant losing one's little money at playing dice games or taking one's turn to buy a coke; and still his arm itched.

When he had enough money he went one evening to the school and said he had been in Standard Three and he wanted to go on with education and had money to buy it. The white man who was the head teacher asked him where he came from. He said from Talane, which was by no means the the name of his village, and also that his father was dead and there was no money to pay for school. The truth is too precious and dangerous to be thrown anywhere. So the man was sorry for him and said well, he could sit with the others and try how he did.

At this time Kobedi worked all day and went to classes in the evening and still he was careful not to become too friendly, in case the friend was an enemy. There was a knife in the shop, but it was blunt, and though he sawed at the sinew on his arm he could not get it off. Sometimes he dreamed about whispering in the night and woke frozen. Sometimes he thought his mother would come suddenly through the door of the shop and claim him. If she did, could the night school help him?

One of the Motswana teachers took notice of him and let him come to his room to do homework, since this was not possible in the shop. There were some books in the teacher's room and a photograph of himself with others at the T.T.C.; after a while Kobedi began to like this teacher, Mr. Tshele, and half thought that one day he would tell him what his fears were. But not yet. There came an evening when he was writing out sentences in English, at one side of the table where the lamp stood. Mr. Tshele had a friend with him; they were drinking beer. He heard the cans being opened and smelled the fizzling beer. At a certain moment he began to listen because Mr. Tshele was teasing his friend, who was hoping for a post in the civil service and had been to a doctor to get a charm to help him. "You believe in that!" said Mr. Tshele. "You are not modern. You should go to a cattle post and not to the civil service!"

"Everyone does the same," said his friend, "perhaps it helps, perhaps not. I do not want to take risks. It is my life."

"Well, it is certainly your moeny. What did he charge you?" The friend giggled and did not answer; the beer cans chinked again. "I am asking you another thing," said Mr. Tshele, "This you have done at least brings no harm. But what about sorcery? Do you believe?"

The friend hesitated. "I have heard dreadful things," he said, "What they do. Perhaps they are mad. Perhaps it no longer happens. Not in Botswana. Only perhaps — well, perhaps in Lesotho. Who knows? In the mountains."

Mr. Tshele leaned back in his chair. Kobedi ducked his head over his paper and pencil and pretended to be busy writing. "There is a case coming up in the High Court," said Mr. Tshele. "My cousin who is a lawyer told me. A man is accused of medicine murder. The trial will be next week. They are looking for witnesses, but people are afraid to come forward."

"But they must have found — something?

"Yes, a dead child. Cut in a certain way. Pieces taken out. Perhaps even while the child was alive and screaming for help."

"This is most dreadful," said the friend. "and most certainly the man I went to about my civil service interview would never do such a thing!"

"Maybe not," said Mr. Tshele, "not if he can get your money a safer way! Mind you, I myself went to a doctor who was a registered herbalist when I had those headaches, and he threw the *ditaola* and all that, but most certainly he did not murder."

"Did he cure your headaches?"

"Yes, yes, and it was cheaper than going to the chemist's shop. He rubbed the back of my neck and also gave me a powder to drink. Two things. It was a treatment, a medical treatment, not just a charm. I suppose you also go for love charms?"

Again the friend giggled, and Kobedi was afraid they would now only speak about girls. He wanted to know more, more, about the man who had cut out the heart — and the liver — and stripped off the fat for rubbing, as he remembered the whispering in the night. But they came back to it. "This man, the one you spoke of who is to be tried, he is from where?" the friend asked. And Mr. Tshele carelessly gave the name of the village. His village. The name, the shock, the knowledge, for it must indeed and in truth be the Good Man. Kobedi could not speak, could not move. He stared at the lamp and the light blurred and pulsed with the strong terrible feeling he had in him like the vomiting of the soul.

He did not speak that evening. Nor the next. He wondered if the Good Man was in a strong jail, but if so surely he could escape, taking some form, a vulture, a great crow? And his mother? And the other women, the whisperers? But the evening after that, in the middle of dusty open space near the school where nobody could be hiding to listen, he touched Mr. Tshele's coat and looked up at him, for he did not yet come to a man's shoulder height. Mr. Tshele bent down , thinking this was some school trouble. It was then that Kobedi whispered the name of his village and when Mr. Tshele did not immediately understand: "Where *that one* who is to be tried comes from. I know him."

"You? How?" said Mr. Tshele and then Kobedi began to tell him everything and the dust blew round them and he began to cry and Mr. Tshele wiped his dusty tears away and took him to a shop at the far side of the open space and gave him an ice lolly on a stick. He had seen boys sucking them, but for him it was the first time and great pleasure.

Then Mr. Tshele said, "Come with me," and took him by the hand and they went together to the house of his cousin the lawyer, which was set in a garden with fruit trees and tomato plants and flowers and a thing which whirled water. Inside it was as light as a shop and Kobedi's bare feet felt a soft and delicious carpet under them. "Here is your witness in the big case!" said Mr. Tshele, and then to Kobidi: "Tell him!" But Kobedi could not speak of it again.

But they gave him a drink that stung a little on the tongue and was warm in the stomach, and in a while Kobedi was able to say again what he had said to his teacher and it came more easily. "Good," said the cousin who was a lwayer. "Now, little one, will you be able to say this in the Court? If you can do it you will destroy a great evil. Modimo will be glad of you." Kobedi nodded and then he whispered to Mr. Tshele, "It will come better if you take this off me," and the showed them the sinew with the medicine. The two men looked at one another and the lawyer fetched a strong pair of scissors and cut through the sinew; then he took it into the kitchen, and before Kobedi's eyes he put it with his own hand into the stove and poked the wood into a blaze so that it was consumed altogether. After that Kobedi told the lawyer the shop where he worked. "So now," said the lawyer, "no word to any other person. This is between us three. *Khudu Thamaga.*"

That night Kobedi slept quickly without dreaming. Two days later a big car stopped at the shop where he was sweeping out the papers and dirt and spittle of the customers. The lawyer came to the door and called him: "You have not spoken? Good. But in Court you will speak." Then the lawyer gave some money to the man at the shop to make up for taking his servant, and when they were in the car he explained to Kobedi how it would be. The accused here, the witness there. "I will ask you questions," he said, "and you will answer and it will be only the truth. Look at the Judge in the high seat behind the table where men write. Do not look at the accused man. Never look at him. Do you understand?" Kobedi nodded. The lawyer went on, "Speak in Setswana when I question you, even if you know some English words which my cousin says you have learned. These things of which you will tell cannot be spoken in English. But show also that you know a little. You can say to the Judge. "I greet you, Your Honour.' Repeat that. Yes, that is right. Your Honour is the English name for a Judge and this is a most important Judge."

So in a while the car stopped and Kobedi was put into a room and given milk and sandwiches with meat in them and he waited. The time came when he was called into the Court and a man helped him and told him not to be afraid. He kept his eyes down and saw nothing, but the man touched his shoulder and said, "There is His Honour the Judge." So Kobedi looked up bravely and greeted the Judge, who smiled at him and asked if he knew the meaning of an oath. At all times there was an interpreter in the Court and there seemed to be very many people, who sometimes made a rustling sound like dry leaves of mealies, but Kobedi carefully looked only at the Judge. So he took his oath; there was a Bible, such as he had seen at his first school. And then the lawyer began to ask him questions and he answered, so that the story grew like a tree in front of the Judge.

Now it came to the whisperers in the midnight room and what they had shown him of their purpose: the lawyer asked him who there were besides the accused. Kobedi answered that one was his mother. And as he did so there was a scream and it came from his mother herself. "Wicked one, liar, runaway, oh how I will beat you!" she yelled at him until a policewoman took her away. But he had turned toward her, and suddenly he had become dreadfully unhappy. And in his unhappiness he looked too far and in a kind of wooden box half a grown person's height, he saw the Good Man.

Before he could take his eyes away the Good Man suddenly shot out his finger over the top of the box and it was as though a rod of fire passed between him and Kobedi. "It is all lies," shouted the Good Man." Tell them you have lied,

lied, lied!'' And a dreadful need came onto Kobedi to say just this thing and he took a shuffling step toward the Good Man, for what had passed between them was *kgogela,* sorcery, and it had trapped him. But there was a great noise from all round and he heard the lawyer's voice and the Judge's voice and other voices and he felt a sharp pain in the side of his stomach.

Now after this Kobedi was not clear what was happening, only he shut his eyes tight, and then it seemed to him that he still wore those sinews which the Good Man had fastened onto him. And the pain in his stomach seemed to grow. But the *kgogela* had been broken and he did not need to undo his words and he was able to open his eyes and look at the Judge and to answer three more questions from his friend the lawyer. Then he was guided back to the room where one waited and he did not speak of the pain, for he hoped it might go.

But it was still there. After a time his friend the lawyer came in and said he had done well. But somehow Kobedi no longer cared. When he was in the car beside the lawyer he had to ask for it to stop so that he could get out and vomit into a bush, for he could not dirty such a shining car. On the way to the Court he had watched the little clocks and jumping numbers in the front of the car, but now they did not speak to him. He had become tired all over and yet if he shut his eyes he saw the finger pointing. "I will take you to Mr. Tshele,'' said the lawyer and stopped to buy milk and bread and sausage; but Kobedi was only a little pleased and he began less and less to be able not to speak of his pain.

After a time of voices and whirling and doctors, he began to wake up and he was in a white bed and there was a hospital smell. A nurse came and he felt pain, but not of the same deep kind, nor so bad. Then a doctor came and said all was well and Mr. Tshele came and told Kobedi that now he was going to live with him and go properly to school in the daytime and have new clothes and shoes. He and the lawyer would become, as it were, Kobedi's uncles. "But,'' said Kobedi, "tell me — the one — the one who did these things?''

"The Judge has spoken,'' said Mr. Tshele. "That man will die and all will be wiped out.''

"And — the woman?'' For he could not now say mother.

"She will be put away until the evil is out of her.'' Kobedi wondered a little about the small sisters, but they were no longer in his life so he could forget them and forget the house and foget his village forever. He lay back in the white bed.

After a while a young nurse came in and gave him a pill to swallow. Kobedi began to question her about what happened, for he knew by now that the doctors had cut the pain out of his stomach. The young nurse looked round and whispered: "They took out a thing like a small crocodile, but dead,'' she said.

"That was the sorcery,'' said Kobedi. Now he knew and was happy that it was entirely gone.

The young nurse said, "We are not allowed to believe in sorcery.''

"I do not belive in it any longer,'' said Kobedi, "because it is finished. But that was what it was.''

Gene Wolfe is one of the best SF writers working today, and, sadly, one of the most undervalued. This situation may be changing, though: his novel The Shadow of the Torturer *(Timescape), the first part of the tetralogy* The Book of the New Sun, *was one of the most critically acclaimed novels of the year, and his short-story collection* The Island of Doctor Death and Other Stories and Other Stories *was hailed as one of the best collections in recent times. Wolfe's other books include the classic* The Fifth Head of Cerberus *(Ace),* The Devil in a Forest *(Ace), and* Peace *(Harper & Row). Upcoming are* The Claw of the Conciliator *(Timescape), the second novel in the* New Sun *tetralogy, and* Gene Wolfe's Book of Days *(Doubleday), a new short-story collection. His novella ''Seven American Nights'' was in our* Eighth Annual Collection. *He lives in Barrington, Illinois, with his wife and family, where he is the editor of the trade publication* Plant Engineering.*

Here he spins a deceptively-simple tale of what seems to be the classic Christmas situation—a quiet Christmas Eve, the child waiting breathlessly for Santa to come, the toys displayed beneath the brightly decorated tree—but somehow we don't think that Clement Clarke Moore would have approved of how everything turns out.

GENE WOLFE
War Beneath the Tree

"It's Christmas Eve, Commander Robin," the Spaceman said. "You'd better go to bed or Santa won't come."

Robin's mother said, "That's right, Robin. Time to say good night."

The little boy in blue pajamas nodded, but he made no move to rise.

"Kiss me," said Bear. Bear walked his funny waddly walk around the tree and threw his arms about Robin. "We have to go to bed. I'll come, too." It was what he said every night.

Robin's mother shook her head in amused despair. "Listen to them," she said. "Look at him, Bertha. He's like a little prince surrounded by his court. How is he going to feel when he's grown and can't have transistorized sycophants to spoil him all the time?"

Bertha the robot maid nodded her own almost human head as she put the poker back in its stand. "That's right, Ms. Jackson. That's right for sure."

The Dancing Doll took Robin by the hand, making an arabesque penché of it. Now Robin rose. His guardsmen formed up and presented arms.

"On the other hand," Robin's mother said, "they're children only such a short time."

170

Bertha nodded again. "They're only young once, Ms. Jackson. That's for sure. All right if I tell these little cute toys to help me straighten up after he's asleep?"

The Captain of the guardsmen saluted with his silver saber, the Largest Guardsman beat the tattoo on his drum, and the rest of the guardsmen formed a double file.

"He sleeps with Bear," Robin's mother said.

"I can spare Bear. There's plenty of others."

The Spaceman touched the buckle of his antigravity belt and soared to a height of four feet like a graceful, broad-shouldered balloon. With the Dancing Doll on his left and Bear on his right, Robin toddled off behind the guardsmen. Robin's mother ground out her last cigarette of the evening, winked at Bertha and said, "I suppose I'd better turn in, too. You needn't help me undress. Just pick up my things in the morning."

"Yes um. Too bad Mr. Jackson ain't here, it bein' Christmas Eve and you expectin' and all."

"He'll be back from Brazil in a week — I've told you already. Bertha, your speech habits are getting worse and worse. Are you sure you wouldn't rather be a French maid for a while?"

"Maize none, Ms. Jackson. I have too much trouble talkin' to the men that comes to the door when I'm French."

"When Mr. Jackson gets his next promotion, we're going to have a chauffeur," Robin's mother said, "He's going to be Italian, and he's going to *stay* Italian."

Bertha watched her waddle out of the room. "All right, you lazy toys! You empty them ashtrays into the fire an' get everythin' put away. I'm goin' to turn myself off, but the next time I come on this room better be straight or there's goin' to be some broken toys aroun' here."

She watched long enough to see the Gingham Dog dump the contents of the largest ashtray on the crackling logs, the Spaceman float up to straighten the magazines on the coffee table, and the Dancing Doll begin to sweep the hearth. "Put yourselfs in your box," she told the guardsmen, and then she turned off.

In the smallest bedroom, Bear lay in Robin's arms. "Be quiet," said Robin.

"I *am* quiet." said Bear.

"Everytime I am almost gone to sleep, you squiggle."

"I don't, said Bear.

"You do."

"Don't."

"Do."

"Sometimes you have trouble going to sleep, too, Robin," said Bear.

"I'm having trouble *tonight,*" Robin countered meaningfully.

Bear slipped from his arms. "I want to see if it's snowing again." He climbed from the bed to an open drawer and from the open drawer to the top of the dresser. It was snowing.

Robin said, "Bear, you have a circuit loose." It was what his mother sometimes said to Bertha.

Bear did not reply.

"Oh, Bear," Robin said sleepily a moment later. "I know why you're antsy. It's your birthday tomorrow, and you think I didn't get you anything."

"Did you?" Bear asked.

"I will," Robin said. "Mother will take me to the store." In half a minute his breathing became the regular, heavy sighing of a sleeping child.

Bear sat on the edge of the dresser and looked at him. Then he said under his breath, "I can sing Christmas carols." It had been the first thing he had ever said to Robin, one year ago. He spread his arms. *All is calm, all is bright.* It made him think of the lights on the tree and the bright fire in the living room. The Spaceman was there, but because he was the only toy who could fly, none of the others liked the Spaceman much. The Dancing Doll was there, too. The Dancing Doll was clever, but . . . well — he could not think of the word.

He jumped down into the drawer on top of a pile of Robin's undershirts, then out of the drawer, and softly to the dark, carpeted floor.

"Limited," he said to himself. "The Dancing Doll is limited." He thought again of the fire, then of the old toys — the Blocks Robin had had before he and the Dancing Doll and the rest had come, the Wooden Man who rode a yellow bicycle, the Singing Top.

The door of Robin's room was nearly closed. There was only a narrow slit of light, so that Robin would not be afraid. Bear had been closing it a little more each night. Now he did not want to open it. But it had been a long time since Robin had asked about his Wooden Man, his Singing Top, and his "A" Block, with all of its talk of apples and acorns and alligators.

In the living room, the Dancing Doll was positioning the guardsmen, and all the while the Spaceman stood on the mantel and supervised. "We can get three or four behind the bookcase," he called.

"Where they won't be able to see a thing." Bear growled.

The Dancing Doll pirouetted and dropped a sparkling curtsy. "'We were afraid you wouldn't come," she said.

"Put one behind each leg of the coffee table." Bear told her. "I had to wait until he was asleep. Now listen to me, all of you. When I call, 'Charge!' we must all run at them together. That's very important. If we can, we'll have a practice beforehand."

The Largest Guardsman said, "I'll beat my drum."

"You'll beat the enemy, or you'll go into the fire with the rest of us." Bear said.

Robin was sliding on the ice. His feet went out from under him and right up into the air so that he fell down with a tremendous BUMP that shook him all over. He lifted his head, and he was not on the frozen pond in the park at all. He was in his own bed with the moon shining in at the window, and it was Christmas Eve — no Christmas night now — and Santa was coming. Maybe he had already come. Robin listened for reindeer on the roof and did not hear the sound of any reindeer steps. Then he listened for Santa eating the cookies his mother had left on the stone shelf next to the fireplace. There was no munching or crunching. Then he threw back the covers and slipped down over the edge of his bed until his feet touched the floor. The good smells of tree and fire had come into his room. He followed them out the room, ever so quietly, into the hall.

Santa was in the living room, bent over beside the tree! Robin's eyes opened until they were as big and as round as his pajama buttons. Then Santa straightened up, and he was not Santa at all, but Robin's mother in a new red bathrobe. Robin's mother was nearly as fat as Santa and Robin had to put his fingers in the mouth to keep from laughing at the way she puffed and pushed at her knees with her hands until she stood straight.

But Santa had come! There were toys — new toys — everywhere under the tree.

Robin's mother went to the cookies on the stone shelf and ate half of one. Then she drank half the glass of milk. Then she turned to go back into her bedroom, and Robin retreated into the darkness of his own room until she had passed. When he peeked cautiously around the door frame again, the toys — the New Toys — were beginning to move.

They shifted and shook themselves and looked about. Perhaps it was because it was Christmas Eve. Perhaps it was only because the light of the fire had activated their circuits. But a clown brushed himself off and stretched, and a raggedy girl smoothed her raggedy apron (with a heart embroidered on it), and a monkey gave a big jump and chinned himself on the next-to-lowest limb of the Christmas tree. Robin saw them. And Bear, behind the hassock of Robin's father's chair, saw them, too. Cowboys and Native Americans were lifting the lid of a box, and a knight opened a cardboard door (made to look like wood) in the side of another box (made to look like stone), letting a dragon peer over his shoulder.

"*Charge!*" Bear called. "*Charge!*" He came around the side of the hassock on all fours like a real bear, running stiffly but very fast, and he hit the Clown at his wide waistline and knocked him down, then picked him up and threw him halfway to the fire.

The Spaceman had swooped down on the Monkey; they wrestled, teetering on top of a polystyrene tricycle.

The Dancing Doll had charged fastest of all, faster even than Bear himself, in a breathtaking series of jetés, but the Raggedy Girl had lifted her feet from the floor and now she was running with her toward the fire. As Bear struck the Clown a second time, he saw two Native Americans carrying a guardsman — the Captain of the guardsmen — toward the fire, too. The Captain's saber had sliced through one of the Native Americans, and it must have disabled some circuit because the Native American walked badly. But in a moment more the Captain was burning, his red uniform ablaze, his hands thrown up like tongues of flame, his black eyes glazing and cracking, bright metal running from him like sweat to harden among the ashes under the logs.

The Clown tried to wrestle with Bear, but Bear threw him down. The Dragon's teeth were sunk in Bear's left heel, but Bear kicked himself free. The Calico Cat was burning, burning. The Gingham Dog tried to pull her out, but the Monkey pushed him into the fire. For a moment Bear thought of the cellar stairs and the deep, dark cellar, where there were boxes and bundles and a hundred forgotten corners. If he ran and hid, the New Toys might never find him, might never even try to find him. Years from now Robin would discover him, covered with dust.

The Dancing Doll's scream was high and sweet, and Bear turned to face the Knight's upraised sword.

When Robin's mother got up on Christmas morning, Robin was awake already, sitting under the tree with the Cowboys, watching the Native Americans do their rain dance. The Monkey was perched on his shoulder, the Raggedy Girl (programmed, the store had assured Robin's mother, to begin Robin's sex education) in his lap, and the Knight and the Dragon were at his feet. "Do you like the toys Santa brought you, Robin?" Robin's mother asked.

"One of the Native Amer'cans doesn't work."

"Never mind, dear. We'll take him back. Robin, I've got something important to tell you."

Bertha the robot maid came in with cornflakes and milk and vitamins for Robin and café au lait for Robin's mother. "Where is those old toys?" she asked. "They done a picky-poor job of cleanin' up this room."

"Robin, your toys are just toys, of course — "

Robin nodded absently. A red calf was coming out of the chute, with a cowboy on a roping horse after him.

"Where *is* those old toys, Ms. Jackson?" Bertha asked again.

"They're programmed to self-destruct, I understand," Robin's mother said. "But, Robin, you know how the new toys all came, the Knight and Dragon and all your Cowboys, almost by magic? Well, the same thing can happen with people."

Robin looked at her with frightened eyes.

"The same wonderful thing is going to happen here, in our home."

Born in Manhattan, Suzy McKee Charnas spent some time with the Peace Corps in Nigeria, and now resides in Albuquerque, New Mexico, with her husband and family. One of the best of the new SF writers, she is the author of the well-known novel Walk to the End of the World *(Berkley) and its recent sequel* Motherlines *(Berkley) Her new novel* The Vampire Tapestry *(Timescape), of which "Unicorn Tapestry" is a part, was one of the most critically acclaimed and talked-about novels of the year, and "Unicorn Tapestry" itself is a Nebula Finalist this year, and a top contender for the award. Her story "The Ancient Mind at Work," a 'prequel' to "Unicorn Tapestry" was in our* Ninth Annual Collection.

Other writers have dealt with the external aspects of the vampire — his fangs, his adversion to light and garlic, his inability to cast a reflection, and so forth — but here Charnas deals with the inwardness *of the vampire (who is depicted as a real being, not a garlic-loathing ambulatory corpse), with his secret thoughts and hidden longings, his fears and aspirations, the very colors of his soul.*

SUZY McKEE CHARNAS
Unicorn Tapestry

"Hold on," Floria said. "I know what you're going to say: I agreed not to take any new clients for a while. But wait till I tell you — you're not going to believe this — first phone call, setting up an initial appointment, he comes out with what his problem is: 'I seem to have fallen victim to a delusion of being a vampire.' "

"Christ H. God!" cried Lucille delightedly. "Just like that, over the phone?"

"When I recovered my aplomb, so to speak, I told him that I prefer to wait with the details until our first meeting, which is tomorrow."

They were sitting on the tiny terrace outside the staff room of the clinic, a converted town house on the Upper West Side. Floria spent three days a week here and the remaining two in her office on Central Park South seeing private clients like this new one. Lucille, always gratifyingly responsive, was Floria's most valued professional friend. Clearly enchanted with Floria's news, she sat eagerly forward in her chair, eyes wide behind Coke-bottle glasses.

She said, "Do you suppose he thinks he's a revivified corpse?"

Below, down at the end of the street, Floria could see two kids skidding their skateboards near a man who wore a woolen cap and heavy coat despite the May warmth. He was leaning against a wall like a monolith. He had been there when Floria had arrived at the clinic this morning. If corpses walked, some, not nearly revivified enough, stood in plain view in New York.

175

"I'll have to think of a delicate way to ask," she said.

"How did he come to you?"

"He was working in an upstate college, teaching and doing research, and all of a sudden he just disappeared — vanished, literally, without a trace. A month later he turned up here in the city. The faculty dean at the school knows me and sent him to see me."

Lucille gave her a sly look. "So you thought, aha, do a little favor for a friend, this looks classic and easy to transfer if need be: repressed individual blows stack and runs off with spacey chick, or something like that."

"You know me too well," Floria said, with a rueful smile.

"Huh," grunted Lucille. She sipped ginger ale from a chipped white mug. "I don't take panicky middle-aged guys any more, they're too depressing. And you shouldn't be taking this one, intriguing as he sounds."

Here comes the lecture, Floria told herself.

Lucille got up. She was short, heavy, prone to wearing loose garments that swung about her like ceremonial robes. As she paced, her hem brushed at the flowers starting up in the planting boxes that rimmed the little terrace. "You know damn well this is just more overwork you're loading on. Don't take this guy; refer him."

Floria sighed. "I know, I know. I promised everybody I'd slow down. But you said it yourself just a minute ago — it looked like a simple favor. So what do I get? Count Dracula, for God's sake! Would you give that up?"

Fishing around in one capacious pocket, Lucille brought out a dented package of cigarettes and lit up, scowling. "You know, when you give me advice I try to take it seriously. Joking aside, Floria, what am I supposed to say? I've listened to you moaning for months now, and I thought we'd figured out that what you need is to shed some pressure, to start saying *no* — and here you are insisting on a new case. You know what I think: you're hiding in other people's problems from a lot of your own stuff you should be working on.

"Okay, okay, don't glare at me. Be pigheaded. Have you gotten rid of Chubs, at least?" This was Floria's code name for a troublesome client named Kenny she'd been trying to unload for some time.

Floria shook her head.

"What gives with you? It's weeks since you swore you'd dump him! Trying to do everything for everybody is wearing you out. I bet you're still dropping weight. Judging by the very unbecoming circles under your eyes, sleeping isn't going too well either. Still no dreams you can remember?"

"Lucille, don't nag. I don't want to talk about my health."

"Well, what about his health — Dracula's? Did you suggest that he have a physical before seeing you? There might be something physiological — "

"You're not going to be able to whisk him off to an M.D. and out of my hands," Floria said wryly. "He says he won't consider either medication or hospitalization."

Involuntarily she glanced down at the end of the street. The woolen-capped man had curled up on the sidewalk at the foot of the building, sleeping or passed-out or dead. The city was tottering with sickness. Compared with that wreck down there and the others like him, how sick could this "vampire" be, with his cultured baritone voice, his self-possessed approach?

"And you won't consider handing him off to somebody else," Lucille said.

"Well, not until I know a little more. Come on, Luce — wouldn't you want at least to know what he looks like?"

Lucille stubbed out her cigarette against the low parapet. Down below a policeman strolled along the street ticketing the parked cars. He didn't even look at the man lying at the corner of the building. They watched his progress without comment. Finally Lucille said, "Well, if you won't drop Dracula, keep me posted on him, will you?"

He entered the office on the dot of the hour, a gaunt but graceful figure. His name, typed in caps on the initial informaton sheet that she proceeded to fill out with him, was Edward Lewis Weyland. He was impressive: wiry gray hair, worn short, emphasized the massiveness of his face with its long jaw, high cheekbones and stony cheeks, grooved as if by winters of hard weather. He told her about the background of the vampire incident, incisively describing his life at Cayslin College: the pressures of collegial competition, interdepartmental squabbles, student indifference, administrative bungling. History has limited use, she knew, since memory distorts. Still, if he felt most comfortable establishing the setting for his illness, let him.

At length his energy faltered. His angular body sank into a slump, his voice became flat and tired as he haltingly worked up to the crucial event: night work at the sleep-lab, fantasies of blood-drinking as he watched the youthful subjects of his dream research slumbering, finally an attempt to act out the fantasy with a staff member at the college. He had been repulsed. Then — panic. Word would get out, he'd be fired, blacklisted forever. He'd bolted. A nightmare period had followed — he offered no details. When he had come to his senses he'd seen that just what he feared, the ruin of his career, would come from his running away. So he'd phoned the dean, and here he was.

Throughout this recital she watched him diminish from the dignified academic who had entered her office to a shamed and frightened man hunched in his chair, his hands pulling fitfully at each other.

"What are your hands doing?" she said gently. He looked blank. She repeated the question.

He looked down at his hands. "Struggling," he said.

"With what?"

"The worst," he muttered. "I haven't told you the worst." She had never grown hardened to this sort of transformaton. His long fingers busied themselves fiddling with a button on his jacket while he explained painfully that the object of his "attack" at Cayslin had been a woman. Not young but handsome and vital, she had first caught his attention earlier in the year during an honorary seminar for a retiring professor. A picture emerged of an awkward Weyland, lifelong bachelor, seeking this woman's warmth and suffering her refusal.

Floria knew she should bring him out of his past and into his here and now, but he was doing so beautifully on his own that she was loath to interrupt.

"Did I tell you there was a rapist active on the campus at this time?" he said bitterly. "I borrowed a leaf from his book: I tried to take from this woman, since she wouldn't give. I tried to take some of her blood." He stared at the floor. "What does that mean — to take someone's blood?"

"What do you think it means?"

The button, pulled and twisted by his fretful fingers, came off in his hand. He put it in his pocket, the impulse of a fastidious nature, she guessed. "Her energy," he whispered, "stolen to warm the walking corpse — the vampire — myself."

His silence, his downcast eyes, his bent shoulders, all signaled a man brought to bay by a life crisis. Perhaps he was going to be the kind of client therapists dream of, and she needed so badly these days: a client intelligent and sensitive enough, given the companionship of a professional listener, to swiftly unravel his own mental tangles. Exhilarated by his promising start, Floria restrained herself from trying to build on it too soon. She made herself tolerate the silence, which lasted until he said suddenly, "I notice that you make no notes as we speak. Do you record these sessions on tape?"

A hint of paranoia, she thought, not unusual. "Not without your knowledge and consent, just as I won't send for your personnel file from Cayslin without your knowledge and consent. I do, however, write notes after each session as a guide to myself and in order to have a record in case of any confusion later about anything we do or say here. I can promise you that I won't show my notes or speak of you by name to anyone — except Dean Sharpe at Cayslin, of course, and even then only as much as is strictly necessary — without your written permission. Does that satisfy you?"

"I apologize for my question," he said. "The . . . incident has left me . . . very nervous; a condition that I hope to get over with your help."

The time was up. When he had gone, she stepped outside to check with Hilda, the receptionist she shared with four other therapists here at the Central Park South office. Hilda always sized up new clients in the waiting room.

Of this one she said, "Are you sure there's anything wrong with that guy? I think I'm in love."

Waiting at the office for a group of clients to assemble Wednesday evening, Floria dashed off some notes on the "vampire."

Described incident, background. No history of mental illness, no previous experience of therapy. Personal history so ordinary you almost don't notice how bare it is: only child of German immigrants, schooling normal, anthropology field work, academic posts leading to Cayslin College professorship. Health good, finances adequate, occupation satisfactory, housing pleasant (though presently installed in a N.Y. hotel); never married, no kids, no family, no religion, social life strictly job-related, leisure — likes to drive. Reaction to question about drinking, but no signs of alcohol problem. Physically very smooth-moving for his age (over fifty) and height; cat-like, alert. Some apparent stiffness of mid-section — slight protective stoop — tightening up of middle-age? Paranoiac defensiveness? Voice pleasant, faint accent (German-speaking childhood at home). Entering therapy condition of consideration for return to job.

What a relief: now she could defend to Lucille her decision to do therapy with the "vampire." His situation looked workable with a minimum of strain on herself.

After all, Lucille was right. Floria did have problems of her own that needed attention, primarily her anxiety and exhaustion since her mother's death more than a year before. The break-up of Floria's marriage had caused her misery, but not the endless depression now wearing her down. Intellectually the problem was clear: with both her parents dead she was left exposed. No one stood any longer between herself and the inevitability of her own death. Knowing the source of her feelings didn't help: she couldn't seem to mobilize the nerve to work on them.

The Wednesday group went badly again. Lisa lived once more her experiences in the European death camps and everyone cried. Floria wanted to stop Lisa, turn her, extinguish the droning misery of her voice in illumination and release, but she couldn't see how to do it. She found nothing in herself to offer except some clever ploy out of the professional bag of tricks — dance your anger, have a dialogue with your young self of those days — useful techniques when they flowed organically as part of a living process in which the therapist participated. But thinking out responses that should have been intuitive wouldn't work. The group and its collective pain paralyzed her. She was a dancer without a choreographer, knowing all the moves but unable to match them to the music these people made.

Rather than act with mechanical clumsiness she held back, did nothing, and suffered guilt. Oh God, the smart, experienced people in the group must know how useless she was here.

Going home on the bus she thought about calling up one of the therapists who shared the downtown office. He had expressed an interest in doing co-therapy with her under student observation. The Wednesday group might respond well to that. Suggest it to them next time? Having a partner might take pressure off Floria and revitalize the group, and if she felt she must withdraw he would be available to take over. Of course he might take over anyway and walk off with some of her clients.

Oh boy, terrific, who's paranoid now? Wonderful way to think about a good colleague. God, she hadn't even known she was considering shucking the group.

Had the new client, running from his ''vampirism,'' exposed her own impulse to retreat? This wouldn't be the first time that Floria had obtained help from a client while attempting to give help. Her old supervisor, Rigby, said that such mutual aid was the only true therapy, the rest was fraud. What a perfectionist, old Rigby, and what a bunch of young idealists he'd turned out, all eager to save the world.

Eager, but not necessarily able. Jane Fennerman had once lived in the world, and Floria had been incompetent to save her. Jane, an absent member of tonight's group, was back in the safety of a locked ward, hazily gliding on whatever tranquilizers they used there.

Why still mull over Jane? she asked herself severely, bracing against the bus's lurching halt. Any client was entitled to drop out of therapy and commit herself. Nor was this the first time that sort of thing had happened in the course of Floria's career. Only this time she couldn't seem to shake free of the resulting depression and guilt.

But how could she have helped Jane more? How could you offer reassurance that life was not as dreadful as Jane felt it to be, that her fears were insubstantial, that each day was not a pit of pain and danger?

She was taking time during a client's cancelled hour to work on notes for the new book. The writing, an analysis of the vicissitudes of salaried versus private practice, balked her at every turn. She longed for an interruption to distract her circling mind.

Hilda put a call through from Cayslin College. It was Doug Sharpe, who had sent Dr. Weyland to her.

''Now that he's in your capable hands, I can tell people plainly that he's on what they call 'compassionate leave' and make them swallow it.'' Doug's voice seemed thinned by the long-distance connection. ''Can you give me a preliminary opinion?''

''I need time to find out more.''

He said, ''Try not to take too long. At the moment I'm holding off pressure to appoint someone in his place. Some of his enemies up here — and a sharp-tongued bastard like him acquires plenty of those — are trying to get a search committee authorized to find someone else for the Directorship of the Cayslin Center for the Study of Man.''

''Of People,'' she corrected automatically, as she always did. ''What do you mean, 'bastard'? I thought you liked him, Doug. 'Do you want me to have to throw a smart, courtly, old-school gent to Finney or MaGill?' Those were your very words.'' Finney was a Freudian with a mouth like a pursed up little asshole and a mind to match, and MaGill was a primal yowler with a padded gym of an office.

She heard Doug tapping at his teeth with a pen or pencil. ''Well,'' he said, ''I have a lot of respect for him, and sometimes I could cheer him for mowing down some pompous moron up here. I can't deny, though, that he's earned a reputation for being an accomplished son of a bitch and tough to work with. Too damn cold and self-sufficient, you know?''

''Mmm,'' she said. ''I haven't seen that yet.''

He said, ''You will. How about yourself? How's the rest of your life?''

''Well, off-hand, what would you say if I told you I was thinking of going back to art school?''

''What would I say? I'd say bullshit, that's what I'd say. You've had fifteen years of doing something you're good at, and now you want to throw all that out and start over in an area you haven't touched since Studio 101 in college? If God had meant you to be a painter, she'd have sent you to art school in the first place.''

''I did think about art school at the time.''

''The point is that you're good at what you do. I've been at the receiving end of your work and I know what I'm talking about. By the way, did you see that piece in the paper about Annie Winslow, from the group I was in? That's a nice appointment; I always knew she'd wind up in Washington. What I'm trying to make clear to you is that your 'graduates' do too well for you to talk about quitting. What's Morton say about that idea, by the way?''

Mort, a pathologist, was Floria's lover. She hadn't discussed this with him, and she told Doug so.

''You're not on the outs with Morton, are you?''

''Come on, Douglas, cut it out. There's nothing wrong with my sex life, believe me. It's everyplace else that's giving me trouble.''

''Just sticking my nose into your business,'' he replied. ''What are friends for?''

They turned to lighter matters, but when she hung up Floria didn't feel cheered. If her friends were moved to this sort of probing and kindly advice-giving, she must be inviting help more openly and more desperately than she'd realized.

The work on the book went no better. It was as if, afraid to expose her thoughts, she must disarm criticism by meeting all possible objections beforehand. The book was well and truly stalled — like everything else. She sat sweating over it, wondering what the devil was wrong with her that she was writing mush. She had two good books to her name already. What was this bottleneck with the third?

''But what do you think?'' Kenny insisted, gnawing anxiously at the cuticle of his thumbnail. ''Does it sound like my kind of job?''

''What do you feel about it?'' she countered.

''I'm all confused, I told you.''

''Try speaking for me. Give the advice I would give you.''

He glowered. ''That's a real cop-out, you know? One part of me talking like you, and then I have a dialogue with myself like a TV show about a split personality. It's all me that way, you're off the hook, you just sit there. I want something from *you*.''

She looked for the twentieth time at the clock on the file cabinet. This time it freed her. "Kenny, the hour's over."

Kenny heaved his plump, sulky body up out of his chair. "You don't care. Oh, you pretend you do, but you don't really — "

"Next time, Kenny."

He stumped out of the office. She imagined him towing in his wake the raft of decisions he was trying to inveigle her into making for him. Sighing, she went to the window and looked out over the park, filling her eyes and her mind with the full, fresh green of late spring. She felt dismal. In two years of treatment the situation with Kenny had remained a stalemate. He wouldn't go to someone else who might be able to help him, and she couldn't bring herself to kick him out, though she knew she must eventually. His puny tyranny couldn't conceal how soft and vulnerable he was . . .

Dr. Weyland had the next appointment. Floria found herself pleased to see him. She could hardly have asked for a greater contrast to Kenny: tall, lean, a fine head that made her want to draw him, good clothes, nice big hands — altogether, a distinguished-looking man. Though informally dressed in slacks, light jacket, and tieless shirt, the impression he conveyed was one of impeccable leisure and reserve. He took not the padded chair preferred by most clients but the wooden one with the cane seat.

"Good afternoon, Dr. Landauer," he said gravely. "May I ask your judgment of my case?"

"I don't think of myself as a judge," she said. She decided rapidly to enlist his intelligence by laying out her thoughts to him as to an equal, and to shift their discussion onto a first-name basis if possible. Calling this old-fashioned man by his first name so soon might seem artificial, but how could they get familiar enough to do therapy while addressing each other as "Dr. Landauer" and "Dr. Weyland" like two characters in vaudeville?

"This is what I think, Edward," she continued. "We need to find out about this vampire incident — how it tied into your feelings about yourself, good and bad, at the time; what it did for you that led you to try to 'be' a vampire even though that was bound to complicate your life terrifically. The more we know, the closer we can come to figuring out how to insure that this vampire construct won't be necessary to you again."

"Does this mean that you accept me formally as a client?" he said.

Comes right out and says what's on his mind, she noted; no problems there. "Yes."

"Good. I, too, have a treatment goal in mind. I will need at some point a testimonial from you that my mental health is sound enough for me to resume work at Cayslin."

Floria shook her head. "I can't guarantee that. I can commit myself to work toward it, of course, since your improved mental health is the aim of what we do here together."

"I suppose that answers the purpose for the time being," he said. "We can discuss it again later on. Frankly, I find myself eager to continue our work today. I've been feeling very much better since I spoke with you, and I thought last night about what I might tell you today.''

"Edward, my own feeling is that we started out with a good deal of very useful verbal work, and that now is a time to try something a little different.''

He said nothing. He watched her. When she asked whether he remembered his dreams he shook his head.

She said, "I'd like you to try to do a dream for me now, a waking dream. Close your eyes and daydream, and tell me about it.''

He closed his eyes. Strangely, he now struck her as less vulnerable rather than more, as if strengthened by increased vigilance.

"How do you feel now?'' she said.

"Uneasy.'' His eyelids fluttered. "I dislike closing my eyes. What I don't see can hurt me.''

"Who wants to hurt you?''

"A vampire's enemies, of course — mobs of screaming peasants with torches.''

Translating into what, she wondered — young Ph.D.'s pouring out of the graduate schools panting for the jobs of older men like Weyland? "Peasants, these days?''

"Whatever their daily work, there is still a majority of the stupid, the violent, and the credulous, putting their featherbrained faith in astrology, in this cult or that, in various branches of psychology.''

His sneer at her was unmistakable. Considering her refusal to let him fill the hour his own way, this desire to take a swipe at her was healthy. But it required immediate and straightforward handling.

"Edward, open your eyes and tell me what you see.''

He obeyed. " I see a woman in her early forties,'' he said, "clever-looking face, dark hair showing gray; flesh too thin for her bones, indicating either vanity or illness; wearing slacks and a rather creased batik blouse — describable, I think, by the term 'peasant style' — with a food stain on the left side.''

Damn! Don't blush. "Does anything besides my blouse suggest a peasant to you?''

"Nothing concrete, but with regard to me, my vampire-self, a peasant with a torch is what you could easily become.''

"I hear you saying that my task is to help you get rid of your delusion, though this process may be painful and frightening for you.''

Something flashed in his expression — surprise, perhaps alarm — something she wanted to get in touch with before it could sink away out of reach again. Quickly she said, "How do you experience your face at this moment?''

He frowned. "As being on the front of my head. Why?''

With a sick feeling she saw that she had chosen the wrong technique for reaching that hidden feeling and had provoked hostility instead. "Your face looked to me just now like a mask for concealing what you feel rather than an instrument for expression.''

He moved restlessly in the chair, his whole physical attitude tense and guarded. ''I don't know what you mean.''

''Will you let me touch you?'' she said, rising.

His hands tightened on the arms of his chair, which protested in a sharp creak. He snapped, ''I thought this was a talking cure.''

Strong resistance to body-work — ease up. ''If you won't let me massage some of the tension out of your facial muscles, will you try to do it for yourself?''

''I don't enjoy being made ridiculous,'' he said, standing and heading for the door, which clapped smartly shut behind him.

She sagged back in her chair; she had mishandled him. Clearly her initial estimation of this as a relatively easy job had been wrong and had led her to move too quickly with him. Certainly it had been too early to try body-work. She should have developed a firmer level of trust first by letting him do more of what he did so easily and well — talk.

The door opened. Weyland came back in and shut it quietly. He did not sit again but paced about the room, coming to rest at the window.

''Please excuse my rather childish behavior just now,'' he said. ''Playing these games of yours brought it on.''

''It's frustrating, playing games that are unfamiliar and that you can't control,'' she said. As he made no reply, she went on in a conciliatory tone, ''I'm not belittling you, Edward. I just need to get us off whatever track you were taking us down so briskly. My feeling is that you're trying hard to regain your old stability.

''But that's the goal, not the starting point. The only way to reach your goal is through the process, and you don't drive the therapy process like a train. You can only help the process happen, as though you were helping a tree grow.''

''These games are part of the process?''

''Yes.''

''And neither you nor I control the games?''

''That's right.''

He considered. ''Suppose I agree to try this process of yours; what would you want of me?''

Observing him carefully, she no longer saw the anxious scholar bravely struggling back from madness. Here was a different sort of man, armored, calculating. She didn't know what the change signaled, but she felt her own excitement stirring, and that meant she was on the track of — something.

''I have a hunch,'' she said slowly, ''that this vampirism extends further back into your past than you've told me and possibly right up into the present as well. I think it's still with you. My style of therapy stresses dealing with the 'now' at least as much as the 'then'; if the vampirism is part of the present, telling me about it is crucial.''

Silence.

"Can you tell me about being a vampire: being one now?"

"You won't like knowing," he said.

"Edward, try to tell me."

"I hunt," he said.

"Where? How? What sort of — of victims?"

He folded his arms and leaned his back against the window frame. "Very well, since you insist. There are a number of possibilities here in the city in summer. Those too poor to own air conditioners sleep out on rooftops and fire escapes. But often their blood is sour with drugs or liquor. The same is true of prostitutes. Bars are full of people but also full of smoke and noise, and there too the blood is fouled. I must choose my hunting grounds carefully. Often I go to openings of galleries or evening museum shows or department stores on their late nights — places where women may be approached."

And take pleasure in it, she thought, if they're out hunting also — for acceptable male companionship. Yet he's never married. Explore where this is going. "Only women?"

He gave her a sardonic glance, as if she were a slightly brighter student than he had first assumed.

"Hunting women is liable to be time-consuming and expensive. The best hunting is in the part of Central Park they call the Ramble, where homosexual men seek encounters with others of their kind. I walk there too at night."

She glanced at the clock. "I'm sorry, Edward, but our time seems to be — "

"Only a moment more," he said coldly. "You asked; permit me to finish my answer. In the Ramble I find someone who doesn't reek of alcohol or drugs, who seems healthy, and who is not inclined to 'hook up' right there among the bushes. I invite such a man to my room. He judges me safe, at least: older, weaker than he is, unlikely to turn into a dangerous maniac. So he comes to my hotel. I feed on his blood. Now, I think, our time is up."

She sat, after he'd left, torn between rejoicing at his admission of the delusion's persistence and pity that his condition was so much worse than she had first thought. Her hope of having an easy time with him vanished. His initial presentation had been just that — a performance, an act. Forced to abandon it, he had dumped on her this lump of material, too much — and too strange — to take in all at once.

Her next client liked the padded chair, not the wooden one that Weyland had sat in during the first part of the hour. Floria started to move the wooden one back. The armrests came away in her hands.

She remembered him starting up in protest against her proposal of touching him. The grip of his fingers had fractured the joints, and the shafts now lay in splinters on the floor.

Floria wandered into Lucille's room at the clinic after the staff meeting. Lucille was lying on the couch with a wet rag over her eyes.

"I thought you looked green around the gills today," Floria said. "What's wrong?"

"Big bash last night," said Lucille in sepulchral tones. "I think I feel about the way you do after a session with Chubs. You haven't gotten rid of him yet, have you?"

"No. I had him lined up to go see Marty instead of me last week, but damned if he didn't show up at my door at his usual time. It's a lost cause. What I wanted to talk to you about was Dracula."

"What about him?"

"He's smarter, tougher, and sicker than I thought, and maybe I'm even less competent than I thought too. He's already walked out on me once — I almost lost him. I never took a course in treating monsters."

Lucille groaned. "Some days they're all monsters." This from Lucille, who worked longer hours than anyone at the clinic, to the despair of her husband. She lifted the rag, refolded it, and placed it carefully across her forehead. "And if I had ten dollars for every client who's walked out on me — tell you what: I'll trade you Madame X for him, how's that?

"Remember Madame X, with the jangling bracelets and the parakeet eye makeup and the phobia about dogs? Now she's phobic about things dropping out of the sky onto her head. It'll turn out that one day when she was three a dog trotted by and pissed on her leg just as an overpassing pigeon shat on her head. What are we doing in this business?"

"God knows," Floria laughed. "But am I in this business these days — I mean, in the sense of practicing my so-called art? Blocked with my group work, beating my brains out on a book that won't go, and doing something — I'm not sure it's therapy — with a vampire . . . You know, once I had this sort of natural choreographer inside myself that hardly let me put a foot wrong and always knew how to correct a mistake if I did. Now that's gone. I feel as if I'm just going through a lot of incoherent motions. Whatever I had once, I've lost it."

Ugh, she thought, hearing the descent of her voice into a tone of gloomy self-pity.

"Well, don't complain about Dracula," Lucille said. "You were the one who insisted on taking him on. At least he's got you concentrating on his therapy instead of just wringing your hands. As long as you've started, stay with it — illumination may come. And now I'd better change the ribbon in my typewriter and get back to reviewing Silberman's latest best seller on self-shrinking while I'm feeling mean enough to do it justice." She got up gingerly. "Stick around in case I faint and fall into the waste basket."

"Luce. This case is what I'd like to try to write about."

"Dracula?" Lucille pawed through a desk drawer full of paper clips, pens, rubber bands, and old lipsticks.

"Dracula. A monograph — "

"Oh, I know the game: you scribble down everything you can and then read what you wrote to find out what's going on with the client, and with luck you end up publishing. Great! But if you are going to publish, don't piddle this away on a dinky paper. Do a book. Here's your subject, instead of those statistics you've been killing yourself over. This one is really exciting — a case study to put on the shelf next to Freud's own wolf man, have you thought of that?''

Floria liked it. "What a book that could be — fame if not fortune. Notoriety most likely. How in the world could I convince our colleagues that it's legit? There's lot of vampire stuff around right now — plays on Broadway and TV, books all over the place, movies — they'll say I'm just trying to ride the coattails of a fad.''

"No, no, what you do is show how this guy's delusion is related to the fad. Fascinating.'' Lucille, having found a ribbon, prodded doubtfully at the exposed innards of her typewriter.

"Suppose I fictionalize it," Floria said, "under a pseudonym. Why not ride the popular wave and be free in what I can say?''

"Listen, you've never written a word of fiction in your life, have you?'' Lucille fixed her with a bloodshot gaze. "There's no evidence that you could turn out a best-selling novel. On the other hand, by this time you have a trained memory for accurately reporting therapeutic transactions. That's a strength you'd be foolish to waste. A solid professional book would be terrific — and a feather in the cap of every woman in the field. Just make sure you get good legal advice on disguising Dracula's identity well enough to avoid libel.''

The cane-seated chair wasn't worth repairing, so she got its twin out of the bedroom to put in the office in its place. Puzzling: by his history Weyland was fifty-two, and by his appearance no muscle-man. She should have asked Doug — but how, exactly? "By the way, Doug, was Weyland ever a circus strong man or a blacksmith? Does he secretly pump iron?'' Ask the client himself — but not yet.

She invited some of the younger staff from the clinic over for a small party with a few of her outside friends. It was a good evening; they were not a heavy-drinking crowd, which meant the conversation stayed intelligent. The guests drifted about the long living room or stood in twos and threes at the windows looking down on West End Avenue as they talked.

Mort came, warming the room. Fresh from a session with some amateur chamber-music friends, he still glowed with the pleasure of making his cello sing. His own voice was unexpectedly light for so large a man. Sometimes Floria thought that the deep throb of the cello was his true voice.

He stood beside her talking with some others. There was no need to lean against his comfortable bulk or to have him put his arm around her waist. Their intimacy was longstanding, an effortless pleasure in each other that required neither demonstration nor concealment.

He was easily diverted from music to his next-favorite topic, the strengths and skills of athletes.

"Here's a question for a paper I'm thinking of writing," Floria said. "Could a tall, lean man be exceptionally strong? I mean a man with a runner's build, more sinewy than bulky.''

Mort rambled on in his thoughtful way. His answer seemed to be ''no.''

''But what about chimpanzees?'' put in a young clinician. ''I went with a guy once who was an animal handler for TV, and he said a three-month old chimp could demolish a strong man.''

''It's all physical conditioning,'' somebody else said. ''Modern people are softies.''

Mort nodded. ''Human beings in general are weakly made compared to other animals. It's a question of muscle insertions — the angles of how the muscles are attached to the bones. Some angles give better leverage than others. That's how a leopard can bring down a much bigger animal than itself. It has a muscular structure that gives it tremendous strength for its streamlined build.''

Floria said, ''If a man were built with muscle insertions like a leopard's, he'd look pretty odd, wouldn't he?''

''Not to an untrained eye,'' Mort said, sounding bemused by an inner vision. ''And my God, what an athlete he'd make — can you imagine a guy in the decathlon who's as strong as a leopard?''

When everyone else had gone Mort stayed, as he often did. Jokes about insertions, muscular and otherwise, soon led to sounds more expressive and more animal, but afterward Floria didn't feel like resting snuggled together with Mort and talking. When her body stopped racing, her mind turned to her new client. She didn't want to discuss him with Mort, so she ushered Mort out as gently as she could and sat down by herself at the kitchen table with a glass of orange juice.

How to approach the reintegration of Weyland the eminent, gray-haired academic with the rebellious vampire-self that had smashed his life out of shape?

She thought of the broken chair, Weyland's big hands crushing the wood. Old wood and dried out glue, of course, or he never could have done it. He was a man, after all, not a leopard.

The day before the third session Weyland phoned and left a message with Hilda; he would not be coming to the office tomorrow for his appointment, but if Dr. Landauer were agreeable she would find him at their usual hour at the Central Park Zoo.

Am I going to let him move me around from here to there? she thought. Shouldn't — but why fight it? Give him some leeway, see what opens up in a different setting. Besides, it was a beautiful day, probably the last of the sweet May weather before the summer stickiness descended. She gladly cut Kenny short so that she would have time to walk to the zoo.

There was a fair crowd there for a weekday. Well-groomed young matrons pushed clean, floppy babies in strollers. Weyland she spotted at once.

He was leaning against the railing that enclosed the seals' shelter and their murky green pool. His jacket, slung over his shoulder, draped elegantly down his long back. Floria thought him rather dashing and faintly foreign looking. Women who passed him, she noticed, tended to glance back.

He looked at everyone. She had the impression that he knew quite well that she was walking up behind him.

"Outdoors makes a nice change from the office, Edward," she said, coming to the rail beside him. "But there must be more to this than a longing for fresh air." A fat seal lay in sculptural grace on the concrete, eyes blissfully shut, fur drying in the sun to a translucent water-color umber.

Weyland straightened from the rail. They walked. He did not look at the animals; his eyes moved continually over the crowd. He said, "Someone has been watching for me at your office building."

"Who?"

"There are several possibilities. Pah, what a stench — though humans caged in similar circumstances smell as bad." He sidestepped a couple of shrieking children who were fighting over a balloon and headed out of the zoo under the musical clock.

They walked the uphill path northward through the park. By extending her own stride a little Floria found that she could comfortably keep pace with him.

"Is it peasants with torches?" she said. "Following you?"

"What a childish idea," he said.

All right, try another tack then: "You were telling me last time about hunting in the Ramble. Can we return to that?"

"If you wish." He sounded bored — a defense? Surely — she was certain this must be the right reading — surely his problem was a transmutation into "vampire" fantasy of an unacceptable aspect of himself. For men of his generation the confrontation with homosexual drives could be devastating.

"When you pick up some one in the Ramble, is it a paid encounter?"

"Usually."

"How do you feel about having to pay?" she expected resentment.

He gave a faint shrug. "Why not? Others work to earn their bread. I work too, very hard in fact. Why shouldn't I use my earnings to pay for my sustenance?"

Why did he never play the expected card? Baffled, she paused to drink from a fountain. They walked on.

"Once you've got your quarry, how do you — " she fumbled for a word.

"Attack?" he supplied, unperturbed. "There's a place on the neck, here, where pressure can interrupt the blood flow to the brain and cause unconsciousness. To get close enough to apply that pressure isn't difficult."

"You do it before or after any sexual activity?"

"Before, if possible," he said dryly, "and instead of." He turned aside to stalk up a slope to a granite outcrop that overlooked the path they had been following. He settled on his haunches, looking back the way they had come. Floria, glad she'd worn slacks today, sat down near him.

He didn't seem devastated — anything but. Press him, don't let him get by on cool. "Do you often prey on men in preference to women?"

"Certainly. I take what is easiest. Men have always been more accessible because women have been walled away like prizes or so physically impoverished by repeated child-bearing as to be unhealthy prey for me. All this has been changing recently, but gay men are still the simplest quarry." While she was recovering from her surprise at his unforeseen and weirdly skewed awareness of female history, he added suavely, "How carefully you control your expression, Dr. Landauer — no frown, no disapproval."

She did disapprove, she realized. She would prefer him not to be committed sexually to men. Oh, hell.

He went on, "Yet no doubt you see me as one who victimizes the already victimized. This is the world's way. A wolf brings down the stragglers at the edges of the herd. Gay men are denied the full protection of the human herd and are at the same time emboldened to make themselves known and available.

"On the other hand, unlike the wolf I can feed without killing, and these particular victims pose no threat to me that would cause me to kill. Outcasts themselves, even if they comprehend my true purpose among them they will not accuse me."

God, how neatly, completely, and ruthlessly he distanced the homosexual community from himself! "And how do you feel, Edward, about their purposes — their sexual expectations of you?"

"The same as about the sexual expectations of women whom I choose to pursue: they don't interest me. Besides, once my hunger is active, sexual arousal is impossible. My physical unresponsiveness seems to surprise no one. Apparently impotence is expected in a gray-haired man, which suits my intention."

A frisbee sailed past them, pursued by a trio of shouting kids. Floria's eye followed the arc of the red plastic disc. She was thinking, astonished again, that she had never heard a man speak of his own impotence with such cool indifference. She had induced him to talk about his problem all right. He was speaking as freely as he had in the first session, only this time it was no act. He was drowning her in more than she had ever expected or for that matter wanted to know about vampirism. What the hell: she was listening, she thought she understood — what was it all good for? Time for some cold reality, she thought; see how far he can carry all this incredible detail. Give the whole structure a shove.

"You realize, I'm sure, that people of either sex who make themselves so easily available are also liable to be carriers of disease. When was your last medical check-up?"

"My dear Dr. Landauer, my first medical check-up will be my last. Fortunately, I have no great need of one. Most serious illnesses — hepatitis, for example — reveal themselves to me by an alteration in the odor of the victim's skin. Warned, I abstain. When I do fall ill, as occasionally happens, I withdraw to some place where I can heal undisturbed. A doctor's attentions would be more dangerous to me than any disease.''

Eyes on the path below, he continued calmly, ''You can see by looking at me that there are no obvious clues to my unique nature. But believe me, an examination of any depth by even a half-sleeping medical practitioner would reveal some alarming deviations from the norm. I take pains to stay healthy, and I seem to be gifted with an exceptionally hardy constitution.''

Fantasies of being unique and beyond fear; take him to the other pole. ''I'd like you to try something new. Will you put yourself into the mind of a man you contact in the Ramble and describe your encounter with him from his point of view?''

He turned toward her and for some moments regarded her without expression. Then he resumed his surveillance of the path. ''I will not. Though I do have enough empathy with my quarry to enable me to hunt efficiently, I must draw the line at erasing the necessary distance that keeps prey and predator distinct.

''And now I think our ways part for today.'' He stood up, descended the hillside, and walked beneath some low-canopied trees, his tall back stooped, toward the Seventy-second Street entrance to the park.

Floria arose more slowly, aware suddenly of her shallow breathing and the sweat on her face. Back to reality or what remained of it. She looked at her watch. She was late for her next client.

Floria couldn't sleep that night. Barefoot in her bathrobe she paced the living room by lamplight. They had sat together on that hill as isolated as in her office — more so, because there was no Hilda and no phone. He was, she knew, very strong, and he had sat close enough to her to reach out for that paralyzing touch to the neck —

Just suppose for a minute that Weyland had been brazenly telling the truth all along, counting on her to treat it as a delusion because on the face of it the truth was inconceivable?

Jesus, she thought, if I'm thinking that way about him, this therapy is more out of control than I thought. What kind of therapist becomes an accomplice to the client's fantasy? A crazy therapist, that's what kind.

Frustrated and confused by the turmoil in her mind, she wandered into the work room. By morning the floor was covered with sheets of newsprint, each broadly marked by her felt-tipped pen. Floria sat in the midst of them, gritty-eyed and hungry.

She often approached problems this way, harking back to art training: turn off the thinking, put hand to paper and see what the deeper, less verbally sophisticated parts of the mind have to say. Now that her dreams had deserted her, this was her only access to those levels.

The newsprint sheets were covered with rough representations of Weyland's face and form. Across several of them were scrawled words: *Dear Doug, Your vampire is fine, it's your ex-therapist who's off the rails*. WARNING: *therapy can be dangerous to your health. Especially if you are the therapist. Beautiful vampire, awaken to me. Am I really ready to take on a legendary monster? Give up — refer this one out. Do your job — work is a good doctor.*

That last sounded pretty good, except that doing her job was precisely what she was feeling so shaky about these days.

Here was another message: *How come this attraction to someone so scary?* Oh ho, she thought, is that a real feeling or an aimless reaction out of the body's early-morning hormone peak? You don't want to confuse honest libido with mere biological clockwork.

Deborah called. Babies cried in the background over the Scotch Symphony. Nick, Deb's husband, was a musicologist with fervent opinions on music and nothing else.

"We'll be in town a little later in the summer," Deborah said, "just for a few days at the end of July. Nicky has this seminar-convention thing. Of course, it won't be easy with the babies . . . I wondered if you might sort of coordinate your vacation to spend a little time with them?"

Baby-sit, that meant. Damn. Cute as they were and all that, damn! Floria gritted her teeth. Visits from Deb were difficult. Floria had been so proud of her bright, hard-driving daughter, and then suddenly Deborah had dropped her studies and rushed to embrace all the dangers that Floria had warned her against: a romantic, too-young marriage, instant breeding, no preparation for self-support, the works. Well, to each her own, but it was so wearing to have Deb around playing the empty-headed hausfrau.

"Let me think, Deb. I'd love to see all of you, but I've been considering spending a couple of weeks in Maine with your aunt Nonnie." God knows I need a real vacation, she thought, though the peace and quiet up there is hard for a city kid like me to take for long. Still, Nonnie, Floria's younger sister, was good company. "Maybe you could bring the kids up there for a couple of days. There's room in that barn of a place, and of course Nonnie'd be happy to have you."

"Oh, no, Mom, it's so dead up there, it drives Nick crazy — don't tell Nonnie I said that. Maybe Nonnie could come down to the city instead. You could cancel a date or two and we could all go to Coney Island together, things like that."

Kid-things, which would drive Nonnie crazy and Floria too before long. "I doubt she could manage," Floria said, "But I'll ask. Look, hon, if I do go up there, you and Nick and the kids could stay here at the apartment and save some money."

"We have to be at the hotel for the seminar," Deb said rather shortly. No doubt she was feeling just as impatient as Floria was by now. "And the kids haven't seen you for a long time — it would be really nice if you could stay in the city just for a few days."

"We'll try to work something out." Always working something out. Concord never comes naturally — first we have to butt heads and get pissed off. Each time you call I hope it'll be different, Floria thought.

Somebody shrieked for "oly," jelly that would be — Floria felt a sudden rush of warmth for them, her grandkids for God's sake. Having been a young mother herself, she was still young enough to really enjoy them (and to fight with Deb about how to bring them up).

Deb was starting an awkward good-bye. Floria replied, put the phone down, and sat with her head back against the flowered kitchen wallpaper, thinking, Why do I feel so rotten now? Deb and I aren't close, no comfort, seldom friends, though we were once. Have I said everything wrong, made her think I don't want to see her and don't care about her family? What does she want from me that I can't seem to give her? Approval? Maybe she thinks I still hold her marriage against her. Well, I do, sort of. What right do I have to be critical, me with my divorce? What terrible things would she say to me, would I say to her, that we take such care not to say anything important at all?

"I think today we might go into sex," she said.

Weyland responded dryly, "Might we indeed. Does it titillate you to wring confessions of solitary vice from men of mature years?"

Oh no you don't, she thought. You can't sidestep so easily. "Under what circumstances do you find yourself sexually aroused?"

"Most usually upon waking from sleep," he said indifferently.

"What do you do about it?"

"The same as others do. I am not a cripple, I have hands."

"Do you have fantasies at these times?"

"No. Women, and men for that matter, appeal to me very little, either in fantasy or reality."

"Ah — what about female vampires?" she said, trying not to sound arch.

"I know of none."

Of course: the neatest out in the book. "They're not needed for reproduction, I suppose, because people who die of vampire bites become vampires themselves."

He said testily, "Nonsense. I am not a communicable disease."

So he had left an enormous hole in his construct. She headed straight for it: "Then how does your kind reproduce?"

"I have no kind, so far as I am aware," he said, "and I do not reproduce. Why should I, when I may live for centuries still, perhaps indefinitely? My sexual equipment is clearly only detailed biological mimicry, a form of protective coloration." How beautiful, how simple a solution, she thought, full of admiration in spite of herself. "Do I occasionally detect a note of prurient interest in your questions, Dr. Landauer? Something akin to stopping at the cage to watch the tigers mate in the zoo?"

"Probably," she said, feeling her cheeks grow hot. He had a great backhand return-shot there. "How do you feel about that?"

He shrugged.

"To return to the point: do I hear you saying that you have no urge whatever to engage in sexual intercourse with anyone?"

"Would you mate with your livestock?"

His matter-of-fact arrogance took her breath away. She said weakly, "Men have reportedly done so."

"Driven men. I am not driven in that way. My sex urge is of low frequency and is easily dealt with unaided — although I have occasionally engaged in copulation out of the necessity to keep up appearances. I am capable, but not — like humans — obsessed."

Was he sinking into lunacy before her eyes? "I think I hear you saying," she said, striving to keep her voice neutral, "that you're not just a man with a unique way of life. I think I hear you saying that you're not human at all."

"I thought that this was already clear."

"And that there are no others like you."

"None that I know of."

"Then — you see yourself as what? Some sort of mutation?"

"Perhaps. Or perhaps your kind are the mutation."

She saw disdain in the curl of his lip. "How does your mouth feel now?"

"The corners are drawn down. The feeling is contempt."

"Can you let the contempt speak?"

He got up and went to stand at the window, positioning himself slightly to one side as if to stay hidden from the street below.

"Edward," she said.

He looked back at her. "Humans are my food. I draw the life out of their veins. Sometimes I kill them. I am greater than they are. Yet I must spend my time thinking about their habits and their drives, scheming to avoid the dangers they pose — I hate them."

She felt the hatred like a dry heat radiating from him. God, he really lived all this! She had tapped into a furnace of feeling. And now — ? The sensation of triumph wavered, and she grabbed at a next move: hit him with reality now, while he's burning.

"What about blood banks?" she said. "Your food is commercially available, so why all the complication and danger of the hunt?"

"You mean turn my efforts to piling up a fortune and buying blood by the case? That would certainly make for an easier, less risky life in the short run. I could fit quite comfortably into modern society if I became just another consumer.

"However, I prefer to keep the mechanics of my survival firmly in my own hands. After all, I can't afford to lose my hunting skills. In two hundred years there may be no blood banks, but I will still need my food."

Jesus, you set him a hurdle and he just flies over it. Are there no weaknesses in all this, has he no blind spots? Look at his tension — go back to that. "What do you feel now in your body?"

"Tightness." He pressed his spread fingers to his abdomen.

"What are you doing with your hands?"

"I put my hands to my stomach."

"Can you speak for your stomach?"

" 'Feed me or die,' " he snarled.

Elated again, she closed in. "And for yourself, in answer?"

" 'Will you never be satisfied?' " He glared at her. "You shouldn't seduce me into quarreling with the terms of my own existence!"

"Your stomach is your existence," she paraphrased.

"The gut determines," he said harshly. "That first, everything else after."

"Say, 'I resent — ' "

He held to a tense silence.

" 'I resent the power of my gut over my life,' " she said for him.

He stood with an abrupt motion and glanced at his watch, an elegant flash of slim silver on his wrist. "Enough," he said.

That night at home she began a set of notes that would never enter his file at the office, notes toward the proposed book.

Couldn't do it, couldn't get properly into the sex thing with him. Everything shoots off in all directions. His vampire concept so thoroughly worked out, find myself half-believing sometimes — my own childish fantasy-response to his powerful death-avoidance, contact-avoidance fantasy. Lose professional distance every time — is that what scares me about him? Don't really want to shatter his delusion (own life a mess, what right to tear down others' patterns?), so see it as real? Wonder how much of "vampirism" he acts out, how far, how often. Something attractive in his purely selfish, predatory stance — the lure of the great outlaw.

Told me today quite coolly about a man he killed once — inadvertently! — by drinking too much from him. *Is* it fantasy? Of course — the victim, he thinks, was college student. Breathes there a professor who hasn't dreamed of murdering some representative youth, retaliation for years of classroom frustration? Speaks of teaching with caustic humor — amuses him to work at cultivating the minds of those he regards strictly as bodies, containers of his sustenance. He shows the alienness of full-blown psychopathology, poor bastard, plus clean-cut logic. Suggested he find another job (assuming his delusion at least in part related to pressures at Cayslin); his fantasy-persona, the vampire, more realistic about job-switching than I am:

"For a man of my apparent age it's not so easy to make such a change in these tight times. I might have to take a position lower on the ladder of 'success' as you people assess it." Status important to him? "Certainly. An eccentric professor is one thing; an eccentric pipe-fitter, another. And I like good cars, which are expensive to own and run.'' (He refuses, though, to discuss other ''jobs'' from former lives.)

We are deep into the fantasy — where the hell going? Damn right I don't control the ''games'' — preplanned therapeutic strategies get whirled away as soon as we begin. Nerve-wracking.

Tried again to have him take the part of his enemy-victim, peasant with torch. Asked if he felt himself rejecting that point of view? Frosty reply: ''Naturally. The peasant's point of view is in no way my own. I've been reading in your field, Dr. Landauer. You work from the Gestalt orientation — ''Originally, yes,'' I corrected; ''eclectic these days.'' — ''But you do proceed from the theory that I am projecting some aspect of my own feelings outward onto others, whom I then treat as my victims? Your purpose then must be to maneuver me into accepting as my own the projected 'victim' aspect of myself. This integration is supposed to effect the freeing of energy previously locked into maintaining the projection.

''All this is an interesting insight into the nature of ordinary human confusion, but I am not an ordinary human, and I am not confused. I cannot afford confusion.''

Felt sympathy for him — telling me he's afraid of having own internal confusions exposed in therapy, too threatening. Keep chipping away at delusion, though with what prospect — it's so complex, so deep-seated.

Returned to his phrase ''my apparent age.'' He asserts he has lived many human lifetimes, all details forgotten, however, during periods of suspended animation between lives. Perhaps sensing my skepticism at such handy amnesia, grew cool and distant, claimed to know little about the hibernation process itself: ''The essence of this state is that I sleep through it — hardly an ideal condition for making scientific observations.''

Edward thinks his body synthesizes vitamins, minerals (as all our bodies synthesize Vitamin D), even proteins. Describes unique design he deduces in himself: special intestinal microfauna plus super-efficient body chemistry that extracts enough energy to live on from blood. Damn good mileage per calorie, too. (Recall observable tension, first interview, at question about drinking — my note, possible alcohol problem!)

Speak for blood: '' 'Lacking me, you have no life. I flow to the heart's soft drumbeat through lightless prisons of flesh. I am rich, I am nourishing, I am difficult to attain.' '' Stunned to find him positively lyrical on subject of his ''food,'' almost hated to move him on. Drew attention to whispering voice of blood.

'' 'Yes. I am secret, hidden beneath the surface, patient, silent, steady. I work unnoticed, an unseen thread of vitality running from age to age — beautiful, efficient, self-renewing, self-cleansing, warm, filling — ' '' Could see him getting worked up. Finally stood: ''My appetite is pressing. I must leave you.'' And he did.

Sat and trembled for five minutes after.

New development (or new perception?): he sometimes comes acrosss very unsophisticated about own feelings — lets me pursue subjects of extreme intensity and delicacy to him.

Asked him to daydream — a hunt. (Hands — mine — shaking now as I write. God. What a session.) He told of picking up a woman at poetry reading, 92nd Street Y — has N. Y. C. all worked out, circulates to avoid too much notice any one spot. Spoke easily, eyes shut without observable strain: chooses from audience a redhead in glasses, dress with drooping neckline (ease of access), no perfume (strong smells bother him). Approaches during intermission, encouraged to see her fanning away smoke of others' cigarettes — meaning she doesn't smoke, health sign. Agreed in not enjoying the reading, they adjourn together to coffee shop.

"She asks whether I am a teacher," he says, eyes shut, mouth amused. "My clothes, glasses, manner all suggest this, and I emphasize the impression — it reassures. She is a copy editor for a publishing house. We talk about books. The waiter brings her a gummy-looking pastry. As a non-eater, I pay little attention to the quality of restaurants, so I must apologize to her. She waves this away — is engrossed, or pretending to be engrossed, in talk." A longish dialogue between interested woman and Edward doing shy-lonesome-scholar act — dead wife, competitive young colleagues who don't understand him, quarrels in professional journals with big shots in his field — a version of what he first told me. She's attracted (of course — lanky, rough-cut elegance, plus hints of vulnerability all very alluring, as intended). He offers to take her home.

Tension in his body at this point in narrative — spine clear of chairback, hands braced on thighs. "She settles beside me in the back of the cab, talking about problems of her own career — illegible manuscripts of Biblical length, mulish editors, suicidal authors — and I make comforting comments, I lean nearer and put my arm along the back of the seat, behind her shoulders. Traffic is heavy, we move slowly. There is time to make my meal here in the taxi and avoid a tedious extension of the situation into her apartment — if I move soon."

How do you feel?

"Eager," he says, voice husky. "My hunger is so roused I can scarcely restrain myself. A powerful hunger, not like yours — mine compels. I embrace her shoulders lightly, make kindly uncle remarks, treading that fine line between the game of seduction she perceives and the game of friendly interest I affect. My real purpose underlies all: what I say, how I look, every gesture is part of the stalk. There is an added excitement — and fear — because I am doing my hunting in the presence of a third person — behind the cabbie's head."

Could scarcely breathe. Studied him — intent face, masklike with closed eyes, nostrils slightly flared; legs tensed, hands clenched on knees. Whispering: "I press the place on her neck. She starts, sighs faintly, silently drops against me. In the stale stench of the cab's interior, with the ticking of the meter in my ears and the mutter of the radio — I take hold here, at the tenderest part of her throat. Sound subsides into the background — I feel the sweet blood beating under her skin, I taste salt at the moment before I — strike. My saliva thins her blood, it flows out, I draw it into my mouth swiftly, swiftly, before she can wake, before we can arrive . . . "

Trailed off, sat back loosely in the chair. Saw him swallow. "Ah. I feed." Heard him sigh. Managed to ask about physical sensation. "Warm. Heavy here — " touches his belly " — in a pleasant way. The good taste of blood, tart and rich, in my mouth . . . "

And then? A flicker of movement beneath his closed eyelids: "In time I am aware that the cabbie has glanced back once and has taken our — embrace for just that. I can feel the cab slowing, hear him move to turn off the meter. I withdraw, I quickly wipe my mouth on my handkerchief. I take her by the shoulders and shake her gently. Does she often have these attacks, I inquire, the soul of concern. She comes around, bewildered, weak, thinks she has fainted. I give the driver extra money and ask him to wait. He looks intrigued — 'what was that all about?' I can see the question in his face — but as a true New Yorker he will not expose his own ignorance by inquiring.

"I escort the woman to her front door, supporting her as she staggers. Any suspicion of me that she may entertain, however formless and hazy, is allayed by my stern charging of the doorman to see that she reaches her apartment safely. She grows embarrassed, thinks perhaps that if not put off by her 'illness' I would spend the night with her, which moves her to press upon me, unasked, her telephone number. I bid her a solicitous goodnight and take the cab back to my hotel, where I sleep."

No sex? No sex. How did he feel about the victim as a person? "She was food."

This was his "hunting" of last night, he admits afterward, not a made-up dream. No boasting in it, just telling. Telling me! Think: I can go talk to Lucille, Mort, Doug, others, about most of what matters to me. Edward has only me to talk to and that for a fee — what isolation! No wonder the stone, monumental face — only those long, strong lips (his point of contact, verbal and physical-in-fantasy, with world and with "food") are truly expressive. An exciting narration; uncomfortable to find I felt not only empathy but enjoyment. Suppose he picked up and victimized — even in fantasy — Deb or Hilda, how would I feel then?

Later: truth — I also found this recital sexually stirring. Keep visualizing how he looked finishing this "dream" — sat very still, head up, look of thoughtful pleasure on his face. Like handsome intellectual listening to music.

Kenny showed up unexpectedly at Floria's office on Monday, bursting with malevolent energy. She happened to be free, so she took him — something was definitely up. He sat on the edge of his chair.

"I know why you're trying to unload me," he accused. "It's that new one, the tall guy with the snooty look — what is he, an old actor or something? Anybody could see he's got you itching for him."

"Kenny, when was it that I first spoke to you about terminating our work together?" she said patiently.

"Don't change the subject. Let me tell you, in case you don't know it: that guy isn't really interested, Doctor, because he's a fruit. A faggot. You want to know how I know?"

Oh Lord, she thought wearily, he's regressed to age ten. She could see that she was going to hear the rest whether she wanted to or not. What in God's name was the world like for Kenny, if he clung so fanatically to her despite her failure to help him?

"Listen, I knew right away there was something flaky about him, so I followed him home from here to that hotel where he lives. I followed him the other afternoon, too. He walked around like he does a lot, and then he went into one of those ritzy movie houses on Third that open early and show risqué foreign movies — you know, Japs cutting each other's things off and glop like that. This one was French, though.

"Well, there was a guy came in, a Madison Avenue type carrying his attaché case, taking a work break or something. Your man moved over and sat down behind him and reached out and sort of stroked the guy's neck, and the guy leaned back, and your man leaned forward and started nuzzling at him, you know — kissing him.

"I saw it. They had their heads together and they stayed like that a while. It was disgusting: complete strangers, without even 'hello.' The Madison Avenue guy just sat there with his head back looking zonked, you know, just swept away, and what he was doing with his hands under the raincoat in his lap I couldn't see, but I bet you can guess.

"And then your fruity friend got up and walked out. I did too, and I hung around a little outside. After a while the Madison Avenue guy came out looking all sleepy and loose, like after you-know-what, and he wandered off on his own someplace.

"What do you think now?" he ended, on a high, triumphant note.

Her impulse was to slap his face the way she would have slapped Deb as a child, for tattling. But this was a client, not a kid. God give me strength, she thought.

"Kenny, you're fired."

"You can't!" he squealed. "You can't! What will I — Who can I — "

She stood up, feeling weak but hardening her voice. "I'm sorry. I absolutely cannot have a client who makes it his business to spy on other clients. You already have a list of replacement therapists from me."

He gaped at her in slack-jawed dismay, his eyes swimmy with tears.

"I'm sorry, Kenny. Call this a dose of reality therapy and try to learn from it. There are some things you simply will not be allowed to do." She felt stronger, better: it was done at last.

"I hate you!" He surged out of his chair, knocking it back against the wall. Threateningly he glared at the fish tank, but contenting himself with a couple of kicks at the nearest table leg he stamped out.

Floria buzzed Hilda: "No more appointments for Kenny, Hilda. You can close his file."

"Whoopee," Hilda said.

Poor, horrid Kenny. Impossible to tell what would happen to him, better not to speculate or she might relent, call him back . . . She had encouraged him, really, by listening instead of shutting him up and throwing him out before any damage was done.

Was it damaging, to know the truth? In her mind's eye she saw a cream-faced young man out of a Black Thumb Vodka ad wander from a movie theater into daylight, yawning and rubbing absently at a sore spot on his neck . . .

She didn't even look at the telephone on the table or think about whom to call, now that she believed. No; she was going to keep quiet about Dr. Edward Lewis Weyland, her vampire.

Hardly alive at staff meeting, clinic, yesterday — people asking what's the matter, fobbed them off. Settled down today. Had to, to face him.

Asked him what he felt were his strengths. He said speed, cunning, ruthlessness. Animal strengths, I said. What about imagination, or is that strictly human? He defended at once: not human only. Lion, waiting at water hole where no zebra yet drinks, thinks "Zebra — eat," therefore performs feat of imagining event yet to come. Self experienced as animal? Yes — reminded me that humans are also animals. Pushed for his early memories, he objected: "Gestalt is here-and-now, not history-taking." I insist, citing anomalous nature of his situation, my own refusal to be bound by any one theoretical framework. He defends tensely: "Suppose I became lost there in memory, distracted from dangers of the present, left unguarded from those dangers?"

Speak for memory. He resists, but at length attempts it: "'I am heavy with the multitudes of the past.'" Fingertips to forehead, propping up all that weight of lives. "'So heavy, filling worlds of time laid down eon by eon, I accumulate, I persist, I demand recognition. I am as real as the life around you — more real, weightier, richer.'" His voice sinking, shoulders bowed, head in hands — I begin to feel pressure at the back of my own skull. "'Let me in.'" Only a rough whisper now. "'I offer beauty as well as terror. Let me in.'" Whispering also I suggest he reply to his memory. "Memory, you want to crush me," he groans. "You would overwhelm me with the cries of animals, the odor and jostle of bodies, old betrayals, dead joys, filth and anger from other times — I must concentrate on the danger now. Let me be.'' All I can take of this crazy conflict, I gabble us off onto something else. He looks up — relief? — follows my lead — where? Rest of session a blank.

No wonder sometimes no empathy at all — a species boundary! He has to be utterly self-centered just to keep balance — self-centeredness of an animal. Thought just now of our beginning, me trying to push him to produce material, trying to control him, manipulate — no way, no way; so here we are, someplace else — I feel dazed, in shock, but stick with it — it's real.

Therapy with a dinosaur, a Martian.

"You call me 'Weyland' now, not 'Edward.'" I said first name couldn't mean much to one with no memory of being called by that name as a child, silly to pretend it signifies intimacy where it can't. I think he knows now that I believe him. Without prompting, told me truth of disappearance from Cayslin. No romance; he tried to drink from a woman who worked there, she shot him, stomach and chest. Luckily for him, small caliber pistol, and he was wearing a lined coat over three-piece suit. Even so, badly hurt. (Midsection stiffness I noted when he first came — he was still in some pain at that time.) He didn't "vanish" — fled, hid, was found by questionable types who caught on to what he was, sold him "like a chattel" to someone here in the city. He was imprisoned, fed, put on exhibition — very privately — for gain. Got away. "Do you believe any of this?" Never asked anything like that before, seems of concern to him now. I said my belief or lack of same was immaterial; remarked on hearing a lot of bitterness.

Steepled his fingers, looked brooding at me over tips: "I nearly died there. No doubt my purchaser and his friends are still searching for me. Mind you, I had some reason at first to be glad of the attentions of the people who kept me prisoner. I was in no condition to fend for myself. They brought me food and kept me hidden and sheltered, whatever their motives. There are always advantages . . . .''

Silence today started a short session. Hunting poor last night, Weyland still hungry. Much restless movement, watching goldfish darting in tank, scanning bookshelves. Asked him to be books. "'I am old and full of knowledge, well-made to last long. You see only the title, the substance is hidden. I am a book that stays closed.''' Malicious twist of the mouth, not quite a smile: "This is a good game." Is he feeling threatened too — already "opened" too much to me? Too strung out with him to dig when he's skimming surfaces that should be probed. Don't know how to *do* therapy with Weyland — just have to let things happen, hope it's good. But what's "good?" Aristotle? Rousseau? Ask Weyland what's good, he'll say "Blood.''

Everything in a spin — these notes too confused, fragmentary —

worthless for a book, just a mess, like me, my life. Tried to call Deb last night, cancel visit. Nobody home, thank God. Can't tell her to stay away — but damn it — do not need complications now.

Floria went down to Broadway with Lucille to get more juice, cheese and crackers for the clinic fridge. This week it was their turn to do the provisions, a chore that rotated among the staff. Their talk about grant proposals for the support of the clinic trailed off.

"Let's sit a minute," Floria said. They crossed to a traffic island in the middle of the avenue. It was a sunny afternoon, close enough to lunchtime so that the brigade of old people who normally occupied the benches had thinned out. Floria sat down and kicked a crumpled beer can and some greasy fast-food wrappings back under the bench.

"You look like hell but wide awake, at least," Lucille commented.

"Things are still rough," Floria said. "I keep hoping to get my life under control so I'll have some energy left for Deb and Nick and the kids when they arrive, but I can't seem to do it. Group was awful last night — a member accused me afterward of having abandoned them all. I think I have, too. The professional messes and the personal are all related somehow, they run into each other. I should be keeping them apart so I can deal with them separately, but I can't. I can't concentrate, my mind is all over the place. Except with Dracula, who keeps me riveted with astonishment when he's in the office and bemused the rest of the time."

A bus roared by, shaking the pavement and the benches. Lucille waited until the noise faded. "Relax about the group. They'd have defended you if you'd been attacked during the session. They'd all understand, even if you don't seem to: it's the summer doldrums, people don't want to work, they expect you to do it all for them. But don't push so hard. You're not a shaman who can magic your clients back into health."

Floria tore two cans of juice out of a six-pack and handed one to her. On a street corner opposite, a violent argument broke out in typewriter-fast Spanish between two women. Floria sipped tinny juice and watched. She'd seen a guy last winter straddle another on that same corner and try to smash his brains out on the icy sidewalk. What's crazy, what's health?

"It's a good thing you dumped Chubs, anyhow," Lucille added. "I don't know that finally brought that on, but it's definitely a move in the right direction. What about Count Dracula? You don't talk about him much anymore. I thought I diagnosed a yen for his venerable body."

Floria shifted uncomfortably on the bench and didn't answer. If only she could deflect Lucille's sharp-eyed curiosity —

"Oh," Lucille said. "I see. You really are hot — or at least warm. Has he noticed?"

"I don't think so. He's not on the lookout for that kind of response from me.

He says sex with other people doesn't interest him, and I think he's telling the truth.''

"Weird," 'Lucille said. "What about *Vampire on my Couch*? Shaping up all right?''

"It's shaky, like everything else. I'm worried that I don't know how things are going to come out. I mean, Freud's wolf man case was a success, as therapy goes. Will my vampire case turn out successfully?''

She glanced at Lucille's puzzled face, made up her mind, and plunged ahead. "Luce, think of it this way: suppose, just suppose, that my Dracula is for real, an honest-to-God vampire — "

"Oh, *shit!*'' Lucille erupted in anguished exasperation. "Damn it, Floria, enough is enough — will you stop futzing around and get some help? Coming to pieces yourself and trying to treat this poor nut with a vampire fixation — how can you do him any good? No wonder you're worried about his therapy!''

"Please, just listen, help me think this out. My purpose can't be to cure him of what he is. Suppose vampirism isn't a defense he has to learn to drop? Suppose it's the core of his identity? Then what do I do?''

Lucille rose abruptly and marched away from her across the traffic, plunging through a gap between the rolling waves of cabs and trucks. Floria caught up with her on the next block.

"Listen, will you? Luce, you see the problem? I don't need to help him see who and what he is, he knows that perfectly well, and he's not crazy, far from it — "

"Maybe not,'' Lucille said grimly, "but you are. Don't dump this junk on me outside of office hours, Floria. I don't spend my time listening to nut-talk unless I'm getting paid.''

"Just tell me if this makes psychological sense to you: he's healthier than most of us because he's always true to his identity, even when he's engaged in deceiving others. A fairly narrow, rigorous set of requirements necessary to his survival — that *is* his identity, and it commands him completely. Anything extraneous could destroy him. To go on living, he has to act solely out of his own undistorted necessity, and if that isn't authenticity, what is? So he's healthy, isn't he?'' She paused, feeling a sudden lightness in herself. "And that's the best sense I've been able to make of this whole business so far.''

They were in the middle of the block. Lucille, who could not on her short legs outwalk Floria, turned on her suddenly. "What the hell do you think you're doing, calling yourself a therapist? For God's sake, Floria, don't try to rope me into this kind of professional irresponsibility. You're just dipping into your client's fantasies instead of helping him to handle them. That's not therapy, it's collusion. Have some sense! Admit you're over your head in troubles of your own, retreat to firmer ground — go get treatment for yourself!''

Floria angrily shook her head. When Lucille turned away and hurried on up the block toward the clinic, Floria let her go without trying to detain her.

Thought about Lucille's advice. After my divorce going back into therapy for a while did help, but now? Retreat again to being a client, like old days in training — so young, inadequate, defenseless then. Awful prospect. And I'd have to hand W. over to somebody else — who? I'm not up to handling him, can't cope, too anxious, yet with all the limitations we do good therapy together somehow. I offer, he's free to take, refuse, use as suits, as far as he's willing to go. I serve as resource while he does own therapy — isn't that therapeutic ideal, free of "shoulds," "shouldn'ts?"

Saw ballet with Mort, lovely evening — time out from W. — talking, singing, pirouetting all the way home, feeling safe as anything in the shadow of Mort-mountain, rolled later with that humming (off-key), sun-warm body.

W. says he saw me at Lincoln Center last night, avoided me because of Mort. W. is ballet fan! Started attending to pick up victims, now also because dance puzzles and pleases. "When a group dances well, the meaning is easy — the dancers make a visual complement to the music, all their moves necessary, coherent, and flowing. When a gifted soloist performs, the pleasure of making the moves is echoed in my own body. The soloist's absorption is total, much like my own in the actions of the hunt.

"But when a man and a woman dance together, something else happens. What is it? Sometimes one is hunter, one is prey, or they shift these roles between them. Yet some other level of significance exists — I suppose to do with sex, and I feel it — a tugging sensation, here — " touched his solar plexus — "but I do not understand it."

Worked with his reactions to ballet. The response he feels to pas de deux is a kind of pull, "like hunger but not hunger." Of course he's baffled — Balanchine writes that the pas de deux is always a love story between man and woman. W. isn't man, isn't woman, yet the drama reaches him. His hands hovering as he spoke, fingers spread toward each other. Pointed this out. Body-work comes easier to him now: joined his hands, interlaced fingers, spoke for hands without prompting: "'We are similar, we want the comfort of like closing to like.'" What would it be for him, to find — likeness, another of his kind? "Female?" Starts to tell me how unlikely this is — No, forget sex and pas de deux for now — just to find your like, another vampire. He springs up, agitated now. There are none, he insists. "But what would it be like? What would happen?"

"I fear it!" Sits again, hands clenched. "I long for it." Silence. He watches goldfish, I watch him. I withhold fatuous attempt to pin down this insight, if that's what it is — what can I know about his insight? Suddenly he turns, studies me intently till I lose nerve, react, cravenly suggest that if I make him uncomfortable he may choose to switch to a male therapist. "Certainly not." More follows, all gold: "There is value to me in what we do here, Dr. Landauer, much against my earlier expectations. Although people talk appreciatively of honest speech they generally avoid it, and I myself have found scarcely any use for it at all. Your straightforwardness with me — and the straightforwardness you require in return — this is healthy in a life so dependent on deception as mine.''

Sat there, wordless, much moved, thinking of what I don't show him — my upset life, seat-of-pants course with him and attendant strain, attraction to him — I'm holding out on him while he appreciates my honesty.

Hesitation, then lower-voiced, ''Also, there are limits on my methods of self-discovery, short of turning myself over to a laboratory for vivisection. I have no others like myself to look at and learn from. Any tools that may help are worth much to me, and these games of yours are — potent.''

Other stuff besides, not important. Important: he moves me and he draws me and he keeps on coming back. Hang in if he does.

Bad night — Kenny's aunt called: no bill from me this month, so if he's not seeing me who's keeping an eye on him, where's he hanging out? Much implied blame for what *might* happen. Absurd, but shook me up: I did fail Kenny. Called off group this week also; too much.

No, it was a *good* night — first dream in months I can recall, contact again with own depths — but disturbing. Dreamed myself in a cab with W. in place of the woman from the Y. He put his hand not on my neck but breast — I felt intense sensual response in the dream, also anger and fear so strong they woke me.

Thinking about this: anyone leans toward him sexually, to him a sign his hunting technique has maneuvered prospective victim into range, maybe arouses his appetite for blood. I DON'T WANT THAT. ''She was food.'' I am not food, I am a person. No thrill at languishing away in his arms in a taxi while he drinks my blood — that's disfigured sex, masochism. My sex response in dream signaled to me I would be his victim — I rejected that, woke up.

Mention of *Dracula* (novel). W. dislikes: meandering, inaccurate, those absurd fangs. Says he himself has when needed a sort of needle under his tongue, used to pierce skin. No offer to demonstrate, and no request from me. I brightly brought up historical Vlad Dracul — celebrated instance of Turkish envoys who, upon refusing to uncover to Vlad to show respect, were killed by spiking their hats to their skulls. ''Nonsense,'' snorts W. ''A clever ruler would use very small thumbtacks and dismiss the envoys to moan about the streets of Varna holding their tacked heads.'' First spontaneous play he's shown — took head in hands and uttered plaintive groans, ''Ow, oh, ooh.'' I cracked up. W. reverted at once to usual dignified manner: ''You can see that this would serve the ruler much more efficiently as an object lesson against rash pride.''

Later, same light vein: ''I know why I'm a vampire, why are you a therapist?'' Off balance as usual, said things about helping, mental health, etc. He shook his head: "And people think of a vampire as arrogant! You want to perform cures in a world which exhibits very little health of any kind — and it's the same arrogance with all of you. This one wants to be President or Class Monitor or Department Chairman or Union Boss, another must be first to fly to the stars or to transplant the human brain, and on and on. As for me, I wish only to satisfy my appetite in peace." And those of us whose appetite is for competence, for effectiveness? Thought of Green, treated eight years ago, went on to be indicted for running a hellish "home" for aged. I had helped him stay functional so he could destroy the helpless for profit.

W. not my first predator, only most honest and direct. Scared; not of attack by W., but of process we're going through. I'm beginning to be up to it (?), but still — utterly unpredictable, impossible to handle or manage — Occasional stirrings of inward choreographer that used to shape my work so surely. Have I been afraid of that, holding it down in myself, choosing mechanical manipulation instead? Not a choice with W. — thinking no good, strategy no good, nothing left but instinct, clear and uncluttered responses if I can find them. Have to be my own authority with him, as he is always his own authority with a world in which he's unique. So work with W. not just exhausting — exhilarating too, along with strain, fear.

Am I growing braver? Not much choice.

Park again today (air-conditioning out at office). Avoiding Lucille's phone calls from clinic (very reassuring that she calls despite quarrel, but don't want to take all this up with her again). Also meeting W. in open feels saner somehow — wild creatures belong outdoors? Sailboat pond N. of 72nd, lots of kids, garbage, one beautiful, tall boat drifting.

W. maintains he remembers no childhood, no parents. I told him my astonishment, confronted by someone who never had a life of the previous generation (even adopted parent) shielding him from death — how naked we stand when the last shield falls. Got caught in remembering a death dream of mine, dream it now and then — couldn't concentrate, got scared, spoke of it — a dog tumbled under a passing truck, ejected to side of the road where it lay unable to move except to lift head and shriek; couldn't help. Shaking nearly to tears — remember mother got into dream somehow — had blocked that at first. Didn't say it now. Tried to rescue situation, show W. how to work with a dream (sitting in vine arbor near band shell, some privacy).

He focused on my obvious shakiness: "The air vibrates constantly with the death cries of countless large and small. What is the death of one dog?" Leaned close, speaking quietly, instructing. "Many creatures are dying in ways too dreadful to imagine. I am part of the world; I listen to the pain. You people claim to be above all that. You deafen yourselves with your own noise and pretend there's nothing else to hear. Then these screams enter your dreams, and you have to seek therapy because you have lost the nerve to listen.''

Remembered myself, said, Be a dying animal. He refused: "You are the one who dreams this." I had a horrible flash, felt I was the dog — helpless, doomed, hurting — burst into tears. The great therapist, bringing her own hang-ups into session with client! Enraged with self, which did not help stop bawling.

W. disconcerted, I think; didn't speak. People walked past, glanced over, ignored us. W. said finally, "What is this?" Nothing, just the fear of death. "Oh, the fear of death. That's with me all the time. One must simply get used to it." Tears into laughter. Goddamn wisdom of the ages. He got up to go, paused: "And tell that stupid little man who used to precede me at your office to stop following me around. He puts himself in danger that way."

Kenny, damn it! Aunt doesn't know where he is, no answer on his phone. Idiot!

Sketching all night — useless. W. beautiful beyond the scope of line — the beauty of singularity, cohesion, rooted in absolute devotion to demands of his specialized body. In feeding (woman in taxi), utter absorption one wants from a man in sex — no score-keeping, no fantasies — just hot urgency of appetite, of senses, the moment by itself.

His sleeves worn rolled back today to the elbows — strong, sculptural forearms, the long bones curved in slightly, suggest torque, leverage. How old — ?

Endurance: huge, rich cloak of time flows back from his shoulders like wings of a dark angel. All springs from, elaborates, the single, stark, primary condition: he is a predator who subsists on human blood. Harmony, strength, clarity, magnificence — all from that basic animal integrity. Of course I long for all that, here in the higgledy-piggledy hodge-podge of my life! Of course he draws me!

Wore no perfume today, deference to his keen, easily insulted sense of smell. He noticed at once, said curt thanks. Saw something bothering him, opened my mouth seeking desperately for right thing to say — up rose my inward choreographer, wide awake, and spoke plain from my heart: thinking on my floundering in some of our sessions — I am aware that you see this confusion of mine. I know you see by your occasional impatient look, sudden disengagement — yet you continue to reveal yourself to me (even shift our course yourself if it needs shifting and I don't do it). I think I know why. Because there's no place for you in world as you truly are. Because beneath your various facades your true self suffers; like all true selves, it wants, needs to be honored as real and valuable through acceptance by another. I try to be that other, but often you are beyond me.

He rose, paced to window, looked back, burning at me. "If I seem sometimes restless or impatient, Dr. Landauer, it's not because of any professional shortcomings of yours. On the contrary — you are all too effective. The seductiveness, the distraction of our — human contact worries me. I fear for the ruthlessness that keeps me alive.''

Speak for ruthlessness. He shook his head. Saw tightness in shoulders, feet braced hard against floor. Felt reflected tension in my own muscles.

Prompted him: '' 'I resent — ' ''

''I resent your pretension to teach me about myself! What will this work that you do here make of me? A predator paralyzed by an unwanted empathy with his prey? A creature fit only for a cage and keeper?'' He was breathing hard, jaw set. I saw suddenly the truth of his fear: his integrity is not human, but my work is specifically human, designed to make humans more human — what if it does that to him? Should have seen it before, should have seen it. No place left to go: had to ask him, in small voice, Speak for my pretension.

''No!'' Eyes shut, head turned away.

Had to do it! Speak for me.

W. whispered, ''As to the unicorn, out of your own legends — 'Unicorn, come lay your head in my lap while the hunters close in. You are a wonder, and for love of wonder I will tame you. You are pursued, but forget your pursuers, rest under my hand till they come and destroy you.' '' Looked at me like steel: ''Do you see? The more you involve yourself in what I am, the more you become the peasant with the torch!''

Two days later Doug came into town and had lunch with Floria.

He was a man of no outstanding beauty who was nevertheless attractive: he didn't have much chin and his ears were too big, but you didn't notice because of his air of confidence. His stability had been earned the hard way — as a gay man facing the straight world. Some of his strength had been attained with effort and pain in a group that Floria had run years earlier. A lasting affection had grown between herself and Doug. She was intensely glad to see him.

They ate near the clinic. ''You look a little frayed around the edges,'' Doug said. '''I heard about Jane Fennerman's relapse — too bad.''

''I've only been able to bring myself to visit her once since.''

''Feeling guilty?''

She hesitated, gnawing on a stale breadstick. The truth was, she hadn't thought of Jane Fennerman in weeks. Finally she said, ''I must be.''

Sitting back with his hands in his pockets, Doug chided her gently. ''It's got to be Jane's fourth or fifth time into the nuthatch, and the others happened when she was in the care of other therapists. Who are you to imagine — to demand — that her cure lay in your hands? God may be a woman, Floria, but she is not you. I thought the whole point was some recognition of individual responsibility — you for yourself, the client for himself or herself.''

''That's what we're always saying,'' Floria agreed. She felt curiously divorced from this conversation. It had an old-fashioned flavor: before Weyland. She smiled a little.

The waiter ambled over. She ordered bluefish. The serving would be too big for her depressed appetite, but Doug wouldn't be satisfied with his customary order of salad (he never was) and could be persuaded to help out.

He worked his way around to Topic A. "When I called to set up this lunch, Hilda told me she's got a crush on Weyland. How are you and he getting along?"

"My God, Doug, now you're going to tell me this whole thing was to fix me up with an eligible suitor!" She winced at her own rather strained laughter. "How soon are you planning to ask Weyland to work at Cayslin again?"

"I don't know, but probably sooner than I thought a couple of months ago. We hear that he's been exploring an attachment to an archaeology department at a western school, some niche where I guess he feels he can have less responsibility, less visibility, and a chance to collect himself. Naturally, this news is making people at Cayslin suddenly eager to nail him down for us. Have you a recommendation?"

"Yes," she said. "Wait."

He gave her an inquiring look. "What for?"

"Until he works more fully through certain stresses in the situation at Cayslin. Then I'll be ready to commit myself about him." The bluefish came. She pretended distraction: "Good God, that's much too much fish for me. Douglas, come on and help me out here."

Hilda was crouched over Floria's file drawer. She straightened up, grim-looking. "Somebody's been in the office!"

What was this, had someone attacked her? The world took on a cockeyed, dangerous tilt. "Are you okay?"

"Yes, sure, I mean there are records that have been gone through. I can tell. I've started checking and so far it looks as if none of the files themselves are missing. But if any papers were taken out of them, that would be pretty hard to spot without reading through every folder in the place. Your files, Floria. I don't think anybody else's were touched."

Mere burglary; weak with relief, Floria sat down on one of the waiting-room chairs. But only her files? "Just my stuff, you're sure?"

Hilda nodded. "The clinic got hit too. I called. They see some new-looking scratches on the lock of your file drawer over there. Listen, you want me to call the cops?"

"First check as much as you can, see if anything obvious is missing."

There was no sign of upset in her office. She found a note on her table: Weyland had canceled his next appointment.

She buzzed Hilda's desk. "Hilda, let's leave the police out of it for the moment. Keep checking." She stood in the middle of the office, looking at the chair replacing the one he had broken, looking at the window where he had so often watched.

Relax, she told herself. There was nothing for him to find here or at the clinic.

She signaled that she was ready for the first client of the afternoon.

That evening she came back to the office after having dinner with friends. She was supposed to be helping set up a workshop for next month, and she'd been putting off even thinking about it, let alone doing any real work. She set herself to compiling a suggested bibliography for her section.

The phone light blinked.

It was Kenny, muffled and teary-voiced. "I'm sorry," he moaned. "The medicine just started to wear off. I've been trying to call you everyplace. God, I'm so scared — he was waiting in the alley."

"Who was?" she said, dry-mouthed. She knew.

"Him. The tall one, the faggot — only he goes with women too, I've seen him. He grabbed me. He hurt me. I was lying there a long time. I couldn't do anything. I felt so funny — like floating away. Some kids found me. Their mother called the cops. I was so cold, so scared — "

"Kenny, where are you?"

He told her which hospital. "Listen, I think he's really crazy, you know? And I'm scared he might — you live alone — I don't know — I didn't mean to make trouble for you. I'm so scared."

God damn you, you meant exactly to make trouble for me, and now you've bloody well made it. She got him to ring for a nurse. By calling Kenny her patient and using "Dr." in front of her own name without qualifying the title she got some information: two broken ribs, multiple contusions, a badly wrenched shoulder, and a deep cut on the scalp which Dr. Wells thought accounted for the blood loss the patient seemed to have sustained. Picked up early today, the patient wouldn't say who had attacked him. You can check with Dr. Wells tomorrow, Dr. — ?

Can Weyland think I've somehow sicced Kenny on him? No, he surely knows me better than that. Kenny must have brought this on himself.

She tried Weyland's number and then the desk at his hotel. He had closed his account and gone, providing no forwarding information.

Then she remembered: this was the night Deb and Nick and the kids were arriving. Oh, God. Next phone call.

The Americana was the hotel Deb had mentioned. Yes, Mr. and Mrs. Nicholas Redpath were registered in room whatnot. Ring please.

Deb's voice came shakily on the line. "I've been trying to call you." Like Kenny.

"You sound upset," Floria said, steadying herself for whatever calamity had descended: illness, accident, assault in the streets of the dark, degenerate city.

Silence, then a raggedy sob. "Nick's not here. I didn't phone you earlier because I thought he still might come, but I don't think he's coming, Mom." Bitter weeping.

"Oh, Debbie. Debbie, listen, you just sit tight, I'll be right down there."

The cab ride only took a few minutes. Debbie was still crying when Floria stepped into the room.

"I don't know, I don't know," Deb wailed, shaking her head. "What did I do wrong? He went away a week ago, to do some research he said, and I didn't hear from him, and half the bank money is gone — just half, he left me half. I kept hoping — they say most runaways come back in a few days or call up, they get lonely — I haven't told anybody — I thought since we were supposed to be here at this convention thing together, I'd better come, maybe he'd show up. But nobody's seen him, and there are no messages, not a word, nothing — "

"All right, all right, poor Deb," Floria said, hugging her.

"Oh God, I'm going to wake the kids with all this howling — " Deb pulled away, making a frantic gesture toward the door of the adjoining room. "It was so hard to get them to sleep — they were expecting Daddy to be here, I kept telling them he'd be here — " She rushed out into the hotel hallway. Floria followed, propping the door open with one of her shoes since she didn't know whether Deb had the key with her or not. They stood out there together, ignoring passersby, huddling over Deb's weeping.

"What's been going on between you and Nick?" Floria said. "Have you two been sleeping together lately?"

Deb let out a squawk of agonized embarrassment, "*Mother!*" and pulled away from her. Oh, hell, wrong approach.

"Come on, I'll help you pack and let's go — let Nick come looking for you. We'll leave word you're at my place." Floria firmly squashed down the miserable inner cry, How am I going to stand this?

"Oh, no, I can't move till morning now that I've got the kids settled down. Besides, there's one night's deposit on the rooms. Oh, Mom, what did I do?"

"You didn't do anything, hon," Floria said, patting her shoulder and thinking in some part of her mind, oh, boy, that's great, is that the best you can come up with in a crisis with all your training and experience? Your touted professional skills are not so hot lately, but this bad? Another part answered, Shut up, stupid, only a dope does therapy on her own family. Deb's come to her mother, not a shrink, so go ahead and be Mommy. If only Mommy had less pressure on her right now — but that was always the way: everything at once or nothing at all.

"Look, suppose I stay the night here with you?"

Deb shook the pale, damp-streaked hair out of her eyes with a determined, grown-up gesture. "No, thanks, Mom. Look, I'm so tired I'm just going to fall out now. You'll be getting a bellyful of all this when we move in on you tomorrow anyway. I can manage tonight, and besides — "

And besides, just in case Nick showed up, Deb didn't want Floria around complicating things; of course. Or in case the tooth-fairy dropped by.

Floria restrained an impulse to insist on staying: the impulse, she recognized, came from her own need not to be alone tonight. That was an inappropriate burden to load on Deb's shoulders.

"Okay," she said. "But look, Deb, I'll expect you to call me up first thing in the morning, whatever happens." And if I'm still alive, I'll answer the phone.

All the way home in the cab she knew with growing certainty that Weyland would be waiting for her there. He can't just walk away, she thought; he has to finish things with me. So let's get it over.

In the tiled hallway she hesitated, keys in hand. What about calling the cops to go inside with her? Absurd. You don't set the cops on a unicorn.

She unlocked and opened the door to the apartment and called inside, "All right, Weyland, where are you?"

Nothing. Of course not — the door was still open, and he would want to be sure she was by herself. She stepped inside, shut the door, and snapped on a lamp as she walked into the living room.

He was sitting quietly on a radiator cover by the street window, his hands on his thighs. His appearance here in a new setting, her setting, this faintly lit room in her home place, was startlingly intimate. She was sharply aware of the whisper of movement — his clothing, his shoe soles against the carpet underfoot — as he shifted his posture.

"What would you have done if I'd brought somebody with me?" she said unsteadily. "Changed yourself into a bat and flown away?"

"Two things I must have from you. One is the bill of health that we spoke of when we began, though not, after all, for Cayslin College. I've made other plans. The story of my disappearance has of course filtered out along the academic grapevine so that even two thousand miles from here people will be wanting evidence of my mental soundness. Your evidence. I would type it myself and forge your signature, but I want your authentic tone and language. Please prepare a letter to the desired effect, addressed to these people."

He took something white from an inside pocket and held it out. She advanced and took the envelope from his extended hand. It was from the western archaeology department that Doug had mentioned at lunch.

"Why not Cayslin?" she said. "They want you there."

"Have you forgotten your own suggestion that I find another job? That was a good idea after all. Your reference will serve me best out there — with a copy for my personnel file at Cayslin, naturally."

She put her purse down on the seat of a chair and crossed her arms. She felt reckless — the effect of stress and weariness, she thought, but it was an exciting feeling.

"The receptionist at the office does this sort of thing for me," she said.

He pointed. "I've been in your study. You have a typewriter there, you have stationery with your letterhead, you have carbon paper."

"What was the second thing you wanted?"

"Your notes on my case."

"Also at the — "

"You know that I've already been to both your work-places, and the very circumspect jottings in your file on me are not what I mean. Others must exist: more detailed."

"What makes you think that?"

"How could you resist?" He mocked her. "You have encountered nothing like me in your entire professional life, and never shall again. Perhaps someday you hope to produce an article, even a book — a memoir of something impossible that happened to you one summer — you are an ambitious woman, Dr. Landauer."

Floria squeezed her crossed arms tighter against herself to quell her shivering. "This is all just supposition," she said.

He took folded papers from his pocket: some of her thrown-aside drawings of him, salvaged from the waste basket. "I found these. I think there must be more. Fetch whatever there is for me, please."

"And if I refuse, what will you do? Beat me up the way you beat up Kenny?"

Weyland said calmly, "I told you he should stop following me. This is serious now. There are pursuers who intend me ill — my former captors, of whom I told you. Whom do you think I keep watch for? No records concerning me must fall into their hands. Don't bother protesting to me your devotion to confidentiality. My pursuers would take what they want, and be damned to your professional ethics. So I must destroy all evidence you have about me before I leave the city."

Floria turned away and sat down by the coffee table, trying to think beyond her fear. She breathed deeply against the fright trembling in her chest.

"I see," he said dryly, "that you won't give me the notes; you don't trust me to take them and go. You see some danger."

"All right, a bargain," she said. "I'll give you whatever I have on your case if in return you promise to go straight out to your new job and keep away from Kenny and my offices and anybody connected with me — "

He was smiling slightly as he rose from the seat and stepped soft-footed toward her over the rug. "Bargains, promises, negotiations — all foolish, Dr. Landauer. I want what I came for."

She looked up at him. "But then how can I trust you at all? As soon as I give you what you want — "

"What is it that makes you afraid — that you can't render me harmless to you? What a curious concern you show suddenly for your own life and the lives of those around you! You are the one who led me to take chances in our work together — to explore the frightful risks of self-revelation. Didn't you see in the air between us the brilliant shimmer of those hazards? I thought your business was not smoothing the world over but adventuring into it, discovering its true nature, and closing valiantly with everything jagged, cruel, and deadly."

In the midst of her terror the inner choreographer awoke and stretched. Floria rose to face the vampire.

"All right, Weyland, no bargains. I'll give you freely what you want." Of course she couldn't make herself safe from him — or make Kenny or Lucille or Deb or Doug safe — any more than she could protect Jane Fennerman from the common dangers of life. Like Weyland, some dangers were too strong to bind or banish. "My notes are in the work room — come on, I'll show you. As for the letter you need, I'll type it right now and you can take it away with you."

She sat at the typewriter arranging paper, carbon sheets, and white-out, and feeling the force of his presence. Only a few feet away, just at the margin of the light from the gooseneck lamp by which she worked, he leaned against the edge of the long table that was twin to the table in her office. Open in his large hands was the notebook she had taken from the table drawer. When he moved his head over the notebook's pages, his glasses threw off pale glints.

She typed the heading and the date. How surprising, she thought, to find that she had regained her nerve here, and now. When you dance as the inner choreographer directs, you act without thinking, not in command of events but in harmony with them. You yield control, accepting the chance that a mistake might be part of the design. The inner choreographer is always right but often dangerous: giving up control means accepting the possibility of death. What I feared I have pursued right here to this moment in this room.

A sheet of paper fell out of the notebook. Weyland stooped and caught it up, glanced at it. "You had training in art?" Must be a sketch.

"I thought once I might be an artist," she said.

"What you chose to do instead is better," he said. "This making of pictures, plays, all art, is pathetic. The world teems with creation, most of it unnoticed by your kind just as most of the deaths are unnoticed. What can be the point of adding yet another tiny gesture? Even you, these notes — for what, a moment's celebrity?"

"You tried it yourself," Floria said. "The book you edited, *Notes on a Vanished People.*" She typed, ". . . temporary dislocation resulting from a severe personal shock . . ."

"That was professional necessity, not creation," he said in the tone of a lecturer irritated by a question from the audience. With disdain he tossed the drawing on the table. "Remember, I don't share your impulse toward artistic gesture — your absurd frills — "

She looked up sharply. "The ballet, Weyland. Don't lie." She typed, ". . . exhibits a powerful drive toward inner balance and wholeness in a difficult life-situation. The steadying influence of an extraordinary basic integrity . . ."

He set the notebook aside. "My feeling for ballet is clearly some sort of aberration. Do you sigh to hear a cow calling in a pasture?"

"There are those who have wept to hear whales singing in the ocean."

He was silent. His eyes averted.

"This is finished," she said. "Do you want to read it?"

He took the letter. "Good," he said at length. "Sign it, please. And type an envelope for it.'' He stood closer, but out of arm's reach, while she complied. ''You seem less frightened.''

''I'm terrified but not paralyzed,'' she said and laughed, but the laugh came out like a gasp.

''Fear is useful. It has kept you at your best throughout our association. Have you a stamp?''

He took the letter and walked back into the living room. She took a deep breath. She got up, turned off the gooseneck lamp, and followed him.

''What now, Weyland?'' she said softly. ''A carefully arranged suicide so that I have no chance to retract what's in that letter, or to reconstruct my notes?''

''It is a possibility,'' he observed, at the window again, always at the window, on watch. ''Your doorman was sleeping in the lobby. He never saw me enter the building. Once inside I used the stairs, of course. The suicide rate among therapists is notoriously high. I looked it up.''

''You have everything all planned?''

The window was open. He reached out and touched the metal grille that guarded it. One end of the grille swung creaking outward into the night air, like a gate opening. She visualized him sitting there waiting for her to come home, his powerful fingers patiently working the bolts at that side of the grille loose from the brick-and-mortar window frame. The hair lifted on the back of her neck.

He turned toward her again. She could see the end of the letter she had given him sticking palely out of his jacket pocket.

''Floria,'' he said meditatively. ''An unusual name — is it after the heroine of Sardou's *Tosca*? At the end, doesn't she throw herself to her death from a high castle wall? People are careless about the names they give their children. I will not drink from you — I hunted today, and I fed. Still, to leave you living . . . is too dangerous.''

A fire engine tore past below, siren screaming. When it had gone Floria said, ''Listen, Weyland, you said it yourself: I can't make myself safe from you — I'm not strong enough to shove you out the window instead of being shoved out myself. Must you make yourself safe from me? Let me say this to you, without promises, demands, or pleadings: I will not go back on what I wrote in that letter. I will not try to reconstruct my notes. I mean it. Be content with that.''

''You tempt me to it,'' he murmured after a moment, ''to go from here with you still alive behind me for the remainder of your little life — to leave woven into Dr. Landauer's quick mind those threads of my own life that I pulled for her . . . I want to be able sometimes to think of you thinking of me. But the risk is very great.''

''Sometimes it's right to let the dangers live, to give them their place,'' she argued. ''Didn't you tell me yourself a little while ago how risk makes us more heroic?''

He looked amused. ''Are you instructing me in the virtues of danger? You are brave enough to know something, perhaps, about that, but I have studied danger all my life.''

216 | SUZY McKEE CHARNAS

"A long, long life with more to come," she said, desperate to make him understand and believe her. "Not mine to jeopardize. There's no torch-brandishing peasant here; we left that behind long ago. Remember when you spoke for me? You said, 'For love of wonder.' That was true."

He leaned to turn off the lamp near the window. She thought that he had made up his mind, and that when he straightened it would be to spring.

But instead of terror locking her limbs, from the inward choreographer came a rush of warmth and energy into her muscles and an impulse to turn toward him. Out of a harmony of desires she said swiftly, "Weyland, come to bed with me."

She saw his shoulders stiffen against the dim square of the window, his head lift in scorn. "You know I can't be bribed that way," he said contemptuously. "What are you up to? Are you one of those who come into heat at the sight of an upraised fist?"

"My life hasn't twisted me that badly, thank God," she retorted. "And if you've known all along how scared I've been, you must have sensed my attraction to you too, so you know it goes back to — very early in our work." Her mouth was dry as paper. She pressed quickly on, anxious to get it all said to him: "This is simply how I would like to mark the ending of our time together. This is the completion I want. Surely you feel something too, Weyland — curiosity at least?"

"Granted, your emphasis on the expressiveness of the body has instructed me," he admitted, and then he added lightly, "Isn't it extremely unprofessional to proposition a client?"

"Extremely, and I never do, but somehow now it feels right. For you to indulge in courtship that doesn't end in a meal would be unprofessional too, but how would it feel to indulge anyway — just this once?" Go softly now, he's intrigued but wary. "Since we started, you've pushed me light-years beyond my profession. Now I want you to travel all the way with me, Weyland. Let's be unprofessional together."

She turned and went into the bedroom, leaving the lights off. There was a reflected light, cool and diffuse, from the glowing night air of the great city. She sat down on the bed and kicked off her shoes. When she looked up, he was in the doorway.

Hesitantly, he halted a few feet from her in the dimness, then came and sat beside her. He would have lain down in his clothes, but she said quietly, "You can undress. The front door's locked and there isn't anyone here but us. You won't have to leap up and flee for your life."

He stood again and began to take off his clothes, which he draped neatly over a chair. He said, "Suppose I am fertile with you; could you conceive?"

By her own choice any such possibility had been closed off after Deb. She said, "No," and that seemed to satisfy him.

She tossed her own clothes onto the dresser.

He sat down next to her again, his body silvery in the reflected light and smooth, lean as a whippet and as roped with muscle. His cool thigh pressed against her own fuller, darker one as he leaned across her and carefully deposited his glasses on the bedtable. Then he turned toward her, and she could just make out two puckerings of tissue on his skin. Bullet scars, she thought, shivering.

He said, "But why do I wish to do this?"

"Do you?" She had to hold herself back from touching him.

"Yes." He stared at her. "How did you grow so real? The more I spoke to you of myself, the more real you became."

"No more speaking, Weyland," she said gently. "This is body-work."

He lay back on the bed.

She wasn't afraid to take the lead. At the very least she could certainly do for him as well as he did for himself, and at the most, much better. Her own skin was darker than his, a shadowy contrast where she browsed over his body with her hands. Along the contours of his ribs she felt knotted places, hollows — old healings, the tracks of time. The tension of his muscles under her touch and the sharp sound of his breathing stirred her. She lived the fantasy of sex with an utter stranger; there was no one in the world so much a stranger as he. Yet there was no one who knew him as well as she did, either. If he was unique, so was she, and so was the confluence here.

The vividness of the moment inflamed her. His body responded. His penis stirred, warmed, and thickened in her hand. He turned on his hip so that they lay facing each other, he on his right side, she on her left. When she moved to kiss him he swiftly averted his face: of course — to him, the mouth was for feeding. She touched her fingers to his lips, signifying her comprehension.

He offered no caresses but closed his arms around her, his hands cradling the back of her head and neck. His shadowed face, deep-hollowed under brow and cheekbone, was very close to hers. From the parted lips that she must not kiss his quick breath came, roughened by groans of pleasure. At length he pressed his head against hers, inhaling deeply, taking her scent, she thought, from her hair and skin.

He entered her, hesitant at first, probing slowly and tentatively. She found this searching motion intensely sensuous, and clinging to him all along his sinewy length, she rocked with him through two hot, swelling waves of sweetness. She felt him strain tight against her, she heard him whine through clenched teeth.

Panting, they subsided and lay loosely interlocked. His head was tilted back; his eyes were closed. She had no desire to stroke him or to speak with him, only to rest spent against his body and absorb the sounds of his breathing, her breathing.

He did not lie long to hold or be held. Without a word he disengaged his body from hers and got up. He moved quietly about the bedroom, gathering his clothing, his shoes, the drawings, the notes from the work room. He dressed without lights. She listened in silence from the center of a deep repose.

There was no leave-taking. His tall figure passed and repassed the dark rectangle of the doorway, and then he was gone. The latch on the front door clicked shut.

Floria thought of getting up to secure the deadbolt. Instead she turned on her stomach and slept.

She woke as she remembered coming out of sleep as a youngster — peppy and clear-headed.

"Hilda, let's give the police a call about that break-in, so just in case something comes of it later we're on record as having reported it. You can tell them we don't have any idea who did it or why. And please make a photocopy of this letter carbon to send to Doug Sharpe up at Cayslin. Then you can put the carbon in Weyland's file and close it."

Hilda sighed. "Well, he was too old anyway."

He wasn't, my dear, but never mind.

In her office Floria picked up the morning's mail from her table. Her glance strayed to the window where Weyland had so often stood. God, she was going to miss him; and God, how good it was to be restored to plain working days.

Only not yet. Don't let the phone ring, don't let the world push in here now. She needed to sit alone for a little and let her mind sort through the images left from — from the pas de deux with Weyland. It's the notorious morning-after, old dear, she told herself; just where have I been dancing, anyway?

In a clearing in the enchanted forest with the unicorn, of course, but not the way the old legends have it. According to them, hunters set a virgin to attract the unicorn by her chastity so that they can catch and kill him. My unicorn was the chaste one, come to think of it, and this lady meant no treachery. No, Weyland and I met hidden from the hunt, to celebrate a private mystery of our own . . . .

Your mind grappled with my mind, my dark leg over your silver one, unlike closing with unlike across whatever likeness may be found: your memory pressing on my thoughts, my words drawing out your words in which you may recognize your life, my smooth palm gliding down your smooth flank . . .

Why, this will make me cry, she thought, blinking. And for what? Does an afternoon with the unicorn have any meaning for the ordinary days that come later? What has this passage with Weyland left me? Have I anything in my hands now besides the morning's mail?

What I have in my hands is my own strength, because I had to reach deep to find the strength to match him.

She put down the letters, noticing how on the backs of her hands the veins stood, pale shadows, under the thin skin. How can these hands be strong? Time was beginning to wear them thin and bring up the fragile inner structure in clear relief. That was the meaning of the last parent's death: that the child's remaining time has a limit of its own.

But not for Weyland. No graveyards of family lay dead behind him, no obvious and implacable ending of his own span threatened him. Time has to be different for a creature of an enchanted forest, as morality has to be different. He was a predator and a killer formed for a life of centuries, not decades; of secret singularity, not the busy hum of the herd. Yet his strength, suited to that nonhuman life, had revived her own strength. Her hands were slim, no longer youthful, but she saw now that they were strong enough.

For what? She flexed her fingers, watching the tendons slide under the skin. Strong hands don't have to clutch. They can simply open and let go.

She dialed Lucille's extension at the clinic.

"Luce? Sorry to have missed your calls lately. Listen, I want to start making arrangements to transfer my practice for a while. You were right, I do need a break, just as all my friends have been telling me. Will you pass the word for me to the staff over there today? Good, thanks. Also, there's the workshop coming up next month . . . yes. Are you kidding? They'd love to have you in my place. You're not the only one who's noticed that I've been falling apart, you know. It's awfully soon — can you manage, do you think? Luce, you are a brick and a lifesaver and all that stuff and that means I'm very, very grateful."

Not so terrible, she thought, but only a start. Everything else remained to be dealt with. The glow of euphoria couldn't carry her for long. Already, looking down, she noticed jelly on her blouse, just like old times, and she didn't even remember having breakfast. If you want to keep the strength you've found in all this, you're going to have to get plenty of practice being strong. Try a tough one now.

She phoned Deb. "Of course you've slept late, so what? I did too, so I'm glad you didn't call and wake me up. Whenever you're ready — if you need some help moving uptown I can cancel here and come down — well, call if you change your mind. I left a house key for you with my doorman.

"And listen, hon, I've been thinking — how about all of us going up together to Nonnie's over the weekend? Then when you feel like it maybe you'd like to talk about what you'll do next. Yes, I've already started setting up some free time for myself. Think about it, love. Talk to you later."

Kenny's turn. "Kenny, I'll come by during visiting hours this afternoon."

"Are you okay?" he squeaked.

"I'm okay. But I'm not your mommy, Ken, and I'm not going to start trying to hold the big bad world off you again. I'll expect you to be ready to settle down seriously and choose a new therapist for yourself. We're going to get that done today once and for all. Have you got that?"

After a short silence he answered in a desolate voice, "All right."

"Kenny, nobody grown up has a mommy around to take care of things for them and keep them safe — not even me. You just have to be tough enough and brave enough yourself. See you this afternoon."

How about Jane Fennerman? No, leave it for now, we are not Wonder Woman, we can't handle that stress today as well.

Too restless to settle down to paperwork before the day's round of appointments began, she got up and fed the goldfish, then drifted to the window and looked out over the city. Same jammed-up traffic down there, same dusty summer park stretching away uptown — not yet the same city, because Weyland no longer hunted there. Nothing like him moved now in those deep, grumbling streets. She would never come upon anyone there as alien as he — and just as well. Let last night stand as the end, unique and inimitable, of their affair. She was glutted with strangeness and looked forward frankly to sharing again in Mort's ordinary human appetite.

And Weyland — how would he do in that new and distant hunting ground he had found for himself? Her own balance had been changed. Suppose his once-perfect, solitary equilibrium had been altered too? Perhaps he had spoiled it by involving himself too intimately with another being — herself. And then he had left her alive — a terrible risk. Was this a sign of his corruption at her hands?

"Oh, no," she whispered fiercely, focusing her vision on her reflection in the smudged window-glass. Oh, no, I am not the temptress. I am not the deadly female out of legends whose touch defiles the hitherto unblemished being, her victim. If Weyland found some human likeness in himself, that had to be in him to begin with. Who said he was defiled anyway? Newly discovered capacities can be either strengths or weaknesses, depending on how you used them.

Very pretty and reassuring, she thought grimly; but it's pure cant. Am I going to retreat now into mechanical analysis to make myself feel better?

She heaved open the window and admittted the sticky summer breath of the city into the office. There's your enchanted forest, my dear, all nitty-gritty and not one flake of fairy dust. You've survived here, which means you can see straight when you have to. Well, you have to now.

Has he been damaged? No telling yet, and you can't stop living while you wait for the answers to come in. I don't know all that was done between us, but I do know who did it: I did it, and he did it, and neither of us withdrew until it was done. We were joined in a rich complicity — he in the awakening of some flicker of humanity in himself, I in keeping and — yes — enjoying the secret of his implacable blood-hunger. What that complicity means for each of us can only be discovered by getting on with living and watching for clues from moment to moment. His business is to continue from here and mine is to do the same, without guilt and without resentment. Doug was right: the aim is individual responsibility. From that effort not even the lady and the unicorn are exempt.

Shaken by a fresh upwelling of tears she thought bitterly, moving on is easy enough for Weyland; he's used to it, he's had more practice. What about me? Yes, be selfish, woman — if you haven't learned that you've learned damn little.

The Japanese say that in middle age you should leave the claims of family, friends, and work, and go ponder the meaning of the universe while you still have the chance. Maybe I'll try just existing for a while, and letting grow in its own time my understanding of a universe that includes Weyland — and myself — among its possibilities.

Is that looking out for yourself? Or am I simply no longer fit for living with family, friends, and work? Have *I* been damaged by *him* — by my marvelous, murderous monster?

Damn, she thought, I wish he were here, I wish we could talk about it. The light on her phone caught her eye; it was blinking the quick flashes that meant Hilda was signaling the imminent arrival of — not Weyland — the day's first client.

We're each on our own now, she thought, shutting the window and turning on the air conditioner.

But think of me sometimes, Weyland, thinking of you.

Honorable Mentions — 1980

Andreissen, David, "If You Can Fill the Unforgiving Minute," *IASFM*, May.

Attanasio, A.A., "The Star Pools," *New Tales of the Cthulhu Mythos*.

Barfoot, John, "The Smell of the Noose, the Roar of the Blood," *Orbit 21*.

Bishop, Michael, "A Short History of the Bicycle," *Interfaces*.

————, "Cold War Orphans," *Their Immortal Hearts*.

————, "One Winter in Eden," *Dragons of Light,*

————, "Saving Face," *Universe 10*.

Bova, Ben, "Vision," *Analog,* January.

Brantingham, Juleen, "My Sister's Eyes," *IASFM,* February.

Brennert, Alan, "Stage Whisper," *New Voices 3*.

Broderick, Damien, "The Ballad of Bowsprit Bear's Stead," *Edges*.

Brunner, John, "X-Hero," *Omni,* March.

Bryant, Edward, "Dark Angel," *Dark Forces*.

————, "Prairie Sun," *Omni,* October.

Busby, F.M., "First Person Plural," *Universe 10*.

C., Peter Santiago, "A Chrysalis Unbroken," *New Dimensions 10*.

Cadigan, Pat, "Criers and Killers," *New Dimensions 11*.

Cador, C.A., "The Shadowed Waters," F&SF, April.

Card, Orson Scott, "Holy," *New Dimensions 10*.

————, "St. Amy's Tale," *Omni,* December.

————, "The Princess and the Bear," *The Berkley Showcase, Vol. 1*.

Chang, Glenn, "The Wizard of Shensi Province," *Chrysalis 6*.

Charnas, Suzy McKee, "Scorched Supper on New Niger," *New Voices 3*.

Chin, Lucie M., "Dragon Ghost," *Ares,* March.

Christensen, Kevin, "Bellerophon," *Destinies,* Spring 1980.

Cook, Paul H. "Proteus," *Chrysalis 8*.

Cowper, Richard, "The Web of the Magi," *F&SF,* June.

Crowley, John, "The Reason For the Visit," *Interfaces*.

Dale, S., "Afternoon for Phantoms," *IASFM,* February.

Davidson, Avram, "Peregrine: Perplexed," *IASFM,* October.

————, "There Beneath the Silky Tree and Whelmed in Deeper Gulphs Than Me," *Other Worlds 2*.

————, "The Other Magus," *Edges*.

Dick, Philip K., "Frozen Journey," *Playboy,* December.

————, "Ravtavaara's Case," *Omni*, October.

Dickson, Gordon R., "Lost Dorsai," *Destinies*, February-March.

Disch, Thomas M., "The Brave Little Toaster," *F&SF*, August.

————, "The Foetus," *Berkley Showcase, Vol. 2*.

————, "The Pressure of Time," *TriQuarterly 49*.

————, "The Vengeance of Hera," *Edges*.

Dunteman, Jeff, "Cold Hands," *IASFM*, February.

Edmondson, G.C., "All That Glitters," *Stellar 5*.

Ellison, Harlan, "All the Lies That Are My Life," *F&SF*, November.

Engh, M.J., "The Oracle," *Edges*.

Embrak, Raymond G., "Underwood and the Slaughterhouse," *Orbit 21*.

Emshwiller, Carol, "Abominable," *Orbit 21*.

Foreman, Lelia Rose, "Hope," *Orbit 21*.

Franson, Donald, "One Time in Alexandria," *Analog*, June.

Gauger, Rick, "Detour," *Analog*, March.

Gotschalk, Felix C., "Among the Cliff-Dwellers of the San Andreas Canyon," *F&SF*, Sept.

Grant, Charles L., "Secrets of the Heart," *F&SF*, March.

Haldeman, Joe, "Lindsay and the Red City Blues," *Dark Forces*.

Hodgell, P.C., "Child of Darkness," *Berkley Showcase, Vol. 2*.

Holdstock, Robert, "Earth and Stone," *Interfaces*.

Hughes, Edward P., "In the Name of the Father," *F&SF*, September.

Ing, Dean, "Vital Signs," *Destinies*, Summer.

Kearns, Richard, "From Bach to Broccoli," *Dragons of Light*.

————, "Love, Death, Time, and Katie," *Orbit 21*.

Kelly, James Patrick, "The Fear That Men Call Courage," *F&SF*, September.

Kennedy, Leigh, "Detailed Silence," *Analog*, January.

Kessel, John, "Animals," *New Dimensions 10*.

————, "The Monuments of Science Fiction," *F&SF*, September.

————, "Uncle John and the Savior," *F&SF*, December.

Killough, Lee, "Bete et Noir," *Universe 10*.

King, Stephen, "The Way Station," *F&SF*, April

Klein, T.E.D., "Children of the Kingdom," *Dark Forces*.

Lafferty, R.A., "Phoenic'," *The Anthology of Speculative Poetry*.

————, "Lord Torpedo Lord Gyroscope," *Berkley Showcase, Vol. 2*.

Lamming, R.M., "The Ink Imp," *F&SF*, May.

Lee, Tanith, "Wolfland," *F&SF*, October.

Le Guin, Ursula K., "The White Donkey," *TriQuarterly 49*.

Leman, Bob, "Feesters in the Lake," *F&SF*, October.

————, "Window," *F&SF*, May.

Lynn, Elizabeth A., "The Gods of Reorth," *Berkley Showcase, Vol. 1*.

————, "Wizard's Domain," *Basilisk*.

Macintyre, F. Gwynplaine, "Martian Walkabout," *IASFM*, March.

Maddern, Philippa C., "The Pastseer," *Interfaces*.

Malzberg, Barry N., "Emily Dickinson — Saved From Drowning," *Chrysalis 8*.

——, "Le Croix," *Their Immortal Hearts*.

Martin, George R.R., "The Ice Dragon," *Dragons of Light*.

McAllister, Bruce, "Their Immortal Hearts," *Their Immortal Hearts*.

——, "What He Wore For Them," *F&SF*, August.

Morris, Janet, "Raising the Green Lion," *Berkley Showcase, Vol. 1*.

Mundis, Jerrold, "Real Estate," *F&SF*, August.

Murphy, Pat, "A Lingering Scent of Jasmine," *Chrysalis 6*.

——, "Don't Look Back," *Other Worlds 2*.

——, "Touch of the Bear," *IASFM*, October.

——, "Wish Hound," *Shadows 3*.

Pangborn, Mary, "The Confessions of Hamo," *Universe 10*.

——, "The Haunting," *New Dimensions 11*.

Pohl, Frederik, "The Gamesman," *Games Magazine*, September-October.

Randall, Marta, "Dangerous Games," *F&SF*, April.

Rasnic, Steve, "City Fishing," *New Terrors 1*.

Roberts, Keith, "The Lordly Ones," *F&SF*, March.

Robinson, Kim Stanley, "On the North Pole of Pluto," *Orbit 21*.

Ryan, Alan, "Comstock," *New Dimensions 11*.

Schenck, Hilbert, "Buoyant Ascent," *F&SF*, March.

Scholz, Carter, "Travels," *IASFM*, April.

Shea, Michael, "The Autopsy," *F&SF*, December.

Sheffield, Charles, "Moment of Inertia," *Analog*, October.

Shirley, John, "The Gunshot," *Oui*, November.

Silverberg, Robert, "Our Lady of the Sauropods," *Omni*, September.

Simak, Clifford D., "Grotto of the Dancing Deer," *Analog*, April.

——, "The Whistling Well," *Dark Forces*.

Singer, Isaac Bashevis, "The Enemy," *Dark Forces*.

Spinrad, Norman, "Prime Time," *Omni*, November.

Sturgeon, Theodore, "Why Dolphins Don't Bite," *Omni*, February-April.

Swanwick, Michael, "Ginungagap," *TriQuarterly 49*.

Tevis, Walter, "Out of Luck," *Omni*, November.

Tiptree, James, Jr., "A Source of Innocent Merriment," *Universe 10*.

Tuttle, Lisa, "A Spaceship Made of Stone," *IASFM*, September.

——, "Bug House," *F&SF*, June.

——, "Sun City," *New Terrors 1*.

——, "Where the Stones Grew," *Dark Forces*.

Varley, John, "Beatnik Bayou," *New Voices 3*.

Vinge, Joan D. "The Hunt of the Unicorn," *Basilisk*.

Wagner, Karl Edward, ".220 Swift," *New Terrors 1*.

Waldrop, Howard, "Billy Big-Eyes," *Berkley Showcase, Vol. 1*.

Watson, Ian, "The World Science Fiction Convention of 2080," *F&SF*, October-ber.

Wellman, Manly Wade, "What of the Night?" *F&SF*, March.

Wolfe, Gene, "In Looking-Glass Castle," *TriQuarterly 49*.
———, "Kevin Malone," *New Terrors 1*.
———, "Suzanne Delage," *Edges*.
———, "The Detective of Dreams," *Dark Forces*.
———, "The God and His Man," *IASFM*, February.
Yarbro, Chelsea Quinn, "Cabin 33," *Shadows 3*.
Yermakov, Nicholas, "Far Removed From the Scene of the Crime," *F&SF*,
    April.
Yolen, Jane, "Cockfight," *Dragons of Light*.
———, "The Sleep of Trees," *F&SF*, September.
Zelazny, Roger, "The George Business," *Dragons of Light*.
———, "The Places of Aache," *Other Worlds 2*.